RITES OF WINTER

INHERITANCE, BOOK SIX

AK FAULKNER

Ravensword Press

RITES of WINTER

A.K. FAULKNER

CONTENTS

THE AWESOME THING ABOUT HAVING HIPPIES FOR PARENTS WAS THAT the family got to travel all around the country, just the three of them, in Dad's camper van, and they could park wherever they wanted.

Eric got to see a lot, and he knew he was lucky. He'd seen the breathtaking beauty of a Montana sunset and the grand majesty of the Appalachian Mountains. They'd driven endless desert roads and winding switchback dirt tracks.

Everywhere they went, his dad played music for money, and his mom grew everything they needed to eat. Between them, they taught him more than most other homeschooled kids could ever learn.

It was the best life possible. He was a Child of Herne, he was learning to use magic, and everywhere he went, there was something amazing to discover.

So why would New York be any different?

His parents weren't dumb. They knew to warn him about certain parts of the city, and he was smart enough to listen to wisdom. So when Dad gave him five bucks and told him he could go out for the afternoon so long as he was back at the RV by five, Eric fully intended to go spend his five dollars on something awesome and make sure he was home on time.

It was more money than he was used to carrying around, so he kept it stuffed deep inside his jeans, with one hand curled around it for safety's sake, while he wandered along and debated what to spend it on. He could buy Mom and Dad a present, maybe? He didn't want to waste it all on food, though a candy store was singing a siren song to him as he stalled outside its windows.

Sure, he could buy presents with the spare change, right?

Or you could buy presents first, then candy with the change.

That sounded horribly sensible. Eric wasn't sure he was on board with walking away from the candy store without anything. And anyway, one bar of chocolate wouldn't kill him.

He bit his lip and tried to resist the pull, but he stepped inside only three seconds later.

Well, at least he knew what it felt like to eat five dollars' worth of candy.

He ate as he walked, digging a bar at a time out of his bag, and then ditching the wrapper in a trash can before he fished out the next, until he was all out of candy and able to toss the bag itself.

Now came the guilt.

He'd really meant to buy Mom and Dad *something*, even if it was just a little trinket to say thanks. Oh, sure, they'd likely sent him out so they could have sex, but even so, he usually only got fifty cents or maybe a whole dollar when he got sent off to entertain himself. Five really was something special, and he'd stuffed it all in his face.

He sighed and bent down to scoop up a stray piece of litter and throw it in the nearest trash can, and continued to do that as he meandered slowly back toward the parking lot Dad had stowed the RV in.

It was in the shadow of a brownstone that he caught sight of something unusual, and after he tossed yet another piece of trash into a can, he headed toward it.

An alley between two buildings was blocked off by a wrought-iron gate, and there was a sign at the top that read *NEW YORK MARBLE CEMETERY*, though Eric was baffled as to what a cemetery was doing down between two apartment buildings.

At the far end of the alley was what had caught his eye. Another wrought-iron gate, just as beautiful as this one, but with a sickly yellow glow twisted around its bars.

He bit his lip and paced back and forth a moment to double-check that what he saw was magic, but there was nothing else it could be. There were no wires, no strings of lights, nothing shiny to reflect the glow from elsewhere.

Instinct told him to stick his nose in, and instinct had proven pretty reliable when it came to chocolate purchases, so he checked around quickly, then climbed up the iron gates and dropped down on the other side. One of the great advantages of being so tall was that he had way less distance to fall than anyone else trying to break into places, and a twelve-foot-tall gate with convenient hand and footholds wasn't going to get in his way.

He glanced under his own shirt to make sure his amulet of protection was still giving off the deep green of his own magic, and then he approached the unknown spell and started searching for any signs of sigils or bindings that were keeping it in place.

There wasn't anything he could see. Not from here. He held his breath and reached out to touch the ironwork, but the spell took no interest in him, so he clambered over and into the grave-yard beyond.

It was a small space, surrounded by apartment buildings and yet cut off from them somehow. Plants hid most of it from the street, but as he circled the outer edges of the cemetery, he could see a few small trees dotted across an uneven lawn, and weathered marble markers embedded in the walls. They were far too eroded to read much of anything.

He felt out of place here. The lands of the dead belonged to Arawn, not to Herne, so he took each step with respect and hoped he wasn't causing any offense.

The sickly glow wasn't restricted to the gate. He found it along the stone walls, which looked to be about as old as Manhattan itself, and it writhed along gaps in fences and between buildings wherever the walls had long since gone to ruin, which he figured meant that the spell was nowhere near as old as the burial site.

Or the spell caster was every bit as old, and just kept patching it up whenever the scenery changed.

He gnawed his lip and dug around here and there, still trying to figure out what this spell was. If he could just find a few anchor points, he might be able to interpret the sigils and work it out from there.

He glanced at his watch. Still just under thirty minutes before he had to be home, so he kept on searching. The candy was starting to disagree with him, too, and he kinda wished he hadn't eaten it all so damn fast, but it was too late for that now. Going over the gates on his way out might be a challenge, though.

"Hey. Kid."

He blinked and turned on his heels, trying not to look guilty as shit. "Huh?"

There was a guy standing a few feet away, his hip leaning against a marker, and Eric was damn sure there wasn't anywhere the dude could've come from. There were no doors, and the gate was still shut.

"How'd you get in here?" The guy's eyes were that same sickly yellow as the magic which surrounded them, and they were glowing softly.

Eric swallowed. All of a sudden he felt like he was in way over his head. "Oh, uh, I kinda just climbed over the gates, dude." He gestured past the guy. "I'm sorry. I can go. I didn't know anyone was here."

"No, it's all right." The guy was a little creepy, but Eric wasn't sure if that was just the way city people were up here. His only encounter so far was with a candy store clerk, so he couldn't really compare notes. "Do you want a leg up when you go again?"

"Oh, man, that'd be handy. Thanks!" Eric smiled. "You want me to leave you alone?"

"I don't mind." The guy shrugged slim shoulders and stepped away from the wall to clear a path back to the gates for Eric. "Tell you what. If I help you, would you help me?"

Eric laughed easily and shrugged. "Sure. What do you need?"

The yellow-eyed stranger motioned toward the gates. "There are some markings outside the restaurant at the end of this alley. If you could deface any of them, I'd call us even."

Eric looked toward the gates. "Oh!"

No wonder he hadn't found sigils near the gates. They were further away than that.

"You want this spell gone, huh?"

The stranger blinked, then sighed with relief. "Oh, thank God. If you wouldn't mind?" He wandered toward the gates and pointed at them. "It's just a stupid prank by my teacher. He reckons I should be able to get out of this shit myself, even though the sigils are intentionally too far away for me to break them. But I figure enlisting help is still me doing it myself, right?"

Eric mulled it over, then laughed cheerfully as he too walked over to the gates and looked at the spell again. "I mean, you're the one who came up with the solution, right?" He grinned at the other witch. "So technically, you've figured it out yourself."

"That's what I thought!" The guy offered Eric his hand. "Ryan McKinley, by the way."

Eric shook it. "Eric Riley."

"Nice meeting you. Okay, you ready?" Ryan laced his fingers together and crouched by the gate.

"Yep!" Eric put his foot in the makeshift stirrup, and Ryan propelled him up just as he leaped.

He was up and over in no time, and looked back to Ryan. "Okay. The restaurant, right?"

Ryan nodded and gave him two thumbs up. "Probably on the front wall. Obviously I've never seen them, because I'm here." He laughed. "Oh, man, this is great. I'm gonna get top marks."

Eric laughed and backed down the alley. "Okay. Give me a few minutes. I'll see what I can find."

Ryan nodded, so Eric hurried away and clambered over the other gates once he was sure he wouldn't get caught, and then he headed under the restaurant's maroon awning and paced up and down, searching for any markings.

It took a few minutes, but then he noticed them, actually carved into a brick at ground level, almost hidden under layers of grime. He wasn't sure how the hell he was going to disrupt a sigil that was chiseled into brickwork. He'd need something hard and sharp, and he'd spent his money on candy instead of hardware.

He glanced at his watch. He had around fifteen minutes or so to fix the problem if he still wanted to get home on time.

Eric looked up at the restaurant, then grinned to himself and began moving silently toward it. One step at a time, looking casual. He'd never tried this without a crowd to blend into before, but he was a Child of Herne, and passing without a trace was a hunter's skill. Not that Eric ever hunted much other than candy, but whatever.

He eased in through the door and made like he was just returning to his table, and idly pocketed a couple of knives before he spotted a heavy salt shaker and grabbed that, too.

Then he turned like he'd forgotten something and wandered straight back outside again.

Eric hunkered down by the brick and placed the edge of one

knife blade against the narrowest part of a sigil, then hammered against the flat edge with the salt shaker. He had to hold the hilt steady with his knuckles against the wall, but each hit chipped loose a little rainfall of old brick.

Just how long had this spell been here, anyway?

He hammered away until the knife blade snapped free of the hilt, and then he swapped knives and kept on going until the cut he'd made in the brickwork was as deep as the sigil itself, and then he dropped his tools and ran back to the gates.

The yellow glow was gone.

"Ryan?" he yelled. "I think I got it!"

He heard howling, eerie and distant, as though a pack of wolves on some faraway mountain had broken into chorus.

Ryan popped into view and scrabbled over the first gate. "Excellent work, Eric," he gasped as he landed on the ground, then he ran toward Eric and leaped at the second gate. "Now I think we better run."

Eric blinked and stepped back so Ryan could land. "Run? From what?"

Ryan pointed back down the alley. "Thanks for your help, man. But I'm outta here. You should go, too."

Eric looked, just in time to catch sight of a streak of blackness as it poured through the gates at the far end.

There was no way to know what it was, but Ryan seemed to have the right idea, so Eric turned on his heel and ran as fast as he could, all the way back to the camper van.

His gut wasn't too happy with all the athletics, and he had to guzzle a glass of water as soon as he made it inside to settle it. When he put the glass down in the sink, he turned and found Mom and Dad staring at him in amazement.

Eric checked his watch.

Bang on time.

"Tah-dah!" He said, arms spread wide, like he'd just done the best trick in the world.

And maybe he had. Because whatever it was that had been chasing Ryan at the cemetery had left Eric alone, and since his folks never seemed to visit places twice, that meant once they left town, it wouldn't be a problem.

Perfect!

1

LAURENCE

LONDON IN WINTER WAS A MISERABLE AFFAIR, AND LAURENCE couldn't wait to leave. It was cold. The whole world was gray. The rain never seemed to stop, not even for a second. Londoners scurried around in gray coats with black umbrellas as though they relished how miserable the world had become.

The problem was, they couldn't leave until they could be sure Quentin could go a day without nightmares.

It was a horrible situation to be in. Laurence had pored over a whole bunch of books about recovering from deep trauma, but there was no getting away from the fact that he wasn't qualified to help.

Quentin needed a real therapist.

And if Laurence was honest with himself, he could use one, too. They'd both been through too much. They'd let Laurence's birthday sail past because Laurence didn't feel like making a fuss, and then Christmas had come and gone much the same way. Now that they were into the new year, Laurence felt like they were stagnating. This was the wrong end of the wheel for him, and spending it in this kind of weather made it doubly hard.

He needed to move.

They were spending time just drifting around. Quentin took him to some amazing restaurants, but neither of them felt all that eager to deal with crowds, so they spent a lot of their time either sitting in hotel rooms, sitting in parks under an umbrella, or sitting in coffee shops watching the world go by.

Still, they weren't under attack. There were no life-or-death fights. And Laurence's cravings had all but subsided.

He had to wonder about that. *Had* Freddy done more for him than he'd insisted he would, or was this really the stage he'd been at before Freddy kidnapped him? It felt like forever ago, and it was hard to compare how he felt now to what he'd felt back then, because there was too much utter horror in between those two times.

Goddess, but he still wanted to kill the duke. Maybe they should get out of the country before his need to hunt took over.

Laurence drew a deep breath and pulled out of his reverie. This was their third hotel in as many weeks, because Quentin was concerned that he might wreck one if he stayed too long. He'd trashed a couple of places already — one before he'd rescued Laurence, and another in Aylesbury afterward — so if moving around made Quentin happier, Laurence was more than willing to do it.

This one was on the north bank of the Thames, overlooking the gray water. Laurence marveled at the fact that even the damn river matched the weather, but it meant the view didn't lift his mood.

He looked away from the window and toward Quentin, who was in another armchair idly reading a book.

Damn, he was still beautiful.

Laurence smiled a little and moved his foot closer so he could rest it against Quentin's.

Quentin blinked, then looked up at him, and mustered a small smile of his own. "Hmm?"

"I was thinking," Laurence began.

Quentin closed the book and set it on the windowsill, then folded his hands together in his lap as he gave Laurence his full attention.

"Mia and Sebastian and Mom are doing great looking after the kids." According to his mom, even Maria, Ethan, and Aiden had been helping out, too. "But we've gotta get home, baby."

Windsor clacked his beak in agreement and hopped from the table up onto Laurence's chair, where he flapped his way along until he was up on the back of it and Laurence could hear him begin to preen his feathers.

"We do," Quentin sighed softly. "Perhaps you should fly ahead?"

"I don't think that's necessary." Laurence sucked on his lip briefly. "I've got an idea."

Quentin's eyebrow arched, and his pale gray eyes matched the outside world far too perfectly. "Oh?"

"Why don't we just do it in hops?" Laurence leaned forward and dropped his elbows to his thighs so that he could brush his fingertips against Quentin's knees. "That way you only have to stay awake for shorter flights, and we can rest between them to make sure we're ready to push on."

Quentin raised a hand to his lips, then gnawed a little on the knuckle of his thumb while he looked at the window. When he dropped the hand again, his gaze remained fixed on some point outside. "What if I have an episode?" he breathed. "I don't want to find out what kind of an effect that might have on an aircraft, darling..."

"I know," Laurence said softly. "But you're doing great when you're awake. I think we just need to travel at quiet times so we're not surrounded by, like..." There was no delicate way to put it that he could think of. "You know, uh... all the noise."

Quentin nodded slowly. "Well, the lounges cut out the noise considerably."

Laurence blinked, then snorted. Of *course* Quentin had lounge access.

"Okay, so let's think it through. The shortest hop from here would be, what, New York?"

"Correct," Quentin agreed. "But it's only around three hours shorter than direct to San Diego."

"But that's three extra hours' rest you could be getting," Laurence countered. "And when we gotta get to the airport three hours ahead of departure, and it takes like an hour to get there, and then Lindbergh Field is like another hour from La Jolla, it all adds up. Believe me, I'd fly direct if I thought it was a good idea, but maybe we just need to take this slow and steady."

Quentin's cheeks pinked a little, and he looked down toward the trees that lined the river.

"Hey. Cut that out. No blaming yourself." Laurence wasn't even going to wait for him to dare try it. "We're safe. The kids are safe. Let's just take precautions and make sure we can get home in one piece, all right?" He smiled as he squeezed Quentin's knee. "It's going to be okay, baby."

Quentin took a breath, then finally looked toward him. "We could spend a couple of nights in New York just to be sure?" he offered.

"Of course. Whatever you need. Hell, whatever we both need, right?" He smiled a little. "Let's face it, we could both use the break. Anyway, didn't you live in New York for a while?"

As tended to be the case, Quentin responded well to the change of subject. His blush faded away, and he lifted his chin as his smile became more certain. "Yes, I did."

"So you can show me around. Maybe we can go to Central Park. Don't they have an ice rink in the winter? Or did I imagine that?"

"They do. And there is one at Rockefeller Center, also," Quentin murmured. "Are you able to skate?"

Laurence laughed at that. "Never tried it on ice. You'll have to teach me. I mean, I assume you can, right?"

Quentin inclined his head. "It is a fair assumption."

"Right. And we can just chill out and be tourists for a couple of days. Once we're in the right time zone, and you're feeling ready, we can do the next hop."

He watched while Quentin mulled it over. He half hoped Quentin would decide to fly direct to San Diego and keep himself awake the extra few hours, because at least then they'd get back to some sunshine.

"We would need to contact Rufus," Quentin concluded, "and ask for the spell he used to send Windsor to us."

"Right. I guess we'd need a license to ship a pet raven anywhere, especially in the hold."

"Poop!" Windsor agreed.

"That, and he's a little bugger," Quentin murmured fondly. "He would likely teach any other birds to say rude words if he were given a few hours to kill in their company."

Windsor ruffled his feathers. "Bugger!"

Quentin's eyes grew wide, and his mouth fell open. "Windsor!"

And like that, the tension in the room seemed to evaporate. Laurence laughed, in part at the look of scandal on Quentin's face, and half with relief that laughter was even possible in the wake of the year they'd shared. The important part was that they *had* shared it, rather than lived through these things alone. Laurence wouldn't have survived his encounter with Jack and remained himself, and sooner or later Quentin's father would have forced Quentin to return home under the duke's conditions, which would only have led to more misery all round.

So what if they had to make the trip home in shorter steps? If that was what it took to get there, then that was what they'd have to do, and griping about it overlooked the fact that they were incredibly fortunate to have made it this far together.

Laurence settled back in his chair and smiled as he curled his toes against Quentin's foot. "Did I tell you — today — how beautiful you are?"

Quentin tore his gaze from Windsor. Some flattery always got his attention, but at least Laurence found his vanity cute. "Er. Possibly?"

"Probably. But it's worth repeating." He grinned. "Okay. I'll contact Ru, you figure out our flights. We can take it from there."

He could see the objection forming in Quentin's eyes, his lips, so he just pulled his phone out and began to tap an email.

Quentin huffed softly, and started talking to Siri.

This was a great plan. It would totally work.

And absolutely nothing could go wrong.

2

QUENTIN

QUENTIN SCROLLED THROUGH SIRI'S RESULTS, AND THE AMOUNT OF options was almost overwhelming. Why on earth did she think he would want to fly via Helsinki? Did anyone really fly to New York via Paris if they were starting in London?

Laurence might well be right. Focusing on this task gave Quentin's brain a way to shut down all the other nonsense it liked to crowd him with, even in quiet moments such as these. But the slew of options seemed only to feed that constant buzz of anger that had become a part of him lately.

Why couldn't these things be *simple*?

It was a flight! A single flight!

He glanced out of the window and fixed his gaze on the Thames while he counted down from ten. He had, he felt, got quite good at calming himself without needing to show Laurence that he was doing it. It worked best in quiet environments, but it was better than making a song and dance out of the whole procedure.

There. He was able to deal with the situation a little more levelly.

Quentin returned his attention to the results and managed to find the filters that cut out options such as multi-stop flights and economy classes. There were, thankfully, so many flights that they could avoid being up at four in the morning to catch one.

If he could arrange a flight at around lunchtime, that meant less time awake in London waiting to fly, which meant less stress, which meant less opportunity for an episode to occur at any point during the travel. Goodness knew what might happen if he went off during immigration at an American airport. Those border control people were humorless enough at the best of times.

He was about to contact an airline when he had a more sensible thought.

Perhaps he should be the one to touch base with his wealth manager for once, rather than the other way around. After all, his finances must have taken quite a knock from his flight to London last month, and then all these hotel stays. The poor man had enough woes without Quentin suddenly buying tickets to and across the United States.

He was almost pleased with himself for even thinking of it, and he scrolled through his limited list of contacts, then tapped the right one. For once, he could also ignore any time zone calculations.

It took a minute to be put through to the right person, and all the while Laurence was being quite provocative by sitting there and looking damn breathtaking. All right, so perhaps Laurence wasn't really *doing* anything, but still, he was quite distracting.

"Lord Banbury! This is Jasper Evans speaking. How may I be of service today?"

"Mr. Evans," Quentin murmured. "I wondered whether we might touch base on my accounts. It could be a nice change from always forcing you to be the one who calls me," he added dryly.

Laurence glanced up at him, eyebrows high, and Quentin imagined poor Evans had a similar look on his face right about now.

If he did, it didn't come across in his voice.

"Of course. It's nice to shake things up every now and then, isn't it?" Evans chuckled. "I'm afraid I do need to go through a few security questions with you, my lord."

Quentin leaned back and answered tedious questions about his date of birth and his mother's maiden name before Evans was willing to speak further. He supposed that anyone with a half-decent grasp of mimicry could call up and pretend to be him, but then surely those people would know enough basic information to pass these security questions too? It was, as Laurence had made clear a while ago now, all on the internet.

"Excellent. If you would give me just one moment for the system to... ah, here we are. Is there anything in particular that you would like to discuss today?"

Quentin gently bit the tip of his tongue and glanced away from Laurence. Now that crunch time had come, he wasn't at all comfortable speaking these words out loud, but what could he do? Hang up like a toddler?

"I would like to check my spending limit for January, please," he murmured through grinding teeth.

"Of course. We have..." Evans tailed off with a soft cough. "Ah, do please excuse me, my lord. Your limit has been raised... quite considerably."

Laurence's fingers landed against Quentin's knee, and Quentin blinked as he looked at them. He found Laurence leaning forward, elbows on his thighs, looking curiously toward the phone.

"How?" Quentin couldn't help but ask.

"Let me see..." He heard some distant tapping or clicking. "You have a new standing order in to your current account, my lord."

Quentin blinked at that. Had Freddy taken pity and decided to throw some money at him for the house renovations after all? "From Frederick?"

"No, my lord. From your father."

Quentin felt his mouth open and shut, but his brain failed to offer any words to go with the motion.

"Would you like the details?"

"Yes, please," he said faintly.

"Fifty thousand pounds, direct into your current account on the first of every month," Evans recounted. "As of the first of January this year."

"So this is the first such deposit," Quentin surmised.

"Yes, my lord. Would you like me to begin investigating suitable investment opportunities?"

Quentin exhaled softly. "Not for the moment. Perhaps in a few months, when we can ascertain whether this is going to stick around for more than five minutes. Thank you, Mr. Evans; you have been most helpful."

He hung up after Evans' goodbyes, then blinked at Laurence.

"That's, what, about sixty-five thousand dollars?" Laurence scrunched up his nose.

Laurence's hearing was far too good. It made phone conversations in his vicinity a non-private affair.

"Something like that," Quentin agreed.

"What the hell is he up to? Does he think he can just..." Laurence waved a hand. "Buy forgiveness?"

"No." He shook his head faintly, too numb to do much else. "He thinks he can buy obedience."

"You think he'll cut you off again?"

"Of course he will. Sooner or later. All he's provided here is a rug which he can whip out from under our feet whenever it suits him to do so."

Laurence gave a soft grunt of agreement. "Still, it'll get us home. At least that's something."

Quentin had to agree. He idly draped his hand across Laurence's and allowed his fingers to drift across the back of Laurence's wrist. He watched as Laurence's eyelashes obscured his eyes, and the American's cheeks flushed.

Perhaps a little sex would keep the anger at bay for another day. Quentin wasn't sure. Sometimes it felt as though sex simply poured fuel on that fire, but at others it was a balm, as though he had opened a tap and allowed just a little bit of his fury to leak out and escape. He couldn't quite identify what it was that he did to push things one way or the other, but he certainly slept better on the latter days, with that rage softly diminished, if only for a while.

He leaned forward, parting his lips and drawing a breath to broach the subject, but Laurence's phone buzzed.

Laurence gasped in shock and grabbed his phone as though it had bitten him. His lips were wet, his throat bobbed as he swallowed, and his hand remained trapped beneath Quentin's while his other thumbed the phone.

"Oh. Wow. Okay." Laurence cleared his throat. "Ru sent the spell over. Looks like I need somewhere with emotional significance in mind to send Windsor to?"

Quentin withdrew so that Laurence could use both hands. It was that or to get away from the device, which now bore a spell. "Mm. That's why I had to go to Paris," he agreed. "It was the closest place to London which bore any significance for Rufus."

"Huh. Wonder why."

"He did not say." Quentin's eye was drawn to Laurence's lap, and he was at least satisfied to note some sign of interest there.

Laurence glanced at him, then snorted softly. "Later, baby. Let me take care of this first."

Quentin tutted as though it were a great imposition, but he rose from his chair and leaned in for a quick kiss. "Very well," he rumbled. "I shall go entertain myself elsewhere for a short while."

"Hang on, whoa." Laurence checked his phone again. "I'm gonna need your help here."

Quentin froze.

"Not to cast," Laurence added quickly. "But this shit's in Latin.

I can't even read it, and I sure as hell don't know how to pronounce half of it."

Quentin narrowed his eyes and pulled away, straightening himself up and checking that his shirt cuffs were neatly aligned. "You wish me to... to..."

"Show me the gestures. Make sure I've got the pronunciations right. Then you can go, and I'll cast it while you're out, baby. There won't be any magic going on while you're here, okay? I promise."

Quentin paced away from Laurence and ran fingers down his shirt front, but his armor was still secure.

All Laurence needed was a little assistance. Quentin didn't have to cast anything, and he wouldn't be here when Laurence did. He'd read through books Rufus had loaned them before, when Laurence was in Otherworld and unable to do so himself, so it wasn't as though Quentin couldn't *read* a spell.

He drew himself upright and turned to face Laurence with a curt nod.

"Very well," he said. "I shall assist."

"Great! Thanks, baby!" Laurence hurried to the desk to grab a notepad and pen, then beckoned Quentin over.

Quentin gave one last, purely demonstrative huff of reticence before making his way to Laurence's side.

Ultimately, he knew that was where he always needed to be.

3

LAURENCE

LAURENCE WOKE TO THE SOUND OF RUNNING WATER, AND HE could tell that Quentin's side of the bed was cooler than it would be if Quentin were still in it. Still, he opened his eyes to be sure.

Empty.

Laurence sat up and yawned as he stretched, grinning weakly as his jaw complained with some residual stiffness.

Yeah, there were benefits to having a telekinetic boyfriend, that was for sure. Especially one who liked to use his gifts to pin Laurence down for sex.

He licked his lips as last night came back to him, then threw the sheets off and padded toward the bathroom.

It had taken a couple of hours to get the spell right, and then Laurence had had to call his mom and make sure there would be someone by the Moreton Bay Fig when he sent Windsor there. Of all the places that meant the most to him, it was the closest to the shop.

It was where he'd first met Quentin.

And then, apparently, after Laurence was successful, Quentin had felt the need to pin him to the bed, suck him off, then fuck his mouth, and there was no way Laurence was gonna say no to any of that, especially when it had left them worn out enough to sleep the whole night through.

If fucking was what it took to help Quentin sleep, Laurence was ready to throw himself on that sword.

He pushed the bathroom door open and grinned toward the shower cubicle. "Hey, baby!"

The side of a hand swiped against the inside of the cubicle's glass and left a clear trail, which Quentin peered through. "I'm sorry. I didn't mean to..." Quentin tailed off, and blinked. "Oh."

Laurence glanced down, then laughed and struck a pose. "Oh, yeah. All natural, baby. Just the way you like it!"

"You are positively *awful!*"

"No, awful would be if you asked me to join you in there."

Quentin snorted at him. "As if I would do such a thing."

"Uh huh." Laurence raised his wrist and looked at it like he was wearing a watch. "Five... four... three..."

There was a huff from the enclosure. "Very well."

"Very well what, baby?"

"Come in."

Laurence dropped his pose and headed to the shower. "Not the sexiest invitation I ever had, but I'll take it."

He pulled the door open and found Quentin waiting, water plastering his ink-black hair to his head, his gray eyes dark like thunderclouds.

Laurence swallowed tightly.

"Okay," he squeaked. "Suddenly it got a lot sexier."

Quentin quirked an eyebrow.

"Sir," Laurence added as he stepped inside.

THEY GOT to Heathrow by taxi. Quentin muttered something about the tube that made it sound like a contagious disease, and

Laurence wasn't going to argue. He'd seen maps, and was kinda glad Quentin wasn't going to use it.

Heathrow was a vast airport. Laurence hadn't been to many in his life, but the freeway had separate exits for different clusters of terminals, and even after the cab took the right one, it took another ten minutes' driving for it to pull up at a drop-off point outside a huge glass-and-white-metal terminal building. Quentin paid the fare by card, and Laurence hefted their sole suitcase out of the trunk.

For once, it wasn't raining. But Laurence's breath hung in the air, and he shivered despite the thick coat he was bundled up in. He wished Quentin had warmed the air around them, then chided himself for being such a baby. They'd be outside for all of thirty seconds. He could cope.

Still, he couldn't help but notice that Quentin seemed utterly unaffected by the cold. So did many of the Brits getting dropped off by taxis or loved ones all around them.

Quentin offered his arm, so Laurence took it, and they strode toward the terminal building.

Inside, thank the Goddess, was way warmer. Laurence reclaimed his arm so that he could unzip his coat, then took Quentin's elbow again as Quentin turned right and sailed past the vast departure boards without paying them the slightest bit of attention.

"Baby? Don't we need to know what zone to check in at?"

Quentin shook his head faintly. "No."

Laurence eyed him. He had a gnawing suspicion that this was some rich person bullshit, and his instincts were proved right a few seconds later, when he spied the far wall of the terminal with its elegant silver curvature and the discreet *First* lettering at head height.

This was only going to get worse now that the duke had decided to throw money at Quentin for whatever reason. Laurence was under no illusion that the asshole had suddenly decided everything was love and cupcakes. Maybe his motive was to drive Laurence away by returning spending power to his eldest son, in which case Laurence was going to have to suck it up and not let any of this get to him.

It was harder than it sounded.

Quentin handed their passports to a warm and friendly desk agent, who called Quentin Lord Banbury without any trace of irony or resentment. She was equally polite to Laurence without speaking down to him for not having a title. And then, once they had boarding passes, she took their luggage, printed a receipt for it, and passed them through to a hidden gap in the silver wall, which in turn led through to a small security area with absolutely no line whatsoever.

Laurence blinked as he shrugged his coat off. "You are seriously shitting me right now."

Quentin laughed gently as he emptied his pockets into a tray, then folded his coat on top of his items. "In what regard, darling?"

"Rich people get their own fucking security line?"

Quentin inclined his head faintly. "I'm afraid so."

Laurence seethed in silence as they passed through the body scanner, and his seething only continued as Quentin led him into a small, private lounge.

With table service.

And a full breakfast menu.

But it *was* nice and quiet.

BOARDING the flight was just as surreal. Their gate agent came into the lounge specifically to let them know in person that their gate would be opening soon, and by the time they arrived, they were able to jump the long, winding line via the priority lane and head straight to their seats.

Laurence felt disconnected from everyone else, as though the whole purpose of his ticket was to keep him as far away from the commoners as humanly possible. Their lounge lacked the chaos and screaming children of the main concourse, and they didn't even have to share a line with the little people. Their gangway had a separate arm to lead directly to the first-class cabin, and once they were on board, their cabin was so shut off from the rest of the aircraft that it felt as though they'd boarded a space shuttle.

He checked his boarding pass and peered to the seat numbers, then shrugged his jacket off and looked for where to put it.

"Ah." Quentin reached past him and tugged on something, revealing a closet tucked into the side of his chair.

Laurence just shook his head, hung the jacket on the hanger inside, and closed the door. "Thanks, baby."

Quentin's seat was across the aisle from his, and Laurence sat while Quentin hung his own jacket and nudged his shoes off.

The cabin had fourteen seats total, laid out in a herringbone pattern. Those in the center had high dividers between them, so Laurence could see why Quentin had chosen for them to straddle an aisle instead, but he still wished they could have sat together somehow.

His seat was more like a self-contained pod. His chair looked way more comfortable than most airline seats, though it was partially hidden by airline-branded bags right now, and there was a footrest built into the end of the pod which looked solid and comfortable enough to be a seat in its own right. Between chair and footrest were an array of buttons, a television screen which he figured could pop out from the pod wall during flight, and what looked like a drawer for storing stuff in, in addition to the coat closet and the overhead bin.

They waited for people to settle down around them, then Laurence crossed the narrow aisle to Quentin's seat and perched on Quentin's footrest. Laurence figured they could do this during the flight, but for now he needed something else. He reached for

Quentin's hands and squeezed them slowly, searching for Quentin's scent on the air.

It was there, vibrant and familiar, overlaid with less well-known hotel toiletries.

Quentin leaned forward and lowered his voice. "Are you all right, darling?"

"Yeah." Laurence cleared his throat. "I'm just... trying to be sure it's you."

He felt Quentin's fingers tighten on his own. Quentin leaned a little further and raised Laurence's hands so that he could kiss them softly.

"I understand," Quentin breathed.

The truth was, Quentin didn't understand. Not all of it. Laurence hadn't told him the full extent of what Freddy had done to him, and his silence might be the only reason Quentin was ever willing to speak to his brother again. Laurence had no way to know whether what his senses told him was real or an illusion, and while he'd resolved to just get on with things under the assumption that Freddy had ultimately told the truth, he still needed to check that this was Quentin, because he'd been fooled before.

He had to have faith. If he were still trapped, he would wake on the Isle of Apples sooner or later. Quentin would rescue him physically, while his mind healed in Otherworld. Freddy *had* to be telling the truth.

Goddess, even while he was torturing Laurence, he'd told the truth.

Laurence took a breath and released his tension as he exhaled, then leaned in for a kiss.

"Thanks, baby," he whispered.

"You are most welcome," Quentin murmured.

Laurence nodded and returned to his own seat in time to be offered a hot towel, and he took it with thanks.

THE FIRST COUPLE of hours of the flight were remarkably busy. There were announcements, drinks, snacks, more drinks, and then a ridiculously large lunch menu was served. Laurence was relieved that none of the cabin crew attempted to push the champagne selection once he and Quentin ordered non-alcoholic drinks, and he wasn't at all surprised to see Quentin struggle to eat half of what they put in front of him. Even Laurence had trouble, thanks to the similarly large breakfast they'd had in the lounge.

They were even given individual salt and pepper mills. Not packets, but tiny little silver twist-top mills to grind salt and pepper with.

Not for the first time, and likely not for the last, Laurence quietly filed away yet another way in which rich people were totally sheltered from the real world. Quentin had probably never even encountered a packet of salt before he met Laurence. Had he ever bought a sandwich off a shelf and eaten it out of the wrapper? Did he know what economy seats looked like, or that there were hundreds of people on the other side of the curtains behind them?

Everything that seemed so obvious to Laurence was an alien concept to Quentin, and this whole flight experience was a sharp reminder of just how different their worlds were. And maybe that was a good thing, because for the better part of last year, Laurence had kind of wondered what century Quentin had stepped out of. But now he could see more clearly, and knowing their obstacles made them easier to face.

He hoped.

Once the remains of lunch were cleared away, the crew began offering a turndown service, and Quentin politely declined on behalf of both of them so that he could slip across to sit on Laurence's footrest. He raised his feet and stretched his legs out to rest his ankles between Laurence's thighs, and Laurence lifted them into his lap so that he could rub fingers across them idly.

Now they just had to pass the remaining five hours or so without anyone or anything triggering Quentin.

Laurence leaned back in his chair and affected a lazy smile. "So how come it always rains in England?"

Quentin blinked, then scoffed at him, crossing his arms loosely. "Utter nonsense. We were there a month."

"Yeah, a month in which it never stopped raining," Laurence teased.

"It was December," Quentin countered. "And a little of January. Honestly, darling, you aren't made of sugar. You won't dissolve."

"I mean—" Laurence leaned toward the window and peeked out. "I'd check from up here whether it's still raining, but I can't see past all the clouds."

"It wasn't raining when we arrived at the airport..."

"Oh, for like five minutes. The clouds probably ran out of water and had to go get a refill."

Quentin laughed, and there was nothing but fondness in his eyes.

All Laurence had to do was keep up the banter, and they'd be in New York in no time.

4

QUENTIN

SITTING ON AN AIRCRAFT FOR UMPTEEN HOURS WAS EVERY BIT AS incredibly boring as Quentin remembered, and while Laurence did his best to mitigate the tedium, Quentin's preferred method of passing the time — lying down to catch a few hours' sleep — was out of the question. By the time the tea-time service passed through the cabin, he was all but chewing the walls.

Thank goodness they landed soon after, albeit in weather no less dreary than they had left this morning.

Laurence scrunched up his nose as they disembarked from the aircraft, and peered out into the gray New York afternoon. He huddled down into his coat even though they were protected by glass and heating.

Quentin took his hand and allowed his thumb to drift across Laurence's skin. "I suppose we must part ways at immigration," he mused. "You'll have your own line."

Laurence blinked and looked at him, then offered a small smile. "It'll be okay. It won't be long."

Quentin couldn't help but laugh a little at that. "I see you haven't flown in through JFK before."

"Oh c'mon. How bad can it..."

They stepped out into a room that was fifty percent queue, and all of that queue was on Quentin's side of the row of border control agents' booths.

Laurence blinked, then bit his lip as his dark eyes scanned the signs for each of the entrances, and his fingers tightened around Quentin's. "Right. I'll stick with you in this line, then I can play dumb and get shoved off to my own line once we reach the front, okay?"

"I'm sure it will be all right."

IT WASN'T ALL RIGHT.

It took three hours to clear the damn queue.

Two hours in, and Quentin was about ready to detonate. Every little thing made his anger crank up another notch. People who didn't move when the queue shifted. People who left their bags on the floor. People who turned their backs on the queue so they could chat with their family.

If Laurence hadn't stayed with him, God alone knew what he might have done. They spent most of the third hour kissing because it at least kept him calm, though he'd sent a few hard stares at anyone who dared comment on two men doing such a thing in public.

Their poor little suitcase, when they finally reached it, was abandoned among a huge pile of every other non-American's luggage from their flight.

The outside world was dark. They'd been in the queue so long that night had fallen, and with it came a sharp and bitterly cold wind, so Quentin flagged a taxi and ushered Laurence into it first.

"Where to?" the driver asked.

"Head to Grand Central for now," Quentin replied. "As soon as I have a hotel name, I'll let you know."

"Sure thing!"

Laurence rested a hand on his thigh while Quentin began quizzing Siri on hotel availability, and once he selected one, he called them to book a couple of nights. He passed the hotel name on to the driver, then caught sight of Laurence taking a deep breath but saying nothing.

Quentin raised an eyebrow and waited.

"Only two nights?" Laurence murmured.

Quentin was sure that his eye twitched again, for all that he tried to stop it from doing so. "Enough to get some sleep for now and decide further in the morning," he replied, "because I suspect that if I do not manage some sleep soon, I may do something I regret."

Laurence's cheeks flushed.

How the devil could the poor boy get aroused by such a statement? Or was he merely embarrassed on Quentin's behalf?

"I better call Mom," Laurence said thickly. "Let her know we landed okay."

Quentin simply nodded and set his hand on top of Laurence's.

***

He'd selected a hotel that overlooked Central Park on the slim hope that if he absolutely needed to get out and let his temper loose, he could do so in the middle of the night without destroying yet another room.

Freddy was still right, damn him. Quentin did need to improve his control, but how could he when these things came to him in his sleep? These memories that he had been free of two months ago, but which now wouldn't piss off and leave him alone?

Worse, sometimes they *did*. And then they came back. In the night, in his dreams, his father waited for him like a rattlesnake.

Of a more pressing concern as they entered their room and

set their things down was the fury he'd accumulated throughout the day, most of which came from their airport queue.

"This is some fancy shit," Laurence mused as he eyed the small chandelier overhead.

"Short notice," Quentin grumbled as he began peeling his clothes off. "Would you like anything to eat?"

"Oh, man, no. I'm stuffed. I think I've eaten like two days' worth of food since we got out of bed." Laurence eyed him, then tugged his own shirt off over his head. "You think you can sleep, baby?"

"No." Quentin glanced across to him. "I was rather hoping you might be interested in *not* sleeping."

"I feel like we've been awake twenty-four hours — oh, you mean sex!" Laurence's grin turned sly as he caught on. "You're naughty, baby!"

"Be that as it may—"

"Yes." Laurence laughed. "Yes, I am very interested in not sleeping, Quen. Where would you like us to not sleep? On the bed? Up against a wall? Overlooking the park?"

Quentin tried to work that last one out, then gasped at it. If Laurence meant to do *that* in full view of the outside world, then... well, Quentin wasn't wholly sure what to even make of the idea. He'd have to shelve it and examine it later, when it was less shocking and more abstract.

"The floor?" Laurence grinned as he slipped his trousers down.

The *floor?*

Quentin crinkled his nose while he finished undressing, and regarded the carpet as though it might just show him whether or not it was too dirty to do anything on, but while he was busy staring at it, Laurence had dropped down onto the pile and rolled to his front, stretching out like a cat with his arse up in the air and on full display.

It was *very* distracting.

Laurence raised his bum higher and reached down to stroke himself, twisting so that he could glance back over his shoulder and up at Quentin. "Goddess," he moaned. "I think if you don't get down here soon enough, I'm just gonna come without you."

Quentin blinked

blood spattered his chest, dripped from a line across his cheek, ran between them in an endless stream which terrified and aroused.

and Laurence's fist continued to bounce, hypnotically, between his thighs

the scream was not unpleasant

and Quentin sank to his knees, trying to push everything else aside and focus just on Laurence. He laid his hands on that ripe, downy arse and squeezed a little more tightly than he might usually, but it made Laurence's moan come even louder, so he did it again.

When he took his hands away, the skin bore the marks of his fingers, if only for a second. They were white against pink.

Red would be better.

He traced his fingers lightly down the backs of Laurence's thighs and was satisfied by the way that Laurence twitched and shuddered under his touch.

"Show me your hands," he barked.

Laurence's whimper was exquisite, but he stopped stroking himself and placed both hands against the carpet instead. "Yes sir."

What would it be like to—

Quentin sucked in air and didn't let that thought go any further. The last time he'd followed his mind down a path like that, he'd liked the result, and so perhaps he should just do things rather than fret about them.

He gripped Laurence's backside again, and pulled it back toward himself, leaning his own hips forward so that his prick could lie in the crease of Laurence's cheeks.

It felt so phenomenally good that he had to clench his jaw and count down from ten, while Laurence whimpered and pleaded with little sounds that couldn't form words.

When he was quite sure he was in control, he began to thrust slowly, carefully, along that dipped line until his tip popped free at the base of Laurence's spine, and the thought of spilling across that beautiful tanned skin was enough to drive him half-mad with need.

That need chased the nightmares away.

He was fully focused. Present in the here and now. His borderline obsession with ensuring that he brought the most pleasure possible down upon Laurence's willing body drove out all other fears and foibles, and gave him a light to cling to in the darkness.

Now that he knew the answer to his unspoken question, he fell forward with care until he was arched over Laurence, arms around him, so that Laurence was forced to bear both their weights. He felt the tremble of Laurence's muscles as they adjusted, and heard the quiver in Laurence's breath as his arousal peaked.

Quentin placed his lips against Laurence's skin and took a moment to center himself. It was exactly like sitting at the piano, and he would not be rushed, no matter how strongly Laurence's body sang to him.

Only once he was ready would he begin.

5

LAURENCE

LAURENCE DIDN'T KNOW WHERE THIS WAS GOING, AND HE WASN'T going to complain. For one brief moment he thought Quentin might try to enter him, despite never having done so before, but it didn't happen.

He didn't know what to think about that. Not while Quentin's cock was nestled up against his ass so tantalizingly. Laurence hadn't had anyone inside him — at least, not with anything more than a finger or two, or a toy — and he didn't want to break off all of a sudden to try and explain how to take it easy and make sure nobody got hurt, so he was relieved he didn't have to.

Quentin wasn't helping him with the weight, either. Laurence had to brace himself to hold them both up without any aid from Quentin's telekinesis, which meant that was exactly what Quentin *wanted* him to do.

Goddess, how was he like this? So desperate to please this man, to do whatever he wanted, to be used by him? Laurence wouldn't think of himself as submissive in a million years, but there was more to Quentin than orders or control. He was no Dan, that was for sure. It didn't make any sense, and the more Laurence tried to unpick it, the more of a tangled mess it became.

What he did know was that he'd spent months fantasizing about Quentin touching him with all the care and attention he lavished on his piano, and whenever Quentin did exactly that, it was more mind-blowing than Laurence had imagined.

Quentin was doing it now.

Those slender, nimble fingers caressed Laurence's chest, demanding his attention almost as much as the balls that rested against his taint, or the hard cock that nestled down his crease. They danced fleetingly across hair and nipples, brushed down across Laurence's abdomen and up to his collarbones. Quentin's chest was against his back, warming his skin, and soft lips and tongue nuzzled between his shoulders.

Laurence's head fell forward and hung helplessly between his outstretched arms. He needed everything about this, and not just because it kept his senses sharp and his gifts potent. No, he needed it every bit as much as he needed air to breathe. It chased the cobwebs away, and it kept his addiction locked up so that he could pass for normal.

The carpet pressed into his palms and knees. His hair almost brushed against it, and he forced himself to straighten his arms properly. His cock hung from his body, weighty and demanding, yet untouched and unsatisfied, and the more Quentin played with everything *but* his dick, the more Laurence desperately needed touch there above all other places.

"Quen," he begged.

He felt Quentin's lips shift against his skin, and the draw of breath before Quentin spoke. "Yes?"

Goddess, he was gonna make Laurence say it, wasn't he?

"Please," he croaked.

Quentin's fingers danced tantalizingly over his abdomen again, twirling through the hairs there without even glancing a touch across Laurence's cock. "What is it that you want?" He asked it dispassionately, as though it wasn't all that important.

"You," Laurence whimpered. "Your touch. Your hands. I want you," he gasped, "to touch me. Please. Goddess, Quen, *please…*"

Quentin laughed lightly. "I am touching you."

Laurence ground his teeth. Sweat trickled from his spine and into his hair, prickling the back of his neck as it went. His arms shook with strain.

"Please, sir," he begged. "I want you to touch my cock."

Fuck, just saying it out loud made his skin tingle and his dick stiffen so hard it came close to bursting. He could feel the moisture accumulating at his tip as each bounce through thin air blew cold air across it.

He couldn't see Quentin, couldn't tell what effect those words might have had on him, and waiting to find out was a sweet torture all of its own.

Quentin began to withdraw, to push himself away from Laurence's body with hands against his back. Cool air rushed into the vacuum and hit the sweat left on Laurence's skin, and Quentin's fingers drew lines down to his ass, right to the point when they eased around him once more.

Laurence held his breath and prayed.

One hand pressed flat over his stomach, and the other caressed his balls.

He whimpered.

Quentin's fingers curled around his dick and squeezed tightly. They held on while Laurence bucked and shuddered, and then they began to stroke. Slowly. Lazily. In no hurry, with no sense of urgency.

"Oh Goddess! Quen! Oh, fuck! Oh, Quentin, fuck yes! Oh, shit, you're so good! Fuck me, oh Goddess, please!"

Words poured out of him in a stream with very little chance for him to pick them apart or analyze them. He begged. He knew that much. Every other word felt like it was *please* or *sir*. He needed to come, needed Quentin to come, and the longer it took the harder he was pushed toward the orgasm that taunted him.

Quentin's hand quickened. The press of his cock against Laurence's ass was insistent but unmoving, and Laurence writhed against it as he thrust into Quentin's fist.

"Oh, fuck," he yelled. "Oh, fuck! I'm gonna come, Quen!"

"Good," Quentin snarled. "Do it."

Goddess, that was the end of him right there! The authority in Quentin's voice, the surety of the command, the hand tight around him, and Laurence came hard into the air, his entire body drenched with sweat and trembling with orgasm.

He gulped down air as his arms finally gave in and he buckled down onto his elbows. His whole frame shook with the aftermath, like ripples still rolling out from a stone cast into a lake, and he pressed his face against the carpet as he swallowed. His breath rasped in his throat, and his fingers dug into the pile briefly when his cock twitched again in Quentin's palm.

Quentin said nothing. He held Laurence in his hands until Laurence was able to draw a deeper breath, and then those hands left Laurence's cock and stomach and returned to gripping his ass.

Laurence sucked his lip and closed his eyes, savoring the sensation of Quentin's cock gliding back and forth along his crease. This wasn't anything Quentin had done before. Laurence hadn't even implied it, and that meant Quentin had come up with it all by himself, which made Laurence incredibly proud. It meant Quentin was *thinking* about sex. He was actually working out what he might like to try, and giving it a go, and that was a huge step forward for him.

He couldn't help but smile weakly as Quentin fucked his ass crack. It felt surprisingly good, now that he was relaxed enough to enjoy it. Quentin's hold on his backside was firm, his dick hard, and the heat between them had made things sweaty and slippery, so that his cock glided with ease. Quentin's balls softly stroked his taint, too, which made him even more of a puddle of goo than he already was.

Quentin's breath became ragged. Needy. He grunted, then let out a primal sound that never failed to make Laurence shiver with pleasure.

That was one of the things he loved the most about Quentin. The man was *loud.* He had no shame, no ability to keep himself quiet during sex, and no desire to, either. He did as he damn well pleased, up to and including waking the damn neighbors when he came.

Laurence felt the heat land heavily against his back, and couldn't help but let out a little moan himself.

Quentin's movement stopped. Hands relaxed, then left Laurence's ass altogether, and only when fingers slipped through the wet on Laurence's skin did he know where they'd gone.

Quentin's weight fell forward again, but this time his hand came to Laurence's cheek, and fingers entered his mouth.

Laurence tasted himself on them, and sucked with renewed vigor, looking up over his shoulder to meet Quentin's gaze as he cleaned his cum from Quentin's fingertips.

Goddess, yeah. Quentin was fucking filthy. All tucked up in that pristine package, hidden away from everyone but Laurence, so perfect and proper to the outside world.

But in private? With Laurence? Fuck, he was unbelievable.

Laurence had once thought Quentin was a bit toppy, but it turned out that wasn't the half of it. He was kinky as hell — kinkier even than Laurence had previously thought he himself might be — and Laurence loved everything about him.

So maybe it was Laurence who needed to push himself more, since Quentin was pretty damn keen on trying anything and making it up as he went.

He grinned as Quentin's fingers slipped free of his mouth and murmured, "That was amazing, baby."

If there was one thing Quentin liked, it was flattery, and his gray eyes creased with genuine warmth as he pushed sweat-slicked hair back from his face. "I'm glad," he murmured.

And like that, all the roughness had gone from him. The stress of the line at JFK, the tedium of the flight, it was all released into the air, and Quentin was back to his gentler, kinder self. He eased back from Laurence with care, then extended a hand to help him to his feet.

Laurence took it, though he needed a while to get his legs under him without them turning to jelly again. Once they stood facing each other, he slipped his arms around Quentin and held him tight.

Quentin held him in turn. There was no rejection there, no distance. He seemed to intuitively understand that Laurence needed contact, both during and after sex, and he gave it freely.

"Seriously," Laurence breathed once he was more able to talk, "have you been asking Siri for sex tips?"

Quentin gasped in shock. "Goodness, no! Oh my word, no! I wouldn't—"

Laurence laughed softly and pressed a kiss to Quentin's sweaty shoulder, taking care not to touch a sensitive scar. "That just means you made it up yourself, and *that* means you're dirty and think about sex!"

Quentin cleared his throat. "So help me, darling, you are the absolute *worst!*"

"Nuh-uh. You are." He pulled back and was rewarded by the pink in Quentin's cheeks and the adoration in his gaze. "I'm gonna shower. Wanna join me?"

Quentin tailed him to the bathroom. "I don't know," he said airily. "Now that I know you are the worst, it would be foolish of me to allow you to lure me into close quarters."

"True, true." Laurence feigned sympathy. "Maybe you can take the bathtub, then. Keep you safe from me."

"Maybe you could take the bath," Quentin argued, "so that I can have a shower."

Laurence laughed as they tumbled into the shower enclosure

together and squabbled playfully over everything from soap to water temperature.

This break might be exactly what they both needed.

6

QUENTIN

Quentin woke as he should.

It had become a pleasant surprise these days, to wake gently and without a care in the world, with Laurence by his side and without any evidence of destruction around him. It was a treasure, to sleep fully throughout the night without screams or nightmares, and he resisted the urge to open his eyes for as long as he could, content to simply lie in bed with his legs coiled around Laurence's.

Perhaps all this sexual activity was doing him some good. He felt at peace in a way that he hadn't in many weeks now, as though he had made a little headway in dialing down the constant rage in his chest. It could be the sex, or the renewed distance between himself and his father, or a combination of factors. He had found in life that things were rarely so simple as to have a single, easily-fixed cause, but he wondered whether this positive outcome worked in some opposite way to triggers. Was he able to ensure a good night's sleep by following a certain routine, or was it all down to avoiding anything that might give him cause to dwell too much on the memories that flickered in and out like a failing light?

He couldn't possibly know. He had been reading a book on the subject of coping with trauma, but it was hard going, and at times he felt that the text was almost as upsetting as the memories themselves.

But he did feel calm and collected enough now to consider how long they might wish to remain in New York, and so he stole a light kiss before he eased out of bed, and used the room's telephone to contact reception and arrange an extension of their stay. A week should be more than enough time to adjust to this time zone and prepare himself for another flight.

"With the storm coming in," the clerk on the phone said, "an extension is a good idea. Once flights start getting cancelled, rooms get booked up fast."

Quentin blinked. "Storm?"

"Yeah. It's coming in tomorrow, but they think it'll get real bad by Wednesday. That's all booked for you now, sir. Is there anything else I can help you with?"

He glanced toward Laurence as his lover began to stir, and shook his head faintly. "No, thank you. That will be all."

"All right. Have a nice day, sir."

"You also." He hung up and sat back in his chair thoughtfully.

"What time is it?" Laurence mumbled as he rubbed his eyes.

"Oh, ah..." Quentin glanced around for a clock and found one on a bedside table. "Oh, I'm so sorry. It's only half four."

"Half *past* four?" Laurence stretched and yawned as he sat up, and the sheets fell to his lap. "Damn it. I guess we're running on British time still. Almost. Kinda halfway there." He sighed, hopped out of bed, and made for the bathroom. "What was that about a storm?"

"Apparently there's a bad one on the way. It's New York in winter. There will likely be a blizzard." Quentin offered a sympathetic smile as Laurence's nose crinkled. "We should nip out and get you some warmer clothing."

"You just want to take me out and dress me up." Laurence chuckled. "I'm not gonna say no, baby."

Quentin laughed softly as Laurence disappeared into the bathroom. He didn't need to answer. They both knew it was true.

THEY KILLED TIME UNTIL SUNRISE, enjoying a lazy bath together and an even lazier breakfast. Quentin's appetite was minimal, but he took his time and managed to get most of the meal down simply by pacing himself.

It was Laurence's theory that Quentin's body was always running at some sort of fuel deficit, and that he made up for this by abstracting energy from the world around him, so if he could force himself to eat a little more, it would likely be a good thing. Laurence didn't mind Quentin drawing on *his* deep wellspring of life force. But if Quentin were subconsciously taking what he needed from those less robust than Laurence, he could be endangering them, which was unacceptable. Eating was so tedious, though, and he had yet to find a middle ground.

Still, once they were done with breakfast, they headed out into the world for some fresh air, and Quentin led Laurence to Central Park for a stroll. They could head south for shopping, or cut across the park to get somewhere with more boutiques. Laurence would likely favor Midtown, so Quentin began to dawdle that way, coiling warmth around them both.

Laurence hung on his arm and breathed deeply, and light touched his smile in a way that Quentin hadn't seen for a while now. It was good, to know that it hadn't gone forever.

"Oh man," Laurence murmured. "This is beautiful. I bet it's gorgeous in the springtime. Look." He gestured with his free hand toward the bare, skeletal trees they passed. "Those are magnolias. I think there's a couple of varieties, even."

Quentin nodded in agreement. Though he didn't recognize

them without their blooms, he was familiar with magnolia trees, and had no doubt that this many of them would look spectacular once they flowered. "I believe there are other flowering trees also," he offered. "It's quite a sizable park."

Laurence nodded, and the farther they walked, the more he picked out, pointing to some Japanese cherry varieties here, or a hawthorn tree there, and he seemed to be enjoying himself a great deal.

And if that were the case, then Quentin was more than satisfied, for despite the leafless trees and the sparse grounds, the park was still eerily breathtaking. An oasis of calm in the heart of a city that was otherwise filled with rush and noise that never seemed to die down, not even in the wee small hours.

"You know," Laurence breathed as he leaned in a little closer, "once we get some clothes and whatever else we wanna pick up, we could have lunch somewhere."

"Mm," Quentin agreed. "There are plenty of restaurants to choose from."

"Right." Laurence grinned at him. "Then after, maybe we could go to a different kind of store."

"Oh? Is there something in particular you are looking for?" He smiled at Laurence, curious.

Laurence's dark eyes flashed with playful intent. "I dunno. But we could track down, like, a sex shop, and I could show you around."

Quentin ground to a halt, and blinked at Laurence. He thought he understood all of those words, but together they didn't make a great deal of sense. "A what?"

Laurence stopped and let go of his arm so he had both hands free to gesticulate, which he did with gusto. "So they're like these stores that sell stuff for your sex life. Not a shop that sells actual sex. There's no sex going on inside the store."

He blinked again. "Well, that's a relief."

Laurence's laugh was damn near contagious. "Right? No, don't worry, baby. It's all surprisingly normal. It's just that what they sell is sex stuff." He shrugged and bit his lip. "C'mon. It'll be fun."

He tilted his head faintly and tried to work out what exactly such a shop might even sell, or how it could be entertaining in the slightest, but Laurence wouldn't want to take him there for no reason. "What is it they even sell?" Quentin licked his lips, then added, "We are already..." he glanced around to ensure that nobody was within hearing range, but leaned closer regardless. "Having sex," he breathed. "Without owning additional... things."

"Oh, man! All kinds of things!" Laurence shifted on the balls of his feet, looking coy as he dipped his head and blushed. "Sexy outfits—"

Quentin arched an eyebrow. "Like Halloween?"

Laurence coughed. "No! Maybe. No, things like... like see-through briefs..." He twirled and patted his own arse as he did so, as though modeling something other than the khaki cargo trousers he wore. "Or leather... uh... stuff..."

He coughed and took Quentin's arm again, leaning into his side. "And then there are toys, and... how about we find one, and we can just take a quick peek inside, and if you wanna leave, we just walk straight out again?" His smile softened.

Quentin eyed him and began to walk once more while he chewed it over.

Laurence might still be feeling a little lewd after last night, which was rather flattering, and Quentin would have to admit that perhaps he too was still basking in the afterglow of their activities. Why else would he even consider this particular shopping experience?

Because I am not a coward.

That thought had considerable merit, truth be told. Control was, in all regards, the name of the game. He had to hold himself in the tightest possible reins, or those around him were in harm's way. He had to work to catalogue and overcome each and every possible threat to that control so that he was prepared in the event of an emergency. He had to devise what the books called a coping mechanism, rather than allow his subconscious mechanisms to come to the fore.

He was prepared for the existence of this shop, and if he had to take it in small doses until he was ready to browse it fully, then there was no shame in that.

"Very well," he murmured.

"Great!" Laurence whipped out his phone and began poking at it.

Quentin blinked at him. "What on Earth are you doing?"

"Just searching for a good one," Laurence assured him. "There's all different kinds, and I figure we don't wanna wind up in a store that isn't relevant." At Quentin's raised eyebrow, he added, "Like, a store that sells stuff for women? They tend not to have such a good selection for guys' things."

He blinked again at that and was somewhat embarrassed at the realization that it hadn't even occurred to him that *other people* might also visit one of these shops. "Oh," was all he said.

"Oh, hey. This one has great reviews!" Laurence said, then tucked his phone away. "But first things first; let's go play dress-up in Macy's." He leaned in to kiss Quentin's cheek, and Quentin felt that warmth even after Laurence's lips left his skin. "Then you can treat me to lunch, and tell me how handsome I am."

Quentin pursed his lips in amusement and raised his chin. "Am I still wooing you, or are we beyond that stage now?"

Laurence gasped in feigned shock, and placed his hand over his heart. "Goddess, Quen, no! You have to woo me for the rest of our lives! It's not a one-time thing, you know! It's ongoing!"

He laughed at that and let his fingers trail over Laurence's forearm. "Very well. Perhaps we should find a venue with a piano, so that I may also serenade you while you eat."

"That would be amazing. But maybe also kinda weird. But awesome." Laurence chuckled, and looked ahead, his curls ruffled by a breeze which swept across the park. "C'mon. Let's get inside somewhere, so you can stop pumping out all this heat. Save your energy for later."

That was it, then. No denying it now.

Laurence was *definitely* still feeling lewd.

How fortunate.

7

LAURENCE

Now that Laurence had a nice, thick coat he'd likely never need again in his entire life, he felt more capable of facing the sharp, cold wind that had whipped up after lunch. It seemed like all these tall, rectangular buildings served to funnel any breeze down into the streets below, and he noticed most people walked fast to try and get to cover quickly.

They wove their way along toward Chelsea as Laurence followed directions on his phone, but every time he looked up to check on Quentin, the earl was still striding along looking confident.

Still, Laurence knew better than to assume that meant every-thing was fine, so when they reached the street the store was on, he pocketed the phone and brushed his fingers against the back of Quentin's hand. "No pressure, okay?" he said gently.

Quentin looked at him, and wind pushed hair back from his forehead, but he still seemed calm. "I understand," he murmured.

Laurence paused to be sure the wind was natural, then smiled and searched for the store itself. When he found it, even he was surprised to find that it was set into another building's basement, with metal stairs leading down past some iron railings, kind of like the basements in London. There were even a few items on display in the window for those who peeked over the railings to see, but thankfully there wasn't anything there that looked too scary. A few mannequins that wore harnesses and jockstraps, or mesh t-shirts, and a couple of rainbow flags behind them, but that was about it.

He pushed the gate open and took the first couple of steps down, then waited, holding the gate open for Quentin.

Quentin took a moment as he fussed over his cuffs and straightened his coat, and then he followed without a word, barely glancing at the window, as though it might offend him.

If that was what it took, Laurence wasn't gonna argue.

He reached the door and opened it, then stepped on in while he held it for Quentin, gaze quickly scanning the inside of the store to identify potential threats and hazards. There were, thankfully, no other customers in here right now, but that meant that both of the guys at the register were available. Sure enough, one of them started to make his way over with a warm, welcoming smile.

Laurence had to intercept this before Quentin took it for what it wasn't.

"Hey!" Laurence left the door and moved toward the clerk with his hand outstretched. "We're just here to browse."

"No problem!" The clerk was in his thirties, with a huge beard and the kind of chest under his t-shirt that suggested he had the ultimate bear body, complete with the belly of a person who loved his food. He shook Laurence's hand with a gentle grip.

Laurence smiled a little more sadly as his mind automatically compared that belly to his dad's, who probably would've already found all the best dives in town and uncovered their secret off-menu items, but he injected a bit more energy into it to try and hide it fast. "Thanks, man. We'll call you if we need any help. Just..." He dipped his head. "My partner's kinda jittery, so he needs a little distance, okay?"

"Completely understood," the clerk assured him. "I'll be right over by the register."

"Thanks. I really appreciate it." Laurence released his hand, then hurried back to Quentin with a grin. "First impressions, baby?"

Quentin looked pretty fucking adorable, with his combination of wide-eyed innocence and scandalized mortification. Whatever he'd seen already hadn't made him lose his shit so far, though.

"I'm at a loss for words," Quentin managed to say.

Laurence grinned and beckoned him toward a section near the door. "C'mon, let's look at the clothes first. They might have some fun stuff we can try out."

Quentin swiveled on his heels to follow. "Fun?" he echoed.

"Yeah. Fun. That thing sex is. It's okay to have fun." He didn't want to spook Quentin with a touch, so he just stopped and rested his hands on a shimmery shirt that looked better for clubbing than bedroom wear. "You... do have fun when we... you know? Right?"

Quentin's cheeks burned bright red. "Well... yes."

"Great!" Laurence picked the shirt off the rack anyway and draped it against his own chest. "How about this?"

There went that eyebrow again, arching as though Laurence had committed some grave fashion error. "No."

He laughed easily and plucked out a few more that he figured would make Quentin reject them, and sure enough Quentin did, but with each shirt returned to the rail, Quentin seemed to be easing up. His shoulders relaxed, and his head rose back to its usual position.

Showing Quentin that Laurence listened whenever he said *no* was hugely important, and Laurence took his time reminding Quentin that he even had that power.

The power Quentin's father had robbed him of his entire life.

Laurence smiled softly at him as he backed further into the store. Quentin was doing great, but now wasn't the time to comment on that. Instead, he gestured to another rail. "Well, what would *you* like to see me wear, baby?"

"I see little need," Quentin grumbled. "You are out of whatever you put on quickly enough."

"True, but until then?" He snapped up a tiny posing pouch and draped it across his crotch. "I could be wearing this under my pants right now, or when we go to dinner, or while I'm at work, and we'd be the only people who knew it."

Quentin blinked, and then his gaze slowly sharpened. "Oh."

"Uh huh." He returned it to the rail and backed further into the store. "Or this, maybe?" He reached for a shelf, and grabbed a thick leather collar.

Quentin still seemed distracted by the posing pouch, probably counting down from ten, and it took a while for him to refocus onto the collar. Once he did, that adorable confusion returned. "What is... oh!" He blinked as he tilted his head a little. "Really?"

Laurence looked and found cuffs that matched it, and grabbed those too. "Sure. You can tie me down, do whatever you want to me, you know?"

Quentin blinked slowly, and when his eyes opened, Laurence felt that invisible hold settle all around him from head to toe.

He swallowed, and his breath quickened. Quentin's unseen touch was *everywhere* on him, freezing him in place, and Quentin stepped in closer.

"Yes," Quentin breathed against his ear. "I can."

Laurence let out a choked, urgent sound as his cock pulsed needfully against his briefs. "Goddess, baby," he whispered past his immobile jaw, "you're so fucking hot."

Quentin brushed lips against his cheek, then stepped back, and his hold evaporated like it had never existed. He even managed to feign a look of casual disinterest. "What, then, does this offer?" He gestured vaguely to the items in Laurence's hands.

It took Laurence precious seconds to fish his brain out of the gutter. That urge to just throw himself at Quentin's feet had almost overcome him again, and his hand trembled as he placed the cuffs back on the shelf. He had to clear his throat before he dared to speak. "Aesthetics?" he squeaked.

When he turned back, Quentin was waiting silently for more explanation, so Laurence buckled the collar around his neck and hooked a finger seductively through the chrome D-ring at the front. He even rested his other hand on his hip and jutted that hip to one side.

"Oh," Quentin breathed again. The sharpness had returned to his eyes, chased by something that looked a hell of a lot like hunger. "I see."

This might have been a mistake. Laurence couldn't move, but this time nothing but Quentin's look held him right where he stood while an electric undercurrent of need jolted between them. Was it the pull of that vortex inside Quentin, or was it pure lust? Fuck, if it wouldn't break Quentin's mind or get them arrested, Laurence would damn well drop to his knees right here and suck him off, no question about it.

Move.

Do something!

Hey, asshole!

Laurence swallowed again and reached back to unbuckle the collar. He returned it to the shelf and bit the inside of his cheek in the hope that it might distract from his rock-hard erection, but his dick wasn't paying attention.

"Anyway," Laurence managed to force his mouth to say, "now you know the kind of stuff you can get in here. Shall we, uh..." He struggled to finish his sentence in a way that was acceptable in a public space. "Head back?"

"Mm," Quentin answered. He even took a step back and turned away, hands folding together behind his back.

Laurence hurried past him and called a thanks to the clerks as he opened the door for Quentin, then trailed up the stairs after him like a puppy. Sure, they could have bought something, but

Laurence didn't want to push his luck. It could be that Quentin had only handled it so well because he'd forgotten the staff were even in the store, or maybe because he was focusing his attention on Laurence.

Either way, Laurence's goal had been a gentle introduction to the existence of sex shops, not causing him any upset or making him black out in public. He felt kinda bad that the clerks had been so great with Quentin's need for space, so maybe he could go back there alone and pick up a couple of items later in the week.

For now, though, enough was enough. He knew not to push too hard, and his instincts were reliable. They'd reached a safe, comfortable limit, and pushing beyond would be counterproductive. To be honest, he was so damn proud of Quentin for coming even this far; why would he want to screw that up?

Besides, he still wanted to unpick whatever the fuck was going on inside his *own* head. What was so different about wearing a collar than just letting Quentin use telekinesis? Quentin might be kinky as shit, but Laurence didn't really think of himself that way, and apparently, he'd been wrong about that.

Quentin was silent as they walked, looking lost in his own thoughts, and Laurence was grateful for it, because it gave him time to chew on the problem without trying to find the words to explain it all. He hoped Quentin's thoughts were good ones, because Laurence's were still lingering on that collar and how it had made him feel.

They pushed on against the savage wind, both hunkered down inside their coats, and the silence stretched on out between them as they went.

8

QUENTIN

QUENTIN LACKED THE WORDS TO BEGIN FRAMING WHAT EXACTLY had just transpired. All he could grasp was that he wanted to have sex with Laurence right this very minute, and yet they were half a city away from their hotel.

A thing had certainly happened, and he wasn't sure whether it was a good thing or not, but the sight of leather against Laurence's throat had caused some kind of absurd arousal for reasons Quentin could not fathom, and now... well, he was quite certain that Laurence was also very interested in having sex right now, too. The florist's features had taken on that keen desperation he adopted so readily whenever Quentin began giving orders.

Still, nothing bad had occurred within the confines of the shop. Despite his reservations, it proved to be quite like any other shop in most regards. Quentin had faced it with courage, and succeeded in leaving the place every bit as intact as he had found it.

He should absolutely reward himself by having sex with Laurence.

Christ, he'd gone from terror to obsession in the span of a few months. Was this a good thing? He thought he had some vague recollection of one of the books Laurence had bought mentioning increased sexual appetite as a result of...

As a means of dealing with...

Quentin sucked in a breath and ground to a halt so that he could screw his eyes shut, but the moment he did

Hands fell on Quentin's shoulders and pushed him to the cold, wet floor. The stench of his own blood was in his nostrils and on his tongue, metallic and salty, pervading his thoughts until all was red.

Ten. Nine. Eight.

Something touched him, and he jerked away from it, but he couldn't tell whether it was real or imagined, and he had to re-start his countdown.

The air was little above freezing. He felt it leech moisture from his cheeks, and latched on to it to help ground himself. It was a sensation that hadn't existed when he—

When Father—

This was now. He was in New York. It was early January, and he was with Laurence.

Seven. Six. Five.

His fingernails dug against his palms as he continued his countdown. Only after he was certain that he was not about to lose control did he open his eyes.

The hunger was gone from Laurence's eyes, replaced by worry as the florist stood two feet away from him with his hands shoved deep into the pockets of his coat. In a way, Quentin was grateful, since his own interest in anything below the waist had brutally evaporated.

"You're doing great, baby," Laurence said softly.

A tremor ran down Quentin's spine, and he set off at a brisk pace, as though he could simply escape the memories he'd left buried for so long.

But those acts... they were what Laurence wanted, weren't they? Deep in his gut, Quentin knew it. He knew that Laurence wanted something more than their current sex life, and it all seemed to lead inexorably to penetration. Quentin couldn't work out how he was supposed to feel about that.

Now that he knew damn well how good it felt to do the rest of it.

No. He was cursed with knowledge now, wasn't he? Trapped by it. He knew not only what an orgasm felt like, but also that he'd done it himself the last time his father raped him.

It made him sick to the stomach to even consider that fact.

Why couldn't this all have stayed buried, where it belonged? Where it was safe?

Where it couldn't hurt him?

"Baby?" Laurence's voice came from his side.

"I'd like to walk," Quentin murmured.

"Sure. Is there a park near here?"

"Yes." He nodded ahead. "Not too terribly far."

Laurence nodded, and they walked the near-freezing streets together as Quentin zigzagged through Chelsea and the West Village toward the High Line. At least Quentin's directional sense didn't fail them, and he showed Laurence to the metal steps that climbed up to the disused railway line, now converted to a park, that stretched toward Midtown.

He didn't envision the park being too busy in this weather. The wind on the streets was cutting enough, but once they were on the elevated park it would likely be too much for most people to bother with, and he took the stairs two at a time in anticipation of the peace and quiet up ahead.

The park was starkly different from that in his memories, but then he had discovered the place in autumn, when he was last in this city. Now the expanse that stretched ahead of him was bare branches and bright red berries, and a cluster of pretty gray birds took flight as he and Laurence popped up like meerkats from the stairs.

"Oh, wow," Laurence breathed. "This is awesome! Look! Witch

hazel!" He pointed to a tree with spidery, bright-orange blossoms that covered bare-seeming branches. "Not actually named after witches," he added with a grin. "Comes from an old English word that meant 'bendy'."

Quentin nodded and mustered what he could manage of a smile as he reached for and clutched Laurence's elbow. "It's very pretty," he murmured.

"It only flowers in winter," Laurence went on as they began to stroll. "Winterberry holly," he added, toward the bushes the birds had flown away from. He went a few more steps before he popped up the collar on his coat for extra warmth. "Do you wanna talk about it?"

He briefly considered being facetious, but what would be the purpose of that? Laurence was offering a shoulder, and it was churlish at best to snap at him for it, so instead Quentin looked ahead to search out the nearest bench. "I cannot say that I do," he admitted.

"I get that," Laurence said as Quentin steered him. "It's up to you, Quen. You know I'm right here if you need me."

Quentin idly brushed a twig from the bench and sat, releasing Laurence's elbow and folding his hands together in his lap as he regarded the bleak shrubs and bushes around them. Laurence settled by his side and left a few inches between them as he leaned his elbows on his knees and looked down at his hands.

"I know what you want," Quentin said quietly.

"I guess it's good that at least one of us does, then," Laurence mused.

He glanced toward Laurence, but found no evidence of sarcastic intent. "Don't you?"

Laurence's dark eyes flitted his way, and he sighed. "I dunno, baby. I thought I did, but then we went into that store, and..."

He shrugged. "I want things with you I've never wanted with anyone else. You make me want to give myself up, and I'm..." Laurence laughed faintly. "I'm not used to it, like, at all. You have this hold over me, and I..." He took a deep breath. "I like it. It's new to me, but now I've discovered it I crave it."

He dipped his head faintly. Laurence had so succinctly managed to describe how Quentin himself felt, in many ways.

"I asked once whether what we had done was sex," he whispered, "and your response was conflicted. You said that it was complicated."

"Sex is complicated," Laurence agreed as he clasped his hands together between his knees. "It can be about so many things. Love, lust, power, play. It can be light-hearted fun, or it can be..." He hesitated. "Well, we've both experienced what else it can be," he finished. "I'm not gonna compare what Mikey did to me with what your dad did to you, though. At least I had some illusion of consent there. I managed to convince myself that I was okay with it as long as it got me what I wanted."

His mouth felt dry, and no amount of swallowing fixed it. His anger simmered back to the surface as though it had never been away. "Mikey?"

Laurence shrugged. "If I couldn't pay, he'd let me suck him off for a bag." He snorted. "Listen to me. 'Let me'. Like he was the one doing me a fucking favor." He rubbed his forehead, then clasped his hands together again. "We were young. Stupid. Mostly just stupid. At least he's sorry. It was one of the things we talked over."

Wind whipped past them. It pulled at their hair and their coats, but it seemed natural. Still, Quentin counted down, lest he be wrong in his supposition.

"How do you..." He shifted his hands to his thighs and gripped them so tightly that he felt the pain of it skitter along the scars beneath his trousers. "How do you do that... with me? Knowing what was done to you?"

"Because with you, it's different. Because I want to. Because I enjoy it." Laurence sat back and wrapped his arms across his chest to tuck his hands under his arms, and he squinted toward the Hudson, though there were too many buildings in the way for any line of sight to the water itself. "But it took time. I didn't do it for years. I didn't even figure out why, I just didn't feel like it." He turned to face Quentin. "You're scared that if we ever have that kind of sex, you'll hurt me, right?"

Quentin pursed his lips, and it was his turn to stare fixedly toward the buildings between them and the river. "I don't know. I'm sure that you're about to tell me that I won't."

"It's possible to cause pain that way," Laurence murmured, "if you don't do it right. You can't just go at it. It takes communication and care. Not gonna lie. And some people straight up just don't enjoy it, even if it doesn't hurt."

The pain remained, but his cock was hard, and pressed into the blood-slick floor again and again as the pressure built inside him. He wasn't there, wasn't present, wasn't in his own body; he just had to survive this, and it would all be over.

But if it felt so good, could it be so bad?

Candelabras crashed to the ground in the black of the void. Glass shattered. The wind howled in triumph.

A wave of heat rippled through his body as he came, adding to the moisture trapped under his body.

"I enjoyed it," he gasped as he dug his nails in harder. The words spilled from him as he screwed his eyes shut and tried to swallow back the nausea that twisted his gut. "Christ, Laurence, I damn well came when he raped me. I wasn't even there, I wasn't *present*, but I must have..." He hiccuped. "How? How could I *possibly...*"

Words failed him. His self-control failed him. As with everything in his life, it all came down to failure.

The wind was no longer natural, and there was nothing he could do. It touched the wetness on his cheeks and damn near froze his tears to his skin.

For god's sake. He was crying again. How did this happen? How could tears just come out of him like this without his say-so?

Treacherous little bastards.

"It wasn't your fault, baby," Laurence said. He spoke so firmly that his voice startled Quentin. "Give me your hands."

He didn't know how. How could he remove his fingers from his own legs? Were they supposed to do what he willed them to, or did things simply happen while he was absent?

"Quen," Laurence said. He didn't raise his voice, didn't sound urgent or tired. Merely soft and kind, as ever.

Quentin blinked, but it flicked more tears down his face, and while he was distracted by them, his fingers twitched free of his thighs and drifted toward Laurence.

Warmth wrapped around his hands. Even in this weather, Laurence was a radiator.

"It's what the body does," Laurence said. "It responds to stimuli. It doesn't mean that you 'wanted' it or 'enjoyed' it. It doesn't mean you deserved what he did to you in any way. None of the blame is on you, baby. None of it. You were a child, you were not responsible for his actions, and ejaculation does not mean consent. Do you understand?"

He gripped Laurence's hands every bit as hard as he had held his own legs, but Laurence didn't so much as twitch.

"How can any of that be true?" And it would have been a beautiful thing if it *were* true, but his gut said otherwise.

And yet Laurence would never lie to him.

Quentin forced himself to raise his head and meet Laurence's gaze, to look into those deep, dark windows and allow himself to become lost in them.

"Because that's how the world works, baby. Do you trust me?"

"You can't trust me!"

He sucked in a sharp breath and screwed his eyes shut. He couldn't cope with that memory right now. Not when he needed to listen, to pay close attention, to cling to the present and drown in Laurence's protection.

"Yes." He swallowed, then repeated it more loudly. "Yes. I trust you, absolutely." He forced his eyes to open.

"Then believe me. We can explore it some time, but for now just trust me and believe me, okay? It was never your fault."

He did what he could to absorb Laurence's wisdom. His very core seemed intent on rejecting it, but Quentin repeated it silently to himself in an attempt to at least commit it to surface-level memory, and perhaps if he repeated it enough it would sink deeper over time.

Laurence released his hands and touched his cheeks instead, tenderly wiping tears from his skin without any hurry. "It was *never* your fault," he insisted.

Quentin exhaled and leaned over until his forehead came to rest against Laurence's, and he wished that he could borrow even a fraction of Laurence's strength, if only for a moment. Instead he simply sat, silent, allowing Laurence's warmth to slowly permeate his skin, anchoring himself to the here and now through touch alone.

The wind died, replaced by spots of something even colder. They landed against his hands, his head, the back of his neck, and he drew breath as though it was his first in hours.

It was snowing.

He blinked as his eyes struggled to focus. Little specks of white drifted down and melted against Laurence's trousers, but more came.

Quentin tipped his head back and looked at the dark clouds above. The snow looked thicker up there as it fell toward him, and he took another breath.

He was alive. Better, he had found love. Whatever else happened, he was more fortunate than most, and he would not allow what he had to be washed away by what he'd lost.

"Thank you," he said. Quiet, but sincere. "We cannot sit out here all day."

"Yeah," Laurence sighed. "C'mon. Let's get back. We can call room service and watch TV all evening, and you can let me look after you, okay?"

Perhaps it wasn't the evening he'd envisioned an hour ago, but it sounded like heaven now, and so he clutched at Laurence's elbow as they stood.

"All right," he said.

The snow began to settle.

9

LAURENCE

LAURENCE WAS NOT A CREATURE MADE FOR SNOW. HE WAS A SOCAL baby through and through, so when he threw open the curtains in the morning and everything he could see was draped in white, for a split second he wondered whether he was dreaming.

He turned his back on the view and checked the hotel room, but nothing seemed out of place. He hadn't been woken in the night, either. He looked at Quentin, still curled up and clutching the sheets tightly, and wondered whether the nightmares hadn't come, or if they were holding Quentin captive in silence this time.

Should he wake Quentin in case, or leave him to rest? He bit his lip, and decided to use the bathroom before he made any decisions.

They'd ordered room service and picked at it while watching a couple of kids' movies. Laurence had scoured the list available through the hotel's entertainment service to make damn sure they avoided anything with overbearing parents or horrible murders, and in the end, they'd put their plates outside the room and gone to sleep.

When he returned from the bathroom, he sat carefully on his side of the bed and trailed his fingertips through Quentin's hair, marveling at its softness and how it would slide against his hands as though made of water. "Baby?" he said gently.

Much to his relief, Quentin stirred slowly, stretching as he yawned before a bleary eye opened. "Mm?"

"You sleep okay?"

Quentin managed to untangle himself from the sheets with grace, and slowly sat up, pushing hair back from his forehead. "Like a log, apparently." He idly straightened his pajamas and draped sheets across his lap.

Laurence smiled and rested the back of his hand against Quentin's knee. "It snowed more overnight."

Quentin turned toward the window, then slipped out of bed, padded quietly to it, and gazed outside. "Oh my word. It's beautiful!"

He should have guessed Quentin would love snow. The guy was like Laurence's polar opposite in every other way, so why not this too?

"Yeah. And kinda Christmassy, I guess. For people who don't live where I do, anyway." Laurence hopped off the bed and wandered over to Quentin's side, and had to admit that the sight of Central Park blanketed in snow really was kinda pretty.

"I don't know that I've seen snow at Christmas for many years now," Quentin mused.

"Well, we've got snow and a few days off," Laurence realized. "How about we make this our own little Christmas break? We didn't really do Christmas in London; we could go out today and pick up, like, a gift or two for each other, then we can have Christmas tomorrow. How does that sound?"

He watched as Quentin's lips pressed together and his eyes narrowed. Quentin's thinking face was super cute, and Laurence felt himself unwinding by his side.

"Only if you allow me to include your birthday," was Quentin's final edict.

Laurence crinkled his nose. "You noticed, huh?"

"I'm afraid so."

He sucked his teeth. "We're pretty good at missing the important stuff, huh?"

"We were preoccupied," Quentin replied with kindness.

Laurence nodded to himself. He'd had a broken rib all through Quentin's birthday last year, and Quentin hadn't said a damn thing about it, just let it slide by while he nursed Laurence back to health. Then, when Laurence's own birthday came, they'd only just gotten free of the crap with Freddy and the duke, and Quentin was having meltdowns pretty much daily, so Laurence had focused on helping him find some stability, and that had lasted all through December. They just hadn't had any time to do anything more than take care of each other.

Quentin was used to his birthdays coming early, or late, or not at all. Those were the times when his father abused him, when he blacked out and lost the whole day, and Laurence had made a promise not to let another one go by without any celebration. All he had to do was make sure they stayed well away from dangerous crap from now all the way through to early March, and he'd keep that promise.

Most of the dangerous crap in their lives came from the duke, so all they needed was for him to uphold his word and leave them the fuck alone, and everything would be fine.

"Yeah," he agreed. "All that's done now, though. We'll be okay." He smiled to Quentin and offered his hand, and Quentin took it. "You know your way around New York, right?"

"I do."

"And shopping's like a national sport for you." Laurence grinned. "If we go out today, we might beat the storm, then we can hole up and look out at the winter wonderland without having to spend any more time in it than absolutely necessary." He let out a small laugh. "I guess all the ice rinks are buried under snow now, anyway."

A sparkle entered Quentin's eyes, humor breaking through. His lips quirked faintly. "The irony," he chuckled. "All right. This seems to be an excellent plan. Shall we have lunch somewhere, and then go our separate ways?"

"And meet back here by five?" Laurence nodded. "You're on. I'm gonna get you something awesome!"

"No doubt." Quentin leaned in to kiss his cheek, then released his hand and backed away toward the bathroom. "Nothing silly," he added with a wag of one finger.

Laurence draped his hand over his heart in faked offense. "Never!"

With a chuckle, Quentin disappeared into the bathroom, and Laurence heard the door lock.

He was beyond any hurt when Quentin chose to lock the door. Sometimes the guy needed his space, and Laurence was okay with that now. He understood it way better than he had when they'd first met; but then, in his defense, Quentin hadn't had these damn memories back then. They were buried too deep.

Laurence never should have gone digging, but what else could he do?

He shook his head and pulled out his phone, then did a little math to make sure he wouldn't be waking his mom by calling her.

She answered promptly. "Morning, Bambi!"

"Hey, Mom! How are you today?"

"Wonderful! It's going to be a lovely day. I hear you have snow in New York?"

"Very funny," he grumbled.

Myriam laughed. "Oh, Bambi. I'm sure you'll have a wonderful time. You both need a vacation. And New York was one of Eric's favorite cities, you know."

"Yeah?" Laurence sat on the ledge by the window, looking at Central Park as he leaned one shoulder against the glass. "I guess he must've come in the summer, though."

"And when a movie ticket cost five dollars," Myriam added. "It was before you were born. Before we even started dating." She sighed, and it sounded wistful. "I hear New York's changed a lot since then. A lot of gentrification and everything that comes with it." She clicked her tongue. "Anyway, how are you both getting along?"

"Not bad. Quen had a bit of a setback yesterday, but I think he's handled it well." He bit the inside of his cheek. "We're gonna need to find a therapist, though. I don't think there's any way around it. How are the kids?"

"They're doing well, but I think they'll be better once you're both home. Mia's not quite the doting parent either of you are. Sebastian had a client over the holidays, so Ethan and Aiden chipped in a lot. We're managing just fine, dear, don't you worry."

He nodded to himself. "And the dogs? You know I can't hang up without an update for Quen."

Myriam laughed again. "They're wonderful. I'll send him pictures later. And on the subject of animals, Windsor appears to have learned a new word, and it sounds like it's one of Quentin's."

Laurence groaned. "It's the accent. Let me guess. He said bugger?"

"He did."

"Mmm. He's got mischief in him, doesn't he?" He chuckled. "Glad to hear everyone's safe. We're gonna have our own little Christmas here in the snow, then we'll be back next week, okay?"

"That sounds wonderful, Bambi! And then we can start organizing this year's Valentine's party, and not invite any gods this time."

"Yeah." He snorted. "Okay. I'm gonna go. Love you, Mom."

"I love you too, Bambi. Have a great time."

"We will. See you soon."

He hung up and started googling ideas of where he might find some good presents for Quentin, and checking how far those places were from the hotel, and whether or not he could take the subway to get to them.

The less time he spent out in the snow, the better.

10

LAURENCE

Snow fell in idle flurries as Laurence parted ways with Quentin after lunch, and he hunkered down inside his thick coat, which was turning out to be one of the most essential purchases he'd ever made.

He watched Quentin head west, then pulled out his phone and checked his short list of potential gift stores. He figured he'd try the Juilliard bookstore for some new sheet music. If he could lure Quentin out of the classical zone, Laurence reckoned he could introduce him to a bunch of modern composers — with the help of the staff, of course, since Laurence's tastes ran closer to folk than Quentin's.

Juilliard was the opposite side of Central Park from their hotel, so he could hit it up on the way back, which meant he had enough time to run back down to the sex shop and pick out a few things. Maybe not for tomorrow, but who knew? Laurence could buy now, then see how they felt in the morning.

He ducked into the nearest subway and swiped his MetroCard through a barrier, then jogged down steps to the southbound platform to get out of the weather.

He took the stairs down to the store carefully. Snow had been brushed off them, but that just meant it had frozen underfoot. Now they were icy as hell. Once he was inside, he stamped slush off his shoes and gave the clerks a cheery wave.

"On your own today?"

"Yeah. Thanks for your help yesterday, man."

"No problem. Was it his first time?"

"Yeah." Laurence grinned a little. "I think I've got an idea of the kind of thing he'd like now, though."

"Okay, well, don't hesitate to call if you need help."

Laurence nodded with thanks and headed straight for the clothes racks, picking through them more thoroughly than he'd had the chance to the day before. There was a whole bunch of stuff he'd pay good money to see Quentin try on, but that was a way off into the future, if it happened at all, so he sighed and focused on things he knew he'd look great in, then narrowed them down to the items he thought Quentin might like to see him in more.

The posing pouch was totally a winner. He couldn't wait to be able to wear that and parade around the bedroom in it, so there was no way he was leaving it on a rack. He also plucked out a mesh shirt and matching briefs, but after some debate, he decided against any other accessories. That was something to leave for another day.

Still, he grabbed some lube and checked for a long expiration date on it, then took it all to the register.

Maybe they'd need the lube one day. Maybe not. But it was better to have some in the house, just in case.

He made it up to Juilliard's bookstore by three o'clock and tried not to dawdle by the guitar music, but he had time, so he rifled through the selection before he moved on to the piano music.

Laurence was feeling pretty good about how things were going. By getting small, personal gifts, it made the disparity in their incomes a lot less obvious, and so long as Quentin didn't go over the top and splash out on something like a diamond or a Tesla, everything should be okay.

Ultimately, he'd come to accept that Quentin's wealth wasn't anything either of them had any control over. It wasn't like Laurence could make the money go away, or like Quentin could buckle down and work harder for more of it. It just existed, like anything else they could have inherited from their parents. Laurence had received gifts and the power to use magic from his lineage, and that was more than the majority of the human race got, so he'd learned to put Quentin's money in that box and not let it bug him so much.

It was probably the time spent with Freddy that had most made Laurence see that Quentin's money didn't define him, that their exposure to the high life only cut them off from the real world. It might be a blessing, but it was one hell of a curse, too. Freddy and Quentin had both had their lives laid out for them by centuries of history, and now that they'd both refused to accept those paths, it would cost their family everything. Quentin probably wasn't going to have kids, and Freddy didn't seem the sort, so that left Nicky, and Laurence hadn't met their youngest brother. He had no idea whether Nicky would continue the line by having children. All he knew was that Annis had tried to warn him about Nicky as she died.

"Can I help you?"

Laurence blinked out of his reverie and smiled at the young lady who had approached him. She seemed polished enough to be a student here when she wasn't working. "Oh, hey. I'm looking for something for my partner. He plays a lot of classical, but I wanna broaden his horizons. Is there anything you'd suggest?"

"Oh, I like a challenge!" She swept dark hair back over her shoulder and leaned toward the shelves. "Soloist?"

"Yeah."

"What are some of his favorites?"

"Uh." Laurence patted his hair while he mulled it over. "He likes Clair de Lune, uh... some Liszt, uh... some Russian stuff? He seems to really like the big sounds, the ones that tear your heart out, are super melancholy or booming, you know?"

She sucked on her teeth a moment, then nodded to herself. "I think he'd like Hans Zimmer. He has that big sound your partner might be looking for. He does a lot of soundtracks. *Inception*, *Gladiator*, those kinds of movies."

"Oh Goddess, that sounds perfect!" Laurence grinned as she plucked out a few examples for him. "Thank you!"

She laughed happily. "You're welcome. Now you get to choose, and I can't help you with that."

"No, this is great! Thank you so much!"

He began sifting through the selection in his hands and narrowed it down to two, then decided to buy them both.

BY THE TIME he made it out of the store and across to Central Park, the snow was coming thick and fast. These weren't the delicate little drops of yesterday. The snow that landed on him was huge, like shaved ice, and if it was gonna melt at all, it wasn't in any hurry to get started.

He tucked his bags under one arm and picked up the pace as visibility decreased. The cloud cover was so total that he felt like he was under one huge, gray roof. Shapes loomed in the snow, some tall enough to be trees, others shorter and walking their own paths through the thickening snowfall.

Suddenly, the white all around didn't seem so beautiful.

He closed his eyes briefly and reached out for Windsor, as

though he could leech some of San Diego's sunlight through that link, but all he got was an excited greeting from his familiar and the strong sense that Windsor was eating, so he opened his eyes and plowed ahead.

A shape emerged out of the snow, on a collision course, and Laurence stepped out of the way before it could happen. The other guy wore glasses that were caked with snowflakes, so Laurence couldn't blame him for the near-miss.

"Oh! I'm sorry!" The guy peered over the top of his glasses, honey-brown eyes wide with embarrassment. "This damn snow!"

"It's okay." Laurence chuckled, and his gaze was drawn to a ring the man wore on his right hand. That and the bright orange nail polish, but mostly it was the ring that stole his interest.

Was it Laurence's imagination, or did the ring have a weak blue glow?

"Laurence Riley," he said, thrusting his hand forward. He affected his best laid-back smile and turned his charm up to eleven.

"Basil Irwin," was the near-automatic reply as the man took his hand and smiled brightly. "You always introduce yourself to strangers?"

"Sure. Why not?" Laurence looked pointedly to the ring, then up to Basil's eyes.

Basil followed his gaze, then gasped. "You think orange is too much for winter?"

"I think your ring glows," Laurence said, giving up on subtlety.

"Oh!" Now Basil's cheeks flushed even redder than the cold had already made them, and he laughed nervously.

"The orange totally goes with your hair, man." Laurence gestured up toward Basil's damp, copper hair. "Who cares if it's winter?" Apart from Quentin, of course, who near religiously believed that fashion came in seasons.

Basil's laugh continued. "Oh, thank God. That's what I

thought!" Then he looked at the ring. "You see it? So you can use magic, right?"

Laurence nodded. There wasn't any way around admitting it, and maybe making contact with a witch who wasn't Rufus would be a good thing. He already knew that he and Ru would disagree on something important in the future, so having contacts — or even friends — to fall back on later in life seemed sensible. If Laurence wanted to sow the seeds of friendship, starting out with lies seemed a bad way to do it.

"Yeah. Hey, look. My hotel's just across the park, and I'm only in town for a few days, but if you wanna get in out of the weather and grab a cup of coffee, you're welcome to join me." He tapped the bags under his arm. "And I can drop these off in my room so they don't get soaking wet."

"Oh, er," Basil pulled a phone from his pocket and checked it, then smiled. "Okay! Let me just—" he poked his tongue out a little as he tapped at the screen with both thumbs. "There we go. Oh my God, this snow is getting worse!" He held a hand up to try and shield his eyes, but his glasses were already caked in the stuff. "Which hotel?"

Laurence started walking, slow enough to check that Basil had fallen in by his side. "The Pierre."

Basil's eyes grew wide again. "Nice," he squeaked.

Laurence wasn't going to deny it. He'd have the same reaction in Basil's shoes. "Yeah. My partner likes his creature comforts, so how he's out in this weather I don't know. He's British," he added, as though that explained the madness.

"Well it's good you're here for a few more days," Basil said, as he hurried along by Laurence's side. "This is going to turn into a blizzard soon enough. Pretty typical New York winter. All the airports shut down, people have to extend their hotel bookings, it turns into this dystopian nightmare of stranded businessmen roaming the streets looking forlorn." He laughed lightly. "Like the bourgeoise zombie apocalypse."

Laurence blinked. "The what?"

"Middle-class." Basil chuckled. "Sorry. I'm a journalist. Words are my business. What do you do?"

"Florist," Laurence answered. "I, uh... sell flowers." He cursed inwardly at making it sound so lame.

"Flowers are cool," Basil argued. "People love them. What brings you to the Big Apple?"

"It's a little break for us. We were just in London... visiting family," he said, doing his best not to sound evasive. "We live in San Diego, but figured it'd be nice to stop off and take like a week to ourselves before we had to get back to the beautiful sunshine and endless beaches, you know?" He flashed a grin. "Sometimes what you really want out of life is impenetrable cloud and a blizzard."

Basil laughed, and lightly patted Laurence's arm. "Oh, this is gonna be great," he cooed. "I've never met anyone else who could use magic. We're gonna have an awesome time!"

Laurence chuckled and hoped Basil was right, 'cause he couldn't deal with another warlock.

Not so soon after the last one.

11

QUENTIN

Quentin drifted in and out of shops without much direction or, in fact, success. He attempted to elicit Siri's assistance in the matter, but it soon became obvious that unless he knew exactly what he was looking for, she was of no use.

Still, he would not be defeated. He was *good* at shopping, for heaven's sake, and he knew New York, to boot.

He ducked into a doorway as the snow grew heavier. He could doubtless keep most of it from touching him, but he was reasonably sure that it would look peculiar to anyone who happened to see it. A little discomfort was preferable to discovery, so he glanced toward the store he'd used as shelter.

It looked as though it might be an arts supply store, and he blinked. The place was sizable, stretching back from the door for what seemed like half the block, so he pushed on the handle and drifted inside.

Goodness, he hadn't so much as lifted a pencil in, what, over a year now? Hadn't painted for far longer. Difficult enough to cart a piano wherever he went, but transporting wet canvases was out of the question.

He found himself wandering along aisles lined with prestretched canvasses and a wealth of paints and brushes. Everything from thinners to mediums, varnishes to solvents were lined along shelves, and he allowed his fingers to drift over bottles and shrink-wrap alike.

He might have allowed his skills to lapse for too long now. Regardless, this was not the time to attempt to find out, so he forced himself away from that section and drifted around others until he reached a shelf of items that caught his eye. A small card proclaimed them to be handmade journals from a local artist, and he reached for one of the leather-bound tomes.

It was good quality. The leather had been dyed purple and embossed with knotwork, and the pages within were hand stitched. He couldn't find a single scrap of loose thread or frayed leather, and it felt comfortable in his hands.

It would make a good spell book.

He bit the tip of his tongue as he placed it back on the shelf and began to scour the others. While he had no wish to encourage Laurence's fascination with magic, neither did he wish to be unsupportive. This could be a good middle ground, to gift him with something he could use in the privacy of his own sanctum or den or whatever word Laurence wished to use for the room on the top floor he had commandeered for his practices.

A flash of green peeked out from behind another, much duller book, and he fished it out. The cover was embossed with a tree whose roots and branches spread out like fans, and knotwork bordered it all.

It was very Laurence.

Still, Quentin checked it over for defects before he took it to the register, and he gratefully accepted when the cashier offered to gift wrap it before bagging.

He checked the time on his phone after he paid. He easily had enough time to drift through a few more shops on his way back to the hotel, so he thanked the cashier for her assistance and headed for the door.

The weather had worsened considerably. He stopped on the warm and dry side of the glass and stared out at the wall of whiteness beyond, swirls and eddies of flakes which made the whole city disappear.

Bloody hell. How was anyone to get anywhere safely in this mess? The snow was already several centimeters deep on the pavement, and if Quentin couldn't see terribly far, he doubted that anyone attempting to drive could either.

If he wished to get back in one piece, he might have to be even more attentive than usual.

Another customer ducked into the store, and Quentin waited for them to pass before he forced himself out into the thick of it. He gritted his teeth as the bitter cold sandblasted his face, and since there was no bloody way anyone could see through this rubbish, he whipped up a faint wind around himself and a slight buffer of warmth to keep the worst of the snow out of his eyes as he pressed on.

Traffic had already ground to a halt. He had to weave past stationary cars at crosswalks, and people appeared and disappeared as though the snow itself were coughing them up and swallowing them whole once more.

The trouble was that he had absolutely no idea where he was now. Had he reached 57th Street yet? If so, surely he should be near Central Park, and yet he was next to — he leaned closer to be sure — a cafe. He frowned and pulled his phone out.

"Siri, how do I get to The Pierre hotel?"

He waited a moment, then frowned as his phone apologized to him. The little bars in the top corner which indicated signal seemed to have disappeared. Perhaps the weather interfered with it somehow, although he had no idea how that might work. Technology was not his strong suit.

Not that he *had* a strong suit.

Still, this city was a grid. All he had to do was get to the next intersection and check the street signs.

Satisfied that he had a plan, he continued on along the pavement to the next junction and peered up into the blizzard, but he couldn't see the signs well enough to read them.

He would have to take a risk and hope that if his sight were this limited, so was everyone else's.

A gust of wind cleared snow out of his way for a couple of seconds. Long enough to note that he was on the corner of 6th Avenue and 57th Street, but the placards were pointing so as to indicate that he had been walking along 57th Street rather than up 6th Avenue. He clicked his tongue as he realized where he must have gone wrong, but at least if he continued along 57th Street, he could just turn left onto 5th Avenue to reach the hotel.

If he overshot the hotel, there were plenty of shops further up 5th Avenue that he could search for a second gift. It was no use to argue in favor of picking up presents for both Laurence's delayed birthday and Christmas surprises, if he then only brought one instead of two back with him.

He listened to be sure that there were no cars in motion, then hurried across 6th Avenue to continue on his way.

Darkness punctured the snow, and for one heart-stopping moment he thought it could be a truck coming at him, but the only thing he heard was the honk of horns and the distant howl of wolves. As absurd as the latter seemed, it certainly wasn't a truck engine, but he did his best to avoid whatever it might be nonetheless.

There was something else in the dark. The dual ember-red glow at head height, which for whatever reason he thought could be eyes, although they left little smoke-like trails of red after-image as they lunged toward him.

Toward him.

Quentin snapped up one hand and slid a foot back as he prepared to deflect whatever on earth this thing was.

There was a flash of teeth. An open maw. The thing was an animal of some sort, made of pitch black, and the inside of its mouth was like a bottomless chasm. It broke free from the cloak of snow and lunged for him.

It was a dog.

A dog the size of a horse.

"Stop!" He darted aside just to be on the safe side, and it was just as well that he had, because the beast didn't obey him in the slightest.

Fear spiked at last, as though the reality of his situation had suddenly set in.

A vast black dog with glowing red eyes that paid no attention to his commands was attempting to attack him in the middle of the afternoon in the heart of Midtown Manhattan. He was certain he was the target, because as the massive flank swept past him, the beast turned around and came for him again.

If it wouldn't respond to a verbal command, his next best solution was telekinesis, but that was about as effective as a chocolate teapot. He didn't even encounter the sort of resistance he had while trying to contain Annis. It was as though the dog simply didn't exist.

Then that maw opened impossibly wide, and it was all over.

12

LAURENCE

Laurence left Basil in the lobby for a few minutes while he went up to his room to drop off the things he'd bought and take off his huge outdoor coat. He double-checked himself in a mirror to make sure he didn't look like a mess, ran fingers through his hair to bring some life back to the snow-drenched curls, then headed back down again.

Basil was still there, looking kind of lost in the huge, fancy lobby, so Laurence beckoned him over and headed toward the bar.

"So you live in New York, right?" Laurence indicated a table for two and followed as the *maitre d'* led them inside.

"That's right. East Harlem." Basil thanked the *maitre d'* as they reached a table, and shrugged his heavy wool coat off before he sat. He looked awkward about letting the *maitre d'* take it away to hang up, but in the end, he relented, and watched it leave. It took a couple of seconds for him to return his attention to Laurence with an apologetic smile. "Where in San Diego are you from?"

"Ah, it's complicated." Laurence laughed. "We travelled a lot when I was a kid, but we finally settled near Mission Trails. Now I live in La Jolla, though."

Basil ran hands through his hair and left it spiked upwards. "Oh, wow. Isn't that..."

Laurence nodded. "Yeah. Again, my partner." He wasn't going to get into it any more than that.

The *maitre d'* returned with menus, which Laurence took with thanks, and he ordered a soda for now, without daring to look down and find out how much that soda cost. For good measure, he showed his room key so the bar tab could be charged to the room. Laurence could sort it out later, rather than sob in public when they got the bill.

Basil also requested a soda, and the maitre d' left them in peace.

"So what does it do?" Laurence pointed toward the ring.

"Oh!" Basil laughed lightly as he looked at the ring. "It just lets me see ghosts." He wriggled the ring off his finger and offered it to Laurence. "I inscribed the sigils on the inside," he explained. "It's a different spell to imbue an item, but..." He waved his hands. "I'm sure you know all that, right?"

"Right," Laurence echoed as he rolled the ring in his fingers and squinted at the sigils within. As with his own amulet, once the ring was beyond the reach of Basil's aura, the glow faded.

Laurence offered it back to him with a smile, and Basil slipped it back onto his finger. The glow returned the moment he reached to take it back.

"I'm a necromancer," Basil explained with almost childish glee. "How about you?"

"Witch," Laurence replied. He paused long enough for a waiter to deliver their drinks, then he poured his soda into the glass he'd been given while he glanced at Basil.

The guy looked nothing like a necromancer. He was small and slim, with wide eyes and a smattering of freckles. He couldn't be much older than Laurence, and he was a lot more femme. None of these things alone screamed ghost whisperer, but taken all together, it was so incongruous that Laurence had to smile. There was a lot to be said for people who did their own damn thing. Speaking as a bisexual florist who'd been beaten up way too often for being a 'sissy,' he felt some small kinship with Basil's dissonance.

"Wow! Is that all, like, nature magic?" Basil sipped his soda.

"Pretty much." Laurence wasn't about to admit to a total stranger that he knew a small handful of spells and had only just discovered that ghosts were even a thing. "You don't, like, make zombies and raise the dead, right?"

Basil's laugh came easily again, and he flapped his hand while he put the soda down. "No. I just try and put ghosts to rest, mostly. My boyfriend is..." He sucked his lip like he was debating what to say. "He's a medium," he admitted. "It comes naturally to him, where I need to use magic to do it. We work together to, like, resolve hauntings and make places safe again."

"Huh." Laurence rubbed his jaw and reached for his glass as he sat back. "It'd be pretty cool to talk to you both, to be honest. My partner's due back by five o'clock and he's not really comfortable talking about magic, but he doesn't mind, like..." He hesitated a second, not sure about the safest way to word it. "You know, other stuff."

"That's great! Maybe we could get together this evening?" Basil pulled his phone out and began to type on it. "Maybe not here, though. I don't know if they'd let Jon in through the door."

Laurence blinked. "Why not?"

"He's, um..." Basil flushed quickly. "People are scared of him. Somewhere this fancy, they might refuse him entry. It's shitty, but we're used to it."

He had to wonder what could be so scary about Basil's boyfriend that a doorman would stop him entering the hotel. It couldn't just be that he was big, surely, or wrestlers wouldn't be allowed anywhere. Maybe he was like Quentin, with that ability he had to seem like he was bigger than his body. It could just be that Basil's boyfriend exuded an air of intimidation, without any ability to dial it down.

"Let me see if Quentin's interested." Laurence whipped out his own phone and tapped out a text. "Just in case he had plans." He glanced toward the doors, then added, "Will anything be open if this weather holds up?"

"You're kidding, right?" Basil gave a little snort. "If you don't show for work, you get fired."

Laurence sighed and examined his phone again, but there was no response. "I guess."

Maybe Quentin was on the subway. Was there signal down there? He'd get the text when he surfaced, but New York was a noisy city, and he might not hear it. Quentin lacked Laurence's sharp senses, and things which stood out a mile to Laurence often flew under Quentin's radar.

No. Sending another text so soon was just Laurence being needy, so he put the phone down and smiled at Basil. "So how'd you get into all this magic stuff?"

"Oh, wow." Basil wrung his fingers together briefly as he looked toward the ceiling like he was lining his thoughts up. "So I was trawling through all these ghost-hunting websites — as you do — and I found a supposed haunting upstate, and I thought it'd make for a fun fluff piece. You know, go there, check it out, find out what was so spooky about it that people thought it was haunted. Well, I was in the house and it really gave me the heebie-jeebies, you know? It just had this awful—" he shook both his hands like he was trying to dry them "—oppressive weight to it that I couldn't shake off, and then I saw a glow under the floorboards, and when I pried one up, there was a book hidden in a cubbyhole down there."

"And the book glowed," Laurence concluded.

"Right!" Basil glanced around before he continued. "I took it home, because who doesn't take home a glowing book they've found in a hidden compartment in a spooky old house, and I found it was all written in another language. I had to go learn Latin just to work out what it was, and it turned out it was a necromancer's Book of Shadows."

Laurence nodded as he listened. He hadn't even begun to write his own Book of Shadows yet, but he understood the concept well enough. A witch would create their own personal journal, a collection of spells, metaphysical musings, and important discoveries all in one single book.

Rather than hit up a whole bunch of books, Basil's discovery was pay dirt. Everything essential distilled into a single tome, without the extra stuff that filled Rufus' entire library. It probably meant Basil had a whole lot of spells at his fingertips, but none of the lore that he might otherwise have access to.

"Wow," Laurence breathed. "That's quite a story."

Basil grinned. "It's kinda awesome. What about you?"

"Oh, uh..." Laurence bit his lip and tried to work out how the hell to even start. "I only found out, like, last year that I could use magic. I didn't have any books, though. I had to find a teacher."

"That must've been hard." Basil was sympathetic. "Especially as you can't just look for one on Yelp."

"Yeah, exactly!" He couldn't help but check his phone, but there was still no answer. "Do cellphones get reception on the subway?"

"Only in the stations. Not in tunnels."

"Huh." He fidgeted with the phone, then sent another text.

Would he be worrying too much if he used his gifts to be sure Quentin was safe, or was it a massive invasion of privacy? What if Quentin was busy buying Laurence's present right this moment, and Laurence spoiled the surprise with his impatience?

What about that time he was nearly killed by a wildfire and you just sat around waiting on him when he couldn't respond?

Quentin hadn't wanted to use the Tube. Why would he turn to the subway?

He pushed his chair back from the table. "I'm just gonna go to the bathroom. I won't be long."

"Oh, sure!" Basil smiled and turned his attention to his phone.

Laurence slipped away to the nearest restroom and locked himself into a stall, then put the toilet seat down so he could sit on it. It took a couple of deep breaths to shut out the world around himself, and he focused on the stream of time, baiting it with his intentions and waiting for the right vision to bubble into his hands.

A flurry of snow with a heart of ink popped out of the stream, and Laurence immersed himself in it.

Quentin pushed through the blizzard with care. Laurence could see him tip his head one way or another as he paused to listen as well as look, and Laurence wanted to reach out and take his arm, as though he could reassure Quentin that the traffic had stopped.

He could hear the mixture of idling engines and distant horns, wrapped around the howl of hundreds of faraway wolves.

Wolves?

In New York?

Quentin seemed to have noticed the odd sound, too. He glanced around as he stepped off the curb and into the street, frowning quizzically to himself.

"Goddess, Quen," Laurence breathed. "Don't tell me you've run off into trouble again."

A shadow loomed in the white, and Laurence narrowed his eyes at it, but Quentin didn't seem to have noticed just yet.

A pair of glowing red eyes followed a snarling maw.

This thing was a monster. It was easily as tall as Quentin, if not taller.

"Goddess! Quen!"

Quentin seemed to spot it at last, and immediately swept a foot back into a defensive position. "Stop!"

The monster didn't stop.

Not until it had eaten Quentin whole and nothing was left.

Laurence screamed as he launched to his feet, and the vision faded to nothing as he slammed his fists against the door of the stall. He hit it so hard that the lock shook loose and the door flew open, and then he kicked it out of his way as he stormed out of the bathroom.

Whatever that creature was, he would track it down, and he would make it pay. No matter how, no matter the cost.

The hunt began now.

13

LAURENCE

HE RAN THROUGH THE HOTEL LOBBY IN A RAGE, TAKING LITTLE CARE whenever anyone was self-absorbed enough to step out in front of him. Laurence mowed down a businessman who yelled at him, and it mingled with another shout.

He ignored both.

The doorman barely had time to open the way for him, and he stormed out onto the street, into a darkening world of blindness.

The sun must already be starting to set. The blizzard was everywhere, and the freezing winds that came with it cut through his shirt and pants to slice the heat right out of him. Laurence halted, fists turned clawlike by his sides, and searched for Quentin's scent.

A hand landed on his shoulder, accompanied by a panting breath. "Laurence?"

He snarled and twisted free of the hold, turning on the hand's owner.

Basil stood there, wide-eyed, half-terrified. He snatched his hand back and used it to further wrap his coat around himself. "Um, I mean…" Then he blinked and huffed. "What's wrong?"

"Quentin," Laurence growled. "He's..." He hiccuped for air. "He's gone, and..."

It all came crashing down around him. He'd just watched some horrible monster distend its jaw and *eat Quentin*.

It couldn't be over. They couldn't have faced the duke, made a truce with Freddy, finally had some breakthroughs with every-thing Quentin was afraid of, for it all to end just like this, could they? It wasn't right. It wasn't fair.

Quentin couldn't be *dead*.

Laurence's breathing shuddered. Wetness touched his cheeks, but it was warm, not the frozen caress of the snow. He howled until his throat was sore, but it just left him feeling hollow, and grief swelled into the void to fill it.

"He can't..." He hiccuped. "He can't be dead..."

All the words did was amplify his grief, and he fell to his knees as his body shook with the force of his sobbing. Every breath lead to a hiccup, every exhale flushed more tears out of him, until everything hurt. His head ached, his eyes were sore, and his skin was near freezing.

Basil's hand was on his shoulder again. "Okay. I don't know what's happened, but you're going to freeze to death out here. Let's go inside and talk."

Laurence's mind's eye flickered to all the things he could do to make Basil stop talking. Entrails were a key feature whenever his thoughts ran this way, and the idea of this nice guy getting those pulled out for trying to help shook Laurence into taking a deep breath.

"What's the point?" he breathed. His fingers dug into his knees through another hiccup, then he had a thought.

That thought blossomed into an idea, and he stared at Basil, grabbing for his arm.

"You can bring him back," he said. "You're a necromancer. You can bring him back!"

Basil's eyes were invisible behind his snow-covered glasses, but his features twisted with doubt. "We need to work out what the problem is, first. C'mon." He hooked an arm under Laurence's and tugged. "I can't lift you, you've got to get up yourself," he added in an apologetic tone.

The chill seemed to run right through Laurence's body and into his bones, and he struggled to stand. The dents he'd made in the snow soon filled in with fresh falling flakes.

He allowed Basil to steer him back into the hotel lobby, and stood numb as the local brushed snow off Laurence's clothes with quick flitting motions of his fingers. The doorman greeted them, but Laurence didn't say a word.

He was too busy clinging to the strand of hope that had flourished before his eyes.

Basil could bring Quentin back.

That meant Laurence couldn't let Basil out of his sight.

Laurence sucked in air to try and stop the hiccups, and he focused all his attention on Basil, who was thumbing away at his phone again.

"Is your coat in your room?" Basil asked.

"Yeah."

"Okay." Basil took his elbow and dragged him toward the elevators. "What floor?"

"Uh. 35." Laurence dug the key card out of his pants as the elevator door closed. He barely even noticed the white-gloved elevator attendant by the buttons. "Why?"

"So we can talk, and you can tell me what's happened, and then we can come up with a plan." Basil tugged his glasses off and pushed his coat open so he could wipe them on his shirt. He glanced toward the attendant, then up to Laurence. "Quentin is... your partner, I'm guessing?"

Laurence nodded, but held his breath. He'd get on top of the damn hiccups if he could just stop for a minute. His dad always made the hiccups go away by telling bad jokes that got him to laugh, but there was no way Laurence would laugh now.

Goddess, he would *really* kill for a hit.

There was no way he could cope with this kind of pain. If he'd thought it was bad finding out about what the duke had done all those years, it was nothing compared to the certainty that his life was meaningless without Quentin in it.

Basil is a necromancer. He had to cling to that.

"Room?" Basil cut in as he steered Laurence out of the elevator.

Laurence gestured, and Basil took the key card from him, then unlocked the door and propelled Laurence inside.

"Sit," Basil barked, despite his mild tenor.

Laurence bristled at being given an order, but he dropped onto the corner of the bed and crossed his arms nonetheless.

"Tell me what happened," Basil's tone turned gentle, and he perched in a chair by the window.

"I—" He snapped his mouth shut.

How much did he want to admit to, here?

How much did he need Basil's help?

Laurence bared his teeth, then turned slightly toward Basil. "I'm not only a witch," he muttered. "I have other gifts."

Basil's eyebrows lifted. "Psychic?"

Laurence nodded. His hiccups had gone at last. "I can see through time. I thought I'd look and find out why Quentin wasn't answering his texts, just in case he'd got into trouble, and there was this huge... this *monster*, and it..." He had to stop and rub his face. "It ate him."

"Oh my god! That's horrible!"

The weight on the bed shifted as Basil came to sit beside him and take his hands, and Laurence didn't fight him.

"It just opened its mouth like a snake swallowing something ten times bigger, and he was gone," Laurence whispered. "He can't be *gone*. I need him!"

"Describe this monster."

He shook his head slowly. Thinking it over, examining it enough to go over the details, wasn't where he wanted to go.

"Laurence, c'mon. You want to find this thing? Then we need to know what it is. Talk to me."

"It's a dog. A wolf, maybe. But, like, it's the size of a horse, man. It was already huge, and then its mouth just—" he drew his arms apart like he was miming a shark's maw. "It just ate him whole, and he was gone."

Basil tutted faintly. "A huge dog? What did it look like? Did it have any markings? Any detail at all could be important."

Laurence snorted and took a hand back to wipe his nose. "I can tell you're a journalist," he muttered. "It was huge and black and had these glowing red eyes. There's no way it was a normal animal." Especially not since it had ignored Quentin's command for it to stop.

"A black dog?" Basil released his other hand and resorted to that phone again. It was like the damn thing was part of him.

"It was massive," Laurence reiterated. *A black dog* made it sound far more mundane than the thing he'd witnessed.

"And it vanished?"

Laurence just bobbed his head and stared at the window. The outside world looked like someone had taped a huge gray canvas across the outside of the glass.

I come?

He blinked and shook his head. *No. Stay there.*

Windsor felt agitated. *I help!*

You can't, he sent back. *Just wait. I'll be home soon.*

Windsor was dissatisfied, but he remained quiet.

"Okay, I thought so." Basil clicked his tongue. "Black dogs are British ghost legends. They're all over the UK. Barguests, Black Shuck, Padfoot, you name it. They tend to have glowing eyes, usually red." The tip of his tongue poked out a little as he scrolled. "I mean, dogs are traditionally gatekeepers to and guardians of the underworld — that's not a British thing, that's pretty global.

Did you know in ancient Persia, the dead were disposed of by feeding them to dogs?"

"What the fuck is wrong with you?" Laurence blinked. The words blurted out of him without any anger, but still. "This thing's eaten the man I love, and you're talking about Persia?"

"Bear with me," Basil murmured. "What I'm saying is that what you saw seems to be some variant of this legend. A hellhound, if you want to call it that. And not all of them are malign. Some come to give warnings, some protect graveyards. And some, er, kill people, but the corpse gets left behind." He peered at Laurence earnestly. "Even when all they do is leave people like shells for the rest of their lives, the people still get left behind."

Laurence felt like Basil's words meant more to Basil than they did to him. "So... what are you saying? Like..." He licked his lips and tried not to get his hopes up too high. "Quentin's not dead?"

"I'm not going to state either way without more facts," Basil sighed. "But this doesn't seem to fit the pattern for a black dog. We should go to where it happened and look for any clues."

Laurence nodded and bounced from the bed, striding over to the closet and grabbing his coat out of it. It still hadn't dried out. "Sure. I can probably find it."

"Great. Jon's almost here. We can meet him outside." Basil hopped up and tucked his phone into his pants pocket, then fastened his coat. "Can I grab some tissues from your bathroom?"

"Yeah, of course." Laurence shrugged.

Basil ducked inside, and returned seconds later with a fistful of tissues, which he started folding one by one, and then he stuffed the lot into his pocket. "For when I run out of dry shirt to wipe my glasses on," he explained with a small smile.

Laurence nodded to that. He didn't really care. He was still wrestling with the idea that Quentin might not have been killed. It was the only thing keeping him from running off on his own now, especially as his mind was still churning over the idea of finding some smack. If he'd had any idea of where to start finding a dealer in New York without getting arrested for it, he'd be a whole lot closer to scoring a hit.

They descended in the elevator together, yet apart, strangers in confinement with the elevator attendant. It felt weird.

This wasn't how today was supposed to go.

They were back out in the snow again before he knew it. He felt oddly adrift, trapped in a limbo where Quentin was both alive and dead, like some paradox from a high school science class. They stopped just beyond the doors and huddled against the blizzard, which had turned icy with the setting sun, and Laurence thrust his hands into the pockets of his new coat.

The one Quentin had bought for him to protect him from this weather.

He blinked rapidly, and darkness appeared in his line of sight. For a moment he thought it could be the black dog, but it came closer, and its eyes didn't glow.

They were almost the opposite of aglow. Black pits of despair in a face so pasty and drawn that Laurence briefly wondered if this was one of the four horsemen. Pestilence, maybe. Or Death himself.

The figure stepped into their little world, and Laurence shivered at the sense of decay that rolled from him, as though this man were every bit as much a sinkhole for life as Laurence was a wellspring for it. His black hair was shabby and drenched with snow, and he was taller even than Laurence, looming over him by a couple of inches.

Laurence recoiled in shock. There was no way this person was anything other than dangerous, if not lethal, yet Laurence felt some glimmer of recognition, like they'd met years ago, far away.

"Jon! You made it!" Basil launched himself at the stick figure of a man and wrapped arms around him.

Jon leaned down for a quick kiss like it was some huge chore, but he did return the hug, skeletal fingers splaying across Basil's back while he eyed Laurence.

"There's a problem," he stated, his voice almost as flat as his features.

"Yeah." Basil quickly gave a rundown of the facts of the situation as he stepped back from Jon's arms, and Jon didn't seem to blink even once while he listened.

Laurence shivered inside his coat while he tried to pick apart where he knew Jon from, and only when Basil stopped talking did it hit him like a freight train.

Sara waved her hands, trying to draw the woman's attention. "Go back!" she screamed. "You have to go back! The hounds!"

The other woman shook her head, wild eyed, and waved her own hands. "Turn around!" She pointed behind her. "Run! The dogs!"

They almost collided at the point where the lands of the dead touched those of the living, and where earth and bramble gave way to soft, lush grass. She grabbed the other woman's arms and gazed into her eyes.

They stood a moment, both desperate for breath, both clutching one another's arms. The other woman was lithe like a mink, with dark eyes and skin as pale as the moon.

"Go back," they both said as one. And then, "I can't."

They let go of each other and ran. She toward the green, and the other toward death.

Laurence stared at Jon, and there wasn't a damn doubt in his mind.

They hadn't met before.

Their ancestors had.

14

QUENTIN

Voices howled within the endless dark. At first they sounded like wolves, but the more Quentin strained to hear them, the more he realized they were people. Desperate, anguished, human voices, overlaying each other in eternity.

Fire didn't help the situation. It was as though he were suspended in a void, with nothing for the firelight to reflect off other than himself.

"Hello?"

His voice sounded flat. Deadened. It hardly seemed to travel beyond his own immediate space.

The voices that weren't his didn't change at all.

He twisted and turned, but had no sense that it meant he had moved in any meaningful way. When he resorted to his phone, it unhelpfully still had no signal whatsoever.

What on earth had happened?

He extinguished the fire. It was a waste of energy, and without knowing more about his present situation, he could ill afford such inefficiency. Following that line of reasoning, he decided to turn his phone off, too, to conserve battery life. If the device was useless to him wherever he now was, there was little point in allowing it to eat through power and leave him without a lifeline when he needed it.

"Hello!" He bellowed it this time, growing mildly irate at being ignored.

Although he *had* been eaten by an enormous creature.

Perhaps he was dead?

He crinkled his nose at the thought. It seemed highly unlikely that death led to one floating around in endless darkness for all eternity. It seemed quite pointless to maintain consciousness for such a thing, and so he discounted it for now. He could revisit it later, should this situation prove insurmountable.

Perhaps that's why everyone else is screaming.

He brushed that thought away. He wasn't ready to examine it any further.

"Laurence?" he called out.

A light breeze touched his cheek, and then he was falling. He yelled, startled, and landed against a surface that was hard and unyielding, and every bit as dark as the rest of his prison.

Quentin splayed fingers across the ground and found brittleness and grit. As he began to push himself to his feet, the dark winked out of existence, and light flooded into his world, making him blink rapidly. He remained still, half hunkered down, waiting for his sight to adjust, but he reached out telekinetically until he could see, so that he at least could develop some numb sense of his surroundings.

It felt like the outside world, with trees and plants all around. Nothing moved, not even in the faint breeze, so he felt safe waiting for his sight to catch up, at least.

The ground came into focus first, dead beneath his outstretched hands. Earth that was dry and almost gray, covered in dead leaves and twigs. He stood with care, brushing hands off against his coat, and raised his head to examine his surroundings.

This was not, by any stretch of the imagination, Manhattan.

The land ahead of him was blasted and barren, a petrified

forest filled with the leafless hulks of long-dead trees and the bitter tangle of lifeless brambles whose thorns were still very much a potential hazard. He heard nothing now; not the screams or howls that had surrounded him, nor the chatter of birds or insects.

The land behind him was no better.

Perhaps flying was damn silly, but he would take it over trudging for miles in the wrong direction, so he cocooned himself and pushed away from the ground, rising into the air without fuss until he was high above the dead forest and could see far more clearly what kind of situation he was in.

In one direction, he saw a very clear demarcation between the forest he hovered above, and one that was lush and green. The line seemed to stretch to the horizon both left and right, and the green forest likewise ran on for many miles.

In the other, mountains rose from the death and were dotted with all kinds of buildings. There were walls, houses, keeps, and castles, all glinting in the cold light from the sky which had no sun.

Wherever he was, he very much doubted that he wished to remain.

The greenery called to him, but there were no buildings among it that he could see, whereas castles atop mountains meant there was some engineering skill involved, and *that* meant people.

Damned if he was going to hike twenty miles through thick brambles to get there, though.

Decision reached, he propelled himself toward the mountains as fast as he was able.

HE DEBATED whether to set himself down inside the walls of one city or outside of its gates and decided that it was more polite to land on the outside.

The cities straddled mountaintops, and each had its own unique flavor. He saw four in total, with distinctive castles that all seemed different from one another. One even looked to be made entirely from glass, while another seemed fanciful and almost French in its construction style, with white walls and delicate spires.

In the end, he simply chose the nearest to him, and landed lightly on his feet on a hefty wooden drawbridge that crossed a ravine with no moat. The fall itself was likely enough deterrent for most assailants.

The gate he approached was topped with the black iron of an open portcullis, spikes looming ominously above as he stepped from the drawbridge and onto solid rock.

While he might be well versed on the etiquette of entering castles in his own world, it was abundantly clear that he was now somewhere else entirely. If he were to make it back home in one piece, he would need to — and he fully intended to — tread carefully. Though, he was loath to admit, if this was Faerie, no amount of careful stepping would save him.

Best hope that it wasn't.

He waited, hands behind his back, just in front of the deep grooves in the ground where the portcullis would land should it be released, and held his head high.

"Who goes there?"

He couldn't determine the gender of the voice, and was none the wiser when the skeletal figure stepped out from a guard post. The accent, however, carried a gentle Welsh lilt.

There was no meat on the bones. Not even tendons. Still, the skeleton moved with purpose toward him, simple sword in one hand, a small buckler in the other. There was even an open-faced helmet and some scraps of what might once have been a tabard.

All in all, Quentin found the effect quite disconcerting, but that was no reason to be rude.

"Quentin d'Arcy," he replied, doing his best to look the guard straight in the empty eye sockets. "Merely a visitor."

The guard stepped closer, crossing to Quentin's side of the portcullis, and the skull tipped down and up as though sizing him up.

"Warrior," the guard mused. "You trespass. Why?"

"It is not my intention. I am not here by choice, and would quite like to know where 'here' actually is, if you would be so kind?"

The guard stared at him, though Quentin supposed it was hard to do anything but.

"You are in Annwn," was the eventual answer. "Come with me."

"Annwn," he echoed as he followed the guard inside. The word felt familiar, and he allowed his brain to fish for it in peace while he looked around the city as he was led through it.

It struck him as reminiscent of the sort of monasterial complexes built on coastal islands in the Middle Ages. The cobbled streets were winding and narrow, and buildings sprang up all around in a chaotic mess that still seemed, overall, quite pleasing. People bustled around in various states of decay, from skeletal remains to bloated corpses, yet each of them seemed quite happy and willing to grimace or wave in his direction.

Thank goodness for many years' practice with a stiff upper lip.

The word *Annwn* finally bubbled to the surface as his memories gave up their treasure, and he gasped. "This is Otherworld?"

"Yes."

He looked down at himself. Everything he would expect to find present was indeed there. If he were in Otherworld, did that mean his body was lying in the street in Midtown, becoming ever more hidden by snowfall with each passing moment?

Could he be dying of exposure right this moment?

Goodness, he wished he knew more about all of this, but it was very much Laurence's field. Thanks to the stories his mother had read him as a child, Quentin might have the occasional word or two that he could identify, but the actual experience was beyond him.

"How have I come here?" he asked, as they began to climb a winding road that he presumed led toward the castle. "I am not descended from a god, nor have I any facility for finding my way here."

"Your trespass is unintentional?" The guard glanced back to him as they walked.

"I'm afraid so." He unbuttoned his coat, since the pace was quick and the ascent steep. "Perhaps if I could simply wake up, I would be out of your way."

"You are physically present," the guard informed him. "Were you merely a projection, you would be unadorned. Were you only a soul, you would be unencumbered."

Quentin blinked.

He had physically entered Otherworld. The creature must have brought him here, but to what end? Could it not at least have lingered a moment to explain itself?

He supposed at least he could be assured that he was not slowly dying in the street in New York, but it did pose a whole new set of problems. Any danger he encountered here was thoroughly real, and he had — to his knowledge — no way of leaving this realm and making his way back to Laurence. Not even any way of communicating with him.

That had to become his priority, then. If he could not find an exit to his world, he should at least find some way of passing a message to Laurence to let him know what had happened.

Satisfied that he had the very outline of a plan, he fell into step alongside his guide and did his best to make a little small talk now and then.

THE CASTLE itself was made of stone. Huge slabs of it, roughly hewn and yet slotted together with precision. Quentin marveled at it as they passed through another portcullis, and through an assortment of tents and stalls that dotted the courtyard. People — very dead people, but people nonetheless — seemed to be hawking everything from weaponry to embroidery.

"I can't help but notice," he said with care, "that everyone appears to be, ah... a little on the deceased side."

"Annwn is the land of the dead," his guard replied, their voice somewhat amused, "and you are here in the height of winter."

"Oh." Quentin blinked. "I see. Well, that explains why you might think I am trespassing."

"Correct, Warrior." The guard actually chuckled.

Quentin smiled faintly as he was led inside the castle keep. Perhaps this would be done with, swiftly and equitably, and he could be back in time to avert any worry Laurence might experience. They could get to the bottom of this mixup, send Quentin back to his world, and things could get back to normal. After all, Laurence had specifically wished them to avoid any stressful situations for a while. He would be relieved to know that Quentin had done just that.

The dead within the keep walls seemed to be in considerably better condition than those outside. Had he not known better, Quentin would be quite certain that they were alive and well, if a little underdressed. He did his best to not look at any once he noticed just how much flesh was on display, and so instead his attention fixed on the decorations. There were wreaths and garlands of holly and mistletoe, with variegated leaves and bright red or white berries nestled among the green. Banners in green and silver hung from the walls, depicting foxes and stags, birds and stoats.

This was, perhaps, some celebration of the winter months. Again, though, Laurence would know far more about these things than Quentin, and he tried not to dwell too much on just how out of his depth he was.

Chatter seemed to turn to more curious sounds the farther Quentin was led into the hall, until a hush fell, and he was not so foolish as to ignore it.

He looked forward, hoping not to see yet more nudity, and was rewarded with an altogether different sight. A large throne, carved from wood and twice the size any human would need, was raised on a small dais which too was smothered with holly and mistletoe.

The person who occupied the throne was tall enough to fill it. Pale, his skin the color of ice, with a crown of holly, and short antlers that rose from his dark curls. He leaned forward and settled black eyes on Quentin.

"A trespasser," he boomed.

"Yes, my king," replied the guard. "A Warrior. His name is Quentin d'Arcy. He maintains that he does not know how he came to be here."

"But a trespasser regardless," stated the king. He rose from his throne, spindly fingers releasing the arms and hanging by his sides as his antlers almost touched the vaulted ceiling. "I am Arawn, Warrior. King of Annwn. You do great insult with your presence."

Quentin couldn't help but take a step back as Arawn towered over everyone present.

"No insult was intended," he murmured, doing his best to sound deferential.

"And yet one was given, and you must face the consequences of invading the lands of the dead."

Quentin glanced over his shoulder, but people who until now had been partying formed a barrier several naked people deep between himself and the exit.

Nope.

He looked at Arawn again, then raised his chin and slid one foot back a little. Just in case.

"All right," he said softly. "And what might those consequences be?"

He was sincerely hoping they would involve being cast out into the lands of the living, but he probably wasn't that lucky.

15

LAURENCE

THERE WASN'T TIME TO FIGURE THIS ANCESTRAL THING OUT RIGHT now. Laurence had to find Quentin. And Jon didn't seem to have any kind of recognition in his eyes, either.

Mind you, he didn't seem to have much of *anything* in his eyes.

"You said you could find where he disappeared from?" Basil looked up at Laurence, above the frames of his already useless glasses.

Laurence sucked his lip, then closed his eyes. "Give me a minute, here."

He delved into the stream again, looking to go just a little further back. Back to before Quentin—

A gust of wind parted the snow, and Laurence could see the street sign as Quentin peered up at it.

He gasped and opened his eyes again, rather than be stuck in that vision. "6th and 57th," he said.

Jon blinked slowly, then set off at a fast pace, his long legs eating up distance. "This way."

Laurence chased after him. The snow crunched underfoot, compressing down to thin slivers beneath his weight, and it was surprisingly easy to walk in. Maybe it'd take a night of freezing over before it became seriously dangerous to pedestrians. He didn't have the most widespread experience with snow, and sure as hell nothing this heavy.

"How did you do that?" Basil gasped. He was having to work twice as hard as Jon and Laurence just to keep up.

"Like I said, I can look through time. I looked back again, when Quentin was by an intersection." Laurence shrugged as he buried his hands in his pockets. There wasn't any need to tell them about Quentin's abilities. Not if he could get away without mentioning it. "Suppose it is this black dog thing. What do we do?"

"I'd have to check my book," Basil said. "We might be able to summon it and ask it what it did."

"And why," Jon muttered.

Laurence wanted to snap that he didn't care *why*, but he knew Jon was right. This shit didn't just happen randomly, or people would get whisked away by mythical black dogs all the time.

"So what's the deal with these black dogs?" he asked Basil.

"It really depends on the regional legend," Basil said, with way too much cheer. "Dogs have been associated with the dead for thousands of years, though."

Laurence nodded slowly. "And human belief shapes the world," he realized.

Basil's eyebrows climbed. "It does?"

"Yeah. We create gods through our faith. We even reshape them once they exist, if what we believe changes over time. If we believed dogs took the dead, then, well... dogs take the dead." Laurence pushed re-soaked curls away from his face. "But it's not a god?"

"No."

"Probably a psychopomp," Jon muttered.

"Which is what, exactly?" Laurence asked.

"A being whose job is to escort the souls of the dead to the afterlife," Basil explained. "Most belief systems have them.

Charon is probably the most famous, which is the name of one of my cats," he added with a quick grin.

"The other is Hades," Jon said, as though that explained anything.

"So this thing made a mistake and took a living person instead?"

"Unlikely, but as good a working theory as any." Jon made a sudden right turn at an intersection, and Basil scurried after him, sticking close.

Laurence followed, listening, but traffic seemed to have hit total gridlock now. "Do storms always come in like this?"

"It's not uncommon," Basil answered. "We'll get a good two or three serious blizzards in the winter. People just use the subway anyway, so it only really affects anyone trying to arrive or leave town."

Jon led them another block, then halted. "You have reached your destination," he deadpanned.

Laurence gritted his teeth. The snow was way too thick to see very far, even with his sight, and it was dripping down the back of his neck as it melted on his hair. He closed his eyes and drew a slow breath, picking over scents and discarding them one by one. Coffee, fumes, pizza...

Quentin.

His eyes snapped open, and he followed the trail. The faint trickle of color was like a thread that was being drenched by snow. He reached glass doors and peered through them into an art store, then turned and backtracked.

Basil scurried at his heels. There was a question in the set of his eyebrows.

"That's where he came *from*," Laurence said, as he stuck with the trail. "He was outside when he got taken."

The trail led him into the middle of a street, and then cut out.

There was no blood, no mess. No sign anything had happened here. The snow was compressed by the feet of hundreds of commuters, but otherwise, there was no evidence that Quentin had even been here. None other than the abruptly terminated trail.

"It happened here," he said, pointing at the ground.

He heard an engine, and a car inched forward; Basil pulled him out of the way as it slowly dawdled along, wheels slipping.

"There is no residual energy indicating a ghost or similar being," Jon muttered. "But it may well have faded by now."

Laurence eyed him once they were safe on the sidewalk again. "You're a Child of Arawn, right?"

Jon just blinked slowly.

"That's why you can sense whether there might've been a ghost? Why you can see them?" He searched Jon's gaze, but it was still blank.

"I don't know what you're referring to," Jon stated flatly.

"Your family doesn't get a dream that tells you..." He trailed to a halt. It was clear that Jon didn't have a damn clue what Laurence was talking about. "Oh, Goddess. Okay. Hundreds of years ago, my ancestor was being hunted by Arawn. She'd crossed into Annwn by mistake, and the Cŵn Annwn were almost on her, but she found the lands of the living, and she met another woman who was being chased by Herne the Hunter." He licked his lips and scanned Jon's gaze, but there was no recognition at all. "They swapped places," Laurence went on. "My ancestor met Herne. She married him. I think the other woman was your ancestor. I think she met Arawn."

"Oh!" Basil snapped his fingers. "There's that story of Pwyll and Arawn. They traded places for a year so that Pwyll could defeat Arawn's enemy, Hafgan. And while Pwyll was there for the whole year, he refused to have sex with Arawn's wife. They were disguised as each other," he added, "so she thought it was Arawn."

Jon's nose crinkled a little. "This sounds like fairy tales," he muttered.

"Yeah," Laurence nodded. "But Herne *is* my ancestor. I've met him. Anyone in Otherworld recognizes me as his Child just by looking at me. I think you might be Arawn's Child. You kinda look a bit like the woman, but you've got this..." He waved his hands toward Jon. "This vibe you give off. Like you're just exuding death." He pointed to his own chest. "Can you sense my energy too?"

At that, Jon's nose crinkled further. "You appear to be leaking life," he groused, as though it personally offended him.

"Yeah. I'm a..." He halted again as footsteps crunched through the snow. Not the hurried steps of someone trying to get home, but something more on a direct line toward them.

The man who joined them was definitely doing exactly that. He stepped into their small huddle and stopped as though he were a part of it.

Laurence blinked at him. He was about to ask if he could help at all, but the energy the guy gave off was all kinds of weird, and Laurence had no idea what to make of it.

Whatever this man was, though, it sure wasn't human.

"You're looking for the dog?" the stranger asked, sounding polite enough. He didn't look a day older than Laurence, and his eyes were an odd shade of amber.

"Yeah." Laurence figured there was little point in lying about it. The stranger felt off, knew about the dog, and hadn't attacked them yet, so it seemed dumb to make an enemy out of him so soon. "You saw it?"

"No. I know it's around, though. Damn thing's a nuisance." He offered his hand. "Ryan McKinley."

Laurence took it, and tried not to wince as he came into contact with a slight fizzing sensation. It wasn't quite like Quentin's perpetual vortex, but there was some faint amount of pull on his own energy. "Laurence Riley."

"Riley. Riley." McKinley sucked on his teeth, then his eyebrows lifted. "Any relation to Eric?"

Laurence's heart leaped into his mouth, and he forgot all

about the shitty weather and the fact that they still didn't know where Quentin was. "You knew my dad?"

"Yeah," Ryan said slowly, like it was all coming back to him. "Man, you kinda look like him, except he was younger."

"You, uh…" Laurence licked his lips. "I hope you don't mind me saying this, but you don't look old enough to have met my dad," he said with some caution. "Did you, like, see a picture or something?"

"No, no. I met him. Owe him a great debt, actually." He took his hand and offered it to Basil, then on to Jon.

"Basil Irwin," Basil mumbled.

"Jon Dwyer." Jon's gaze lingered on Ryan's hand even after it withdrew.

He must've felt it, too.

What did it mean?

"If the dog manifested recently, it won't be around for at least a day," Ryan said as he turned back to Laurence. "We should get out of this blizzard before it freezes us all to death. Well, okay, before it freezes Basil to death. I figure the rest of us are probably okay."

"Why me?" Basil squeaked.

"Because you're the only human here," Ryan countered. "If you're here for the dog, then it took someone you know. If it's taken someone you know, we can't just run after it to find them. So why don't we hole up somewhere warm and dry where we can talk in private, and figure this thing out?" He eyed Laurence. "Since I owe your dad, I figure it's okay to transfer my debt to you?"

Laurence bit his lip. He knew what Ryan was really asking, so he gave a faint nod.

"I'm sorry," Ryan murmured.

"It's okay." He took a breath to steady himself. "My hotel's near here. Like, three blocks away. Unless you've got somewhere closer, it's probably the best place we have." He glanced at the snow that piled up around their feet. "If the dog's taken someone, are they alive?"

"Yes and no." Ryan sighed faintly. "They're in Annwn."

The cold began to seep through Laurence's thick coat and toward his chest.

Quentin was in the land of the dead.

He was in Otherworld.

16

QUENTIN

ARAWN DIDN'T ANSWER HIM RIGHT AWAY. QUENTIN WASN'T troubled by that in the slightest. He had read and reread *The Book of Five Rings*, which Mia had downloaded onto his phone last year, so many times that he was sure he could recite passages from memory. In this instance, he was well aware that he had to be patient.

He was quite good at waiting, so he folded his hands together behind his back and swiveled on the balls of his feet to watch Arawn as the god walked a slow circle around him.

"I am not unaccustomed to striking bargains with Warriors," Arawn mused as he drifted to a halt with his back to the throne. He had come full circle, and not a step farther. "If you are willing to aid me, I will return you to your world and consider your debt paid."

"And if I am not willing?"

"Then you remain here." Arawn shrugged. "There is no food in Annwn that can sustain a living body. No guard who will allow you to leave the castle. Your insult was grave, so I would not do you the mercy of a swift death."

This was all rather convenient for Arawn, but Quentin was

not so foolish as to say as much to a god's face. Not when that god held the key to Quentin ever seeing Laurence again.

Still, that didn't mean Arawn held all the cards.

"What would you like me to do?" he murmured.

"I have an enemy." Arawn settled back onto his throne and rested his hands on the ornately-carved arms. "For hundreds of years, his role was simply to guide the dead to Annwn so that they may rest, but eventually he decided that he should become king. He influenced mortals, convinced them that he had already defeated me, and that he was now king."

Quentin quirked an eyebrow and took a step toward the throne, his head tilting aside faintly. "Yet you remain unchanged," he mused. "How did the shift in belief not bring about his desired outcome?"

"What he failed to understand is that everyone already here is a believer." Arawn gestured to the room at Quentin's back, but Quentin chose not to look. "And they see the truth. It is they who have sustained me."

Quentin pursed his lips. "That's quite a sizable advantage," he admitted. "Why not simply influence people to revert to the older belief?"

Arawn blinked slowly. "I cannot enter your world without a bargain. A mortal to exchange places with."

"And you wish to exchange places with me?"

"You are most perceptive, Warrior." Arawn raised his hands to steeple his fingers. "I will care for your world and your loved ones in your absence. Protect them as though they were my own. Should you have a wife, her virtue will remain intact in my presence."

It took him a couple of seconds to understand that Arawn was stating that he wouldn't sleep with any wife Quentin might have, and he cleared his throat. "No," he murmured. "No wife. I have a..." he hesitated.

What was the word? They were not married. They were not even engaged. And *boyfriend* seemed so understated.

"Lover," he concluded. "A man," he added for clarification.

Arawn raised his head. "Then your lover's virtue will remain intact."

"I should hope so. Why would I think otherwise?"

At that, Arawn's lips twitched. He rose from the throne, yet did not grow any taller. Instead he shrank as he approached, and his clothes darkened. His hair seemed to recede and straighten out, and his flesh took on an ivory-pink tone.

In under five seconds, Quentin was eye level with a man who now looked in every way identical to himself.

"Because," Arawn said in Quentin's voice, "I will take your place."

***

UNSETTLING DIDN'T BEGIN to describe the sensation of watching a god mimic him so perfectly. Everything was flawless, from the eye color to the cut of the coat, and Quentin suddenly felt eminently replaceable.

Yet if he were to flinch, he would lose whatever game Arawn was playing with him.

He had to examine the situation calmly and wring what benefit he could from it, and if a god was going to keep him prisoner in Otherworld unless Quentin agreed to do as he asked, then the very best Quentin could do was ensure that Arawn was up to the task of protecting Laurence in Quentin's absence. He couldn't lead with that, though. It would show his hand.

Quentin inclined his head. "Tell me about this enemy of yours."

"He is Gwyn ap Nudd," Arawn said, casually sloughing off Quentin's appearance and resuming his own. "King of the Tylwyth

Teg. Hunter, trickster, false king of Annwn. He has tortured men and slain their kin. Those under his rule are twisted creatures, defiled by his power. He brings the dead to Annwn to be their ruler, not their defender. He has no nobility despite his noble birth, Warrior. To destroy him is to free the countless souls under his heel."

At that, Quentin risked a glance around the throne room. The people had drifted away from the door again, but their attention was still mostly on Arawn, and while they were predominantly naked, they also seemed so very human. Even the skeletal guard felt human, whether by personality or posture Quentin couldn't determine.

These were all people. Dead, but people, and if Gwyn ap Nudd had held even half as many as prisoners against their will for hundreds of years...

He rocked his jaw faintly.

He was but one man. To think otherwise was dangerous only to himself.

"He occupies one of the other castles?" Quentin returned his attention to Arawn.

"The Four-Peaked Fortress," Arawn responded. "It is best you do not approach by air, for Gwyn masters his own Wild Hunt, and he has many of the Cŵn Annwn at his command. You will have more advantage on land, where you may use the terrain in your favor."

Quentin glanced away while he mulled that information over. If Gwyn ap Nudd's forces were airborne, then flying would indeed allow them to outnumber him while presenting them with clear line of sight. Arawn's advice appeared sound.

"You are essentially asking me to single-handedly kill someone for you," he finally sighed. "Someone I have never met, and the sole word against him is yours. I am not a killer, and certainly not a murderer."

"He may have been raised by human parents, but do not

mistake him for one. He is of the Tylwyth Teg, a crimbil. A changeling."

Quentin's gut began to twist into a knot. He might not know the first two terms, but he understood the implications of the third. A human child had been kidnapped by fair folk and they had left one of their own in exchange. The creature that had replaced the real Gwyn ap Nudd was nothing remotely human.

He was something infinitely more frightening.

"He's a fairy?" he breathed. "You wish for me to kill a *fairy?*"

Arawn finally shifted his stance and blinked.

He *knew* what he was asking.

"You are a strong Warrior. It will be well within your ability." Arawn sounded certain, but he didn't meet Quentin's eye until after he spoke.

Which meant that now was the time for Quentin to play his card.

"Then I expect a great deal from you in my place," he sniffed. "You are offering to protect those I love? Then you must swear to do so with your very existence if necessary. You *cannot* ask me to risk my life for you without agreeing to do the same for me."

Arawn towered over him as he leaned in, but Quentin had been subject to his own father's attempts at intimidation over the years. More importantly, Arawn *needed* him, for if Arawn were capable of defeating Gwyn ap Nudd, he would have done so already.

So Quentin simply lifted his chin to maintain eye contact.

"You are trespassing," Arawn rumbled.

"Those are my terms," Quentin murmured.

Arawn loomed for a couple more seconds, and then he clicked his tongue and offered his hand. "I accept."

Quentin reached for it, and his own disappeared into Arawn's massive palm. "As do I."

"So mote it be," Arawn rumbled. "You are a wise Warrior." He released Quentin's hand. "But wisdom will not be enough. Annwn is unknown to you, and holds many dangers for the living. It is best if I provide you with a guide."

Quentin smiled a little. As though setting off to hunt down a fairy wasn't dangerous enough already? "I hope I don't have to negotiate for the services of this guide?"

Arawn laughed and patted his shoulder so heavily that Quentin's frame shook under the blow. "Do not tempt me, mortal. What more do you have to offer?"

"You have a point," he murmured as he gently rolled his shoulder. "Very well. I had best get started. Where may I find this guide?"

Arawn turned to the guard. "Bring me the last Hunter."

"Yes, my king." The guard held their fist to their chest briefly, then turned and marched from the room.

Quentin frowned faintly. Did Arawn mean Hunter the way he meant Warrior, or was it simply a turn of phrase?

Arawn looked at him. "Warriors are at their best when paired with a Hunter," he explained, which answered Quentin's unspoken question. "I would do you grave dishonor to offer a guide who did not also complement your strengths. Indeed, it could be construed as sabotage for your guide to work against those strengths. I am not dishonorable."

"Then I appreciate the kindness." He inclined his head, but felt as though any moment now the panic might set in. The moment he allowed himself a few minutes to examine the ramifications of the deal he had struck, he would probably scream for half an hour straight, but what else could he do? He had no way out of Otherworld, and Laurence had no idea Quentin was here in the first place.

This was a bloody unfair situation, and no amount of anger would change that.

He maintained his stiff upper lip while Arawn retook the throne and the people behind him returned to their party, or whatever it was dead people in throne rooms got up to when left to their own devices. He didn't wish to look. Half of them were barely wearing a translucent skirt and the rest hadn't bothered with clothes at all, so he left them to it and stared at a spot on the wall instead.

He estimated that only a few minutes had passed when Arawn stood once more, and Quentin focused on the god.

"Hunter," Arawn rumbled warmly. "You have my gratitude. The task has been explained to you?"

"Yeah, dude." The accent was the first American one that Quentin had heard here. "This sounds like a blast!"

"Then I thank you for your assistance," Arawn murmured with a slight bow.

"No worries!" The Hunter stepped up alongside Quentin, then turned to face him.

Quentin would have to hope that there were clothes involved. He turned on his heel and offered his hand, then felt as though the breath had been punched from his lungs.

The man was far taller than Quentin, with a head of thick honey-blond curls and a touch of graying stubble along his jaw. His eyes were dark and brown, earthy and kind, and he looked to be carrying significantly more weight than was strictly necessary. He was, thankfully, wearing jeans and a loose, cream linen shirt.

Quentin had seen this man before, in photographs on the walls of Myriam's home.

"Eric Riley?" he whispered.

17

LAURENCE

THE SNOW WAS EASILY APPROACHING A FOOT DEEP BY THE TIME they made it back to the hotel, and everyone stopped just inside the foyer to shake themselves off like wet dogs. Basil pulled a tissue out and wiped his glasses, then used another to get the streaks off the lenses.

Laurence stamped white from his boots as he led the way toward the elevators. While he wasn't wildly excited about taking a stranger to his room, the fact was he barely knew Basil or Jon any better than he did Ryan, and they couldn't have this conversation in a public area.

"Fancy," was all Ryan said as the elevator attendant pushed the button for them.

Laurence didn't say anything until they were all crammed into his room, and once he'd shed his coat for the second time that day, he moved to the window and slumped into a chair, sprawling his legs out as he kicked his boots off.

Basil and Jon moved to the bed and sat on the end of it, and then all three of them faced Ryan expectantly.

Ryan leaned his ass against the desk and placed his palms either side of his hips. "I couldn't even begin to guess why the dog took your friend," he started without preamble. "I presume that he, like you, is extraordinary in some way? Dogs like witches in particular."

Laurence saw Basil swallow nervously. "Yeah," Laurence admitted. "Yeah, Quentin's... pretty special."

Ryan nodded faintly. "It doesn't happen often. Usually, they stick to what they're supposed to do. I think if they step out of bounds with their duties escorting the dead, then it's under orders, you know?"

Jon's stare was unblinking. "Why would anyone command a black dog to take a living person to Annwn?"

"Depends on who did it, and whether your friend was targeted for anything more specific than his abilities. Does he have enemies?" Then Ryan paused. "Of course he does. Everyone does. What I mean is, does he have enemies who have the skill and motive to send him to the lands of the dead?"

Both Basil and Jon looked at Laurence with expectation, as though they hoped Laurence would pop out a single name that could solve all this mystery, but he had nothing.

The duke sure as hell had the power, but what motive? Revenge for his defeat at Quentin's hand? Then surely, he would set out to kill either Quentin, Laurence, or both of them, rather than pack his son off to Annwn. Frederick couldn't use magic, and if he was at all honest about the love he held for Quentin, he wouldn't do it anyway. Jack was dead, but Laurence doubted that Jack would want anything to do with Annwn. Kane also couldn't use magic, and was just as dead as Jack.

Quentin wasn't the kind of guy who *made* enemies. He'd spent most of his life drifting between parties, drunk as a skunk, engaging too fleetingly with people to have any of them hunt him down.

Laurence shook his head. "I honestly can't think of anyone," he admitted. "Maybe it wasn't personal?"

"Then it's someone who wants a witch?" Basil nudged his

glasses up his nose, then frowned at his own fingers at a chip in his nail polish.

"Not a lot to go on," Ryan mused. "It'd have to be another witch to be able to control a dog, though."

"Not a necromancer?" Basil tore his attention from his damaged polish and back up to Ryan.

"Witch, necromancer, it's all the same." Ryan shrugged. "The words they use to describe themselves just specify their area of expertise, nothing more."

Laurence swallowed tightly. "So the dog might take a warlock?"

Ryan turned to face him and blinked slowly. "He's a warlock?"

"No, he..." Laurence shook his head. "No."

No. They didn't know *what* Quentin was, because he refused to learn magic.

Ryan just shrugged. "Okay, so if he was taken at random, that means motive's harder to figure out, so we can't focus on that. All we know is where he's gone, so we're gonna need another witch — or a necromancer, if you want to get specific — so we can go get him back."

Laurence and Jon both turned their attention to Basil, who laughed nervously.

"You can't seriously want to..." Basil licked his lips. "You *do*," he sighed as he met Laurence's eyes.

"We're going to get him back," Laurence said, with every ounce of determination he had. He didn't know how Quentin made people do what he wanted by declaring that those things would just happen, but if he could echo even ten percent of Quentin's will, it might be enough.

Basil's cheeks reddened, and he nodded. "I mean, the book—"

"Yeah, I know. I understand. If you don't have the spell, we'll have to find one. Worry about that later."

Laurence ran his tongue along his teeth as he tried to hide the little flicker of excitement that had stirred inside him. Now wasn't the time to get thrilled at the prospect of a hunt, and he wasn't all that comfortable that he *was* excited by it. Not when that hunt was for his own lover, in the depths of Otherworld.

"Okay. First we check the plan. If you have the spell we need, we go to Annwn. If you don't, we find the spell you need."

Basil nodded. "How?"

"I have some connections; let me worry about that." Laurence pushed himself from his seat and shoved hair back from his forehead. "East Harlem, right? How far is that?"

"Approximately three and a half miles," Jon stated. "The 6 train is the fastest route from here."

"Okay. Let's go." He started toward the closet, but Basil bounced to his feet, hands up, in Laurence's way.

"Wait. Hold up! We'll go, you wait here."

Laurence stared down at him. "What? Why?"

"My place is kinda small and shitty, okay?" Basil's blush returned to his cheeks, and he glanced down. "There's not a lot of room in there for Jon and me, and four of us aren't going to fit easily. Just wait here, please? I'll go, grab the book, then bring it right back. By the time I've been reading it on the train for half an hour, I should have found whether or not the spell's in there."

Laurence bit the tip of his tongue. The urge to demand that Basil allow Laurence to accompany him was profound. This was Quentin's *life* they were trying to save, and Laurence had to rely on total strangers to help him do that.

But from Basil's perspective, Laurence was also a stranger. One who could use magic, and had other powers at his disposal. Basil couldn't be sure that letting Laurence into his house wasn't dangerous, or even deadly.

"How about a compromise," he rumbled. "We go together, then Ryan and I wait for you at the subway. Nobody needs to get into your apartment, and I don't feel like a third wheel sitting here doing nothing for the next hour, while my partner is trapped in a land he has no experience or understanding of. Deal?"

Basil bit his lip as he glanced at Jon, but whatever Basil saw in Jon's empty gaze, Laurence missed it.

"Okay," Basil said. "Deal."

THEY ALL SAT in strange silence on the subway. There was no small talk, no idle comment. Basil held Jon's hand, Ryan inspected the people and places around them like it was all fascinating to him, and Laurence gritted his teeth every time the train's wheels screeched against the rails.

Chatter would only worsen his mood, and he was already pretty frustrated. Relieved that Quentin wasn't dead, but something still tugged on his thoughts, and it took most of the journey for him to put a finger on it.

They left the train at 125th Street. Basil promised he'd be back in ten minutes, so Laurence found himself a big red metal box to sit on. He figured it housed some kind of emergency equipment, but it was nearby, and it let him monitor the platform's entrance for Basil's return.

Ryan sat next to him.

"So this Quentin is your lover?"

Laurence pursed his lips and looked toward him. "Yeah."

"Then I understand your sense of urgency." Ryan nodded. "I'm sure we'll figure this out between us."

"We will." Laurence sucked briefly on his teeth. "What did you mean when you said that Quentin was both alive and not alive at the same time?"

"Ah." Ryan sighed. "He's a living creature in the lands of the dead. It will begin to seep into his soul if he stays too long. Like your friend Jon, there." Ryan gestured toward the stairs. "He has death inside him. Your soul is touched by Annwn too, isn't it?"

Laurence crossed his arms. "You can sense that?"

"Yeah. You've nearly died, I assume?"

Laurence bobbed his head. He wasn't going to go into details, and he hoped Ryan wouldn't push for them.

"There's no food in Annwn that can sustain life," Ryan continued. It looked like he'd taken the hint, since he didn't ask more questions about Laurence's near-death experience. "If he eats anything, it'll bring him closer to death. If he doesn't eat anything... well, that brings anything living closer to death, by nature. There's no food, no water. Only the dead can subsist on what's there."

Laurence rocked his jaw slowly. "Then we need to take supplies," he concluded. "Especially water."

"That would be wise. How long has he been gone?"

He withdrew his phone, then huffed. "I don't think any longer than three hours," he said after a little mental arithmetic. "So he should be fine right now."

"Assuming nothing bad has found him."

Laurence's heart skipped a beat. "Like what?"

Ryan shrugged slightly. "I don't know. A lot of Arthurian lore says that Annwn is riddled with demons, over which Gwyn ap Nudd has full control. If he sends them after Quentin, I doubt even a witch could survive such an attack."

Laurence jumped off the locker and headed for the turnstiles. There was no way he could sit around waiting for Basil if there was a more immediate threat to Quentin's life. To hell with Basil's worries about the inside of his apartment, or whatever else might be spooking him out. Nothing got in the way now.

"Hey!" Ryan ran after him and fell into step at his side. "Wait up. Where are we going?"

"We're gonna get Basil, and we're not letting him out of our sight again," Laurence muttered. He pushed through the turnstile and took the stairs to the surface, grabbing the handrail tight. The further up the stairs he got, the more slush was on them, with a thin layer of fresh snow on the top of it all.

"He wanted us to wait—"

Laurence spun on his heels at the top of the stairs and bared his teeth.

Ryan just lifted his eyebrows as though Laurence were a toddler in the middle of a tantrum.

"I'm going," Laurence growled, "to find him."

Ryan squinted up at the snow, then sighed. "If you do, he won't trust you ever again. Nobody trusts an oathbreaker."

Laurence turned away and took two steps, then came to an abrupt halt.

Who said *oathbreaker* when *liar* would do?

Gods. Daemons. Pagans.

So which was Ryan?

He turned slowly back to face Ryan. The man had met Laurence's dad, yet hadn't aged a day since. His hands fizzed with some strange power, totally unfamiliar to Laurence. And he seemed to know a lot about everything that was going on right now.

"Who are you?" Laurence said. "Really?"

Ryan squinted again, but this time at Laurence. "Hunters are perceptive," he said softly. "I'm not your enemy, Child of Herne. Your father did me a great favor, and I intend to repay his debt. As such, I will do you no harm. I will even do all that I can to protect you. But I owe you no more than that. And you know that my counsel is true. If you breach your friend's trust, break the promise that you have made to him, he will not trust you. And you need him, Laurence. You need his knowledge if you are to recover your beloved."

Laurence licked his lips and caught the wetness of snowflakes on his tongue.

Ryan — whoever and whatever he really was — was right. As much as it grated on Laurence's need to do *something*, he'd made a deal with Basil, and breaking it could have lasting ramifications.

"Fine." He scowled, and stomped back down the stairs. "But if anything happens to Quentin, I'm holding you responsible."

It might well be a hollow threat, and he sure didn't feel better after he'd made it, but he was damned if he was going to let Ryan weasel out of his questions without consequences.

Ryan followed without a word, and Laurence stared belligerently at a MetroCard vending machine while he waited for Basil to come back.

18

QUENTIN

"Oh, hey, dude!" Eric grinned. "Have we met?"

Quentin shook his head numbly. If Arawn was playing some sort of game here, Quentin couldn't see what it might be. "No," he breathed. "I'm afraid we have not. But it is an honor." He shook Eric's hand firmly.

"Okay." Eric squeezed his hand in return, then thumbed toward the door at his back. "We're off to kill Gwyn ap Nudd, yeah?"

"That is the task, yes." Arawn placed his hands on his knees and leaned forward. "I would like you to be the Warrior's guide."

"Right on. I guess we better get started. You look alive to me," Eric added, "so I reckon we don't have a whole lot of time."

"To descend one mountain and climb another?" Quentin nodded grimly. "I'm afraid you are correct. If you do not mind," he said to Arawn, "we will be on our way."

Arawn nodded. "Blessed be."

"Blessed be," Eric agreed. Then he took Quentin by the arm and steered him toward the exit. "Oh this is gonna be a riot!"

"God," Quentin murmured. "I hope not."

"So, like…" Eric idly stretched his arms together over his head as he sauntered along the corridor which led out of the keep. "How'd you know who I am, huh?"

"I know your son," Quentin murmured. "Laurence. Bambi." He hesitated, then added, "Cricket."

Eric dropped his arms and laughed as he wrapped one of them around Quentin's shoulders. "Man, he told you about that? You guys must be close."

Quentin inclined his head. "I would concur."

"Oh, *that* close, huh?" Eric's smile softened. "Well, I've known you all of two minutes, but you seem a decent guy. I hope you're treating him right."

"I hope so, too." Quentin raised a hand to shield his eyes a moment as they stepped out into the cold mountain light. "He misses you terribly."

"Yeah. I can imagine." Eric released Quentin's shoulder. "Losing the people we love is so hard. We all go through it, but we can't make it any easier for others. Isn't that weird?" He eased his hands into the pockets of his jeans. "How's Cricket doing? Is he happy?"

"I think he's faring remarkably," Quentin replied. They drifted along cobblestoned streets, exchanging nods and smiles with people going about their daily deaths, and Quentin slid his hands into his own pockets. "He has endured so much, and yet he is still kind, still so full of life. You should be proud."

"Oh, I've always been proud." Eric chuckled briefly. "From the day he was born to the day I died, he was a ray of sunshine in a dark world. You treat him well, kid, and he'll be your sun." He looked at Quentin. "How's Myriam?"

Quentin smiled himself, and allowed his fondness for Laurence's mother to show through. "Absolutely wonderful," he assured Eric. "She still loves you very much, and is everything one could hope for in a mother."

"And in a wife, I promise you." Eric smiled fondly. "I'm waiting here for her. If we get through this, could you let her know that? Even if she moves on, I'll always love her."

"I strongly suspect that she will always love you," he said. "But I promise you I will pass it along." He bit his lip as they moved through the town square. "Perhaps it would be wise if I were to obtain some warmer clothing, if such a thing is available?"

Eric eyed him. "Oh, yeah. That coat looks pretty thin. Nice, though. Are you rich?"

Quentin pursed his lips. "Comparatively."

"You better be spending all that money on my boy."

Quentin laughed. "Of course."

"Then I guess it's okay. C'mon, let's find something that isn't made of pig skin."

Quentin crinkled his nose as Eric led him off toward the marketplace.

<hr>

It wasn't made of pig skin.

Quentin wasn't entirely certain what it *was* made of. The decaying corpse at the stall had insisted it was armor made from spider silk and nightmares, neither of which sounded like suitable clothing material; but it was light and thin, and it fit under his coat like a tunic, trapping his body heat and keeping him far warmer than the wool coat alone.

What bemused him was that it cost nothing.

"Are you absolutely certain?"

The stallholder laughed warmly. "What would I do with money?" He gestured to the rest of the market with grisly hands. "We create because it pleases us, and because fulfilling the needs of others brings us joy, not because it makes us wealthy. Annwn has everything that we need, Warrior. Now it has what you need, too. Please, take it, with my gratitude. May the Goddess watch over your journey."

"You are most kind." He hesitated just long enough to summon the courage, then offered his hand.

The stallholder shook it, his fingers reforming skin and taking on a healthy tone just long enough for the contact, and his smile was genuine.

Quentin was thirty feet away from the stall before he checked his hand, but there was nothing present that shouldn't be, no residual matter from the contact. Despite the dreadful state of the stallholder's body, no unwanted bits had been left on Quentin's skin.

"You start to see how mutable a soul is once you're free from your body," Eric said as they headed for the outer gate together. "Some of us like to play around with decomposition, to wear away our fear of death and accept ourselves for who we are. Others like to decompose along with their bodies until there's nothing left. We're all just soul, at the end of the day. None of it's gonna end up on your hands." He grinned and squeezed Quentin's shoulder.

Quentin crinkled his nose. "Does this mean that everyone here appears however they choose to?" He glanced back toward the market, then at Eric. "They wish to, ah..."

"To explore what it means to be alive?" Eric nodded. "Yeah. Why do you think I look intact, bro? I got told you were a breather, and I didn't wanna freak you out."

He blinked at Eric. "You mean you... ah, you aren't usually..."

"Naw. Wanna see?"

Quentin debated the question. His initial, gut response was one of revulsion. How could Eric possibly think that Quentin might want to see whatever state of decay he might usually spend his time wandering around Annwn in?

But Quentin was no longer a man who would be ruled by his

fears. Eric was not even a physical, living person. He was spirit, or soul, or whatever people here were constructed from. Quentin might be able to touch them, but there was no body. And even if there were, what on earth would it matter?

These were people, and people deserved dignity.

He took a breath, then nodded. "Would you mind?"

"Dude, I wouldn't offer if I minded." Eric laughed warmly, and his skin melted away.

So did his clothes. His hair.

His eyes.

Quentin halted and tried to parse this. It was one thing to have encountered skeletons and decomposing bodies while here, but another to see a face so hauntingly close to Laurence's suddenly turn to rot.

Tears pricked his eyes, but blinking only made it worse. "Oh," he breathed faintly.

Eric reformed in a heartbeat, his skin flush with false life and his golden-brown curls restored to full glory. His deep, dark eyes were creased with concern. "Quentin?"

"I'm..." He held his breath as wind whipped around them, bitterly cold and with a touch of frost in the air. "I don't..."

He had no idea what to say, or even how to feel. This *felt* like grief, but that seemed foolish. Eric was still here, he wasn't... well, he *was* dead, but...

But he looked so much like his son. So much so that it had been dangerously like watching Laurence...

Quentin cast around for somewhere to sit before his legs gave out, and he found a low wall a few feet away, so he hurried to it. His backside hit it hard, and he screwed his eyes shut while he fought for control, waiting for the winds to end.

Laurence would come here when he died.

And Quentin would not.

The sense of loss that claimed him was so profound that it left him shaking. There was no hope of stopping the wind, and he gave up trying. The afterimage of Eric's awful corpse was burned into his brain, so he forced his eyes to open and scrubbed his tears away with cold, numb hands.

Mama wasn't here either, was she? No. She'd raised her sons to be as faithless as she herself was, and so she would have received the death she believed in. There was potential for everyone in the mortal world to go to a place that welcomed them, and instead she was nowhere, just as he would be.

He hiccuped.

"Hey, now." Eric sat by his side. "Wanna hear a good joke?"

Quentin shook his head. He didn't even want to hear words right now.

"Here we go. What do you call a fake noodle?" Eric grinned, his eyes alight with excitement.

"Um..."

"An impasta!" Eric laughed and slapped his own thigh. "Did you know that milk is the fastest liquid in the world?"

"Er—"

"It's pasteurized before you even see it!"

Quentin rubbed at his nose and frowned.

"Why don't you ever see elephants hiding in trees?" Eric leaned toward him.

"I don't—"

"Because they're so good at it!" Eric howled with laughter. "Oh man, I've got thousands of these. You may as well surrender now, dude. What do you call a fish with no eyes?"

Quentin blinked.

"Fsssshhhhh!"

"This is horrible," Quentin muttered.

"What do you call a deer with no eyes?"

"You're horrible," Quentin added.

"No idea! Get it? No eye deer! What do you call a deer with no eyes *and* no legs?"

"I take it all back. You're a terrible father," Quentin grumbled without malice.

"*Still* no idea!" Eric crowed. "Because it's got no legs! So it's not moving. It's still!"

"Yes, I got that..." Quentin pursed his lips, then sighed and rested his elbows on his knees. "Thank you," he added.

The wind faded, and Quentin was left with little more than a bone-deep sense of exhaustion, but at least the grief had passed. For now, at least. It really was difficult to retain his upset in the face of Eric's gentle, awful jokes. He could see how Laurence would have responded so well to them.

"Any time." Eric's tone softened, and he too leaned forward, elbows on his knees, mimicking Quentin's posture. "Wanna talk about it?"

Quentin bit his lip a little.

Did he want to talk about it? About anything, in fact? He didn't know Eric, other than the fact that the man was the father of the person Quentin loved, but on the other hand, Eric was offering.

If Quentin ever wished to speak with a therapist, the first step was learning to speak at all, and Eric was far too dead to tell anyone about the unwell chap with the impossible powers.

But perhaps he should start with the more immediate topics.

He drew a breath and glanced toward Eric. "What happens to those who do not believe in..." He gestured toward the world around them, palm toward the sky. "All of this?"

Eric shrugged. "Same thing as happens to us all in the end. Rebirth. You just cut out the vacation in between, which seems like a poor choice to me."

Quentin blinked at him and sat up straighter. "You mean... into new lives? Forgetting everything?"

"Yeah." Eric shrugged. "The vacation option's better all around. You get to work out your lifetime's bullshit and deal with it, instead of just carrying it with you into the next life with no idea where it came from." He stood up and offered his hand to

Quentin. "C'mon. We can't spend too long hanging around. You've got a fuel conservation problem."

With a soft sigh, Quentin heaved himself to his feet. Eric was quite correct. Quentin's functional time was limited by being alive, and if he wished to remain that way, he had to complete his task within a small handful of days at most. Worst, he had been warned not to fly, so he would be expending more fluid than he might like by climbing mountains the hard way. He did not have time to sit around fretting, and he certainly couldn't afford the tears.

"Do you know the way?" he asked of Eric.

"Sure. Kinda. I mean, we just point toward the right mountain and keep on walking, right?" Eric grinned and marched toward the gates. "C'mon. You can tell me all about how you met Cricket on the way!"

It was a safer topic, certainly. And a story Quentin had recounted before. As they passed through the gates and waved farewell to the guards, he fell into step alongside Eric and slipped his hands into the pockets of his coat to keep them warm.

"I suppose it all began at Balboa Park," Quentin said. "For me, at least. For Laurence, it started three years before that. Before you had passed, too," he mused.

Eric's eyebrows climbed. "Now that's a hook. Go on."

And so, as they followed a winding path away from the castle, Quentin launched into the story of how he'd met Eric's son.

19

LAURENCE

Laurence turned toward the clatter of footsteps in time to
see Basil and Jon descending the stairs into the subway station,
and he was standing by the time their heads came into view.

Basil had a courier bag over one shoulder, the strap draped
across his chest, and he clutched that strap with both hands.
"Sorry it took a while," he began the moment he got close. "I had
to feed the cats."

"Before they ate us," Jon said, as though it were a real threat.

Laurence narrowed his eyes. He was starting to think Jon
might be joking half the time he said anything, but his tone was
so flat and his features lacked almost any animation, which made
him hard to read, even for man with Laurence's senses.

Basil must've thought it was humor, because he smiled briefly
as he plucked his MetroCard from a pocket. "Okay," he breathed.
"Back to your hotel?"

"For now," Laurence agreed. "Beats hanging around in this
weather."

He waited for Basil and Jon to pass through the turnstiles
before he followed. Whether he just wanted to make sure they
didn't run off once he was the wrong side of the barriers or not

he couldn't be entirely sure, but he stuck to them like glue as they waited for the next train, keeping only the most tangential attention on where Ryan was.

Basil didn't pluck his book from the courier bag until they were safely on a train. There weren't initially four seats available together, but once Jon had stared at people for sixty seconds, mysteriously a whole section of seats opened up, which Basil slotted himself into like he was used to his boyfriend clearing space for him.

Laurence sat opposite and eyed the blue glow of the pages. Even the cover glowed blue, and rippled softly, like water in a swimming pool. He didn't recall seeing any books at Rufus' where the covers themselves glowed, but Basil had a task, and Laurence wasn't going to interrupt it.

They sat in silence. Only Basil could read Latin, and besides, there was only one copy of the book to go around. All Laurence could do was wait.

He hated waiting.

***

"OH!" Basil sat forward sharply as their train pulled in at the 68th Street station. "I think this might be it!"

Laurence tore his attention from the view out of the windows and leaned forward. "Think?"

"I'll have to google a few of the words to make sure they don't have some different meanings, but yes." Basil beamed widely. "It should send us to the lands of the dead."

"Which lands of the dead?" Laurence frowned at him.

"Er. Well." Basil adjusted his glasses, then sighed. "Yes. But I think we can just tweak the spell to make sure we go to Annwn and not, like, Valhalla and Fólkvangr, or Duat, or Tartarus—"

Laurence cut in to stop Basil listing every single faith's underworld since the dawn of time. "You sure you can do that?"

"Well, like I say, I just need to google a few words. But yes. I believe it's possible."

Laurence nodded. "Okay. Let's go get some wifi."

Basil tucked the book away into his bag with care, fastening the bag's straps to keep it secure, and puffed out his cheeks. He looked toward Jon and then took his hand.

Did Laurence imagine it, or was there the faintest note of concern in the set of Jon's mouth?

But then the train rattled into 59th Street station, and it was gone.

THE TIME TAKEN to get to East Harlem and back had cost them the last of whatever daylight might have been lingering above the impenetrable cloud cover. When they reached the street, any light that came through the increasingly thick snow was artificial. Lights from hotels and cars, from street lamps and cellphones.

Jon set off unerringly along the street without checking around, and Basil chased at his heels, his hands tightly clutching the strap of his bag.

Ryan eyed Laurence as they followed. "You're absolutely sure you want to do this?"

Laurence rocked his jaw. "Am I absolutely sure that I want to rescue my partner from a world he can't possibly escape on his own? Yes. Does anyone else have to come with me? No, of course not. But I'm going anyway."

Ryan nodded slightly, but whatever he might have said next was forestalled by Basil letting out a startled squeak.

Everyone stopped walking.

Basil was staring fixedly at his ring, and he began turning in a circle, his hand outstretched, palm facing away from himself.

"Again?" was all Jon said.

"What is it?" Laurence stepped back out of Basil's radius.

"Ghosts," Basil breathed. "So many of them. This happened earlier..." He tailed off and blinked to Laurence above the frames of his glasses, then sighed.

"It's been happening off and on ever since I made the ring," he admitted. "There's like this huge pack of ghosts in Manhattan, but I never seem to find them. Either they're too fast, or they dissipate, or otherwise are gone whenever I get there."

He licked his lips. "I was looking for them earlier, when we met. That's why I was in the area, but I figured talking to you would be more important."

Laurence stamped his feet to try and keep warm. Why would Basil prefer to talk to a total stranger, instead of hunting down this army of ghosts he'd spent months trying to track?

Then it hit him.

For exactly the same reason Laurence had reached out to Basil.

Basil didn't know any other necromancers, or witches, or anything else. He'd literally learned all his magic from one single book that he'd found under a floorboard, and here was his one chance to maybe learn more, make a contact, feel less alone in his world. And if he'd failed to find these ghosts for months already, what was once more in the face of a future as the only magic-user he knew?

Laurence let out a breath. "Okay. Any idea how close?"

Basil shook his head. "No. And they don't usually stick around for long."

He knew what Basil was begging for, and Laurence crossed his arms while he considered it. He didn't want any delay in getting to Quentin. Also, running into possibly hundreds of ghosts all at once seemed like one hell of a bad idea.

Knowing Laurence's luck, this would be the one time Basil found the damn things, and Laurence wasn't prepared to fight ghosts in the slightest. He couldn't see them, and he sure as hell didn't know how to kill one, or if it was even possible.

"I think it's a bad idea," he concluded. "Can you both handle that many ghosts at once?"

Basil bit his lip. "Er—"

"Not if they're antagonistic," Jon replied bluntly.

"And can I get to Annwn without you?" Laurence looked at Basil.

"Well—"

"No," Jon concluded.

"Thanks," Laurence said. "Then if it's okay with you, I'd really like to get to Annwn. If you wanna go chasing ghosts once I'm gone, that's obviously up to you, but I can't do this without you, and Quentin's in danger. The longer we leave him, the more in danger he's gonna get, because that's exactly the kind of guy he is." Laurence sighed. "I'm sorry. I'd be more than happy to help you track down ghosts when we get back, but if Jon was stuck, you'd do everything you could to rescue him, right?"

Basil's cheeks were already red from the bitter cold, but he winced faintly and dipped his head. "I'm sorry. You're right. I just got carried away. Let's—"

Laurence held his hand up.

There was darkness in the snow.

It had red eyes.

Worse, he knew the others hadn't even seen the monster yet. He pointed to it, in the hope that someone here could deal with something that Quentin hadn't been able to protect himself from. Maybe between the four of them, someone had whatever it took to tackle giant black dogs who ferried witches to Annwn.

"Black dog," was all he said.

They all turned toward it, and Basil raised his hand.

"Oh my god," he gasped. "It's the ghosts! The dog! It's..."

Basil squeaked in terror and stopped talking, so Laurence figured the necromancer must have seen the dog at last.

"It *is* ghosts," Jon mused, sounding for all the world as though a beast the size of a horse was not bearing down on them right that very moment. Even worse, he too reached a hand toward it.

"Goddess, I hope you know what you're doing," Laurence gasped.

The dog let out the howl of a thousand distant wolves, throwing its head back even though the sound echoed down the streets from distant points, and then it dove headfirst into the sidewalk, passing through it as though it wasn't at all solid.

It left a pillar of darkness in its wake. Tall and slender, with hair like ink and skin almost as white as the falling snow.

Laurence's pulse raced, and he pushed past Basil and Jon, unsure whether to believe his eyes.

"Quen?"

Except it wasn't Quentin. Despite the pale gray eyes, the soft lips, the flawless facsimile of Quentin's clothing and features, the steady churn of the vortex within him was absent, replaced by nothingness.

Not-Quentin turned his gaze on Laurence.

"Ah," was all he said.

20

LAURENCE

Laurence balled his hands into fists and took a step closer to Not-Quentin. "Where is he?" he snarled. "What have you done with him?"

Not-Quentin glanced around, his features impassive, unruffled by Laurence's approach. He was in no hurry, it looked like, as he idly swept those familiar eyes across the crowd around Laurence. His gaze lingered briefly on Ryan, but settled on Jon. "The irony is that if he had forewarned me that you were a Hunter, I would not have troubled with the disguise," Not-Quentin mused, pale eyes still fixed on Jon. "No matter. You are the son of Eric Riley, yes?" The eyes returned to Laurence.

Laurence clenched his jaw.

Just what on earth had his dad been up to while he was in New York, that all these people were able to pick Laurence out of the crowd?

"So this *isn't* Quentin?" Basil squeaked, still clutching his bag. "Where did the ghosts go?" Then he gasped. "Are they in the black dog? Were you controlling it? Did you send it to kidnap Quentin in the first place?"

"Where is he?" Laurence repeated, stepping in until he was looming over Not-Quentin, taking full advantage of that one-inch difference in height between them.

"He is in Annwn," said Not-Quentin. "I have sworn to him that I will protect you in his absence." He tipped his head back a little to maintain eye contact with Laurence. "Though perhaps you require less protection than he believes, Hunter. You are a Child of Herne, more than capable of defending yourself. And you keep such interesting company."

"Yeah, well, if there's no need to babysit me, there's no need for him not to be here himself, is there?" Laurence jabbed a finger against Not-Quentin's chest and tried to ignore just how much like Quentin this being felt. "Take me there. Or bring him back, I don't care which."

"I cannot." Not-Quentin shrugged. "Not until his task is complete, at which point we will automatically return to our correct worlds. All you must do, Hunter, is wait."

"Then what is his task?" Goddess, Laurence felt like he was losing his mind, playing twenty questions with an unknown being who was posing as the man he loved. "No, forget it. Tell me who you are."

Not-Quentin finally allowed a small flicker of a smile to touch the corners of his mouth. "I too am a Hunter, child. I am the very cause of your existence. And of his." He sidestepped Laurence and approached Jon, lashing out with one thin arm and snatching Jon's hand before Jon could do more than step backwards. "And yet the disparity is astonishing. Three thousand years. Perhaps Herne's offspring have been interbreeding." He pursed his lips, then placed the palm of his free hand against Jon's forehead.

Jon arched back, mouth opening with no sound, but Not-Quentin remained in contact, even while Basil ran in to grab his arm and try to pry him off.

Laurence darted in and tackled Not-Quentin around the

waist, but he was immobile, rooted to the spot, and Laurence's feet slipped in the snow. He snarled and attempted to straight up lift Not-Quentin off the ground. "Let him go!"

Jon fell to the sidewalk, landing heavily in thick snow, which cushioned his fall.

"I am Arawn," Not-Quentin finally said, brushing both Laurence and Basil off himself with barely a shrug. "King of Annwn. God of the dead. Master of a Wild Hunt. Long is my waiting."

Laurence backtracked a step and stared at Arawn in growing horror.

He was a god, and he'd just dropped Jon to the ground like Jon was utterly meaningless.

Basil fell to his knees by Jon's side and felt for a pulse, then his eyes grew wide. "You killed him," he whispered, full of disbelief and only barely audible to Laurence. Then he spoke again, more loudly, with anguish chasing away his disbelief. "He's dead! You killed him!"

It was like everything happened at once. Basil began sobbing as he shook Jon's shoulder and begged him to wake up. Ryan lunged forward and tackled Arawn, pushing him back several feet, until Arawn grabbed for his throat. The dog returned, flowing out of the sidewalk as it engulfed Jon and Basil, but then it split apart like ink spilled in water and vaporized into the snow.

Laurence's gut instinct was to follow Arawn, so he plunged after the god, wishing he had a damn thing on him that could so much as lay a scratch on a deity. Instead all he had was his hands, and they'd have to do.

"You bastard!" Ryan yelled. "He didn't do anything to you! I'll kill you! I'll fucking kill you!"

"You may try," Arawn said, sounding bored.

Sounding like Quentin.

Laurence dove after them with gritted teeth. The last time he'd fought Quentin was when Freddy controlled Laurence's body.

Now it was when it wasn't even Quentin, but a god in disguise. A disguise he could only have gained by taking Quentin in the first place.

Arawn had taken Quentin. He'd killed Jon. And Laurence wouldn't let Ryan face him alone.

HE PLUNGED through the blizzard and followed Ryan's scent, but it was quickly tainted with blood. There was nothing like it, no smell that came even close to the familiar touch of metal and life that marked blood apart from the rest of the world.

Red stained the white, and Laurence plunged on until he found Ryan sprawled on the ground, blood pouring from him in so many places that Laurence didn't know where to begin. Sure, he had some first aid training, but he didn't have any equipment.

He'd have to improvise.

Laurence crouched and began to assess Ryan's airway. There was a routine. He couldn't just skip straight to the bleeding parts. Airway. Breathing. Circulation. Only once he was sure they were about as good as could be expected did he start evaluating wounds.

Goddess, so many wounds. They were jagged and torn, and Laurence couldn't begin to figure out what weapon could have caused them.

"Hey," he grunted. "Ryan? Are you with me?"

Ryan's eyelids fluttered softly. His lips parted.

"Okay. It's me. It's Laurence. I need to check you over, see if I can move you, okay? You can't stay on the ground in this weather. I'm gonna do what I can to patch you up fast, then get you inside."

Fuck. This was the worst possible time to have a dead body and a dying person on his hands. Could ambulances even get through the gridlock right now? He doubted it, but he also doubted the hotel would appreciate Laurence walking in with a bleeding body in his arms.

Screw 'em. They'd have to deal with it.

He ran top to bottom down Ryan's body, doing what he could to try and tend to each injury, though it fast became apparent that there wasn't anything he could do without bandages at the very least, so he scooped Ryan up into his arms. "Basil!" he yelled, hoping the necromancer could hear him. "Ryan's hurt! I have to get him inside. I'll come back for you, okay?"

He didn't hear an answer, but Ryan was running out of time, so Laurence gritted his teeth and jogged forward, praying to the Goddess that Jon had been right about which direction the hotel was in.

LAURENCE DIDN'T EVEN GET an argument from the doorman, which surprised him. Instead, calls went out over radios for security to come with a first-aid kit, and Laurence was guided into a ground-floor office where Ryan could be laid out on the floor and tended to by the security guard who rushed in to join them.

"I can't stay," Laurence gasped. "He's not the only one. I need to go get the other."

"What even happened?" the guard asked as he began assessing Ryan's injuries.

"Man, if you think I saw shit in this weather, I got news for you." Laurence wiped blood off his hands and onto his wet coat. "I'll be back as fast as I can."

He ran out into the darkness and followed the scent of fresh blood all the way back to where Ryan had fallen, and then continued on, hunting for Jon and Basil in the murk. "Basil? I'm back! Where are you?"

There was no response. Only the sound of relentless sobbing, of heartbreak made loud and awful.

Laurence swallowed. It was a terrible sound, not for the noise itself, but for the meaning it carried. It was grief, and anyone who had made that sound themselves in their lives would be a monster to remain unaffected by hearing it from anyone else. It was beyond words, and instead touched the soul, one heartbreak to another.

It made Laurence's nose run and his eyes fill with tears.

He had felt that loss.

He tried not to get blood in his eyes as he wiped them with the wrist of his jacket, and he stumbled toward the sound just as Basil's sobs turned to weak gasps as his energy began to leave him.

"Basil," he croaked. "Basil, I'm here. We need to get inside. We can't stay out here."

"Jon," was all Basil said.

"We can take him inside." Laurence found them at last, huddled on the ground, and he crouched by Jon's side. He checked for life signs, even though Basil hadn't found any, but there was nothing.

"I'm sorry," he breathed.

Basil's eyes were so reddened that they looked painfully sore. He didn't take his gaze from Jon, didn't let go of Jon's arm.

Jon's eyes flicked open.

Laurence jerked his hand back, startled. There hadn't been a sudden reappearance of a pulse, no color in Jon's cheeks, but Laurence hadn't heard of people's *eyes* opening once they were dead. Was that a thing?

If it was, it was a damn freaky thing.

Basil yelped, too. "Jon?"

Jon sat up slowly, eyes almost entirely black, his skin gray and hollow. "This is new," he mused. He turned to face Basil, then blinked and added, "Have you been crying?"

Basil flung his arms around Jon and squeezed tightly. "I thought you were dead!"

Laurence sat on his haunches and rested his elbows on his thighs while he watched.

He still felt nothing from Jon, so he remained unconvinced that Jon was anything *but* dead.

But if he *was* dead, how on earth had he sat up and spoken to them?

21

QUENTIN

These were entirely the wrong shoes for mountaineering.

Quentin had to resort to telekinesis more than once to keep himself from slipping as they descended the mountain. Perhaps chatting with Eric should have taken a back seat to paying attention to the ground, but in truth, it helped to give him something to talk about with the father of his lover.

This was bonding time, and only a fool would waste such a rare opportunity. And from Eric's perspective, this could be his only chance to hear news of his family while he waited for them to join him — hopefully not for quite some time yet. And so Quentin could endure the occasional slip, since telekinesis didn't seem to drain him a great deal. Nowhere near as much as generating heat or fire, anyway.

He left out a few details that he felt served no purpose in sharing, other than to enrage a man Quentin felt didn't deserve such anger — that, and sharing that information would only infuriate Quentin himself, and he was in no position to deal with that anger at the present time. He had been fortunate enough to enjoy several days, of late, with a much more tolerable level of wrath inside his own head, and he would rather prefer to continue at a degree where a smile did not feel like a betrayal or a lie.

No matter how long they walked for, they only seemed to get further away from the castle they had left, and yet no nearer to the one they aimed toward. While it took little energy to descend, Quentin did not eagerly anticipate the amount it would require to climb, if this was how long it all took.

Yet the sky did not change.

He frowned up at it briefly, then looked at Eric. "Is there ever night here?"

"Nah." Eric shook his head. "No sun, no day or night."

"If there is no sun—"

"Where does the light come from?"

Quentin nodded.

"You got me," Eric chuckled. "It doesn't matter. Otherworld is a result of human imagination. At some point, people started believing the sky of Annwn had no sun, so that's the way it is."

He grappled with that notion for a few minutes. "Then how does belief not shape the living world in the same way?"

"Ah, now that's the question, isn't it?" Eric's smile faded away. "I don't know. Maybe matter isn't all that malleable, or maybe we just believe it isn't, and that's what makes it so solid. We're all made of gaps and empty space, when you really get down to it. Atoms and molecules and all that jazz. Maybe we imagine these worlds with their weird rules, so that we can live in a place that makes some kind of sense. I don't know; I'm not nearly as much of a philosopher as you seem to be."

"Oh, I'm not..." Quentin slipped and caught himself again, and paused to set his footing straight with a soft exhale. "I'm no philosopher," he murmured. "Merely rather new to all this, and attempting to understand. Before I met Laurence I had no idea any of it was possible, let alone existed, and I certainly did not know of the presence of my own abilities."

Eric scratched his stubble in a gesture so familiar that it made

Quentin's heart ache. "Yeah. I wish I'd known about this, like, this need to hunt you described. I figure it might've saved me from a few candy bars, you know?" He patted his stomach. "I figured I just had this addictive personality, and Cricket inherited it from me. Still, can't have too many regrets. I still met Myriam, still had a wonderful son. I had a life filled with love and laughter, you know? And in my defense, chocolate is *so* good." His smile slowly returned as he spoke, both to his lips and his eyes. "Yeah. I had a good life. I think maybe that's the best thing we can ever hope for, right?"

Quentin smiled a touch. "I think you may be more philosophical than you give yourself credit for."

"Ha!"

They continued down, sometimes forced off the main path due to a rockfall or a tangle of weeds, and continued their chat.

Eric was every bit as easy to talk to as his son, and Quentin was beginning to find the entire experience quite pleasant.

<hr>

THIS TIME his slip was more of a slide, and he coasted a good three feet downhill before he came to a halt, his arms outstretched.

"Bloody hell," he breathed.

"Dude, are you okay?" Eric jogged to catch up, then grabbed Quentin's shoulder. "Man, you look beat!"

"I look—" Quentin broke off to cover his mouth as he yawned. "I'm sorry, what?"

"Tired, Quentin. You look tired. I'd say dead tired, but I don't wanna get misunderstood here." Eric looked around.

Quentin blinked several times, but the action didn't seem to restore any moisture to his eyes. He stifled another yawn and followed Eric's example in examining his surroundings.

They were, at last, off the rock and into woodland. Or, rather, the long-dead petrified remains of woodland that he had flown over many hours ago. The ground underfoot was formed of untrustworthy, lifeless dirt that shifted and slid around with each step.

The hill was still steep, too, although not as aggressively so as the rock had been. These were undoubtedly the foothills of the mountain, and all Quentin and Eric need do was continue along, up and down hills, until they could begin climbing the next mountain.

All right. When he assessed the full magnitude of the task ahead, perhaps he *did* feel a little tired.

"We can continue," he murmured.

Eric eyed him as they set off walking. "Let me guess. This is the British stiff upper lip thing, right? Dude, you don't hafta prove anything to me. It's okay to take a rest. I can keep watch."

The insistence that Quentin must be tired only seemed to make him yawn even harder, and his shoulders sagged. "This is ridiculous," he muttered. "What am I to do? Sleep on the ground?"

"Uh. Yeah?"

Quentin snorted at him. "And ruin this coat? Not bloody likely!"

THEY MADE it a whole two miles further, by Quentin's reckoning, before he had to admit defeat. His eyes were so dry that even blinking had become painful, and his mouth was almost as parched. His limbs ached, as did his head, and it was a genuine struggle to even focus on where he was placing his feet.

He needed to rest, but rest seemed like a waste of his time. It would be hours with no food or water *and* no further progress.

Eric squinted up at their target through blackened and bare branches. "We're gonna need cover."

"From what weather?" Quentin's sarcasm rose to the challenge, where his brain failed to supply a reasonable explanation for this need.

"From their line of sight," Eric explained. "Otherwise, they're gonna see us while you're napping and maybe come down out of the sky to chew our faces off or whatever."

"Cover," Quentin muttered as he glanced around. He uprooted dead trees and dragged them nearer, then arranged them in a sort of conical shape, their branches splintering as he crammed them together with enough force that slippage wasn't an option.

"Whoa!" Eric blinked as he took a step back. "Dude, did anyone ever tell you that you can get pretty intense?"

"It has been mentioned." He swept the dead earth aside to clear any rocks or brambles out from beneath the canopy, then crawled inside and used his arm as a pillow. "For which I can only apologize."

"That you get intense, or that people have noticed it?"

It was too difficult a question for him to grapple with at the moment, so he merely grunted in agreement and closed his eyes.

Eric was right. Just a few minutes with his eyes closed would be for the best. They would be up and away again in no time.

"What do you think you are doing?"

Quentin snapped the book closed quickly. It was far too large for his hands, too heavy for him to hold steady, and it tumbled to the floor with a loud smack of leather hitting wood.

Father never came to the door. Quentin always had to wait for him. He hadn't expected to get caught nosing over the shelves in the little library that sat between the corridor and Father's office.

His heart raced. He swallowed. He felt rooted to the spot, unable to leave his chair and pick up the book, yet it sat on the floor with its pages open like the clearest imaginable indicator of guilt.

"Pick it up," Father snapped.

At last, Quentin could move. He jumped down from the chair and grabbed the book, then closed it more gently.

"Put it back where you got it from."

Quentin didn't want to turn his back on his father, so instead he sidled along the shelves and stood up on his tiptoes to slide it back into place, one eye still on Father. "I'm sorry," he mumbled.

"Speak up, boy!"

"I said I'm sorry," he blurted.

His hands were shaking.

Father's eyes lingered on the book. Then he crouched in front of Quentin and spoke with unexpected softness. "Why did you choose that book, Quentin?"

Quentin teetered on the hope that he might have done something good for once. Something Father approved of. He gasped and bit his lip, and met his father's gaze. "The spine was pretty," he said, speaking loudly lest he be told off again.

"And what made it pretty?" Father's eyes were almost gleaming. There was something desperate in them, maybe even hopeful, but Quentin didn't know what.

He glanced at the book, then back to his father. "The color."

Father leaned forward. "What about the color?"

"It's purple." Quentin knotted his fingers together and tried not to panic. Was this the right answer? He had no way to know what Father expected, or even why he was speaking so kindly all of a sudden. "I liked the pattern pressed into it."

"Embossed," his father corrected. But he sighed as he stood, and he reached for Quentin's hand.

Disappointed.

Father was always disappointed.

"It is your birthday," he said, his voice returning to a dispassionate monotone.

And, soon enough, Quentin began to scream.

22

LAURENCE

"WE CAN FIGURE THIS OUT LATER," LAURENCE BREATHED AS HE pushed himself to his feet. "I got Ryan to the hotel. They've got security giving him first aid, but we should get back. Here." He offered Jon his hand, and Jon reached for it.

Their skin met.

Numbness swallowed Laurence's fingers. It shot up his arm and across his collarbone as, within a fraction of a second, the life in his body began to abandon him.

Jon's eyes widened. He snatched his hand back at the same time as Laurence threw his whole body away from the contact.

"What the fuck!" Laurence gasped. He tried to flex his fingers, but they were unresponsive.

Gray.

Dead.

His own energy swirled down his arm, and the first sensation to return was the discomfort of pins and needles.

"Interesting," was Jon's sole comment.

"No, not fucking *interesting*," Laurence gasped. The discomfort turned to pain, but it was soon washed away.

Color returned to his hand, and he cradled it in his other arm while he tested his fingers.

"Oh my god!" Basil looked between them, trying to see past his soaking wet lenses. "What was that?"

"I don't know." Jon turned away from Basil to slowly stand. "It might be best if you don't make skin contact for now."

Basil blinked. "What? Why not?"

"Because he damn near killed me," Laurence said as realization dawned.

Jon hadn't drained him. Not the way Quentin could. He had simply negated Laurence's energy, blotted it out of existence like it was meaningless. If Laurence didn't have a perpetual flow of life force inside of him, his whole arm would be dead now, and might never have recovered.

They'd both reacted fast enough for Laurence to still be alive, and he wasn't sure Basil stood a chance.

Basil bit his nails briefly, but all that managed to do was flake off another chip of his polish, and he huffed as he coiled his arms around himself instead. "You mean when I hugged you just now, if I'd touched your skin, I could've just died right then and there?"

"So it would seem." Jon patted snow from himself, then dipped his hands into his coat pockets. He was far too lanky for anyone to accidentally touch his face, and it looked like he was going to protect them all by putting his hands similarly out of reach.

It wasn't a good enough solution. They were about to go into a crowded hotel. Sooner or later, Jon had to touch *something*.

Laurence stamped his feet as he pocketed his own hands and his thoughts began to nag at the problem. "You're a Child of Arawn," he said, trying to put his thought process into words. "Well, that was Arawn. He seemed kinda unimpressed that I was more..." He hesitated. "More like Herne than you were like Arawn, so maybe he's done something to turn you up to eleven."

Jon's thin eyebrow raised, and he looked unimpressed with this line of logic. "This theory is weak."

"Yeah, early stages. C'mon." Laurence jerked his head toward the hotel, then started walking that way, skirting the blood that was already disappearing below fresh snowfall. "He said the disparity was astonishing, right?"

"Correct." Jon fell in at his side.

Basil caught up and strode along next to Jon. "You think he evened the disparity by, what? By doing something to Jon to make him more powerful?"

"Yeah, pretty much." Laurence huffed. "He's eradicated the disparity by making us equal, and he chose to level Jon up rather than strip me down. Maybe he can't affect me like that. It could be he can only affect Jon due to lineage."

"Then it must be possible to control this," Jon murmured. "If your logic holds."

"Right. So just..." Laurence shrugged. "I dunno, man. How would you normally not kill everything you touched?"

"By not drawing the life out of it," Jon said dryly.

"But this didn't feel like you were pulling. It felt like you just flat-out negated my arm." Laurence shook droplets from his curls. "Does that make sense?"

Basil and Jon exchanged a glance.

Which meant that it *did* make sense, for some reason. To both of them.

"Normally, when you disperse a ghost," Basil began, his voice picking up some excitement.

"It requires that I nullify their energy with my own," Jon completed.

"So if the dog is made of ghosts—"

"—And if Jon is nullifying whatever he touches—" Laurence realized.

"—That explains why the dog just fell apart when it touched him," Basil concluded.

Jon looked between them both, then stopped walking. He almost looked like a ghost himself, nothing but a pale head floating in the darkness, eyes almost hidden, cheeks hollow and gaunt.

"I see," he said.

"Arawn is the god of death," Laurence said as he stopped and turned to face Jon. "It'd make sense if your gifts were kinda, you know." He swallowed. "A bit deathy."

"I was perfectly accustomed to my gifts as they were," Jon groused.

"But you learned before, right?" Basil smiled eagerly. "Just... do it again!"

Jon blinked slowly at him. "I had a teacher then," he murmured.

Basil's smile faltered. "Yeah. But..." He let out a deep sigh. "I know you can do it."

"Logically it must be possible," Jon agreed. He closed his eyes and adopted a slight frown.

Laurence closed his own eyes a moment and reached for Windsor.

I come?

He pursed his lips to hide a smile. *No. Do you know of Arawn?*

Scary! Windsor's tone was one of awe. *A Hunter!*

Yes. Laurence agreed with both sentiments. *Do you know more?*

No. Windsor was apologetic. *Born here.*

Laurence understood. Windsor had only been an egg when Laurence brought him here from Otherworld. Despite Windsor knowing a smattering of information about Otherworld, he couldn't possibly know everything. He was still young, and had never been back. Any knowledge he did have had come from either intrinsic means — whether by dint of being a creature of spirit, or a gift from Herne, Laurence didn't know — or whatever he had overheard since his birth.

Okay, he replied. *Thank you. I hope we'll be home soon.*

I hope so too!

Laurence opened his eyes in time to catch Jon doing the same.

There was tone to Jon's skin. Color. Life. Not a huge amount, sure, but as much as he'd had before Arawn touched him and then ditched him on the sidewalk.

Laurence tilted his head, and picked up the faint traces of Jon's energy. It wasn't as strong as Basil's, but then it hadn't been before, either, and in comparison to absolutely nothing it was like a bonfire.

"Is that better?" Jon asked, sounding doubtful.

"I think so." Laurence hesitated, and then he withdrew a hand from his pocket to offer to Jon. "Let's try it."

Jon nodded, and Basil stepped back as Jon's own hands emerged.

The fingertip that touched the end of Laurence's pointer finger was cold, but it didn't make his hand numb. They looked up at each other, then shifted their hands forward until they clasped each other's palms.

Laurence let out a breath of relief. "Way better," he said. He hadn't been looking forward to a numb arm, but this was far safer than letting Jon touch Basil and kill him outright.

Basil eyed Jon's hands. "No offense, baby, but I think I'd rather wait until you touch a plant or something?"

"None taken," Jon agreed. "That would be the most sensible next step."

Laurence nodded. "You've got a lid on it for now though, right? Whatever it was?"

"Yes."

"Okay. 'Cause it'd suck if they kept Ryan alive only for you to kill him."

Jon's eyes gleamed briefly, and Laurence struggled to be sure whether it was in amusement, or out of some sadistic desire to murder people.

No. He was being unfair. It was probably the former.

It seemed nicer to believe it was the former, anyway.

IT WAS GETTING hard to wade through the deepening snow, and they made it back to the hotel just as the effort became tiring.

Or maybe it was the adrenaline crash.

Laurence huffed as he stepped into the warmth, and he unfastened his coat. "Thanks, man," he said to the doorman. "The guy I brought in. Is he…" He licked his lips. "Is he okay?"

The doorman, whose name badge read *Tony*, nodded toward the office Laurence had carried Ryan through to earlier. There were already cleaners discreetly trying to get blood out of the carpet in the space between Laurence and that doorway. "I don't know, sir. Go on right through, though. Wait, hold up there, son." He put a hand up to Jon, then his features contorted.

It was the face of a man who realized he'd made a terrible mistake, like he'd just reached for a rattlesnake.

He took his hand back and smoothed his features a little. "Guests only," he said. His voice shook as he said it.

"He's with me," Laurence snapped. "C'mon." He ushered Basil and Jon toward the cleaners, stepping around them and then continuing on toward the doorway. "Guests only, my ass," he muttered. "You guys get shitty customer service in this city. My mom would fire anyone who spoke that way."

"We're used to it," Basil sighed. "This is what I meant when I said they might not let Jon in."

"It's not okay, though." Laurence clenched his jaw.

"Everyone fears death," Jon said.

"Still doesn't make it okay!" He knocked on the office door, and then pushed the door open so that he could poke his head in and see whether it was appropriate to speak.

The reek of blood hit him like a wall. Confined to this office for the few minutes he'd been gone, it permeated the air and almost overpowered all the other smells. Cologne, soap, sweat, perfume, coffee, it all seemed so unimportant compared to the blood. Maybe it was the quantity, or he figured it could be possible that Hunters were more attuned to blood than other aromas, but he had to hold his breath while he got used to it.

Security was nowhere to be seen.

Hell, Ryan was nowhere to be seen.

"What the fuck?" Laurence shoved the door all the way open and strode inside.

There wasn't any sign of a scuffle that he could see. The furniture hadn't been kicked over; papers were still on desks. The blood was in a vaguely human shape on the carpet, still wet, but growing dark now.

"Here," Basil breathed. He crouched near the doorway and pointed.

There was half a footprint, dark red and quickly oxidizing, facing the doorway.

"Whoever it was, they went out the door," Basil said. "Either Ryan, or the first responder who might have stepped in some of the blood."

"Did an ambulance arrive?" Jon mused.

Laurence shook his head. "No sirens nearby. Traffic's gridlocked. There's no way an ambulance crew got in here, patched Ryan up, and took him away in the time I was gone."

"So he left," Basil said.

"Yeah." Laurence gritted his teeth and shot out of the room again, this time jogging to reception and pushing to the front of the line. At the chorus of objections, he simply snarled, then turned to the clerk. "The security guard who was doing first aid on the guy I took through there—" He pointed to the office. "Where is he?"

She blinked up at him, then gasped. "The guy with all the blood?" She waved a hand at herself as though indicating that blood. "He just took off, sir, a few minutes ago. I believe Ramirez went after him."

"Damn it. Thanks. Thank you, really." He nodded to her, then darted away from the desk. "He's gone," he said when he returned to Basil and Jon. "Just ran off, apparently. Problem is, the security guard went after him."

Basil tugged his glasses off and wiped them on a tissue from his pocket. "This seems bad. Or is that just me? Anyone?"

Laurence flexed his jaw.

If Ryan had gone to chase Arawn again, and Ramirez was following what he thought was a patient in desperate need of aid, Ramirez would be following Ryan straight into a lethal battle with a fully manifested god. Arawn wasn't in a weakened state, not like Jack had been, and he wasn't worn down into a daemon, the way Black Annis was.

No.

Arawn might look like Quentin right now, but unlike Quentin, he could and would kill. He was a god of death, for crying out loud. What death god pulled their punches?

If Ramirez wasn't dead already, he could be soon.

"Yeah," Laurence said. "This is bad."

Mainly because the only person who could track Ryan and Ramirez in this weather was Laurence, and he was scared sick at the prospect of entering that battle.

But if he didn't, an innocent man would die.

"Goddess," he whispered. "Please watch over me, 'cause this shit's gonna get hairy."

23

QUENTIN

QUENTIN WOKE TO SCREAMING AND THE VIOLENCE OF A TEMPEST. He shouldn't have been surprised that he was the source of both, and yet every bloody time it happened, it terrified him.

He intended to grab the sheets, but there were none. Instead there was nothing but dry dirt beneath his hands, and his fingers dug into it even as it was swept away by the winds.

Annwn bubbled up from the depths of his brain. *You're in Annwn.*

He gasped. His throat was sore, and he had little saliva to remedy the issue with.

"Quentin? Dude, what's happening?"

Quentin gritted his teeth and screwed his eyes shut. It sounded like Laurence, almost, but it wasn't.

The wind howled. Uprooted trees crashed and cracked against more ancient deadwood. Dirt sounded like rain against wood and earth alike.

He had to regain control, but snatches of the nightmare still lingered. He thought he had a handle on things, but then there would be a flicker, and he lost it all.

No.

This was not good enough.

He slowed his breathing and released his grip on the earth. If simply counting down would not work, then he must resort to meditation.

Quentin focused on the sound of his own breath. He measured it as it entered and left his lungs, and allowed himself to let go of the little things that didn't matter right now.

In, two, three, four.

Out, two, three, four.

He either managed to tune out the sound of chaos, or it died down. Either way, he remained focused on his breathing.

The last dregs of the nightmare evaporated.

In, two, three, four.

There was nothing left but his breaths, slow and calm.

He finally opened his eyes.

There was no storm.

He sat in the center of a vast bowl, shallow and yet perhaps a hundred feet in diameter, with gently-curved waves running around the edges. Beyond, there were few trees remaining that weren't splintered, jagged wrecks.

Quentin dusted himself off as he stood and walked to the edge of the bowl he'd carved from the ground.

Littered around were branches and trunks, twigs and splinters, spread out from the bowl like the rings of a dartboard.

He frowned.

In his panic, he had effectively drawn a huge target all around himself.

He heard footsteps slipping through dirt and swiveled on the balls of his feet, only to see Eric scrambling toward him from the other side of the bowl.

Quentin frowned faintly. This was not the way to make a good impression on your lover's father.

"Dude, did you *see* that?" Eric puffed as he jogged up to

Quentin's side. "What was it?" He held a hand over his eyes to shield them from the nonexistent sun and scanned the landscape. "Whoa. You fucked up some shit right here, my man!"

"I can only apologize," he croaked. "I didn't mean for this to happen."

"What *did* happen?"

Quentin pressed his lips together tightly and avoided Eric's gaze. "Did I get much sleep?"

"No, I can't say you did. A couple of hours at most."

He sighed and stepped away from the bowl. "That will have to do for now. I have... nightmares," he added as Eric joined him. "Now and then. And when I do, I tend to..." He gestured to the destruction all around.

Eric let out a low whistle. "You could hurt someone, you know?"

Quentin knew exactly what Eric meant.

"Yes," he agreed. "I take every possible precaution not to."

"Maybe wearing armor made of nightmares was a bad idea, huh?" Eric looked at him with a sympathetic smile.

Quentin frowned and unfastened his coat so that he could look down at the silk-thin tunic beneath it. It looked darker than when he had obtained it. Where before it had been flimsy and translucent, with no particular color to it, now it was cloudy and gray. "Do you suppose that is the problem?" he asked as he buttoned his coat once more.

"I don't know. It could just be tissue paper. I'm not into all this crafts stuff." Eric shrugged. "So you're, what? Telekinetic?"

"The current working theory is that I am psychokinetic," Quentin murmured as his voice slowly began to grow less scratchy. "I am telekinetic, but I can also alter temperature, create and control fire, that sort of thing. I don't believe that a demonstration would achieve much other than to drain me of valuable energy," he added, lest Eric ask to see a fireball.

"That's amazing! And you lose control over it when you have these nightmares, right?"

"Correct."

Eric pursed his lips. "Can I ask if they're, like, a trauma thing?"

After he safely ensconced his hands deep within his pockets, Quentin gave a slight nod. "Yes. They are. But I would rather not discuss the matter further, if it's all the same with you?"

"No, I totally get it." Eric smiled. "Hey, how does a penguin build a house?"

Quentin blinked. "I don't—"

"Igloos it together!" Eric grinned. "Why can't two elephants go for a swim together?"

"Er—"

"Because they've only got one pair of trunks!"

Quentin flexed his jaw and sighed. "You are terrible," he murmured. "I see where Laurence gets it from."

"The good looks? The rugged charm? The amazing sense of humor?" Eric laughed.

"No," Quentin chuckled. "His awfulness."

"Oh, burn. Are the kids still saying that these days?"

"I may have heard it once or twice." Most likely from Soraya, he suspected.

"Buuurrrrnnnn!" Eric crowed.

There were, Quentin supposed, far worse people to be trapped in another world with.

"I don't wanna be, like, teaching you to suck eggs, dude, but how much do you know about all this stuff?" Eric waved at the landscape around them.

Quentin huffed softly. They had begun a gentle ascent of yet another hill, and they were trying to stick to the lowest points between each mound to minimize Quentin's effort, but after such little sleep he was already flagging.

"Not a great deal, if I'm to be wholly honest," he murmured.

"That's okay. Not everyone's into religions that are thousands of years old." Eric smiled. "Have you heard the story of Pwyll and Arawn?"

"I cannot say that I have."

Eric rubbed his hands together. "I'll keep it short. The legend is that Pwyll, the Prince of Dyfed, was out hunting one day, but he got separated from his companions and came across these hounds that were feeding on a fallen stag. The hounds were pure white, with red ears, the Cŵn Annwn, but he didn't recognize them. He waded on in and shooed the hounds off the stag so that his own hounds could eat, and of course he's pissed off Arawn, 'cause it was Arawn's kill and Arawn's hounds."

Quentin frowned as he listened. "This is pre-medieval, I presume?"

"Oh, yeah. Arawn gets pissed, and to appease him, Pwyll agrees to switch places with him."

Quentin felt his eyebrows slowly climb.

"Yeah, I know, right? Except in this case it's for a year and a day, and they swap appearances. Arawn goes out into the world disguised as Pwyll, and actually improves Pwyll's reputation. Meanwhile, Pwyll has to not only stay here, but also kill Arawn's enemy, Hafgan."

"Is this a frequent occurrence?" Quentin muttered. "Does Arawn always use people to bump off his foes?"

"Uh-huh." Eric didn't smile. "You see what I'm getting at? Pwyll not only did like he was asked, but he also refused to sleep with Arawn's wife, and when Arawn returned, he was especially pleased with that."

"I should bloody hope so!" Quentin stared at Eric in dawning horror. "Did he not consider that before he made his bargain?"

"No, apparently it hadn't occurred to him. But he's a god, and gods can be weird."

Quentin ground his teeth. "Are you suggesting that he intentionally tricks people into Annwn so that he may trade places with them and have them deal with his problems for him?"

Eric spread his hands. "It looks like a pattern, is all I'm saying."

"Then how did Pwyll survive here for a year and a day?"

"I have no idea."

"Where is Arawn's wife now?"

"Don't know." Eric shrugged. "Cricket ever tell you about the dream of Herne?"

"He did, yes."

"In that dream, our ancestor is on the run from Arawn's dogs, but there's another woman running from Herne. I think she's Arawn's wife, or at least, I think she became his wife after Sara escaped and met Herne. If that's true, then she was human, so she's probably long since dead. Might even have been reborn hundreds of times since then."

Quentin scowled as they crested the hill and began to descend toward the next one. "Then he expects me to fulfill this task in a very short amount of time, which is perhaps for the best. We might have come to a disagreement if he had insisted on a year and a day."

"Ha." Eric nodded at him. "And he wants you to kill Gwyn ap Nudd, King of the Tylwyth Teg, King of Winter, wannabe King of Annwn. No big deal. We just march up to a faerie's mountain fortress stronghold, dispatch his guards, then stab him, right? You got a sword?"

Quentin shook his head.

"A knife?"

"No."

"Something sharper than just your wit and those cheekbones?"

"Alas not."

"This looks like an oversight." Eric sucked his teeth. "Either

Arawn thinks you can defeat Gwyn ap Nudd without a weapon, or he's sent you off to get turned into mulch."

"Let's hope it's the former rather than the latter, hmm?"

"Yeah. Wait—" Eric stilled and threw his arm across Quentin's chest as he tilted his head.

Quentin froze and listened, but it was a few more seconds before he heard it.

Twigs and scrub crunched underfoot. Faint grunts accompanied the sound.

Both Quentin and Eric lowered themselves into a crouch, but there was little cover to hide behind other than a low, long-dead tangle of brambles.

And then it crested a hill and howled.

Quentin gasped softly. "What is it?"

The creature was twisted, with one broken wing and legs that didn't seem capable of all reaching the ground at once. Half its body was covered in peeling scales, and the other half with patchy feathers, and its mouth was a wide maw filled with jagged teeth like those of a shark. All in all it wasn't much larger than Quentin, but it looked like it was a cobbled-together mess from at least three distinct creatures.

It was almost unbearable to watch. Every motion went against the joints in its limbs or the logic of a living four-legged creature, and yet it barreled toward them with an unearthly screech.

The closer it got, the more human its eyes seemed.

"I have no damn clue," Eric whispered. "I'm just glad it's alone. Anyway, I'm just the Hunter here. You're the Warrior." He squeezed Quentin's shoulder. "Good luck, dude."

"Bloody hell," he breathed. "You had best stay here."

"Seems wise," Eric agreed.

Quentin rose from his crouch and stepped around the brambles. He rolled his shoulders and put several strides between himself and Eric so that he had room to maneuver, and then he adopted a loose stance with his hands raised, ready.

He had no desire to get into a fight, least of all with whatever this poor unfortunate thing was, but he very much doubted that it felt the same way, and Sebastian had drummed into him time and again that regardless of how Quentin felt, any opponent who was willing to kill him was already one step ahead.

It screeched, and then launched itself at his face with unexpected speed.

24

LAURENCE

He didn't like tracking blood. It made him feel like a hound, like he had some kind of lust for hunting a wounded creature.

He certainly had a lust for hunting, though, and it was so powerful that it had driven him to addiction, because he couldn't find anything else to quiet that need. It had pushed his dad toward candy, too, and that was what had killed him so young.

Laurence found a deeper irony in the mechanics of his existence. If he failed to hunt, he would die. Not through lack of sustenance, but because he would turn to all the wrong substances to fulfill his needs. He had to wonder whether his grandpa on Dad's side had died young for the same reasons.

Damn it. There was so much he hadn't gotten to ask Dad about before he died.

He stuck to the bright gleam of blood as he ran after it. The weather had blotted out many weaker scents, crushed them beneath layers of freezing flakes of snow, but the blood was fresh. Either Ryan was spilling it, or whoever had stepped in some was laying a nice, neat trail for Laurence to follow. It didn't matter.

All he knew was that this was a hunt, and the thrill of it made him come alive.

Laurence wove through gridlocked traffic at each intersection. He darted around people so quickly that he doubted they saw him in the murk.

Basil and Jon panted at his heels, but Laurence didn't look back. If he lost them, he could find them again on the way back.

His prey came first.

He came up on Ramirez fast. The guard's uniform was dark and smattered with white across the shoulders, and he was growing weary of the chase.

The scent was not his.

Laurence reached out to tap his shoulder. "Hey! Ramirez, right?"

Ramirez stumbled to a stop and rested his hands on his thighs as he took a breather. "He... he just ran! Took off like... a bat out of hell!" He gulped air, then pushed himself upright. "I thought if I caught up with him I could get him back to the hotel, but if he's gonna outrun me the guy probably doesn't need any more first aid, you know what I'm saying?"

Laurence nodded. "Yeah. I get you. It's insane. I would have sworn he was ten seconds from death when I left him with you." He pushed soaking-wet curls out of his eyes and blinked at Ramirez. "You're okay, though, yeah? He didn't hurt you?"

Ramirez shook his head. "No. Like I say, he just got up and ran. Didn't even say a word. I swear to God, he was not in any condition to move like that. He'd lost so much blood, had such bad injuries, he should've been passing out, or worse!" The man sighed and rubbed his jaw. "God damn it. I can't have duty of care for a guy who sprints away like that, right?" He sounded uncertain.

Laurence patted Ramirez' elbow lightly and put on his best sympathetic face. "You did your best, man," he agreed. "You're the hotel's security, not a paramedic. I don't think anybody'd blame you if you went back to the hotel. I'll go see if I can find him, and since I'm staying in that hotel anyway, I'll let you know what I find, okay?"

Ramirez' shoulders dipped, and his head rose in gratitude. "Thanks, man. I really mean it."

"No worries." Laurence gestured back the way he'd came, just as Jon and Basil caught up. "You wanna go that way. Eight blocks."

"Thanks." Ramirez shook his hand, then began a much slower jog toward the hotel.

Basil was ruddy cheeked, and his glasses were opaque yet again. "Nobody's dead yet?" he puffed.

"Not that I can tell. You ready?"

Basil gave an exasperated little shrug. "Do I have a choice?"

"Technically, yes," Jon said.

Basil shot him a look, and Laurence turned his back on them to double down on his sprint.

The blood was close now.

THREE MORE BLOCKS, and he caught them. Ryan and Arawn, throwing each other around the sidewalk like they were toys. The sight was made more terrible by the fact that Arawn still wore Quentin's appearance, and so for one awful moment, it looked as though Quentin was getting the stuffing knocked out of him.

Laurence had caught up with his prey, and that was almost satisfying. If only he didn't also have the urge to rip someone's head off now that he was here.

"Hey!" He skidded to a halt a few feet outside their radius of violence. They ignored him, so he tried again, bellowing at the top of his lungs. "Hey!"

"This does not concern you, Child of Herne," Arawn snapped as he drove his hand into Ryan's gut and pulled something wet and gross out of it, which he threw aside.

Laurence felt his gorge rise, and he covered his mouth. "God-dess, stop! Just stop for one minute!"

Ryan roared and swept a backhand at Arawn so powerful that it knocked the god clean off his feet and into a snowbank.

Basil and Jon caught up again and skittered to a stop, with Basil grabbing Jon's arm to hold himself upright. "Oh shit!" Basil squeaked. "What's going on?"

Ryan glanced toward them. His amber eyes were aglow now, giving off an unnatural luminescence that was eerie in the dark-ness. "You've all been great, kids," he said. "Really, I can't thank you enough. But you gotta step back and let the grown-ups sort this out now, okay?"

"Your intestines are hanging out," Jon said. He sounded about as disinterested in that as he was about everything else. "This is inefficient. If you need to resolve a problem, it is less costly to negotiate than to fight over it."

Arawn laughed as he rose from the snow, white stuff show-ering to earth from his back. "And what if the problem may only be resolved by the death of one of us?" He reached inside his coat and withdrew a sword that was far too long to have fit inside it, and far too heavy for someone with Quentin's strength to lift.

It looked like a damn claymore. It was easily six feet long, and Arawn raised it as he grasped the hilt in both hands.

Ryan snarled and pulled a sword forth from the hole left in his gut by Arawn's attack. It came out bloodied and wet.

Laurence's gut twisted, and he took a step back, arms out to drag Jon and Basil with him.

"Magic?" Jon asked quietly.

Laurence and Basil both shook their heads.

"I don't think so," Laurence said. "No spellcasting."

"Maybe it's a prepared item. Like my ring?" Basil bit his lip.

Now wasn't the time for Laurence to worry about whether or not you could enchant an entire sword to live inside your stomach on the off chance that your opponent ever ripped your guts out. All he knew was that they were way out of their league.

And then Ryan's sword caught fire, and he swung it at Arawn with a snarl of fury.

"This is insane," Laurence breathed. "Even if they don't kill each other, someone's gonna get hurt, and it's probably going to be us."

Fire whooshed through the air. Metal slammed against metal. If people hadn't heard the fight yet, they sure would now.

"I have a theory," Jon said.

"I'm all ears," Laurence replied.

Jon stepped away, disengaging himself from Basil. He held up his hands, palms toward Basil as though instructing a dog to stay, and then he walked toward Ryan and Arawn.

His energy flickered out of existence.

"Jon!" Basil lunged after him, but Laurence grabbed his coat collar and held him back.

"You can't touch him," he breathed. "Not right now."

"Let go of me!" Basil squirmed, but Laurence's grip was too strong. "Jon!"

"This theory better be fucking good," Laurence muttered.

Jon waded right up to the battle and stepped in between the two combatants.

Ryan and Annwn swung their swords toward him, but both snapped their hands back at the last moment, withdrawing a pace each from Jon's presence.

Basil screamed.

"Stop," Jon said, sounding almost bored. "You can't do this here."

They stared at him like a bug had just walked between two fighting tomcats, and then Ryan threw his head back and laughed.

"Your child has some balls, Arawn!" Ryan rested the tip of his sword against the ground. The flames made the snow hiss and melt around the blade, yet his hand was untouched by them. "How about I cut them off?"

"How about you do?" Arawn shrugged. "While you are distracted with that, I will take your head. It seems an excellent plan."

For a second, Laurence thought they'd talked each other into a standoff, with Jon standing awkwardly between them. He even took a step forward, ready to try to talk some sense into them both.

"Look. Whatever your beef is with each other—" Laurence began.

"Wait," Ryan cut in. "Hold on there, kid." He held up his hand. "Before you go any further."

Laurence blinked. "Sure. What?"

Ryan raised his sword.

Then he ran it straight through Jon's chest.

25

QUENTIN

QUENTIN SWEPT THE CREATURE TO ONE SIDE, TO HIS RIGHT WHERE Eric was to his left, so that the two would not collide. He turned lightly to keep it in his line of sight and kept his hands raised.

"Stop," he called out.

It did not, which only lent further credence to the uncomfortable notion that this was no animal. It rolled across the dusty earth and writhed back to its feet, only to launch again.

This time, Quentin captured it in midair. He cocooned it in his telekinetic grip and held it steady without applying pressure. It was only a temporary measure, of course. He could not remain here holding this creature forever. But it allowed him to step closer, to meet its gaze.

The eyes *were* human. They were a soft shade of brown, and creased in anguish.

He felt sick to his stomach.

"Can you speak?" he asked of the... creature? He knew no kinder word for this poor thing, which was obviously suffering a great deal.

The open maw shuddered, and the creature let out a pitiful wail.

"It's all right." Quentin took another step and raised his hands to show that they were empty. "I don't know how to help you. I'm sorry. But I will do my best, I promise you."

"Dude." Eric's voice was trembling. "What're you doing?"

Quentin glanced back toward him. "I think this is — or was — a person," he murmured. "They seem to be in extraordinary pain."

Eric nodded. "Well, anything in pain can still bite your arm off. Especially with those teeth!"

"Agreed." Quentin looked at the creature once more, taking note of its one, damaged wing. There was no other, not even a stump where one might have been. "This must have been done to you," he realized. "Oh my goodness, I am so sorry." He reached out and gently placed his hand between the creature's eyes, resting his palm there.

The eyes closed briefly, and the creature's frame shuddered with a deep sigh. It warbled out a pitiful sound, somewhere deep in the back of its throat.

"Let me set you down." He withdrew his hand and gently lowered the creature to the ground, but he wasn't so foolish as to release it from his grasp. Once it was there, he crouched in front of it, sitting lightly on his heels. "I know that you can't speak," he murmured. "That's all right. I will find out who did this, all right? I will see if there is a way to... undo it somehow."

He heard Eric come closer, but didn't turn to watch him.

"Oh, Goddess," Eric groaned as he crouched by Quentin's side. "I think you're right."

Quentin frowned softly. "What makes you say that?"

"I dunno, man. I'm good at reading people. Always have been. I figure it's a Herne thing." Eric shrugged. "And you're definitely a person, aren't you?" he said to the creature with a sigh. "We gotta fix this."

Quentin nodded grimly, then met the creature's gaze. "If I release you, will you let us leave?"

There was another little wail of despair. The creature blinked tears from its eyes.

"That's a no, then, huh," said Eric.

Quentin pressed his lips together tightly and rose to his feet. "Then we must risk some flying after all," he murmured.

"Wait, what?" Eric launched to his feet. "Flying? With what?"

"Well, quintessentially, I suppose that it isn't actually *flying*, since all I am really doing is applying my telekinesis to my own body," Quentin murmured. "More importantly, are *you* capable of flight?"

"Uh..." Eric looked around like he thought Quentin might be talking to someone else. "Why would you think that?"

"Because your form is wholly malleable?"

Eric blinked. His jaw worked a moment. "Right, but... Dude, I don't know the first thing about aerodynamics!"

Quentin nodded. "Then I shall have to carry you."

"You are *kidding* oh shit no you're not kidding at all, are you?" Eric eyed him.

"Not remotely." He turned away from Eric and crouched down slightly. It seemed somewhat more dignified than bearing the man in his arms, or over his shoulder the way Laurence carried bags of topsoil.

"Okay, but I just wanna go on record as saying this is the weirdest shit I've ever been involved in, and that's including that one time in Vegas with the strippers and — wait, no. Don't tell Myriam any of that."

"I suspect that she would not mind," he said dryly.

The weight of Eric clambering onto his back was almost too much, until Quentin brought his telekinesis to play in propping Eric up.

"Yeah, you're right," Eric said.

Quentin launched into the air and aimed directly at the fortress, with Eric squealing into his ear like a child on a trampoline.

The creature they left behind wailed mournfully.

THEY MADE it halfway up the mountain before the sky began to grow dark.

"I don't wanna alarm you," Eric yelled to be heard over the wind, "but I think we're screwed."

Quentin raised his gaze up to the sky and saw the source of the darkness.

Thousands of creatures were streaming from the fortress and into the sky, bringing with them dark clouds that partly obscured and partly supported their forms.

"That," Eric shouted with utter certainty, "is a Wild Hunt."

There were white dogs with red-tipped ears. Twisted creatures with odd numbers of limbs or wings. Naked women with bows and arrows, most of which were starting to be aimed at Quentin and Eric.

"Bugger," Quentin breathed. Then, more loudly, for Eric's sake, he added, "I'm going to land."

"Yeah," Eric agreed. "That'd be good!"

Quentin sank toward the mountainside feet first, his eyes mostly still on the Wild Hunt. He didn't want to find out what one of those arrows could do, and as they began to rain down on him, he had to split his attention between landing safely and deflecting the projectiles.

Eric slid off him once they touched down, and he pressed up against the side of a tree. "You know, I reckon we might be slightly outnumbered," he said.

"I couldn't agree more." Quentin tore a few more trees up and levitated them together over his head to blot out the arrows, then he beckoned for Eric to join him under the shelter. "Ready for a sprint?"

"If you'd asked me that when I was alive, the answer would've been no." Eric hurried to join him under the makeshift shield. "Let's go."

Quentin nodded, and they began a race toward the fortress while they still had the ability to cover some ground.

Once those creatures caught up, though, they'd need a better plan.

"Everything here," Quentin gasped as he leaped a dead tangle of branches. "Other than me, of course. It's all dead, yes?"

"I mean, other than Arawn and Gwyn ap Nudd, yeah," Eric agreed.

"Ah, yes." Of course Gwyn ap Nudd had to be alive; otherwise, how could Quentin be expected to kill him? "So these creatures, these people..." He gestured over his head. "They are all already dead?"

"I'd guess so, yeah." Eric shook his head. "What're you getting at?"

"Nothing vital to you, I don't think," Quentin answered. "More a matter of principle for myself. I'm not wholly comfortable with doing harm to others."

Eric was quiet for a few feet, then he burst out laughing. "You're a pacifist?"

"I suppose so, yes." It fit about as well as any word, he imagined.

"And a Warrior," Eric added.

"Allegedly." Quentin winced as arrows began to slam into the trees he held overhead, each one hitting with a *thunk* which reverberated through the dead wood. "I never claimed to be any such thing."

"But gods don't see what you say. They see what's in your heart." Eric gave him a slight shrug as they sped along. "Maybe even what's written on your soul. I dunno, I'm just a dead dude." He grinned softly at Quentin. "Besides, what's better? A warrior who's always eager to fight, or one who avoids a fight at all costs?"

Quentin wove around trees and didn't answer immediately.

Obviously he felt that avoiding fights was for the best, but that might seem too egotistical a response. He was fully aware that he usually considered his way to be the prime choice in any situation, but he had to admit that it wasn't, not always. Laurence held perspectives that were thoroughly different from his own, and from which Quentin had learned a great deal.

But even Laurence would rather nobody got into a fight.

"The latter," he sighed.

"Whoa, congratulations. You're exactly the kind of Warrior I'd want by my side," Eric laughed. "Man, I don't wanna get dragged into a fight if there's another way. Who shoots first and asks questions later? Assholes, that's who. Assholes who think everything can be solved by spreading their violence outward into the world."

"I wouldn't go quite *that* far," Quentin murmured.

He heard a crack overhead and glanced up in time to see one of his trees finally splinter from the impact of one too many arrows.

When he looked forward again, the Wild Hunt had begun to land. Even the clouds came down to the ground, like an unnatural mist. The Hunt touched down in a spiral around them, those closest landing first. The rain of creatures came in thuds and hoofbeats, screeches and howls, and the clouds rolled around them, obscuring legs and feet, lending the Hunt a dreamlike air.

There were so many of them that they formed rows, and before the last had landed, the first began to rush forward.

Quentin used his arrow-infested trees as the foundations for a wall, and tore more out of the earth to add to the pile. It wasn't truly a wall without his telekinesis to back it up, but it would save him from being forced to attend to each and every arrow or spear that came at them.

It would do for now.

And then his resolve would be tested.

26

LAURENCE

TRUE TO HIS WORD, ARAWN USED THE DISTRACTION TO SWEEP HIS sword at Ryan's head, and sliced his throat wide open.

Jon wiped the blood from his face and flicked it aside, then reached for Ryan's hand, still coiled around the hilt of the blade that was jammed clean through Jon's body.

"I don't..." Basil trailed off, but he was still squirming to try to get to Jon, so Laurence kept hold of him.

"Yeah, me either," Laurence breathed.

Ryan's face contorted in rage, but it was short-lived. Rather than fall to the ground, he dropped out of existence entirely, sword and all. One second he was there, and the next he was gone, and all that remained was the smell of singed clothing and fresh blood.

"Shit," Arawn said.

"Jon!"

Jon idly turned to face them, while peering down at the hole in his clothes. "Do you think we can find a thrift store that's still open?"

"What the hell do you think you were doing, man?" Laurence

strode toward Jon, still not about to let Basil go. "That wasn't a theory, that was suicide!"

"Almost literally," Jon mused. He dug his fingers into the hole, then looked at Arawn, eyebrows raised.

Arawn sighed and shoved his own sword back into his coat, which was still far too small to disguise an entire claymore. "My Child cannot be killed while in this form," he explained, pale eyes flitting toward Laurence. "Nor is he alive. It is the most profound of the gifts my children bear, though they be few and far between. My children reproduce rarely, compared to the children of others." He glanced at Jon. "You may be among the last," he mused.

Basil finally shook himself free of Laurence's hold. He'd cheated and slipped out of his coat, leaving it hanging from Laurence's hand so that he could run toward Jon, but he stopped two feet away and wrapped his arms around himself. "Are you okay?"

"The question is, will I be all right if I turn back?" Jon asked of Arawn.

Arawn shrugged. "So long as your head has not been removed, yes."

Jon nodded, and then life returned to his body and he drew a breath.

Basil bit his lip, then flung his arms around Jon and began to scold him. "You could have been killed! If you were wrong, I mean. And sometimes you *are* wrong, you know! You can't just assume you've got it all figured out all the time."

Laurence folded the coat over his forearm and looked at Arawn. "What the hell was that all about? Why did Ryan attack you?"

Arawn huffed. "It would be best for you if we were to find shelter."

"You promise not to cut our heads off?"

A smile tugged the corners of Arawn's lips in an expression so like Quentin's that it made Laurence stall.

"I promise," Arawn said.

THEY MADE it back to the hotel, and Laurence stopped off to assure Ramirez that they'd found Ryan and taken him to a hospital. It was bullshit, of course, but Laurence excelled at selling bullshit to strangers, and it'd be a weight off Ramirez' mind.

Did he want to take a death god up to his bedroom?

Where else could they talk about the sword swinging and murder, though? The lobby was out, and the restaurant was just as bad.

It'd have to be the room.

Arawn seemed fascinated by the inside of the elevator. Even more so by their white-gloved attendant.

"Can you not press buttons yourself?" he asked.

"It's a rich people thing," Laurence sighed.

"Are you rich?"

"No, Quentin is."

"So you can press buttons," Arawn reasoned.

The doors opened, and Laurence was first out of the elevator. "I dunno, man. I'd be happy to press my own damn buttons, but he gets paid to do this, and it's hard enough already to find work in this economy." He carded his door to unlock it, and ushered everyone inside. Once he shut the door, he moved over to the window to sit. Jon and Basil went into the bathroom, and Laurence heard running water while they left the door open.

"All right. We're off the street." He unfastened his coat, but didn't bother taking it off. "Spill the beans, because I'm pretty much at the end of my patience here."

Arawn stood by the end of the bed with his hands hanging loosely at his sides. "You say you know him as Ryan?"

Laurence nodded.

"He is Gwyn ap Nudd," Arawn sighed.

Laurence knew that name, though it took him a few seconds to dredge it up.

Fuck. Ryan was the one who'd mentioned it. He'd stood there and said it right to Laurence's face.

"He's Gwyn ap Nudd," Laurence said slowly. "Does he control a whole bunch of demons in Annwn?"

Arawn pursed his lips, then crossed to the chair by Laurence's side and sat. His pale eyes fixed on Jon and Basil as they finally took a seat on the edge of the bed, both of them wiping themselves dry with towels that were stained with Ryan's blood.

"You are aware of how faith shapes us?" Arawn murmured.

"Yeah," Laurence said. Then for Basil and Jon's sakes, he added, "What people believe in is what creates and molds gods, right?"

"Correct. It also shapes entire realms. Annwn was created by faith, and faith sustains it. But Gwyn ap Nudd is not a god. He is of the Tylwyth Teg. The word your lover used was fairy."

Basil sucked in a breath. "As in, a cute little guy with wings who sprinkles fairy dust and magic wherever he goes?" He fixed a fake smile in place that became more of a grimace. "No. You mean those hideously powerful and unpredictable creatures from lore that like to murder people and steal babies, don't you?"

"I do," Arawn admitted. "Gwyn ap Nudd is also a psychopomp. Long has it been his whim to steal souls destined for Annwn and bear them away to his fortress to do with as he will. He enjoys playing into the more modern ideas of Annwn — that it is akin to Hell, and that the dead who reside there are deformed and malicious. He torments those he should protect until they are incapable of passing on, and so his army only grows larger as the years pass, and the darkness compounds itself. But one day he departed for this realm, and he never returned."

Laurence crossed his legs as he leaned back in his chair. It was a lot to take in all at once. "Where did he go?"

"I do not know. I suspected that he was attempting to lure me out of Annwn for a confrontation, but the years passed, and still he did not return." Arawn hesitated. "I am not able to leave Annwn as and when I wish. I am only able to depart if there is another to take my place while I am gone."

"Which is where Quentin comes in," Jon said.

"Yes." Arawn nodded. "When he arrived in Annwn, I took my opportunity and offered him the deal. He accepted, and I came here to find Gwyn ap Nudd and destroy him once and for all so that I might recover those souls from their imprisonment and restore them. Without his army, it would be a simple matter of one of us against the other, with Annwn as the prize."

Basil blinked. "You sent the black dog?"

Arawn shook his head. "I did not. It is not impossible that Gwyn ap Nudd sent it so that I would have a mortal with which to exchange places."

"But he's dead now, so you and Quentin can just—" Laurence abruptly swept his hands past each other "—switch back." There had to be a catch. He knew there was. Not only was there always a catch where gods were involved, but if Arawn could swap places again, why hadn't he done it already?

"No," Arawn mused. "The magic is dependent upon Gwyn ap Nudd's death, and he is not dead. What is enough to kill a mortal is only enough to return a Tylwyth Teg to Otherworld. Even the touch of cold iron merely returns them to their realm. It is only when cold iron touches a Tylwyth Teg in Otherworld that it may truly be destroyed."

"But now that he's in Otherworld, he can make his way to Annwn and Quentin can kill him, which fulfils your bargain and brings him back?" Basil bit his lip.

"He cannot. There is no cold iron in Otherworld. It exists only here, in this world. I did not expect that Quentin would actually face Gwyn."

Laurence ground his teeth, but he didn't feel a great deal of anger.

Instead, what was growing in him was anticipation.

He could see the path ahead.

"Then here's what we do," he barked. "We go get supplies. This is the city that never sleeps, right? So stores will be open?"

Basil nodded. "It depends on what you want."

"Food. Water. Something to carry it in. Cold iron. Where do we get that from?"

Jon raised his head. "Cold iron is an anachronistic term for wrought iron, which is obtained by puddling pig iron while it is molten. It has a very low carbon content compared to cast iron, and as such remains malleable."

Laurence stared at him as he turned into a human encyclopedia. Partly because he was pretty sure he still didn't know what wrought iron was, and partly because Jon seemed to genuinely relish regurgitating his facts.

"He's an engineer," Basil said with a chuckle, smiling fondly at Jon.

"Sweet." Laurence grinned. "Where can we get some?"

"Lowe's, or any hardware store that sells goods that could feasibly be constructed from wrought iron. Stair balustrades, ironwork gates, and so on. However, I have not seen wrought iron in stock in stores here," Jon said.

Laurence rubbed his jaw. "Wait, this stuff is used for gates, right? And fences and stuff?"

Jon nodded. "Particularly ornamental, or..." His eyebrows raised.

Laurence grinned at him. "Or from buildings that are old enough," he completed. "What do we need to take a piece of fence from out front of a store?"

"A hacksaw is affordable, but requires manpower and time. If you favor speed, a handheld circular saw is best, but costs at least fifty dollars. However, it would minimize the odds of our remaining in place long enough to get caught."

"Okay. We get food, water, and a circular saw thing, then we bag ourselves some cold iron and go to Annwn to kick Gwyn ap Nudd's ass. Anything I'm missing?"

Arawn shook his head. "So long as there is no darkness within the Warrior's heart, he will prevail until your arrival."

Laurence hesitated. "What?"

Arawn blinked. "Oh," he said. "Then I suggest that you move with haste."

Basil looked between them and clutched his bag to his chest. "What's the problem?"

Laurence glanced at Jon, who met his gaze.

"The problem," Jon began, "is the dead who reside within Gwyn ap Nudd's fortress."

"The darkness compounds itself," Laurence quoted. "They're at critical mass. I figure Gwyn ap Nudd only steals those dead who already carried some darkness?"

Arawn nodded. "He cannot influence a heart that is pure. There must already exist that which can be drawn upon." He frowned at Laurence. "The Warrior is not a Tyrant."

"No, but he's..." Laurence drew breath. "He's going through some stuff right now." He bounced to his feet and pulled his wallet out, then fished out a handful of cash and thrust it at Basil. "You guys go get the saw and a backpack or something. Get a new shirt and coat, too." He pointed toward the holes in Jon's clothes. "I'll get food and water. Meet back in the lobby, and then we can go get the iron, okay?"

Basil's eyes widened at the cash in his hands, and he rose to his feet. "Do you know where to find some?"

Laurence nodded. "Yeah. I know just the place."

Goddess, by the time he was through in this city, he'd never be welcome back.

27

QUENTIN

"GREAT," ERIC SAID. HE SOUNDED ENTHUSIASTIC. "GOOD MOVE. I like this. What's our next step?"

"I hadn't got quite that far," Quentin admitted. "I was hoping something would have come to me by now."

Eric's smile faltered. "Okay, well, I don't wanna alarm you, but out of the thousands of people here right now, only one of them can die."

Quentin nodded grimly. The trees he held in place around them shuddered under the assault of weapons far heavier than arrows. At first he'd supposed they were spears, but as time went on, the sound grew deafening.

Swords and axes must have come into play, which meant that they were completely surrounded, with only a few feet between them and their attackers.

He took a deep breath.

What did *The Book of Five Rings* say about being outnumbered? *Waiting is bad.*

He clicked his tongue faintly. To his recollection, Musashi's book specifically said to pick out those nearest to you and wade in with both swords. All waiting did was allow the enemy to come to you instead.

Which it had.

In large-scale strategy, it is important to cause loss of balance.

Quentin narrowed his eyes. Musashi hadn't meant literally. He meant to disrupt an army's equilibrium, whether by damaging their morale, causing surprise, or through stripping their resources.

He knew how to cause a surprise, but the cost would be tremendous.

"All right," he nodded. "Stay close."

"Dude, I am on you like fleas on a dog."

Quentin nodded and threw the trees in front of him straight forward, pushing as hard as he could to fling them away from him. At first it was easy, but the resistance grew quickly as more and more people behind it were crushed together.

Creatures fell away from the trees like bowling pins. Some tried to run, and others were simply swept aside. But before they could regain their balance, he threw a jet of flame into the path he had cleared, igniting the rest of the wall around himself while he was at it.

"Fuuuuck," Eric said.

"Quickly." Quentin darted forward, using the flames and shadows as cover. He had to trust that Eric was sticking to him as closely as he'd said he would.

He built a tunnel of fire, and drew some heat back into himself to create a bubble of cool air so that he could pass through it. While fire didn't seem to harm him, heat was another matter, and drawing some of the fire's temperature back allowed him to retain more energy.

Quentin ran. He bolted down the tunnel and left it in place so that they couldn't tell where along it he and Eric were. He pushed more fire forward, hoping that it didn't cause too much pain to those who were caught in its path, but ultimately Eric was correct.

Only one person here could die, and Quentin had no intention of doing so.

THEY RAN until the sounds of the Hunt died down, and only then did Quentin rescue as much of the fire's heat as he could. It wasn't much, but it would have to do.

He had burned a lot of energy, and he couldn't afford to use that tactic twice, which was just as well, since it wouldn't be a surprise the second time.

He didn't stop. Didn't even give Eric time to allow himself to be picked up gracefully. They had to cover more ground, and Quentin hoped it would take a while for an army that size to get airborne again. He grabbed Eric and flung them both into the air at high speed, but this time he didn't shoot straight up. He elevated them just enough to skim across the treetops, then sped over them as low as he could in the hope that the army wouldn't even notice that their prey was flying again.

The problem there was that mountains, by their very nature, were not flat.

"This is still the plan?" Eric bellowed.

"I have even more plan," Quentin yelled back. "They came from the top of the fortress. If we can fly in there, we can seal it so they can't get back in."

"Here's my problem." Eric glanced behind them, then up ahead to the fortress. "Hunters lead Wild Hunts. Did you see Gwyn ap Nudd back there?"

"I haven't a clue what he looks like."

"Me either."

They glanced at each other, then burst out laughing.

It was a welcome relief, but Quentin knew it couldn't last.

———

"THEY'RE UP!" Eric informed him.

Last time, Quentin and the Hunt had been flying directly toward each other. This time they were at his back, and he didn't have much farther to go. So long as they didn't travel at the speed of lightning, he should make it.

"Find me that entrance," he ordered.

"Oh, sure thing!" Eric looked ahead as they sped up the outer walls. "Guards," he barked, his free hand darting forward to point.

Quentin swept them off the ramparts with a thought. It took little effort to throw them telekinetically from their otherwise safe positions, and they yelled as they plummeted to the moat.

He was, he felt, getting quite used to everyone here being too dead for him to do lasting harm.

"There!" Eric swung his arm up, toward the keep.

The keep was enormous, with one tower on each corner. The towers were ridiculously tall, like the spires of a French château but beyond whatever limits the engineering or resources of the time might have placed on them. It was more like the drawing of a fairytale castle one might find in a book for children.

Perhaps that was exactly what it was. Gwyn ap Nudd was, after all, a fairy, and this was his stronghold.

Eric pointed to the keep's drawbridge, which was still down, crossing a moat that looked sickeningly deep from up here. The problem, as Quentin now saw it, was that a fortress was not designed to defend against air attacks, only from forces on the ground. This form of castle was a quintessentially medieval concept, when not even the hot air balloon had been invented. The best weapon at the time was some sort of siege engine for helping invaders scale the outer wall.

Even if they got into the keep and raised the drawbridge, nothing would stop the army from landing inside the outer walls and entering through the keep's windows, or demolishing the drawbridge.

But again, it put a barrier between them and him, and every second's delay he could inflict upon them gave him another second in which to come up with a better idea.

He dived for the drawbridge with the wind howling in his ears.

THEY MADE it through and into the keep by tossing another couple of guards outside, and Quentin quickly located the counterweight and dropped the portcullis, which drew up the drawbridge until it was flush against the heavy metalwork grid. He then threw the wooden doors shut and dropped the solid oak beam into its cradles to lock them.

Only then did he step back and evaluate their surroundings.

Eric was still gawping at the doors, one finger pointing vaguely toward them. "That right there is some Jedi bullshit," he breathed. "How do you even know how castle doors work?"

"Past experience," Quentin said.

"Riiiiight."

Quentin sighed and planted his hands on his hips. "I'm an earl, Eric. While I didn't grow up in what one might traditionally call a castle, I knew plenty of people who did."

Eric finally turned to stare at him instead of the doors. "So if you marry my son, he becomes... what? An earl-ess? Earl squared? Are you some kind of royalty?"

He opened his mouth, but his brain abandoned him, so he shut it again.

Everyone seemed inordinately fascinated with the idea of

marriage. Eric barely even knew him, and he was already on the subject.

Eric just laughed and clapped a hand on Quentin's shoulder. "I'm playing with you," he grinned, and started off down the hall. "C'mon. If Gwyn ap Nudd is in here, we better go say hi."

Quentin bit the tip of his tongue lightly, then strode rapidly after Eric, holding his head high.

Marriage, indeed.

How utterly preposterous.

THEY MOVED SIDE BY SIDE, and it seemed an excellent arrangement. Eric's senses were preternaturally sharp, and he was able to forewarn Quentin of any noises or movement as they picked their way through the keep. Eric also moved with astonishing silence for a man his size, although doing so slowed them down to the point where Quentin doubted they had a great deal of time before the Hunt landed in the castle's courtyard.

Eric held up two fingers, then gestured forward and left, making eye contact with Quentin for a moment.

Quentin nodded and held a hand up for Eric to wait, then brazenly walked toward the potential hazard, making no effort to move with any stealth.

"You might as well surrender," he said. "I haven't time to mess around."

The guards that leaped out at him seemed almost human, other than the decaying flesh and empty eye sockets. Not at all like the monstrous forms of the Hunt's participants, or the guards outside the keep. Both were lightly armored with little more than padded gambesons beneath chainmail shirts, and both held swords that looked far sharper than strictly necessary.

"Splendid," he said. "Would you be so kind as to tell me where I might find Gwyn ap Nudd?"

The guards actually paused, faces turning toward each other as though they might have misheard.

Quentin waited, his hands hanging loosely by his sides.

"He's not here," one guard said, turning back to Quentin.

Quentin arched an eyebrow. "Then where might I find him?"

The other shrugged. "He went to the living realm and never returned."

One eye began to twitch as the ramifications unfolded before him. He suspected that, were he less exhausted, he might have been able to keep a lid on his worry, but nothing he did made his eye stop.

Arawn had sent him on a mission that he could not possibly complete. Gwyn ap Nudd was not here, and Quentin had no way to reach him, but Arawn's deal was for them to switch places.

Did Arawn know where Gwyn ap Nudd was?

Had he switched with Quentin to chase after Gwyn ap Nudd himself?

He sighed softly and shook his head. He had to hope they couldn't see the spasm in his eye, but he turned to look at them side-on to obscure that side of his face. "Very well. Who is in charge in his absence?"

The guards exchanged a look again.

"No one," they both said at once.

Eric came closer, though he still hung back out of range of the swords. "This is a wild goose chase?"

"So it would seem." Quentin eyed the guards.

Fragments of a plan were falling into place. It was bold. Audacious, even. But he had thousands of very angry dead people at his back, and he could only see one way to survive the next thirty minutes.

"Would you be so kind as to guide me toward the throne room?" he asked.

The guards laughed.

"Why would we do that?" one asked.

"Oh, that's simple." Quentin smiled. "So that I may claim the throne."

They laughed again, and Quentin laughed along with them.

And then he took their swords.

28

LAURENCE

Laurence eyed Arawn as they stepped outside. "Do you have to come with me?"

Arawn shrugged. "I can hardly go with them."

"Jon's your child."

"I'm not a family sort of god," Arawn muttered.

Laurence crinkled his nose as they made their way through the piled-up snow. The blizzard had died down to a more leisurely kind of snowfall, but New Yorkers already seemed to have had enough and gone either indoors or underground. "Have you spoken to any of your children over the past three thousand years?"

Arawn's shrug was faint, and so like Quentin's that Laurence glanced away so he didn't have to keep looking at the god who was wearing his lover's face. "Usually, once they die, they come to me."

Laurence sighed. He supposed he couldn't really lay into Arawn for being the god that humanity had invented him to be. "Do you miss them?"

"I miss *her*," Arawn mused. "I see her from time to time, but there is no guarantee that she will rediscover the faith she held when we first met. Each time could be the last."

Laurence dug his hands into his pockets and frowned. "That's gotta be hard."

"It is the price we all pay for love," Arawn countered. "The cosmos is such that we always lose all that we have and all that we are. But first we must gain those things, and that's what gives them beauty."

He snorted. Trust a death god to think that way. "You think nothing can stay beautiful forever?"

Arawn laughed. It even seemed genuinely warm, as though Laurence had just done something adorable. "Even gods do not know everything," he admitted. "We are as much a part of the cosmos as our creators. If you wish us to serve you, we do. If you wish us to be capricious, we are. But you cannot wish immortality upon us, because you yourselves are not immortal. Once the last of you are gone, even your immortal gods will fade away without faith to feed them. If there is something that is eternal, I know not what it is."

"I am never inviting you to a party." Laurence spotted a Walgreens and headed for it. It might not be the best food in town, but it was the closest, and it was portable. "Can I ask what she was like? When you first met her, I mean?"

"She preferred to enter Annwn than be torn apart by Herne's hounds." Arawn's lips quirked faintly and his eyes shone. "She had immense courage, but she was also kind and wise. I loved her, and I hope that I always will. My ability to hold on to that love is in the hands of those whose faith sustains me."

Laurence grimaced as he pushed the store's door open and led Arawn inside. He was starting to understand the god's perspective a little, even if he didn't agree with it. Maybe that was because of who he was. Herne was a Hunter. Death was a fact of life. But it didn't mean Laurence was willing to throw everything away just yet.

He was going to kill Gwyn ap Nudd and get Quentin back.

Love was worth fighting for.

"Okay. When we go to Annwn, you have to stay here, right? Is that how it works?" He grabbed a basket and searched for the refrigerators to fill it with bottled water and sandwiches. "Then you'll switch places and send Quentin home?"

"I will return home and, once the situation is confirmed, I will send him here, yes. Though this is not where he belongs, correct?"

Laurence tilted his head as he eyed Arawn. "What makes you say that?"

"His accent differs from those in this place."

Laurence nodded. "He's a long way from home. We've got farther to go, too. But once he's here, we can figure that out. Hire a car and drive if we have to. It'll be okay."

Arawn gave him a speculative look, then nodded to himself and began to wander the aisles of the store as Laurence returned to stocking up on food.

Laurence gave silent thanks for the place being almost totally deserted.

***

THEY ALL MET up back at the hotel lobby, and Laurence stuffed everything he'd bought into the backpack Basil handed to him.

Jon was, he couldn't help but notice, still covered in dried blood and singed clothing, despite his quick wash in the hotel bathroom.

"No thrift store?"

Jon shook his head. "Not that was open. Besides, there is a reasonable possibility that there will be more clothing damage before this is dealt with."

"Story of my life," Laurence agreed. He gestured to the plastic bag in Jon's hand. "Is that it?"

"Cordless, partially charged," Jon said.

"Partially?"

Jon blinked slowly. "They do not guarantee a full charge, because it is likely that a small percentage of charge has dissipated in storage. However, this is a new model, so cannot have been on the shelf for longer than six months. Even if the batteries were manufactured and stored prior—"

"It should be more than we need," Basil cut in with a grin.

"Great. Here's the plan." Laurence hoisted the pack over his shoulders and made for the exit. "I'll take us to the railing. Then Arawn, Basil and I will keep watch while Jon checks that it's the right kind of metal. If he's satisfied, he goes ahead and carves out a piece, and we get away as fast as we can. If we get separated, we meet back here in the lobby."

Basil nodded eagerly. "What about security cameras?"

"We keep our heads down and our faces covered and hope it's enough," Laurence said.

"No offense, but your hair's pretty distinctive." Basil pointed to Laurence's curls.

"Ten minutes walking in this snow and it won't be." He patted it down while it was still damp to show what he meant.

"And what about the god who, for all intents and purposes, strongly resembles your boyfriend?" Jon gazed impassively at Arawn.

Laurence followed the look and frowned. Jon had a point. Quentin was distinctive enough, but once the fact that he was an aristocrat was added to the mix, and that he had a whole bunch of Twitter fans without even knowing what Twitter was, the chances that Arawn was wearing an identifiable face were pretty damn high.

"I can keep my distance," Arawn offered.

"That's probably the best we can do," Laurence said. "I'm hoping this doesn't even lead anywhere, and we can stop by and pay them for the damage once all this is done."

Basil nodded. "Then let's go break the law."

"Do we think Gwyn ap Nudd caused the blizzard?" Basil murmured as they threaded their way downtown.

Laurence tilted his head. Basil must have had a reason for asking, but Laurence looked at Arawn for clarification.

"King of Winter," Arawn said. "It is plausible that he wished to operate under protection from mortal eyes."

"Yes!" Basil fist pumped the air. "I googled him," he added with a shy grin to Laurence. "There's this whole Arthurian myth about Gwyn ap Nudd locked in eternal combat with Gwythyr ap Greidawl — am I saying that right?"

Arawn shrugged. "Close enough."

"Okay, so the theory is that Gwyn got merged with the whole King of Winter legends, and Gwythyr the King of Summer, so during their fight, the back and forth heralds the changes in the seasons."

Arawn rolled his eyes.

"Not a thing?" Basil peered over his glasses.

"Gwyn ap Nudd is not shaped by faith, and has thus remained free from that prison," Arawn said, his nose crinkled slightly. "Though he is more than happy to play into said beliefs, as they give him power. As such, it is not beyond the realm of possibility that he may have worsened the weather to serve his purpose."

"Thank you." Basil gave a smug smile, but it quickly turned sheepish.

"Okay, this is it. Arawn, you stay here." Laurence glanced around, but he couldn't see anyone out on the street but them.

Arawn nodded and stood still.

Laurence beckoned Jon and Basil to follow and led them toward the railings.

Basil gasped. "Wait, is this—"

"Yeah," Laurence cut in.

"What?" Jon looked at Basil.

Basil was bright red. "Nothing, hon."

Jon eyed them without blinking, and Laurence gestured to the railings.

"We'll keep watch. C'mon, Basil."

They marched past until Laurence was satisfied that they didn't look too suspicious, and he made sure his wet hair was patted down around his face to hide as much as possible. He kept his head dipped and his ears open.

It wasn't long before the sound of a motor and screeching metal invaded his world, and Laurence winced a little. He spared a glance toward Jon and saw sparks flying, and a second later, all the energy cut out of Jon like he'd just switched himself off to avoid any damage from the sparks.

Laurence let out a soft breath. He doubted he'd really get used to this gift Arawn had awakened in Jon. It jarred his sense of balance, and he turned his back on it all to try and focus on his job here.

If they got arrested, Laurence wasn't entirely sure that Arawn wouldn't kill whoever stood in their way. Not with his relaxed attitude toward death. That meant it was on Laurence to not only make sure they weren't caught, but also to stop Arawn murdering their way to freedom.

The screeching stopped, and Laurence glanced back in time to catch Jon scooping a short metal bar out of the snow.

"All right," he breathed. "Showtime."

***

Jon ditched the saw in a trash can on the way back to the hotel. Laurence saw no sign of them being tailed. Arawn fell into step with them two blocks from the scene of the crime, and Basil was almost bouncing on his toes with excitement.

"It's wrought iron?" Basil squeaked.

"I would not have taken it if it was not what we required." Jon eyed Basil as he offered up the piece of metal.

Laurence reached for it. It was only a foot long, and the cuts at either end left those ends looking dangerously sharp around the edges. The metal was hefty, and reminded Laurence uncomfortably of the chandeliers the duke had in his sanctum.

He grimaced and handed it to Basil.

"Have we got everything you need for the ritual?" Laurence dug his hands into his pockets to try and warm them up.

"Yeah. No problem." Basil patted his bag with his free hand as he gave the iron back to Jon. "We're all set."

Jon sneaked the bar into the depths of his coat.

Laurence grinned as they strode into the hotel lobby. The thrill of the hunt was clawing its way through him, and now that this first step was almost complete, he allowed himself to luxuriate in the feeling of success. They'd done it. Laurence had made a plan that actually paid off, and the glow that filled him with was worth the risks they'd taken.

They were closer to their prey, and that prey wasn't some petty duke who thought abusing a child was the way to ensure that child's future success. No. This prey was one of the Fair Folk, with an army of dead on his side, capable of going toe to toe with a god and not getting killed just yet.

This prey was so beyond his reach that he had to assemble a team just to try.

They crossed to the elevators and headed for Laurence's room, and all the while Laurence didn't even try to wipe the smile off his face. He felt so alive that he wouldn't have succeeded, so he didn't see the point.

"Okay!" Once they were in Laurence's room, Basil pulled his book out and began to sift through it. "Jon, baby, I need a sheet off the bed."

Jon nodded and began to strip the bed with calm efficiency, and Arawn watched his Child just as placidly.

"Laurence, I'm gonna need a few heavy things for the corners of the sheet to hold it in place."

"What, like..." Laurence looked around, then his eyes settled on the chairs and table by the window. "Easy," he said.

"Great!" Basil put the book on the desk, open, its blue glow gently radiating from the pages as he skimmed it. His hands fished around inside his bag while his eyes kept working on the book, and soon he had dug out a Sharpie from the depths.

At this point, Laurence was beyond caring about getting billed by the hotel for drawing all over the bedsheet. The faster they got to Annwn, the sooner they could rescue Quentin and put an end to Gwyn ap Nudd's plans.

Between them, he and Jon spread the sheet across the floor and used furniture to spread it out and weigh it down, so that Basil could get to work with his pen. Laurence did what he could to help Basil get the sigils right, but mostly it amounted to holding the book so that Basil didn't have to go back and forth every time he came to a new one.

This ritual was way outside Laurence's wheelhouse. In a way that scared him, even though he was already fully aware that there were sorcerers in the world who operated very differently from Laurence and Rufus. Seeing just how different was a little discomfiting.

There was no way Laurence could learn all this. It was overwhelming. He'd barely managed to remember how to ward rooms in a building.

Wards.

Laurence cursed under his breath and reached inside his shirt to grab the thong from around his neck. He eased it off over his head, pulling his talisman free. The last thing he needed after all this effort was to get left behind when Basil cast his spell, so he stepped away and draped the necklace across a pillow.

"Huh?" Basil looked across, then nodded. "Oh shit, yeah. Good idea. That would've been awkward."

"Yeah." Laurence looked the sheet over and did what he could to assess the concentric circles filled with sigils and symbols. "Are we good to go?"

Basil nodded. "Everyone inside the outer circle. Well, everyone who isn't a god." He looked apologetically toward Arawn.

Arawn sat on the edge of the bed and crossed his legs as he watched impassively. "I wish you luck," he murmured.

Laurence stepped onto the sheet. "We'll fix this."

At least, he *hoped* they'd fix it.

They *better* fix it.

29

QUENTIN

QUENTIN WEIGHED THE SWORDS IN HIS HANDS AS HE KEPT HIS EYES on the guards. While he was not familiar with this style of weapon and doubted very much that fencing with them would work terribly well, he suspected that holding on to them would appear far more intimidating than tossing them aside. And if his eye didn't damn well stop twitching soon, he might not be able to focus well enough to scare his way out of a paper bag.

The guards' laughter had subsided. For a moment, they both looked at their empty hands and then to Quentin's full ones as they tried to work out how their swords had leaped from their grasps and through the air, but then they raised their heads.

"We *are* already dead," one said.

"A sword isn't all that much of a threat," said the other.

Quentin shrugged, doing his damnedest to maintain a controlled exterior. "And yet you carry them. You clearly believe they are useful for defending a castle. But if it makes you feel any better, I shall let go of them."

He held his arms out, sword tips toward their original owners, and then made a display of letting go of the hilts. His fingers splayed, his hands up as though in surrender, while he telekinetically held the swords rock solid in midair.

The guards hissed slightly and stepped back.

Quentin lowered his hands to his sides. "The throne room," he prompted, more sharply than he had intended. "If you would be so kind."

"Kindness?" One guard laughed. "This is not the fortress for that."

"I would say that whoever sits on that throne is the one to decide," Quentin murmured, "wouldn't you? Now. Onward. I wouldn't wish to do you any harm, especially not as you are this close to your own freedom."

They faced each other again, and their shoulders eased a little.

"Fine," one said. "But if Gwyn ap Nudd returns, we won't protect you."

"He'll make us join the Hunt for treason," the other added.

"Not if he doesn't survive his return." Quentin gestured for them to proceed.

After another moment's hesitation, the guards led further down the corridor.

Quentin risked an exchanged look with Eric. He could feel the hunger churning his gut, feel the thirst that parched his throat, and Eric frowned at him.

"Are you okay, bud?" Eric whispered.

"I don't have the luxury of being anything but," he breathed. "We should hurry."

He set off after the guards, jogging a moment to catch up with them, but even that seemed to drain him further.

It really had cost an awful lot of energy to escape the Hunt. He couldn't afford to waste any now.

ERIC LET out a low whistle as they entered a vast hall even larger than Arawn's had been. "I guess you need high ceilings when you turn everyone under your thumb into big-ass monsters, huh?"

The guards shifted nervously on the spot.

Quentin stepped cautiously into the hall as he examined it. "Are there hidden passages or cubbyholes?"

"Of course," chimed the guards.

"Search them, please."

The guards shrugged to each other, then parted ways and began to circle the walls around the room.

The throne was at the far end, as Quentin had expected, but he did not rush toward it. There could be any number of dangers between him and it that he was unaware of. While he doubted they had a great deal of time before the Hunt arrived, he refused to get himself killed through impatience.

"Thoughts?" Eric murmured.

Quentin allowed his gaze to wander. "It's not impossible that the room could hold traps in Gwyn ap Nudd's absence," he said softly. "I would rather proceed with caution."

"Yeah. Give me a sword."

Quentin arched a brow, but he released one into Eric's hold as Eric's fingers closed around the hilt. "Don't do anything foolish," he said.

Eric laughed. "A Riley? Do something foolish? It's like you know us!" He patted Quentin on the shoulder and began to walk toward the throne, using the sword to wave through the air and poke at flagstones as he went.

It wasn't the worst plan, Quentin supposed. In theory, nothing could harm Eric.

Quentin examined the room in more depth as he stood still.

The walls were paneled in the same dark wood that stood in the petrified forest and, as such, the great hall was a gloomy affair. There was little natural light, as the windows were tiny and high up the walls. Quentin suspected they were more for allowing fresh air to circulate when fires and candles were lit, rather than for any potentially stunning views of the mountains around them.

Banners bearing unfamiliar crests hung along those walls, shadowed but looking clean enough. Above the banners, running along the walls like bunting, were garlands of fresh holly, with bright red berries gleaming in the dark. The air smelled musty, aged, as though none of the fires had been lit in a long while.

He chose not to question where the dead got so much holly. Gods made very little sense, and Quentin suspected that their worlds were equally lacking in logic.

The throne itself was also carved from black wood, too far away for Quentin to make out fine details, but it looked far too big for a human form.

Eric was halfway to the throne, and paying very close attention to not getting himself hurt, which Quentin was grateful for.

What this place needed was some light, though. Eric's eyesight might be sufficient to see into every little nook and cranny, but Quentin could only make out the bigger picture. Where otherwise he might readily have used his gifts to light each and every candle and fireplace here, the thought of doing so in his current state only made his eye worse, and he rubbed at it to try and get it to calm down.

He made his way with care toward a candelabra and ignited a single candle, which he then lifted from the candelabra and used to light each other candle. If they generated enough heat after a while, he could absorb it back into himself and take the edge off the worst of his fatigue, but that would require more than a single candelabra's worth of tiny flames.

"If there are any traps," Eric said as he stepped up to the throne and turned to face Quentin, "they aren't set off by the dead."

Quentin nodded as he planted his first candle back where he'd gotten it. "Thank you, Eric," he murmured. "Would you be so kind as to light some more candles? Let's see if we can't brighten this place up somewhat."

Eric nodded, and they locked eyes on each other before they slowly crossed the hall to switch places.

Quentin took his sword from the air and used it much as Eric had, poking and prodding his way across the floor, alert to anything that might leap out of the shadows at him. He laid down a blanket of telekinesis, too, lest he miss anything with the sword, but he stepped up on to the throne's dais without incident.

Perhaps Gwyn ap Nudd had not intended to be gone terribly long, and had not thought to lay traps before his departure.

Perhaps the throne itself was the danger.

Quentin eyed it, then poked it with the sword. Finally, he grasped it in his telekinesis and applied pressure little by little, until he was sure he was replicating his own bodyweight.

Nothing.

He drew a breath and placed the sword on the floor, then hoisted himself onto the seat, half expecting it to try to eat him.

Nothing happened.

The throne dwarfed him. Even Eric would not fill it. This was made for someone of Arawn's stature, which didn't fill him with excitement for Gwyn ap Nudd's return. Still, the size of his opponent was almost immaterial, especially if said opponent wasn't even here.

"Nothing," one guard declared.

"The hall is safe," said the other.

"Thank you." Quentin's back didn't even reach the back of the throne, so he sat upright and rested his hands in his lap. "My name is Quentin. I would be honored if you would care to share your names with me, so that I may address you correctly."

The guards reconvened in front of the throne, clearly still uncertain about the whole situation.

"I am Bleddyn," said one.

"I am Tegan," said the other.

"Eric, could you return Tegan's sword, please?" Quentin raised the other and sent it through the air, hilt first, toward Bleddyn and set it on the floor by his feet. "You may wish to reclaim your weapons," he continued. "I would like for you to advise the remaining guards of the new situation in this fortress."

Eric brought a candle with him as he offered his sword to Tegan. He eyed Quentin briefly, then continued on to light another candelabra.

The guards picked up their swords and sheathed them.

"Which new situation, exactly?" Tegan asked.

"Tell them that I have taken the throne," Quentin replied. "If they wish to refute my claim to it, they are welcome to issue a challenge. Otherwise, I consider it an act of treason for them to resist the position which I have fairly and rightfully claimed."

Bleddyn clasped his fist to his chest and bowed, and Tegan followed suit a second later.

"Yes, my liege," they said as one.

Quentin watched them go, and only once they were out of the hall did he allow himself to let out a sigh while his shoulders sagged. "Bloody hell," he said. "That was tense. Thank you, Eric."

Eric shrugged. "You really think this is a good idea?"

"I think it's the only way to narrow a whole army down into one-on-one challenges," Quentin said. "Otherwise, they're simply going to pour in through the doors and overwhelm us."

"They still might." Eric gestured toward Quentin with his candle, and a drop of wax spilled to the floor. "You're gonna need a crown if you want to pull this off."

Quentin frowned at that. It felt as though a crown would be crossing some invisible boundary line. Crowns were for actual royalty, not earls who were out of their depth. Yet it was the way things used to be. Once you defeated a king, you claimed his crown as well as his throne.

No. It still felt wrong. Quentin was no king, and certainly not in this place, where he didn't belong.

He shook his head faintly and raised a hand to stifle a yawn behind. "I think a crown would be a step too far," he said.

Eric sucked on his teeth, then his eyes widened. "Wait. Dude. I know exactly what you need. The only question is whether or not we can find or make one in the next, like, ten minutes."

Quentin lifted an eyebrow. "What is it?"

"What you need," Eric said with a conspiratorial smile, "is a torc."

Quentin tilted his head faintly. The word seemed familiar, but he couldn't quite put his finger on why. His brain felt sluggish after his interrupted sleep and subsequent expenditures.

"It's an ancient Celtic piece of jewelry," Eric explained. "Some were for everyday wear, but it's theorized that some were for nobility or for ceremonial use. It's kind of like a necklace, except it's a circle of metal that you have to bend open to get on or off."

Quentin blinked. "Like a collar?"

"I am *not* gonna ask for context on that question." Eric raised a hand while he continued to light candles with the other. "What you and Cricket get up to is none of my business."

"Um—"

"Am I pondering what you're pondering?" Eric shrugged. "I think so, Brain. But where are we gonna find a torc at this hour?"

Quentin didn't know what to do with that one, so he pursed his lips. "Perhaps there is a vault?"

"And you know your way around castles. If there is a vault, where's it most likely to be?"

"A treasury is most usually found at or below ground level within the keep," Quentin said. "Sometimes beneath a chapel."

"Yeah, there won't be a chapel here." Eric chuckled.

"Then a basement," Quentin said.

Eric blew his candle out, set it down on the floor, and clapped his hands together. "Let's go."

Quentin eased himself off the throne with some reluctance.

He'd been getting quite comfortable for a moment there.

———————

THEY HURRIED through the corridors together, Eric listening out for trouble, and Quentin doing his best to figure out the interior layout of an unknown building.

He supposed that, if it came down to it, they could always lock themselves in the treasury and narrow the Hunt down by dint of only having a door wide enough for one or two at a time, but he vastly preferred not to allow things to get that far.

"Down there." Eric pointed toward a doorway, and they sprinted for it.

Quentin glanced around, then through the arch. There was no door, no sign that there should have been one, and beyond was a spiral staircase which led both up and down.

They must have reached one of the turrets.

"Perfect," he breathed, and eased past Eric to lead the way down.

"Are you sure you should go first?"

"Spiral staircases are designed to be defensible by sword," Quentin said as he hurried down the stone steps. "They ascend clockwise so as to force assailants to expose more of their bodies if they wish to use their dominant hand, which was usually the right." He patted the center column with the back of his hand to demonstrate. "But it also means that should assailants be descending, as we are doing, they have the advantage. It's best if I go first to deflect any possible defense."

"Why would you make it easier for your attackers to come down to you if that's where you keep all your swag?"

"Because you have a killing zone at the bottom that those attackers must pass through if they wish to reach your treasure," Quentin explained. "Your attackers are funneled into a controlled area over which you have the upper hand."

Eric grabbed the back of his coat and brought Quentin up short. "You know what? Maybe we don't need a torc! You can just do the whole telekinetic floaty sword thing and that ought to do it!"

Quentin glanced back over his shoulder and up at Eric. "Eric," he said softly. "If we require some symbol of authority to quell what might otherwise become a very short and very violent protest at the sudden change in ruler, I'm not wholly certain that a couple of swords will cut the mustard."

Eric eyed him, eyes creased with worry, but he sighed and let go of Quentin's coat. "Yeah. You're right. Just... please try not to get killed?"

"I always try my utmost, I assure you."

He turned to face the steps and resumed his descent, hoping that Bleddyn and Tegan had already spread the word this far.

The alternative didn't bear thinking about.

30

LAURENCE

THE HOTEL ROOM WAS GONE IN THE BLINK OF AN EYE. THE moment Basil's recitation of the ritual was complete, the glow that rose from the bedsheet grew intense and then dissipated, and was replaced with what looked and sounded a whole lot like a party.

A super naked party.

Sure, some people had gossamer-sheer gowns or shirts on, but they were as good as nude, since the material hid nothing.

The place they were in was huge, like some old castle's hall. Quentin would probably call it a proper castle, since his own place was more of a stately home despite the name.

Laurence rocked his jaw and drew his thoughts back to the reason they were here.

"Hey!" He lifted his hands into the air. "Sorry to interrupt. Did anyone see the good-looking British guy Arawn traded places with?"

Slowly, the edges of the party turned toward them, and Laurence put on his best, friendliest smile as he dropped his hands.

The party quickly turned to curious chatter.

"A Hunter?"

"Wait, who is *that?*"

"Is it Arawn?"

"Are they alive?"

A middle-aged woman stepped forward, clad only in her birthday suit, and she clasped Laurence's hand. "Yes," she said. "We saw him. He has gone to the Four-Peaked Fortress to defeat Gwyn ap Nudd."

"That's great. Thank you!" Laurence smiled at her. It was almost a relief to have his usual Otherworld position reversed, to be the clothed one amongst all this nudity. If the air weren't so chilly — and he didn't have a rescue underway — he'd be willing to drop his own clothes and join in. "Could you show us the way?"

She laughed softly and patted his arm. "You are a Hunter."

Laurence opened his mouth, then smiled wryly. "Yeah. Good point. Thank you. I'm sorry we crashed the party."

"Don't be." She leaned in to kiss his cheek, then sailed away to a table to reach for some grapes.

"This is, er," Basil cleared his throat as he stepped up alongside Laurence. "Not what I expected?" He closed the book and stowed it in his bag, then fastened the straps to keep it safe.

"Me either," Jon muttered. "We should go."

"Hold on." Laurence closed his eyes and drew a slow breath, searching for Quentin's scent.

It stood out like a beacon, as though it had waited for him. There were so few other scents here that it was easy to latch on to, and when his eyes drifted open, he could see it lead out of the hall.

Laurence grinned and patted Basil's arm.

"Let's go."

THEY SPRINTED through a bustling marketplace as Laurence tailed Quentin's scent around a variety of stalls. Why was he not surprised that Quentin had managed to find shops, even in Annwn?

People out here had significantly less flesh on their bones. Some were literally just bones that were held together by absolutely nothing that Laurence could make out, not even a tendon. It was kind of weird, but not as weird as the way almost everyone was fascinated by Jon.

"Can they tell?" Basil whispered.

"They identified Laurence as a Hunter immediately," Jon mused. "It is not unreasonable to extrapolate that they are fully capable of somehow detecting my nature."

"Yeah," Laurence agreed. Even people on Avalon, who had left the mortal world of their own accord and were still alive and well, could tell Laurence was a Child of Herne. "It's pretty common in Otherworld. Seems like if you're either from here, or have been here long enough, it's something you develop."

"But nobody seems to think I'm anything?" Basil glanced around as they walked.

"Don't take it personally. I don't think magic is necessarily handed down from gods, unlike Jon's and my gifts."

The trail left the square in the end, and Laurence led Basil and Jon through winding streets until they reached a wall with a medieval-looking gate in it. The gate was open, and the view beyond was a mix of stunning and horrifying all in one.

They were at the top of a mountain. They had to be, since beyond the gate everything only went downward until more mountains rose from the depths.

That was the stunning part.

What was horrifying was the way a stream of monsters filled the distant sky around another castle on top of the next mountain. They were descending on it like a swarm of bees around a ruined hive, and they looked horribly like some twisted interpretation of a Wild Hunt.

"Uh." Basil pointed toward the mass of flying things. "That can't be good?"

Laurence knew that was where Quentin had to be. The man was a trouble magnet. That, and the castle in the distance had four spires that stretched toward the sunless sky.

"Fuck," he breathed. "That's gotta be, like, miles away!"

"Three to five," Jon said. "In a direct line." He glanced behind them, then toward the distant mountaintop. "On the assumption that the curvature of Annwn matches that of the Earth, and that the size of that castle matches the size of this. Otherwise, it is impossible to calculate without more data."

Laurence nodded in thanks. "And we can't go in a direct line."

"More data required," Jon muttered. "I cannot even begin to determine the cross-country distance without topographical information."

"Yeah," Laurence agreed. "There's no way we're gonna get there today. Not without a fucking helicopter."

"Or another Wild Hunt."

Laurence spun on the spot toward the new voice.

A skeleton in some kind of armor approached, with a somewhat jaunty tilt to their head.

"Sorry," Laurence said. "I don't wanna sound ungrateful, but where am I gonna find one of those?"

The skeleton laughed gently. "You are a Hunter. Call one."

Laurence narrowed his eyes. "I, uh. I can't say that I know how."

The skeleton's head dipped slowly, then turned toward Jon, at which point the skeleton bowed deeply. "A Child of Arawn and a Child of Herne," they mused. "And a friend. I have not seen so many living in such a short span of time for many years."

"You saw Quentin?" Laurence gestured toward the other castle. "Did he go there?"

"Yes, and yes. The Warrior has gone to kill Gwyn ap Nudd."

"Except Gwyn ap Nudd isn't there," Basil said.

The skeleton turned toward Basil. "Then the Warrior faces a Wild Hunt alone." They tapped fingerbones against their teeth with a jarring, clacking sound. "You are in Otherworld, Hunter. You should be able to summon a Wild Hunt. I do not know how, though. It seems the sort of thing horns are used for?"

At least the armored skeleton sounded apologetic, and Laurence nodded his thanks. "Is there some way I can get up there?" he said, pointing to the battlement over the top of the gate.

"Yes. Please, follow me."

The skeleton led to a door by the gate, and Laurence glanced at Jon and Basil as they began to follow.

"Have you got a horn?" Basil asked, his voice low.

Laurence shook his head. "No. But I'm hoping I've got the next best thing."

"Which is?" Jon looked at him, the faintest hint of curiosity in his near-black eyes.

Laurence grinned wolfishly and took the steps two at a time, his long legs easily carrying him up as fast as the skeleton ahead of them.

"Instinct," he said.

THEY MADE it up to the battlement and out into open air, and Laurence could see the small town they had walked through to get here on one side of the thick walls, the mountains stretching out before them on the other. Far below, in the valleys, was a forest of petrified trees and blackened earth, much like he had seen in his dream of Herne and Sara.

He looked along the walls, topped with walkways so that

guards could patrol them, and saw what he wanted directly above the gate.

The bell was huge. It hung from black wooden beams embedded into the walls of a stone building built to hold it. Along the walls were other such outbuildings, which he had to assume also held bells.

He gestured for Basil and Jon to stay where they were, and headed in to grab the bell rope and unfurl it from the hook it was woven around.

And then he tugged on it.

The bell swung slowly at first. It took Laurence a little experimentation to figure out how hard he had to pull, and when exactly to pull again to work with the weight of the bell instead of against it, but soon it was pealing out so loudly that he had to let go of the rope and back out of the building.

As his bell began to die down, others along the wall picked up the call, and it continued to ring out around the castle for another couple of minutes.

Laurence waited for it to dissipate, and then he cupped his hands around his mouth and bellowed at the top of his lungs. "I am Bambi Laurence Riley. Son of Myriam and Eric Riley. Child of Herne the Hunter. God-Killer. Daemon-Slayer. I call upon all that is wild and true. I call for the end to a great evil. I call," he yelled, "for a Wild Hunt."

A hush fell as he let out the last words of his shout. He swallowed to take the edge off the soreness in his throat, though it would heal soon enough.

"You're the son of Eric Riley?" The skeleton looked at him with empty eye sockets, yet somehow still managed to look curious.

Laurence nodded.

At first it seemed simple. He'd been asked a question, and the answer was yes, so a nod would do. But then his brain kicked in.

The question wasn't whether he was Myriam's son.

Laurence whirled on the skeleton. "You know my dad? He's here?"

The skeleton nodded. "A fine Hunter. A good man. He has not been with us long, but he warms us with his presence."

Laurence swayed. He reached for the stone wall and gripped it, while the world under his feet continued to spin so fast he wasn't sure he could stay upright.

Dad was here.

He felt the stab of tears prick at his eyes, the crush of grief in his chest. He didn't know whether to feel elated or stricken, and all he could think of was the sight of Dad lying in that hospital bed, slowly fading away while Mom clung to his hand.

"Oh my God! Laurence? Are you okay?" Basil rushed to his side and gripped his arm, leaning in to try and make eye contact.

"I watched him die," was all Laurence could think to say. His voice cracked as the tears rolled slowly down his cheeks. "Goddess, I watched him die so many times, and I... He's here. He's right here!"

"Well," said the skeleton, with some trace of apology. "Not here, really."

Laurence wiped tears away and stared at the skeleton. "What?"

The skeleton stepped aside and stretched an arm toward the Four-Peaked Fortress. "He is there," they said softly. "Arawn asked him to guide the Warrior. They travelled together."

The distant Wild Hunt seemed smaller now. There was less of it in the sky.

That meant more of it in the fortress, where Dad and Quentin had gone together.

He couldn't lose his dad yet again. He'd watched Dad die during his overdose, he'd watched Dad die in real life a year later, and he'd watched Dad die in a too-real nightmare soon after he first met Quentin. There was no way Laurence was ready to do it a fourth time, and he sure as hell wasn't going to lose Quentin.

He swiped the wetness from his cheeks and rubbed his nose, then pushed himself away from the wall and pulled his head up straight.

He was the Hunter, and nothing would stand in his way.

31

QUENTIN

The trouble with basements, Quentin quickly realized, was that they were underground. Far away from any light source.

He stopped on the bottom step and hesitated, one hand on the central column of the staircase. "Do you hear anything?" he whispered.

"No," Eric breathed. "But if someone's down here, they're as dead as me. All they gotta do is stand still. Just use some fire."

"I would prefer not to overextend myself." Quentin rubbed at his eyes again, careful not to tug too tightly on his own skin, though frankly, if he didn't make it out of here, early wrinkles would be the least of his concerns.

His vision was no clearer for it.

"You sure you're okay?" Eric's hand rested against Quentin's back.

Quentin automatically tried to reach out for any sense of warmth, but there was none. Perhaps Laurence's theory was correct. If Quentin were constantly drawing on his environment to some minuscule background level, then the utter absence of any energy around him could be having more of an effect than the lack of food, sleep, or water, combined. But if there were no energy whatsoever, how was it that things here were not frozen solid?

Neil was correct about even ice containing some degree of heat energy, and Quentin had frozen Annis' surrounds to the point where she had been almost incapable of motion; yet here he was now in a world which could not sustain him, and yet nothing was frozen.

Was it possible that the energy was there, if he only bothered to look for it?

"Keep watch," he whispered. "I want to try something."

"Okay. Try not to take too long."

Quentin nodded and closed his eyes, then took slow, deep breaths. He reached out, searching for anything that he could take into himself. Anything at all. The faintest hint of warmth or life.

There was nothing.

"You're out of time," Eric muttered.

Quentin snapped his eyes open, and seconds later he heard the faintest echo of thunder from up above. "What on Earth is that?"

"That's the sound of an army landing in a courtyard. We gotta go."

With a grim nod, Quentin alighted on the bottom step and strode swiftly across the empty room, laying down his telekinesis as a rudimentary replacement for eyesight.

No arrows came at him from murder holes. There was no hot oil delivered from above.

He found a wall sconce and gently pushed just enough heat into it to ignite the candle wick, then tore the sconce from the wall and held it aloft as the flame caught and gained in strength.

God, he ached to pull that little flame right back into himself, but he needed it where it was.

Light glinted from a door handle. He crossed to it and twisted, but the door was firmly locked, so he tore it off its hinges and beckoned Eric to move.

Eric hurried across the floor to join him, and Quentin jammed the door up against the staircase, but it was the wrong size to fit in as any kind of lasting barricade, so Quentin left it there as best he could and darted through the doorway. They ran through the next room and he tore yet another door away, jamming it in the hole left by the first, and then he held the sconce overhead as he stepped through.

Light bounced off metal.

A lot of metal.

"Goddess," Eric said. "Would you look at all this."

Quentin nodded numbly. He'd seen a lot of precious metals and jewels in his lifetime, but never had it been piled up as though it were worthless. Despite being behind two locked doors and a killing zone, the treasure in here was heaped into piles as though it had simply been dumped.

"It's a hoard," he realized.

"Holy shit," Eric said as he stepped toward the nearest pile. "Celts used to do this, didn't they? Nobody knows why. They'd toss all their gold into a hole in the ground and just bury it together, not with the people it had belonged to."

"Not only the Celts," Quentin murmured as he began scanning the hoard for anything resembling a torc. "It was quite a habit across the entire British Isles."

"There!" Eric pointed, then leaned forward to pluck something from a pile, which shifted slightly as he tugged it free. "That should do." He turned and held it out to Quentin.

Quentin took it from him and gazed down at it. An almost-complete circle of intricately twisted gold, capped at the ends, with terminals shaped like the heads of dogs. The wirework was truly spectacular, with several cords twisted around each other and then plaited together into a larger rope-like circlet.

The workmanship was astounding, particularly for something that would have been handmade.

"Why does Gwyn ap Nudd need treasures such as these?" he mused. "People don't bring them with them in death, surely?"

"No. But he collected the dead from battlefields," Eric said, one ear turned toward the door. "He had plenty of opportunity to loot, if he wanted to. Ah, someone's coming! Put it on!"

"How?" There was no way Quentin could get his neck through the inch-wide gap between the terminals.

"Just pull it open. Gold's really bendy, dude."

Quentin could hear the thunder coming down the staircase. He was out of time. He tugged on the terminals, but it took a little telekinesis to really make the torc open up, and he parked the sconce in midair so that his hands were free to put the torc on.

He managed to close it up again just as the door to the intervening room was destroyed in a shower of splinters.

"Oh boy," Eric gasped as he backed toward the hoard. "You're up, Warrior. I hope you're good at this."

"Bloody awful," Quentin admitted. "Take the sconce. Let's not lose the light."

Eric grabbed it, and Quentin went to the doorway.

Thundering toward him was a creature the likes of which he had only ever seen in children's books. Easily eight feet tall and three feet wide, it was a wonder the thing had fit down the staircase. It had skin like rhino hide and biceps wider than Quentin's head, but he felt nothing from it. It was every bit as dead as Eric.

Deep within the matted hair that fell across its face, it had human eyes.

Quentin gritted his teeth and stepped out of the treasury. If he was wearing a torc, and it was some sort of status symbol, then he had best act worthy of whatever status it might convey.

"Stop," he barked.

It worked about as well as it had in Manhattan.

<hr>

HE DIDN'T WISH to think of this person as a monster. Somewhere beneath all the armor and matted hair, there was the soul of a human being who had been twisted by however long they had spent in Annwn, but that didn't preclude that soul from attempting to kill Quentin.

He darted aside as the creature rushed him, unfastening his coat with a deft flick of his fingers so that he could move more freely.

His opponent turned and flicked a limb outward. It flowed and lengthened, then reformed into a scythe of flesh and serrated bone.

Quentin blinked and grabbed his assailant telekinetically, taking steps back as he held them in place.

"There is no need for this," he called across the intervening space. "Gwyn ap Nudd is gone. I can help you."

The creature — the *person* — laughed. A mouth formed somewhere under the bedraggled hair. "He will return, and he will destroy you." The eyes swiveled down toward Quentin's chest, and then doubt entered the voice. "A Warrior cloaked in nightmares."

Quentin glanced down to the tabard he wore beneath his coat. It glinted faintly in the flickering candlelight. "Apparently so."

"No matter." His attacker sounded uncertain, but leaped at Quentin regardless of whatever doubts they weren't sharing.

It felt like Annis slipping through his grasp all over again. One moment Quentin held the creature steady, and the next it was through his metaphorical fingers like he was squeezing yogurt.

The bone scythe sliced through the air toward him.

Quentin threw himself out of the way and into a forward roll, then allowed his momentum to propel him right back up to his feet, but he didn't stand still. He darted across the room as the creature mutated even further, hide becoming chitinous, limbs spawning from its torso, until it was something truly nightmarish. The body of a man born aloft on eight black legs that were draped with matted hair and tipped with serrated bones.

"Fucking hell," Eric yelped.

Quentin had to agree.

There was no way to win this fight. The creature was able to become insubstantial at will, and he had no doubt that it could reappear once it made contact with him. Annis had shown that to be possible within a fraction of a second.

Quentin also suspected that his opponent would not tire, whereas Quentin was already at his very limits. The dive across the floor had left him slightly dizzy, and his head began to pound in time with his heart.

If he could make it back to the great hall, there might be enough heat in the candles to give him more of an edge.

It was the best he could think of, so he turned and ran for the stairs as fast as he could, putting on a burst of speed that was not his absolute best, but certainly the best he could manage under the circumstances.

He heard the *clack-clack-clack* of bones skittering across the flagstones behind him, and he glanced over his shoulder.

It was gaining on him.

Quentin all but threw himself up the spiral staircase. It was far too narrow for the creature's current form, and he fervently hoped that if it wished to follow, it would have to mutate once more, which would chip a few seconds off its speed and allow him to gain some distance. Eric should hopefully follow, and then together they could tackle the problem. Eric had mentioned that their forms were malleable, and perhaps Eric could attack the creature if it phased out of any sort of physical form again, since they were both equally dead.

It was the best he had right now, and he allowed himself a brief glimmer of satisfaction at his ability to adjust his plans on the fly in a way he couldn't possibly have managed before he'd met Laurence.

Maybe he *was* a Warrior. Or, at the very least, could be, should he last long enough.

He all but flew up the stairs and out into the corridor, and he got halfway to the hall before he heard the skittering of bones against the floor. He threw a glance back over his shoulder in time to see his pursuer resume their monstrous spider-like form, and wished he hadn't.

There wasn't time to mess around, so he launched himself from the ground and opted for a more literal flight. It was far faster to propel himself telekinetically, no matter how quickly he could sprint, and he burst through into the great hall in a matter of seconds.

Candelabras and fireplaces were lit. What had begun as one tiny flame was now a battery he could pull from to sustain himself, and he had a momentary debate as to whether it was best to take it all now or to save for emergencies.

It was best to use it now. Flames might be extinguished during a protracted battle, whether through a draft of air or being knocked over, and their heat would be lost to him for good.

He reached for all of it and tugged.

Flames flickered and died out. The fireplaces sputtered and died. His headache subsided, though it did little for his thirst or hunger.

It was a start.

Darkness swept outward from him like it was a living thing, and when it reached the doorway, it met the monster which had come to kill him.

Quentin raised himself to his full height and turned his body side-on toward his opponent. He lifted his head and raised his hands.

"You will not win," he said, with all the confidence he could muster.

The monster stepped warily inside, each tap giving away its position in the dark.

"You are alive," it rasped. "You have no power here."

"Stand down, or you may find out just how much power I

hold." Quentin barked his order so loudly that it echoed across the hall.

For one second, he thought the creature might consider it.

And then those hopes were dashed.

32

LAURENCE

It began as a rumble.

Then it became a roar.

Laurence pushed away from the wall and turned toward the noise that flowed toward him from the castle.

"Oh my God," Basil whispered. "Do you hear that?"

"I do," Jon muttered.

The roar turned to thunder.

Laurence's pulse raced. His blood sang. From tip to toe, his skin tingled with a thrill he intuitively knew to be interwoven with the oncoming hunt.

The Wild Hunt poured through the streets toward him, running in rivulets down the mountain's peak and becoming an unstoppable tide, a river of horses and riders and red-eared dogs that surged toward the gates but took to the air before reaching them.

A horse the size of Herne's landed atop the battlements and dipped its head to Laurence. It made a snorting sound and turned side-on to him in invitation.

"Are we—" Basil squeaked.

"Grab a horse." Laurence grinned. "Be part of the hunt."

Whatever Basil said next was lost to the thunder as it passed overhead. Laurence didn't wait. He climbed the edge of the battlements so he could jump across to the horse's back. The moment he grabbed hold of its mane, it leaped into the sky, ploughing through the Wild Hunt toward the front. Laurence was the Hunt's leader, and his horse was taking him to his rightful place.

The thrill was electrifying. The horse beneath his legs, the wind in his hair, and the roll of thunder as they sped through the sky. Even Windsor had sensed the thrill across their bond and yelled in excitement.

Laurence threw his head back and his arms wide, and screamed his triumph to the sunless sky.

HE COULD SEE the other Wild Hunt in the distance, the last of it landing within the fortress' walls.

They weren't going to make it. Not unless Quentin had managed to barricade himself inside one of the fortress' inner buildings.

"C'mon, Quen," he muttered under his breath. "Hold on. I'm coming, baby."

From the corner of his eye, he saw a horse begin to draw parallel with his own, and he looked toward it. It was enormous, a bay with a pale mane, and Jon and Basil on its back. Jon clung to the mane as wind slapped it against his face, and Basil's arms were tight around Jon's waist.

"This is amazing!" Basil yelled. "What happens when we get there?"

Laurence flashed his teeth. He could barely wait to land and catch his prey, and couldn't stop grinning. "We find Quentin and kill Gwyn ap Nudd."

"How do we get in?" Jon seemed to have no inclination to

shout, and so his voice was barely enough to be heard over the thunder of the Hunt and the rush of the winds.

Laurence gestured toward the fortress. To the massive, monstrous army within its outer walls. "We trample his Hunt with ours."

Basil's eyes grew wide and he looked where Laurence pointed. "That's insane!"

"We're airborne," Laurence countered. "They've landed. We'll crush them!"

Basil gawped at him and said nothing.

Laurence's grin wasn't going anywhere.

THE FORTRESS RUSHED up to meet him.

Laurence's hold tightened more than he thought possible. His hands ached with the strength of his grip, and his nails dug against his palms. Landing on an army had seemed like such a great idea two minutes ago, but now that they were meters away from impact, it suddenly looked like suicide.

Horses neighed and hooves clattered. Horrific faces below turned to the sky and mouths opened — whether to scream, or in readiness to attack, wasn't clear.

And then the two forces collided.

Laurence was thrown from his horse with the force of the impact, and bounced off something squishy before he fell enough that the ground was in sight. He grasped at the nightmare he had landed against and used its hair to slow his descent.

The instant his feet touched the ground, he darted away to find some space before he could get flattened. He ducked and wove amid the chaos, wincing at the sounds of tearing flesh and snapping bones.

A muffled yell sounded more human than the rest of the cries, and Laurence whipped his head toward it in time to see Basil go flying through the air.

There was no sign of Jon.

Laurence cursed and began to force his way toward Basil. Without a weapon, all he could do was avoid getting hit, and thankfully he was pretty small compared to most of the combatants. He was able to slip under their notice without slowing himself down.

All it would take was a bad landing or a careless hoof, and Basil would be toast. Since Basil had brought them this far, Laurence couldn't leave him to fate.

"Basil!" he yelled. "Are you okay?"

Basil didn't answer.

Hooves slammed down inches from Laurence's feet. He yelped as he twisted past the massive horse, which kicked one of the monsters so hard that it cleared a path through three more.

Laurence gave silent thanks and scrambled over the fallen monsters toward the splash of amber beyond them.

"Basil!" He landed by Basil's side and crouched over him, feeling for a pulse.

Basil's glasses were gone, and so was his bag.

"Goddess." Laurence looked around, but he couldn't make out either. "Basil, you gotta get up, man."

There was a pulse beneath Laurence's fingers, so he heaved Basil up and over his shoulder. Basil's weight landed across the backpack, which tugged harder on the straps over Laurence's shoulders, but this wasn't the time or the place to try and wake Basil up.

If Laurence couldn't find Basil's bag, Basil would be powerless.

If he didn't find Quentin fast, Quentin would be dead.

Laurence gritted his teeth in frustration and sped toward the outer edges of the fight, arms clamped around Basil's legs to keep him from falling. Once he found a wall, he was able to follow it toward the main building without getting kicked or torn apart.

He exhaled slowly and looked toward the battle.

It was among the most dreadful sights he'd ever witnessed. Monsters fought against the dead, horses kicked and screamed, and while there wasn't a single speck of blood, the sounds of pain made it horrible enough already.

Laurence had made this happen. He'd brought a war to the Four-Peaked Fortress just to satisfy his own goals.

With a shake of his head, he dismissed that thought. He had to get to Quentin, so he sprinted toward the drawbridge that spanned the eerily-deep moat.

A tall, pale figure with dark hair emerged from the fight, and for brief second Laurence held his breath. But it was Jon, not Quentin. Jon, who had switched off being alive for now and looked like he'd received the injuries that proved it had been the right choice.

"Jon!" Laurence ran toward him.

Jon turned to face them, his skin white as a sheet and his eyes almost wholly black. He nodded, then looked out toward the fight himself.

Laurence caught up, panting for breath. A backpack of supplies and the dead weight of a small necromancer added up pretty fast. "I didn't see his bag," he said.

"I'll go back in," Jon said. "Take him to safety."

Laurence nodded. "Are you sure?"

Jon shrugged at him. "They cannot harm me, and any who try are destroyed instantly. It is the safest option. Go inside."

"I'm not gonna argue. Good luck."

Jon gave him a look that made it very clear that he didn't believe luck existed, and simply walked back into the melee.

Laurence backed toward the drawbridge, then turned so he could run across it.

Beyond the open gates stood two rows of guards. Most were little more than skeletal remains, but some still had meat on them. All wore a variety of armors, from padded jackets to chain mail.

Each and every one held a sword, which was pointed toward Laurence.

"Halt, Hunter," they said in unison.

There weren't enough of them to prevent either Wild Hunt from entering the building, but there were enough to put plenty of holes in Laurence and Basil.

"I hunt Gwyn ap Nudd." Laurence slowed and held his head high. "I cannot be stopped."

"He's not here," said one of the guards.

"We are already free," said another.

"We protect our liege," said the third.

"To some extent," added a fourth.

Laurence grit his teeth. He wasn't in the mood for games, and he wasn't going to let a bunch of guards who didn't even seem to know whether or not they had a job to do get in his way.

He took a breath and latched on to Quentin's scent.

It led past the guards and into the fortress.

"If Gwyn ap Nudd isn't here, who is your liege?" Laurence finally stopped walking.

"The Warrior," said a skeleton near the back. "His name is Quentin."

Laurence felt his mouth hang open, and he shook his head. Quentin hadn't seriously walked right into Gwyn's own castle and stolen his fucking throne, had he? Though now that he considered it, Laurence could picture it with such ease that it was probably exactly what had happened.

Basil groaned and began to twitch. There weren't any words, and he wasn't fighting against Laurence's hold on him, but Laurence didn't want either to become a problem, so he put Basil down on his feet and coiled an arm around his waist to hold him up. He dragged Basil's arm across his own shoulders to distribute the weight.

Basil sucked in air and slowly lifted his head, eyes squinting. There was one hell of a road rash across one cheek. "Whugunun?"

"You got thrown from your horse," Laurence muttered. "You think you can stand?"

"Nnnhhh."

The guards shifted their stances slowly to make sure their swords pointed toward both Laurence and Basil.

"Swords?" Basil rubbed his eyes.

"Yeah. But they're calling Quentin their liege." Laurence eyed the guards, and spoke more loudly. "Take us to Quentin. We demand a, uh... meeting."

"Aud'nce," Basil mumbled.

"Audience," Laurence clarified.

The guards shifted their positions again, then lowered swords and stepped aside.

"Come," said one. "Follow me."

Laurence eyed the blades as he practically carried Basil past the defensive line, and he didn't let himself take another breath until they were safely inside.

The only question now was that if Gwyn ap Nudd wasn't here yet, where was he?

33

QUENTIN

THE CREATURE RAN TOWARD HIM AS FAST AS HE HIMSELF HAD flown here, and Quentin did what he could to waylay it, but it was like trying to stop water with a sieve. He could dart aside, run around the room, even dash outside again, but this monster was able to evade him, and he could not evade it.

Not forever.

If he managed to lure it into the courtyard, he might be able to lose it among the Wild Hunt, but there was the risk that they would kill him the moment they saw him. But if he headed to the very top of the keep, he might be able to make his escape without any of the Hunt spotting him right away.

Where the hell was Eric?

Quentin couldn't wait any longer. He pursed his lips and made a break for the hall's entrance.

The monster pivoted and mutated as it flung tendrils toward him. Chitinous arms gave way to rope-like limbs, each tipped with those razor-sharp edges.

Bone sliced through his coat and snagged him off his feet, and he yelped in surprise as the creature hauled him backward through the air.

More arms coiled around him, like vines from an overgrown plant, and

Jack laughed and peeled himself away from the wreck of the greenhouse. He plucked glass from himself and tossed it into the wind. "You're not half as scary as you think you are, you sanctimonious little prick. Not when I know exactly how to beat you."

he gasped in shock and tried to remember where he was.

This was not Jack.

They were not in San Diego.

The vines dragged him closer as more curled around his body

"Quen!" Laurence's voice was a gasp. "Stay with me!"

and he blinked rapidly, focusing on the monster.

It was inches from his face now. Had he lost time, or was the monster that much faster than he had realized?

But they were in physical contact, and that meant he could affect it.

He seized it, and it slipped his grasp. It blinked out for a second, and when it blipped back into physical form it was a fraction of an inch out of place. Bones sliced his skin, and in that instant he wasn't sure who yelled the loudest. He cried out in pain, but so did the creature, and it recoiled from him, unable to pull away. It thrashed like a cat with its claws stuck in carpet.

"Release me," it sobbed. "I beg you, Warrior. I yield. I yield!"

Quentin shook his head numbly and tried to push the creature away, but its bones were still trapped within his coat. He reached for one and tried to pry it free, careful not to touch the sharp edge.

Tendrils of shadow had bled through the gash in his coat, and were wrapped around the bone, holding it fast.

They came from his armor, and the more he looked at it, the darker it got.

"Oh my god," he breathed. "I'm so sorry! I don't know how to make it let go of you!" He ran his fingers over the tiny threads to feel his way around them. If he could find some weak points, maybe he could tear them off.

They recoiled from his touch and bled back inside his coat. The bone slid free.

"All right. Shh. I think I've got it. Try to hold still." Quentin ran his fingers across more of the pieces of bone that were wedged into his armor, and one by one they leaped away the moment they could, whipping away from him as though burned.

The last broke loose, and Quentin pinched his nose briefly. If he approached the creature, it might well shy away from him, so he resisted the urge. Instead, he stepped around it, walking a wide circle until he reached the throne.

He turned his back on the seat and slid up into it, eyes on the creature.

"Are you all right?" he said softly.

His skin twitched as trickles of blood from his wounds spread across it, trapped beneath his shirt and aided by sweat. He shifted in his seat and grimaced, but did his best to ignore the sensation.

The creature undulated. The multitudinous limbs withdrew into its body. Instead of chitin or hide, the mass grew skin. Grimy, white skin without a scrap of clothing, half unseen beneath the overgrown and tangled hair.

"I think," the creature — the *man* — rasped, "I might be." Hair parted just enough for one blue eye to peek out at Quentin, and he fell to one knee, bowing his head, which had the blessed side effect of obscuring the parts of other peoples' bodies that Quentin preferred not to see. "My liege," he gasped.

Quentin tilted his head slightly. The sight of someone bowing to him snagged his attention, but before he could work out why, there was movement at the door. Quentin snapped his head up and refocused his attention.

Eric sneaked slowly into the room, but paused once he was inside. "Whoa. I thought you might, like, need some help. But, uh."

He gestured to the man who was kneeling between them. "You look like you've got this covered."

"Apparently," Quentin mused. He plucked at his coat and drew it aside to show Eric the tabard. "This actually *is* armor after all."

Eric eyed it, then hurried across the hall toward Quentin. "Yeah. What's the plan?" He waved a hand toward Quentin. "Great as you look sitting on a throne and wearing a torc, there's gotta be more to it than that."

Quentin shrugged. Now that the stress and adrenaline was leaving him, he felt quite comfortable up here. He couldn't really justify leaving this poor fellow on his knee for so long, though. "You may rise."

"Thank you, my liege."

Quentin turned his attention to Eric so that he didn't see anything he shouldn't, and lifted his eyebrows in surprise. Eric had closed the distance fast, and was beside him on the dais now. He really did move quickly for a man of his size.

"C'mon," Eric said, offering his hand. "We can't stay here."

"Why not?" Quentin smiled faintly. "The guards are passing the message along. If anyone wishes to challenge me for the throne, they must come here to do it. And now that we know I can hold it, it is best to remain exactly where we said that I would be."

Eric switched his gesture to patting Quentin's arm instead, and he nodded. "Okay. Or," he added, and gripped Quentin's wrist, "you step down and give me back my throne, and I let you live."

Quentin's eyes widened as Eric's grip grew uncomfortably tight. "What?"

Eric leaned in, and those eyes, which were so like Laurence's, were alight with malice. "So you are the Warrior that Arawn thought could kill me," he snarled. "Pathetic. You think yourself a king? You believe that a gambeson of nightmares is enough to save you?"

Quentin shook his head in confusion and reached out with everything he had to try and push Eric away.

There was heat within that tall, large frame.

Eric was alive, but he most certainly had not been earlier.

"Gwyn ap Nudd," Quentin realized.

Sodding hell. This was *not* how this was meant to go at all, and now Quentin had been snared by a bloody fairy king in his own castle, sitting on his own throne.

Eric's form shifted and grew. His face blackened as though it had been burned to ashes, and antlers sprouted from his head. Holly leaves bristled from platinum hair that fell in waves around a void-black face and pointed ears. There was a neat, red gash across Gwyn's throat, but no blood came from it.

Silver plate emerged from nowhere. A thick green cloak spawned at his shoulders and unfurled as it fell to his heels.

Gwyn was easily twice Quentin's size, and the antlers made him seem all the larger.

"You are one of the Old Ones," Gwyn snorted in his face, his breath dry and without odor, "but that does not give you the power you would need to defeat me. Your journey ends here."

Quentin gritted his teeth and met Gwyn's eye. "I can always get more power if need be."

There had been nothing alive enough in Annwn to sustain him, right up until the moment Gwyn had grabbed him by the wrist and pinned him to the throne, so Quentin reached for that warmth and pulled on it with as much haste as possible.

Gwyn howled in rage and wrenched Quentin to his feet, reaching for Quentin's throat, but Quentin batted his hand away with a thought and reached for Gwyn's arm instead. If he could grab it, and if a fairy had the same muscles as a human, then he should be able to break Gwyn's hold on him, and they would be on much more equal footing.

Gwyn yanked on Quentin's arm and smashed his head into

the side of the throne, then bore him to the ground and straddled his prone body.

Quentin reeled from the blow, and his headache flooded back with a vengeance. Blood flowed from his nose. The weight that pressed down on him was immense, and he struggled just to breathe. His shoulder and arm burned with pain when Gwyn twisted them up behind his back, and he groaned against the floor.

"Your mistake, Warrior," Gwyn snarled against his ear, "was in allowing me to see you. There is darkness in your heart, and that makes you mine."

He could just about ascertain which way was up, and he managed to reach out telekinetically, feeling for and then grasping Gwyn, ready to throw the fairy king off him and suffer the consequences to his trapped arm.

Pain seared along his nerves. It radiated out from his heart in ice-cold glaciers that sliced him apart and left him screaming with what little air he had. The darkness around him turned black, and then to nothing at all, and his screams fell into the void with nobody to hear them.

Fury bubbled and seethed its way to the surface. Red hot, like lava, it chased the glaciers and devoured all in its path. It burned his kindness to a crisp and incinerated his compassion as it flowed inexorably toward his love.

"Your darkness will consume you." Gwyn's voice rattled around inside his head. It seemed to bypass his ears altogether. "And then you will be every bit the monster you were born to be!"

Quentin's shrieks became howls of rage, and still they weren't enough to drown out Gwyn's laughter.

LAURENCE

Laurence was barely past the line of guards when he heard the terrible sound that echoed along corridors like it had some-place better to go than where it had come from. He heard laughter — cruel, vicious — dancing with howls, which he imme-diately knew to be Quentin's despite never having heard him make such a noise before.

Quentin was in trouble.

Laurence hissed in anger and dragged Basil to a wall, then lowered him to the ground, careful not to bang Basil's head against anything on the way down. "I gotta go," he breathed. "Stay here. Jon's coming, okay?"

Basil sagged against the wall. His eyes rolled toward the noises, and he winced. "I think I lost my glasses."

"You did. And the book. Jon's gone to find them. You just have to wait here." He squeezed Basil's shoulder, then burst into a sprint to track the bright trail of Quentin's scent.

The room he ran into was an assault on the senses, despite having only the weakest of light trickle in through tiny windows high overhead. There were bold colors hanging from embroidery on the walls. Some naked white guy, who looked like he'd been growing his hair out for the past hundred years, prostrated on the floor, giving Laurence the kind of view he used to only get after a night on the town.

And a giant with holly-covered antlers laughing manically as he held Quentin facedown against the floor next to a black throne.

Laurence skidded to a halt by the stranger's side. He couldn't see Quentin's face, but he could see Gwyn ap Nudd's, pitch-black features alight with his laughter.

"Gwyn!" Laurence held his hands up to show that he was unarmed. "Let him go!"

Gwyn's laughter faded. He turned his massive head to face Laurence, and his eyes were as black as night. There was a gash across his throat from Arawn's sword, though it seemed nowhere near as bad as it had when Arawn made it.

"Bambi Laurence Riley," Gwyn said. Although his voice matched Ryan's, the accent had shifted to British. "You made it."

"Let him go," Laurence snapped.

Gwyn tipped his head forward. A cascade of white-blond hair spilled over one shoulder and draped across Quentin's head, and then Gwyn released Quentin and rose to his feet. "Take him," Gwyn said as he stepped back. "If that is what you want."

Quentin's howling died down into a sob, and then to labored breathing. The arm that had been twisted up behind his back still lay there, like it had been abandoned.

Laurence licked his lips and assessed the scene. If he approached, he'd be within Gwyn's reach. There was no sign of that flame-doused sword, but Laurence knew Gwyn could pull it out of his ass if need be, which meant Gwyn was armed while Laurence had nothing.

Not that Laurence had any idea what to do with a damn sword even if he'd had one.

He took cautious steps toward the dais Quentin and Gwyn

were on. It was only a few inches high, easy enough to hop up onto, and he kept the throne between them as he did so.

Gwyn eyed him, smiling with malice, his teeth and armor glinting in the faint light.

"Where is my father?" Laurence snarled.

"Restrained in the treasury," Gwyn said. "But you are here for your lover, aren't you? So take him." Gwyn leaned against the throne and sneered. "I dare you."

Laurence licked his lips. "You said that you would do no harm to me, that you would protect me. You owed me that."

Gwyn's grin was fixed in place. Immobile.

Laurence took a deep breath and then stepped around the throne, eyes on Gwyn until he reached Quentin.

Gwyn leaned in and ran a thick finger down the side of Laurence's neck. "That was a debt I owed to your father," he whispered.

"But one you transferred to me," Laurence snarled, doing his best to keep a lid on the fear that threatened to make him piss himself.

Gwyn's eyes fixed on his for a moment, and then Gwyn turned away and stepped off the dais. "Rise, Iolo ap Huw," Gwyn snarled to the figure still bowed against the floor.

Iolo's frame shook as he stood, and his head remained low.

"With me."

Gwyn swept from the hall, his cloak billowing behind him, and Iolo ap Huw ran at his heel to keep up.

Laurence listened until their footsteps were gone, hoping that Jon had already moved Basil to safety, but the moment there was silence he turned his attention to Quentin.

"Quen?" He eyed all the tears in Quentin's coat. Neat, like he'd been in a swordfight and taken a few blows. Laurence smelled blood, too, though didn't see any. "Baby? Are you with me?"

Quentin groaned again, which meant he hadn't noped out of whatever Gwyn was doing to him, so Laurence reached for the arm which still lay at an awkward angle across the small of Quentin's back and tried to move it carefully and make sure it wasn't broken.

After flexing his fingers, Quentin moved the arm himself, and it flopped against the ground; then he twisted his legs and rolled onto his side. His face was contorted with a snarl, blood trickling from his nose, and he eyed Laurence.

"About bloody time you got here," he snapped. He wiped at the blood with the back of his hand.

Laurence swallowed. They weren't a great many words, but they stung, and he sat back on his heels. "I'm sorry, baby," he whispered. "We need to get out of here."

Quentin sat up. There was a golden torc around his neck, and some kind of shirt beneath his coat that looked like it was made of oil. "In a minute," he said as he grabbed one of the straps to Laurence's backpack and used it to jerk Laurence toward him for a rough, demanding kiss.

Laurence whimpered and clutched Quentin's shoulders, but there was nothing sensual to their contact. He felt the vacuum inside Quentin as it reached out and snared his life force, then dragged it out of him so hard that it hurt. He cried out in pain, but his cry was muffled by Quentin's mouth.

Quentin raised his other hand to Laurence's throat and gripped it, squeezing as he continued to drain the life from Laurence's body.

Laurence sagged against him, his head spinning as he tried to come up with a reason for keeping his clothes on. He tried to make eye contact, to beg Quentin to fuck him without any power to say the words, and his whole body tinged with need, with arousal. He whimpered again.

"Let go of him." A deep voice, sounding almost bored, reverberated around the hall.

Quentin bit Laurence's lip with a scowl, his pale eyes

narrowed with lust or anger, Laurence couldn't tell. But he broke contact and looked toward the newcomer.

The drain on Laurence's energy stopped.

Laurence's chest heaved as he gasped for air, and he clung to Quentin as though just hanging on tight enough could save him from drowning.

"You must be Quentin," the voice intoned. "We did not come all this way for you to kill Laurence. Let him go."

Jon. It had to be Jon. Laurence had trouble tearing his gaze off Quentin, but when he finally managed it, he could only turn his head slightly toward Jon. It was enough for him to see that Basil was with him, leaning against Jon for support, bag across his chest but still without his glasses.

Quentin pushed Laurence aside, and Laurence landed hard on his ass. He winced and rolled onto all fours so that he could lift himself off the ground, and staggered to his feet, arms out for balance.

Jon eyed him blankly, then looked back to Quentin.

"I do," Quentin growled softly, "whatever I wish with him, and it is none of your business."

Laurence's gut tightened. He didn't know whether to be horny or not, and his instincts were screaming at him that horny would be a bad idea right now.

There was something deeply wrong.

He took a deep breath, but the scent was correct. The trail led right to Quentin and clung to him like perfume, yet the behavior was like nothing Laurence had seen in him. It was more like Freddy, or even the duke.

Laurence raised his hands. He didn't like the feeling of walking on eggshells. He'd had enough of that shit from Dan. "My dad's in the treasury," he said, hoping to derail whatever this was before Quentin attacked Jon. "Do you know where that is, baby?"

Quentin turned his cold stare on Laurence. "Eric was supposed to back me up," he sneered.

Laurence's heart skipped at hearing his dad's name spoken out loud. "I don't think he could. Gwyn said he's restrained."

Quentin curled his lip, but his gaze flickered. "He must have trapped Eric there so that he could disguise himself without incident." A flash of his teeth, and then Quentin wreathed his hands in fire. "You release Eric, I will destroy Gwyn."

Laurence yelped and hopped back as flames flared in the darkness. "You can't. Goddess, Quen, what did he do to you?"

"I can," Quentin spat.

"No," Jon sighed. "You can't. Only cold iron can kill him, and you don't have any."

Laurence turned away so he could adjust his pants; then he frowned at Quentin and hopped off the dais. "Can you put the fire out, baby? Please? You know I don't like it."

He thought he'd already endured the most horrible feelings possible in his life. He'd exchanged sex for heroin. He'd watched the duke abuse his own son. He'd seen his father die, then fought a whole year to get Dad to change his ways and prevent that future from taking place, and failed.

Nothing cut as deeply as his sense of betrayal when Quentin ignored his request and stalked toward the exit.

Tears pricked his eyes, and Laurence felt lost, floundering in a strange land with the sickening feeling that the man he loved was no longer in love with him, or even the same man that he'd been when they'd landed in New York just two days ago. The future they had together was in tatters, shredded by whatever Gwyn had done.

Laurence had gotten here too late to save Quentin, and the worst part was that Quentin hadn't even been killed.

Not on the outside.

He rubbed his face and hurried after Quentin, ignoring Jon's and Basil's eyes on him as he passed them. He could feel their judgement without looking for it, and knew damn well what they had to be thinking.

We came all this way for him?

Are you crazy?

No. Gwyn had done something, and once they destroyed Gwyn, they could undo whatever it was, and Laurence could have his Quentin back again. Kind, compassionate Quentin who cared about him and wouldn't ever look at him the way this Quentin did, wouldn't treat Laurence's fear of fire like it was inconsequential.

Laurence bared his teeth and clung to the hope that they could figure it out. He'd spent nearly an entire year working his ass off to earn Quentin's trust, and he wasn't going to throw it all away for some Tylwyth Teg who pretended to a throne in a realm that didn't belong to him.

He could deal with this, because this wasn't Quentin. Not really. In body, but not in heart or soul. They'd kill Gwyn, Arawn would return, and then Laurence could find a spell to fix everything.

He broke into a run to catch up, grateful to have a plan in place. All he had to do was make sure Quentin didn't kill him before he could put it into action.

35

—

QUENTIN

THERE WAS NOTHING INTRIGUING ABOUT THIS EXPERIENCE. Nothing worth holding on to. Everything irritated him, from the look on the face of the short copper-haired man Quentin sailed past to the voice of the other one, the one who had *dared* issue an order to him.

They were both extraordinarily fortunate that Quentin had decided against retaliation. For now, at least. The way the little one squinted at him as he passed was another log on the inferno of his anger, and Quentin came close to just smacking him and having done with it.

Put the fire out.

He curled his lip at the tiny voice that urged him to do something which went against his wishes.

Laurence is terrified of fire. Put it out!

He snarled at himself. Who gave two damn hoots what Laurence was afraid of? Quentin would show him what fear truly was.

But first he would show Eric, for leaving Quentin to face Gwyn alone.

He walked briskly along the corridor toward the nearest

turret, only to see a dozen or more guards jog toward him, their weapons readied. It took him barely a second to piece together what must have happened.

They knew Gwyn was back, and that meant they were no longer on Quentin's side.

Well, that was their mistake.

"Halt!" One of them called out.

Quentin cut loose without so much as a warning. They didn't deserve one. He blasted fire along the length of the corridor, filling it from floor to ceiling and charring everything in his path.

"Holy shit!" squeaked the shorter of the two strangers.

Quentin glanced over his shoulder and eyed the trio at his back. "Who are they?"

Laurence had a trickle of sweat down one cheek. Or it was a tear? "This is Basil," he said in a shaking voice. "And Jon."

"Why are they here?"

"Apparently, I am a Child of Arawn," Jon intoned. "Basil is a necromancer."

Quentin cancelled the fire and turned to face Basil, eyeing him with suspicion. "You use magic?"

Laurence darted between them, his hands up in surrender. "Baby, we couldn't have gotten here without him. Don't hurt him, please?"

He stared at Laurence. "Do we need him to get home again?"

"Yes," Laurence said quickly.

Quentin rocked his jaw and turned back to the guards. The necromancer could live for now, he supposed.

The guards, burned and blackened, were still on their feet, so he threw them all down the corridor into a pile, then breezed on toward the doorway.

The rest would have to hurry if they wanted to keep up.

HE TOOK the stairs two at a time, jogging down with hardly any effort. While he still felt a little thirsty, his hunger and headache were distant memories. Now he was nothing more than a shell filled with unbridled wrath, ready to burn whatever so much as sneezed in his direction.

He jumped over the trashed remains of the door that he had used to block the stairs, and through the killing zone, past the remains of the second ruined door and into the treasury itself, where he pulled forth another fistful of flame to cast light on the proceedings.

Eric was in the middle of the room, bound with silvery rope that wrapped around his ankles and wrists, tethering them together behind his back. Quentin ground his teeth at the sight.

Perhaps Eric had had a reasonable rationale for not being there when Quentin needed him.

Quentin huffed and gestured toward Eric, willing to not incinerate him for the time being. Any more slip-ups, though, and he would change his mind.

"Dad?" Laurence ran past Quentin and collapsed to his knees, working feverishly at the rope.

Now Quentin was certain that Laurence was crying.

Help them!

He curled his lip and turned his back on Laurence, instead eyeing Jon. "You have cold iron."

It was a logical extrapolation. If Laurence required Basil to get them into Annwn, and Gwyn could not be killed without cold iron, then one of them had brought some along. It was plausible that Laurence carried in that backpack he wore, but as Jon had been the one to raise the issue, it was more likely that he was also the one who carried it.

Jon's face was expressionless, but Quentin didn't need him to react to know that his deduction was correct. Where Jon was carved from stone, Basil was malleable and eminently readable, and his wide-eyed gasp told him everything.

"Give it to me."

"Don't," Basil breathed.

Quentin plucked them apart. It was easier than lifting kittens away from their mother, and he didn't have to raise a finger to do so. Basil squealed, so Quentin settled a coil of telekinesis around his neck and began to squeeze while he made eye contact with Jon.

Jon blinked slowly while Basil struggled to breathe.

"It is in my pocket," Jon intoned. "I need to move my left arm to get it for you."

Quentin shrugged and released the arm in question, and Jon dug a foot-long piece of metal from his pocket, which Quentin wrenched from his grip. He dropped the Americans to the floor and made his way out without looking back.

He had what he needed to kill Gwyn. After that, he would have no need for the necromancer. Arawn would swap places and send Quentin back home. From there, Quentin knew exactly what to do to make this rage go away.

He would seek out his father and take the vengeance he had idiotically refused to enact when he had the opportunity.

Satisfied with his plan, he sprinted up the stairs and left everyone else behind.

He continued past the ground floor, running up the stairs without any fatigue whatsoever. He must have taken more than enough from Laurence to make up for his earlier lack of stamina.

Laurence.

Bloody hell, he'd been about ready to fuck him right there on the dais. If Laurence had survived the drain on his life, of course. As much as Laurence maintained that Quentin was welcome to take as much as he needed at any time, surely it was a finite resource? It took time to replenish, which meant that Quentin had drained him more quickly than Laurence could refuel himself, which suggested that it was entirely possible to kill him if Quentin was careless.

Did it matter, so long as Quentin got what he needed?

Of course it matters!

He gritted his teeth. "Shut up!"

You need to regain control!

Quentin just laughed. If he was out of control, he wouldn't be able to use any of his gifts. It was self-evident that he had all the control required, and then some.

The torc weighed heavily around his neck, and he slowed his ascent as a thought came to him.

Did he truly want to go home?

If he stayed here, he could remain on the throne. Command an army. He would be a king in his own right, not merely hold an inherited dukedom. He would rule over hundreds of people, and each one of them would have no choice but to obey him. Better still, Arawn clearly had no intention of killing his own enemies, and Quentin could mount a surprise attack and destroy Arawn to claim all of Annwn as his own, rather than sit around and wait for Arawn to send a patsy to do his dirty work for him.

He stopped by a doorway, emerged into a corridor, and found a window to look down at the courtyard from.

It was chaos. A battle raged, monsters against corpses, horses fighting demons, and dogs savagely biting anything that they could get their teeth into. The Wild Hunt that had chased him was locked in combat with what looked like Arawn's people.

But where was Gwyn?

He seethed in irritation and began to pace up and down the corridor, glancing down to the courtyard every few seconds while he tried to work out whether he had some way of enticing Gwyn back into another confrontation. He even patted down his pockets, in case there was anything he could use that he'd forgotten he owned.

Phone. Wallet. Iron bar.

Book.

He frowned and reached into his inner breast pocket to withdraw the leather-bound journal, still wrapped in the store's bag. Bone had sliced one edge of the bag and through the gift wrap, leaving a scored line across the leather itself, and he snarled.

All the time he had spent ensuring that he found a journal with no flaws, wasted.

"I expected better."

Quentin froze. The dread which clawed at his insides was made of ice and tore through him like a tornado. It pulped his muscles and ruined all self-control.

The book fell from his hands, clattering as it hit the stone floor. The iron rod fell a second later.

"Stand up straight," the duke barked.

Quentin jerked upright. His thighs burned with the effort.

Christ, he felt ten years old all over again.

He had to be asleep. He had to be imagining this. Hallucinating. He'd finally snapped. Being clinically insane would be better than the alternative.

Father couldn't be here!

It couldn't be over.

"You have duties, Quentin." The duke's gaze never wavered. There wasn't an ounce of respite on offer. "You will return to them."

"No." It came out of him like the last gasp of a dying man.

The duke snorted. "You are a not a child any longer. You will cease to behave as one. Come home, Quentin. I shall not repeat myself."

His legs buckled and he fell to his knees. Pain shot up his legs as kneecaps met stone. He dropped forward, hands out to catch himself, then scrabbled for the book. He didn't know whether to hold it or throw it away, and once his fingers landed on it he remained frozen with indecision.

He'd bought it for Laurence.

But Laurence didn't matter.

Except Laurence was *everything*.

No! He is nothing! A commoner! You owe him nothing! He's only interested in your money, your status!

Your body!

He's a disgusting, filthy wretch, and he's using you!

Quentin gritted his teeth and dragged the book closer.

There was something he had to say. Words that meant something, if only he could get them out. There was something beneath the hatred and wrath that boiled in his veins, and it refused to shut up, let alone die.

His armor rippled like a wave of tar.

The more his fury spewed bile to defile Laurence's memory, the more those words screamed to be heard.

To be spoken.

To stand against the storm and draw a line in the sand.

He clutched the book to his chest and sat on the floor with his back to the wall. Uneven stone pressed against him, making his wounds itch, and he sucked in a breath as he fought against the fury.

"I love him," he whimpered.

The words fell out of him, weak. Insipid. Rage tried to swallow them, and he screwed his eyes shut and banged his head back against the wall a few times, as though he could smack the anger out of himself.

Like it could ever be that easy.

"I *love* him," he snarled.

The anger that surged forth seemed to be behind his words this time, as though he had reclaimed a scrap of it for himself and turned it toward the unfettered violence in his head.

"Your darkness will consume you. And then you will be every bit the monster you were born to be!"

He gasped in horror as Gwyn's words came back to him.

Gwyn had done this. He'd set loose Quentin's anger, the constant companion he kept under lock and key. Quentin didn't know how, but he also didn't think it mattered. Fairies were completely alien creatures, with powers and whims beyond mortal comprehension, and Quentin wasn't about to waste the time trying to figure it out.

Gwyn had messed with Quentin's self-control, and seemed to think that would make Quentin follow him, and maybe it would have worked if Laurence hadn't interrupted the process. Who knew what just a few seconds more would have achieved? Even now, Quentin couldn't compare the feelings he had for Laurence to those he had held in the real world. He'd used the word love because it had power, but that power was slow to respond, and Quentin needed it right now.

He was a danger to the only man he loved. Out of control, running on all the wrong emotions, the best he could do was stay right here and pray that Laurence found a way to fix everything.

He curled his arms around the book and blinked away tears, then began to sob quietly.

36

LAURENCE

Laurence stared at the body in the room.

Everything he thought he knew about life and death was wrong, because he'd been so damn sure he'd never see his dad again, and yet here he was. Right here, right now, tied up like a Thanksgiving turkey in the middle of a room that was full of gold and jewels.

"Dad?"

Tears flowed freely as he met his father's eyes. Laurence hiccuped and ran over. He fell to his knees as he scrabbled to find an end to the silvery rope that bound and gagged Eric. He heard Quentin start to interrogate Jon, but it was hard to listen in when his own sobbing got in the way.

Right now, he couldn't take his eyes off his father, and the feeling looked like it was mutual.

"Shit," he muttered under his breath.

Where the fuck was the end?

He hissed as he finally spotted it, wedged between Dad's ankles, and he dug for it with fingers and teeth alike until he worked it loose. After that, it was way easier to start unthreading all the knots, one by one, even if it was pretty painstaking. His fingers slipped now and then on his own fallen tears, and he paused to wipe his nose on his sleeve.

The more that he unraveled, the easier it got to loosen the rest. He let the rope fall when he freed Dad's mouth, and Eric grabbed him in a bear hug and held him tight.

"Cricket," Eric sighed. "Oh, man, it's good to see you."

"Dad!" Laurence hiccuped again. His chest ached, and he grabbed hold of his dad in case this was some kind of fucked-up dream. "Goddess, you're... you're really here!"

"Yeah. Yeah, I am. But so is Gwyn ap Nudd." Eric patted Laurence's hair with one hand and cradled him against Eric's chest with the other. "Cricket, you can't beat him. You need cold iron."

"We have some," Laurence cut in.

Jon cleared his throat.

"Actually, we don't," Basil said.

Laurence hesitated, then turned to look toward them.

Quentin was nowhere to be found.

Basil rubbed at his own throat, and Jon was midway through standing up.

They were several feet away from each other.

Laurence released his dad with one hand and rubbed at his eyes. "What happened?"

Basil flapped his hands. Even more of his nail polish had been lost, so there were just patches of orange left now. "Quentin. He, like, fucking force-choked me and made Jon hand it over, then he went that way." He waved back toward the stairs. "I don't wanna be that guy, Laurence, but your boyfriend is a psycho."

"No, he isn't," Laurence said at the same time as Eric.

"I've just spent a whole lot of time with Quentin," Eric explained as Laurence stared at him, "and he's a good man. A man I felt confident about having in my son's life. Gwyn got to him, didn't he?"

Laurence nodded numbly. "Yeah. I don't know what he was doing, but Quentin was yelling like someone just killed his dogs."

"I heard." Eric loosened his hold on Laurence, but didn't let go. "Gwyn draws darkness out of people, puts it in the driver's seat. It's how his people look the way they do. When you come to Annwn, you're supposed to use your time here to make peace with the life you lived, so you can move on to the next one, but there's no peace in Gwyn's ranks. He rules by fear and hatred, and none of his dead can go forward."

Laurence hissed and stood up, offering a hand to his dad to help him up. "Quen's got... some unresolved issues," he breathed. No way was he going to tell everyone more than that. He hadn't the right.

"I know. And those issues are in charge now." Eric patted himself down, then rose to his full height.

Laurence suddenly remembered what it used to be like not being the tallest member of his family.

"Hey," Eric added as he put a hand on Laurence's shoulder and grinned. "Wanna hear a joke?"

"No." Laurence frowned up at him.

"Okay." Eric's grin faded to a smile, then he nodded. "Then hear some truth instead. Whatever Quentin's done since Gwyn touched him, that isn't the man you know. He loves you, and while I wouldn't for one minute suggest you ever love a man like *that*—" he pointed toward the stairs "—I was happy to hear you'd found love with the man he was when I met him. Let's go get him back, yeah?"

Laurence sniffed and rubbed his nose again, and then he nodded. "Yeah."

"Right on," Eric agreed.

———

THEY MADE it halfway to the stairs when the sound of footsteps reached Laurence, and he stopped and put a hand across Basil's chest at the same time Eric did the exact same thing to Jon.

It was a bit uncanny, if Laurence was being honest with himself. Did Dad have more than just magic at his disposal? Did he have the acute senses, too?

"What is it?" Basil breathed.

"Guards," Eric said.

Laurence nodded in agreement. There were way too many footsteps for it to be Quentin. "Shit. Is there another way out?"

"Doubt it." Eric shook his head. "The whole point of hoarding your treasure underground is to make it harder to steal."

Laurence looked around quickly and spied a door. "Where does that go?"

"I suggest we find out!" Basil sprinted towards it.

"No need." Jon shrugged as the guards poured out of the staircase and into the room. The life cut out of him, and he turned to face them.

Eric blinked. "What just happened?"

Laurence huffed. "He's a Child of Arawn," he breathed. "He can, like... I dunno. Kill himself at will, kinda. Except when he's like this, he'll kill whatever he touches, too."

"Bro," Eric called out. "They're already dead."

Jon nodded, then stepped toward a guard and let it run him through so that he could touch its chest lightly.

The guard made a rattling sound for all of two seconds, then faded out of existence.

"Oh my fucking god!" Basil backed up against the door. "What did you do?"

Jon drew the sword out of himself and waded through the guards.

Two more disappeared.

Eric narrowed his eyes. "Are they, like, *gone* gone, or do they come back?"

"I do not know," Jon said, as he dispatched a fourth.

"'Cause if you're, like, ending them, and they're Gwyn's guards, you're basically tossing them out of Annwn to go be reborn," Eric added.

Jon glanced over, his black eyes unreadable.

"Before they're ready," Eric said. "Like, all the emotions in control of them at the moment, they aren't getting purged or dealt with. They're gonna be reborn into the mortal world with all that fear or anger or whatever, and they're never gonna know where it came from, and they're just gonna inflict it on everyone around them for, like, their entire lives. What I'm sayin', dude, is you gotta stop doing whatever that is. Like, right now."

Jon frowned, and while he did, two more guards stuck swords into him.

"Then what do you propose?" he said, as though he hadn't even noticed.

"Wait. Wait! Are they ghosts?" Basil unfastened the buckles on his bag and drew his book out. The blue glow seemed all the stronger for the lack of light down here. "I mean, forgive me for saying so, but you all seem more, um, fleshed out than ghosts?"

"Naw. We're souls," Eric said.

"Right. Okay." Basil began to hunt through the pages. "Actual dead people, not echoes," he muttered.

Laurence winced as another guard disappeared. Jon hadn't done a damn thing, but the guard had gone for a punch now that his sword was embedded in Jon's body, and that had been enough.

"We can't wait around doing nothing," he muttered. "Jon, come over here. Get those damn swords out and hand me one."

"You know how to use a sword?" Eric blinked.

"No clue, but that didn't stop me from stabbing the shit out of a couple of people who really pissed me off." Laurence scooped a sword off the floor after Jon slid one toward him hilt-first. "Mom says trust my instincts, and my instincts say grab a sword."

He stepped forward, swapping places with Jon just as he felt Jon flicker back to life.

"Well, I guess if Myriam says to do it, who are we to argue?" Eric stepped in and picked up another fallen sword. "I never got anywhere in life without her by my side, so I'm not gonna start ignoring her counsel now."

Laurence weighed the sword in his palm and grinned, and with his father next to him, he waded into the fray.

<hr>

SWORD FIGHTING without any training whatsoever was, Laurence wasn't surprised to discover, really fucking hard. He had to rely on his keen senses and quick wits to evade incoming blows, and whenever he used his own sword to parry, the shock ran down his blade and through his arm, and it damn well hurt.

His dad was doing the same, and they both darted around, engaging the guards and doing their best to keep them away from Basil while Basil searched through his book, though if Basil could find some way of going faster, Laurence's arm would super appreciate it.

Goddess, he was tired.

He still had the backpack on, but it wasn't that. It was the way Quentin had drained him and left him reeling in the aftermath. His strength was coming back, but not as fast as he'd like given the circumstances.

"Any time you're ready, Basil!" he yelled as he ducked another swing from a sharp edge.

"I mean, we're really only hoping there's a spell for this—" Basil began.

"Not helping, kiddo!" Eric called out as he stepped in to shield Laurence from another swipe. "Man, I'm a lover, not a fighter."

"Yeah," Laurence panted, as he took a second to switch his sword to his off hand and shake his right arm to loosen it up. "Me too."

"Right?" Eric chuckled as he parried awkwardly and used his shoulder to shove a guard back a few paces. "So who'd you stab?"

"Uh." Laurence winced and ducked a blow. He kicked the guard away from himself and parried another, but his left hand wasn't so good at hanging on to a vibrating sword, and he dropped it with a curse. "Just, uh. A god."

Eric handed Laurence his own sword, then darted across to scoop up the one Laurence had dropped.

"And then a psychic," Laurence admitted. "Oh, and a daemon."

"This is sounding less like a thing you do when you need to, and more like anger management issues," Eric chided.

"Hey. The god was most of the way through killing Quentin, and it was the best I could do." Laurence scowled. "The psychic was trying to blow up a yacht full of innocent people, and after I stabbed him, I lost the knife and had to break his neck with my bare hands. And the daemon was gonna eat some kids she'd stolen if we didn't stop her."

"I guess." Eric clicked his tongue. "Sounds like you live in interesting times, Cricket."

"Way more interesting than I'd like," Laurence agreed.

"But all the stabbing—"

"Yeah, I know." Laurence grimaced as a blade snipped one of the backpack's straps cleanly in two and drew a thin line through his coat. "We were supposed to be leaving that behind us, Dad. Then this black dog stole Quentin right off the street, and we've been trying to find him ever since. I don't *want to* be here, and I sure don't wanna be in a fight! I just want some peace and quiet for once in my life, without any of the stabbing, or kidnapping, or drug dealers, or weird shit—" He gulped down air and used his sword to smack the hell out of a guard, even though it was with the flat side. The idea of slicing up a guy who was a prisoner of his own negative emotions just made him feel sick, and he couldn't do it.

"Eric!" Basil yelled. "Get out of the way!"

"But Cricket—"

"Move!"

Eric ignored Basil, and continued to use himself as a shield for Laurence.

Laurence huffed as he noticed Jon pick up a sword and wade into the fray.

"Dad," Laurence bellowed. "You gotta back off. If Basil's got a spell it'll affect you, too."

"Laurence is correct," Jon said as he stuck his sword through a guard's forearm and twisted, tossing the guard to the floor.

Eric blinked. "Well, apparently the ninja arrived, so…" He began to back toward Basil. "You two stay alive out there."

Laurence stared at Jon, who simply shrugged as he wedged the sword between two flagstones.

"Physics," Jon muttered.

Laurence shook his head and ducked his way around in a circle. He could hear Basil reading out a spell, but he didn't dare look over. The moment he took his attention off the fight would be the moment he got killed, and he didn't have time for that crap.

The air stilled around him. He knew that sensation well, the feeling of the entire universe holding its breath as it prepared to do a witch's bidding.

Then time snapped back into place as lines of faint blue glow whipped across the room and made the air vibrate as they snaked around the guards and rooted them to the ground.

Laurence dropped his sword as he stumbled back toward Basil, and he flexed both his hands to try and bring sensation back. "Goddess," he breathed, still gazing at the guards. "Nice work. How long will that keep them?"

"Until the sigils get broken or I fall asleep, whichever comes first." Basil snapped his book shut, and the sound of it made Laurence look his way at last.

There were sigils scribbled on the door behind Basil in Sharpie ink, hard to make out in the gloom, and no sign of Eric.

"Uh." Laurence licked his lips. "Basil?"

Basil buckled his bag closed. "Yep?"

"Where's my dad?"

"Behind the door," Eric called out. "I should be able to meet you upstairs. I just can't go through that room."

Laurence gnawed the inside of his cheek briefly. He'd only just found his dad; he didn't want to lose sight of him again. But what choice did they have? Either they released the guards and started the fight all over again, or he took this risk.

"Fine. We're gonna go find Quentin. Hopefully he didn't get far. Don't you dare get caught, Dad!"

"You either, Cricket! See you on the flip side!"

Laurence huffed and checked around the floor in case they'd left anything behind. He caught a faint gleam of silver from the treasury, and darted through to scoop the rope off the floor. If it was capable of holding his dad, it might come in handy if they got into a situation with some other guards, so he quickly coiled it into a loop.

He grabbed the one remaining strap of his backpack to stop it sliding off his shoulder as he jogged past the frozen guards, and beckoned to Basil and Jon with a jerk of his head. "C'mon. Let's get out of here before Gwyn comes back."

They ran up the stairs so fast it made him dizzy, and he was about to run out at the first floor when a sound echoed down the stairs and squeezed his heart.

Someone was crying.

Someone he loved.

Laurence ground his teeth, then turned his back on the exit and hurried farther up.

But he would've been lying to himself if he thought he really wanted to find out what could possibly make Quentin cry while he was ruled by rage.

37

LAURENCE

He shrugged the backpack off and handed it to Jon as they drew nearer to the sound of sobbing. "Take this," he whispered. "And this." He offered the length of rope.

Jon took both and shouldered the bag. "I'm pretty sure a psychokinetic could untie himself," he muttered, eyeing the rope skeptically.

Laurence snorted. "We're not using it on Quentin, Jon. Stay here and wait for my dad, okay?"

Jon tutted faintly and turned to look down the stairs.

Laurence hesitated, then continued up to the next doorway and peeked around the edge.

Quentin was sprawled across the floor, something clutched against his chest as he cried quietly. The iron bar was a couple of feet away from his feet. Laurence couldn't make out Quentin's face, only the shaking of his body and the underside of his shoes.

He took a deep breath and hung back, trying to mentally prepare himself for another round of verbal assault from a man who wouldn't harm a fly, but it was no good. The tug on his heart was too powerful, so he slipped silently around the edge of the door and crept closer.

There was no way he was going to announce his presence unless he could be sure Quentin wouldn't set him on fire for it.

Laurence placed each step with care, pausing only when he heard Eric's voice in the stairwell. He glanced back that way in time to see his dad give him a thumbs up before ducking back out of sight, then looked back to Quentin.

At any other time, there'd be no need for all this creeping around. He'd be in like a shot without hesitation, because Quentin was in pain and needed him. But what if this was a trick of some kind?

His gut said it wasn't.

Still, Laurence wasn't ready to get his heart crushed again. He sneaked closer, easing past Quentin's outstretched legs to see what it was that Quentin was holding on to so tightly.

It looked like a bag of some kind, torn like someone had hit it with a knife.

Or like it'd been sliced up, just like the gashes in Quentin's coat.

Laurence frowned faintly as the dominoes fell softly into place.

Quentin had left an arts supply store before the black dog had taken him. They'd been out shopping for their Christmas-in-January gifts.

The bag held the gift Quentin had bought for Laurence, and it had been damaged by whatever attacked him. The only reason to cry about that was that Quentin still cared. Somewhere, locked away inside that skull of his, he still clung onto a feeling that wasn't fury.

Laurence's heart skipped a beat. He didn't want to get his hopes up to have them crushed again, but he couldn't just crouch here doing nothing.

"Quen," he whispered.

Quentin groaned, and his legs curled up toward his chest as his eyes flickered open. They were red-rimmed, glossy with tears, and he took a second to spot Laurence, even though Laurence was right in front of him.

Laurence bit his lip and stayed still.

Quentin gulped down air as he tried to stop crying, and he shuffled away a few inches before he wriggled to sit upright. He shifted his hold on the bag, and then stuffed it away inside his coat again, doing his best to hide it. "Go away."

Laurence shook his head gently and eyed the rippling black armor beneath Quentin's coat. "Can I join you?"

"No."

Laurence pursed his lips, then put on his very best Bambi eyes. "Please?"

Quentin hesitated, his fingers skittering across his coat like he might be able to make himself presentable if he could just brush a little dirt off.

"Very well," he huffed.

Laurence moved slowly, turning to sit by Quentin's side and stretch his own legs out. He rested his hands in his lap and looked down at them to give Quentin a bit of personal space. Appearance mattered a hell of a lot to the earl, and if Laurence stared at him while he looked a mess, it might set off whatever part of him Gwyn had dialed up to eleven.

They sat together, Laurence taking slow breaths and Quentin sniffling now and then, until Laurence heard light thumping and looked over to find Quentin banging his head back against the wall.

"Quen—" Laurence began.

"It helps," Quentin breathed.

Laurence grimaced and reached for Quentin's hand, but didn't take it. He just set his own down on the floor beside it, an inch away, and tried not to watch what Quentin was doing.

The thumps continued for a while longer, then stopped.

A finger brushed against Laurence's, and Laurence looked

down to see Quentin's hand nestled alongside his, their pinkies side by side. He drew a breath and held onto it.

"He said there was darkness in me," Quentin croaked. His voice sounded raw from crying. "Said that it would consume me, and make me the monster I was born to be. Said that made me his."

Laurence remained still. The last thing he wanted to do was spook Quentin by making a move that Quentin didn't expect. "You're not a monster, baby," he said as gently as he could.

Anger flickered in those pale eyes, and Quentin began to bang his head against the wall some more. "I'm not my father," he whimpered. "I'm not."

"You're not," Laurence agreed. "Baby, I love you. I love you so much, and I know you can fight this. You're the strongest person I know. If you want something, you tear the world apart for it, and you make it happen." He hesitated, but he didn't want to give Quentin the impression that Laurence was telling him what to do. That might just aggravate him even further. "I love you," he said again, trying to inject as much feeling as possible without it sounding aggressive.

"I needed you," Quentin breathed. He screwed his eyes shut and gritted his teeth as his feet pushed against the floor, like he could somehow disappear into the wall if he shoved hard enough. "I needed you and you weren't here and now it's too late." He was speaking far faster than he usually would, and his words were dipped in pain.

Laurence hung his head and rubbed his face with his free hand. This wasn't Quentin talking. Not really. It was the darkness. The darkness that was already part of him. All Gwyn had done was let it out.

"Annis saw it," Quentin said.

Laurence frowned and looked at him again. "Saw what?"

"This." Quentin's eyes were still closed. "She said that I was bright like the sun, but with darkness in my heart." He ground his teeth again. "You should go. Run from here. Be safe. I'm not... I'm not good for you, Laurence."

Heat rushed to Laurence's cheeks as his own anger flared into life. He bit it back, but it was impossible to keep it all from his voice. "You're the best fucking thing that ever happened to me, Quentin, and don't you dare ever think otherwise!"

Quentin's eyes snapped open and he shifted his hand to cover Laurence's, gripping tightly. His head rolled against the wall, and his gaze was hard as he met Laurence's eyes. "You have no idea," he snarled. "None!"

"Try me!" Laurence bared his own teeth. "Herne told me our souls were in balance. That we protected each other from becoming tainted by the darkness. I need you, Quen! I need you, and you need me, so don't you even think about telling me you're no good for me! I'm sober! I'm fucking *sober*, baby, because of you!"

"I see blood," Quentin growled. "Every time I close my eyes. I see blood and fire and I want to lash out. I want to—" He cut himself off and turned his face away to smack his head against the wall, harder this time. "I'm not well, Laurence. I'm not well, and I don't want to hurt you."

"You think telling me to leave doesn't hurt me?" Laurence scoffed at him. "Stop banging your head against the wall, baby, you're going to hurt yourself."

The banging stopped, and Quentin dragged Laurence's hand into his lap, then clutched his arm and clung to it like it was a life preserver. "I can't hold it back."

"You can. I know you can." Laurence shuffled a little closer so his arm was more comfortable. "Whatever he did to you, we can undo it, okay? I promise you." He licked his lips. There was no damn way he could make that promise, but it was too late now, and if he were in Quentin's place, he'd want to know there was some hope. "We can undo it. You just gotta hold on."

Quentin shook his head and drew his knees up to his chest,

which just helped to trap Laurence's arm more completely. "You don't understand," he whispered. "It isn't just Gwyn. This is... this is me. I *am* a monster."

"Bullshit."

Quentin lifted his head and searched Laurence's gaze, and he traced one hand along Laurence's trapped arm until his fingers reached Laurence's shoulder. Then they drifted along the coat over Laurence's collarbone and to his throat.

Laurence swallowed tightly. He didn't take his eyes off Quentin's, but he didn't know where this was going.

The fingers curled around his throat, resting there lightly, yet it felt deeply possessive.

They sat in silence. Laurence didn't resist, didn't attempt to free his arm or make Quentin release his throat. Whatever Quentin was figuring out, it was keeping him quiet, stopping him from hitting his damn fool head against the wall, and if that meant Laurence had to sit here like a museum specimen, then that was what he was going to do.

"I want you," Quentin finally breathed.

Laurence swallowed again. "Yeah," he groaned. "Goddess, baby, you're so fucking hot. I wanna throw myself at your feet every single day, you know that? You just look at me, the way you're looking at me right now, and it makes me want to give myself to you. Nobody's ever made me feel that way. Not before I met you. But you?" He arched his back a little and let his head fall back to expose more of his throat. "I wanna be yours, Quen. I want you to *make* me yours. The way you look at me, the way you touch me, the way you kiss me, it's everything I never knew I needed, and I'm never letting it go. I'm never leaving you. I know you're not well, I've known that almost since the day I met you, and I'm not walking away from you. You sat by my bed when my ribs were broken. I stand by you when your mind is broken. That's what love is, Quen. We protect each other. We take care of each other. And we always will."

He felt Quentin come closer. His arm moved as Quentin's chest pressed against it. Breath touched his cheek.

Laurence turned his head slightly, not wanting to move so much that Quentin released him.

"I would not argue," Quentin sighed, "if you were to prostrate yourself at my feet once in a while."

Laurence blinked and dropped his head forward so he could search Quentin's gaze.

Quentin gently released both Laurence's arm and his throat and rested his hand against Laurence's chest. There was no anger in his eyes now, only exhaustion. Weariness. "I love you," he said. His words were quiet, but had lost the raw edge from his crying. "My God, Laurence, I love you. I'm so sorry. I can't... I can't make this go away..."

"Shh." Laurence finally moved his arm of his own volition, lifted it out of the way, and carefully draped it across Quentin's shoulders. "Oh, baby, it'll be all right. You're so tired. It's okay." He drew Quentin against his chest and tucked Quentin's head beneath his own chin, and drew in the scent of his lover, stained as it was by blood and sweat. "It's gonna be okay. Why don't you rest? Then one day, when this is all fixed, we can talk about this whole prostrating business."

Quentin snorted softly against his chest and slid arms around Laurence's waist. "Now you're being silly," he sighed.

Laurence chuckled with relief and shook his head. "I dunno. Like I said, we'll talk about it. Later. Once you've had some rest. I'll be right here with you, baby, I swear."

He ran fingers through Quentin's hair to soothe him, curled a leg around Quentin's to help him feel safe, and scowled when he looked down the corridor and found Basil, Jon, and his dad standing there staring at him like they'd just stepped out of an elevator and into an orgy. Basil's eyes were brimming with tears and his hands were clasped together over his mouth.

Laurence glared at them, daring them to say a single word, but they seemed to know better, and tiptoed along the corridor until they could disappear into a room and out of Laurence's sight, Jon ducking down to scoop up the iron bar on his way.

They didn't have time to hang around in corridors waiting for Quentin to get a good night's sleep, but frankly, Laurence couldn't see that they had any other choice.

Everything else would have to damn well wait, because Laurence held the most important man in his life in his arms right now, and he wasn't going to let go.

38

LAURENCE

Laurence held Quentin, tenderly running his fingers through that silky hair, and occasionally humming a lullaby. The longer he sat, though, the more he realized that the floor of a medieval castle wasn't the best place to do this.

His ass was going numb. The uneven stone of the wall dug against his body.

Quentin was out like a light.

Laurence moved as silently and slowly as he could to scoop one arm under Quentin's legs and the other farther down his back, and then he began the most awkward maneuvering to get his feet under himself. Once he had feet against the ground and his legs braced to do the lifting, he raised Quentin off the floor and up against his chest, then heaved himself to his feet.

Thank the Goddess he was used to lugging heavy sacks of soil and fertilizer around.

Quentin stirred and mumbled wordlessly, so Laurence brushed lips against his hair and whispered soothing words while he glanced out the windows and down to the courtyard.

The battle had worn itself out. There were still a few fights here and there, but the area was littered with fallen monsters.

Laurence could see the hunt he'd brought here flying off toward their original castle, moving in clumped groups rather than one cohesive whole.

It meant Laurence had no quick way out of here, but that was okay. Unless he took care of Gwyn, no amount of running away would help.

He turned and carried Quentin through the doorway the others had passed through, and blinked at the sight that greeted him.

Basil was sitting on the edge of a four-poster bed, flicking through his spell book, with Eric beside him, peering over his shoulder. Jon had opened up the backpack and was chewing on a sandwich while he sat in a wooden chair, the iron bar across his lap.

Laurence used his foot to quietly nudge the door shut. "Hey," he whispered.

Jon blinked.

"Hey, Cricket," Eric whispered as he looked up. "Your guy Basil here has a whole bunch of spells, but I don't think any of them will work on Gwyn."

"Yeah," Basil breathed in agreement. "They're all about the dead. Ghosts, souls, corpses, you name it. But Gwyn isn't dead."

"No," Laurence said. He carried Quentin toward the bed and gently laid him down on the opposite side from where Basil and his dad sat. He settled beside Quentin and took his hand so that there was still some contact between them. He kept his voice low to give Quentin the best possible chance at more rest. "But he will be, once this is through."

"You have a plan?" Jon murmured.

Laurence glanced at Quentin a moment, then looked at Eric. "Mom said you were the one who could use magic." He whispered the last word so quietly he was all but mouthing it instead.

Eric nodded. "Right, but I don't know anything for dealing with fair folk. You only learn that kind of spell if you want to get drowned in a lake or whisked away for a hundred years. And I don't think what I know would jive all that well with Basil's skills."

"I meant for me," Laurence said.

Eric blinked, then cracked a wide smile. "Oh, Cricket! That's awesome!"

Quentin stirred, eyebrows furrowing in his sleep.

Eric clapped a hand over his mouth, then lowered his voice again. "That's awesome," he whispered. "Oh, dude, if only we'd known sooner. I could've taught you so much stuff. Have you got a teacher?"

He nodded. "Yeah. Rufus Grant. Paula and Todd's little boy?" he added, figuring Dad was more likely to know their names than that of their son.

Eric nodded slowly. "Oh yeah. Wow. I guess he's all grown up too now, huh? Man, Paula and Todd were real nice. It was a shame."

Laurence hesitated, then leaned in a little. "Do you know how they died?"

"Yeah. Auto wreck." Eric gave a brief nod.

"Right, but Rufus thinks they were murdered. You know anything about that?"

Eric narrowed his eyes and rubbed his jaw. "Man, it was a long time ago. I can't say I heard anything that said they'd been..." Then he blinked to Laurence. "Of course, if anyone had used magic, it wouldn't show up in any forensics report. Is this what you're working on? Finding out if Rufus is right?"

"It's the price of his mentorship," Laurence agreed. "He teaches me, I find out how they died, but I wasn't ready to look back in time and watch a car wreck just yet, you know?"

Eric nodded a little. "Oh man. I wish I knew the answer, Cricket. I'm sorry. But I can give you a backup plan."

Laurence raised his eyebrows. There was no way they had enough time for his dad to teach him everything he knew. Not while Gwyn was still out there, especially as they didn't even know what he was doing or what his plans were. His thoughts raced along, almost tripping over each other, until he worked it out, and then he gasped.

"You kept a Book of Shadows," he hissed.

"You betcha I did." Eric grinned.

"But Mom would've given it to me. She doesn't know about it?"

Eric shrugged. "We don't really share with those who can't use magic." Then he looked at Basil. "You ever let Jon read your book?"

Basil blinked and reached up to adjust his glasses, then huffed when they weren't there and he nearly poked himself in the eye. "He looked at it once?" he offered. "But he's not really into stuff he can't use..."

Jon nodded. "It holds no value to me."

"Right," Eric agreed as he turned back to face Laurence. "And I didn't use a whole lot of magic once I grew up. It was mostly something I dabbled with as a kid. But it might be of use to you, and if nothing else, you can read all the stupid spells I thought were important at the time."

Laurence smiled widely. "I'd love to have it. It'd mean a lot to me. I don't have to, like, wrestle a bear for it or anything? Go on some epic quest?"

Eric was about to laugh, but slapped hands over his mouth and choked against them instead, his shoulders shaking. He stood up so he didn't jiggle the mattress, and paced away to splutter more quietly from a distance. "Oh, dude, no," he finally managed to say. "No. It's at the house. Myriam hasn't sold the farm, right?"

Laurence shook his head.

"Great. It's in our bedroom, under the floorboards. You ought to be able to make out the glow. Just lift up that rug, and it's right there."

Laurence gaped at him.

His father's Book of Shadows had been in the house the whole time, and Laurence never knew. Goddess, even Mom didn't know. Dad had buried it and left it there to be forgotten, like it was a part of his life he didn't need any more. And maybe he was right. The life he lived with Mom hadn't been fraught with danger or adventure, the way Laurence's seemed to be.

That, or they really were a collection of stupid spells; but even so, they'd be Eric's stupid spells, full of all the love and warmth and good humor his dad had approached life with.

Just to have that connection, once Laurence was back home, would be utterly amazing.

"Thanks," he whispered. He cleared his throat as softly as he could and sniffed slightly. "Hey. Gwyn said he owed you, like, some huge favor or something. Do you know why?"

Eric shook his head. "No, but fair folk are pretty good at lying."

"I dunno. He said he owed you a debt, and for that reason he wouldn't harm me. Even said he'd protect me. And I think it could be why he tied you up instead of killing you. He's sticking to that debt, even now."

"Then maybe I met him and never knew it," Eric mused. "I mean, fair folk go around in disguise a lot, too. That's kind of their thing, isn't it? That, and all the torture and murder, obviously."

"Ryan," Basil breathed. "When we first met him, he said his name was Ryan McKinley."

Eric shrugged again, then began to pace slowly. "Ryan McKinley," he muttered. "Ryan... Ryan. Oh, Goddess! Oh!" He hushed himself immediately and eyed Quentin, then looked at Laurence. "Yeah. I was, like, seventeen or something? Mom and Dad took me to New York."

"We were in New York," Laurence said. "That's where we met him."

"I was out on my own. Mom and Dad gave me five bucks to

leave them alone so they could, you know." He grinned. "I bought a bunch of candy, ate the lot, then saw some magic and went to go check it out, and there's this dude Ryan, trapped in a little hidden graveyard by this spell. He said his teacher trapped him there, and he had to figure his own way out, and I helped him wreck the sigils that kept the spell in place, 'cause they'd been put way out of his reach." He ran a hand through his curls and puffed out his cheeks. "It struck me as kinda weird, 'cause those sigils were carved into brick, and they didn't look fresh, either. But I figured, one guy helping another, you know? I scratched away at a sigil until the spell broke, then we ran like our asses were on fire. There was this thing, like, this black shadow that howled and started to chase Ryan, and I ran the other way. I never saw him again."

"The black dog?" Basil squinted across at Eric. "Why would it be chasing Ryan?"

"To bring him back to Annwn?" Laurence shook his head. "Either way, I think we have to assume that Ryan's stayed in New York since then, and he wasn't behind that spell of his own free will or he wouldn't owe Dad that debt."

"And once a fair folk owes you a debt, they won't break it," Eric added. "They're not like gods, who can choose to break their oaths. Fair folk are bound by them."

"So he can't hurt either of us." He frowned to Quentin and lightly ran his thumb across Quentin's knuckles. "Physically. But I'm gonna guess he doesn't care about emotionally, or he wouldn't have done this."

"Which means we can't assume you guys—" Eric gestured to Jon and Basil "—are remotely safe."

Basil eyed Quentin. "Yeah, I think that's been made super clear already."

"Then our plan is to kill Gwyn," Jon drawled. "And our best weapon is you," he said to Laurence, "as he can't hurt you in any way."

"Agreed." Laurence smiled dryly. "I am the Hunter. This is what I do. You can all hole up in here while I go take him out, and when I'm done I'll come get you."

"No, wait. You're not going alone, dude," Eric said.

"It seems foolish," Jon added. "Gwyn may be unable to harm you, but that does not go for his guards or other servants. You require protection if you are to reach your target."

"We can't bring Quentin." Laurence shook his head faintly. "He won't be able to take it."

"Then he stays here, and I will keep watch," Jon said.

Basil huffed. "I'm not leaving you."

"You have the spell for restraining the dead," Jon reasoned. "Gwyn cannot harm Eric or Laurence. I am the only disposable one, yet I also have the facility to remain unharmed and to remove an opponent if truly necessary. Logically, it is the best allocation of our resources."

"Kid's right," Eric sighed. "Sorry, Basil. It's the best way if we're gonna split the party."

"Party?" Basil blinked.

"What, you never played D&D? What are kids doing with their time these days?" Eric wandered over and patted Basil on the shoulder. "But he's right. And we'll get this done as fast as we can."

Basil chewed a thumbnail as he hunkered down on the bed, then he leaned forward and grabbed a bottle of water from the backpack. "Fine. But I don't like it."

"I don't think any of us are in love with the idea," Laurence murmured. "But it's all we've got." He leaned over and raised Quentin's hand so he could kiss it, then set it down and reluctantly let go.

He stood and eased silently away from the bed, then swooped down to scoop up the discarded length of silvery rope off the floor. He stuffed it into a coat pocket and took the iron from Jon's lap.

"Okay. Let's go kill a fairy," he said.

39

LAURENCE

"Uh," Eric said.

Laurence paused, the door already open, handle against his palm. He looked toward his dad, but Dad was staring at the bed and shaking his head, so Laurence followed his stare.

Quentin was twitching in his sleep. Little flinches that suggested he was dreaming. But the oil-like shirt he had under his coat was rippling like water.

"Quen?" Laurence darted back to the bed and motioned to the shirt. "What is this stuff?"

The closer he got to the material, the more he could see it had grown hair-thin tendrils that were undulating like seaweed in the water of the cloth.

"It's armor," Eric said. "Annwn isn't warm, so we grabbed another layer before we set off."

"Then what's it doing?" Laurence reached out to touch it lightly, and the waves gently parted for his hand. It felt soft, like velvet, but it didn't hurt or lash out at him.

"It's made of spider silk and nightmares," Eric whispered. "It did this last time he tried to sleep. Though it was way more transparent back then." His eyes grew wide. "It was right before he, uh…"

Laurence gritted his teeth. "We need to get everyone out of this room right now."

"Yeah," Eric agreed. "C'mon, kids, get outside." He grabbed Basil's arm and hauled him to his feet.

Basil squeaked as he spilled some of his water. "What? What's going on?"

Jon stood and gazed at Eric until Eric released Basil's arm, and then he made his way toward the door.

"What's going on is it's gonna turn into a tornado in here—"

Wind whipped the last of Laurence's words right out of his mouth, and furniture began to shake. The drapes around the bed snapped free of their little clips and billowed out, snapping like the sails of a boat.

"Out!" Laurence propelled Basil through the door just as Quentin began to scream, and he managed to drag the door closed before it could get torn from its hinges.

The noise was horrible. Wood and fabric slammed and cracked and rattled. The door was shaken with every impact against it. And through it all, snatches of screams that gripped Laurence's heart and made him want to charge into the storm and hold Quentin tight.

"Guys?" Basil sounded worried.

"Suboptimal," Jon muttered.

Laurence tore himself away from the door and found Basil and Jon staring at the courtyard, so he hurried across the corridor and looked down.

Beyond the drawbridge, on the far side of the ominous moat, Gwyn stood staring directly up at him, teeth forming a humorless white grin in the void of his face.

Monsters were flowing around him like water and surging across the drawbridge.

Is bad? Windsor's concern was strong.

Yeah, Laurence replied. *It's bad. I gotta go.*

I come!

No!

He pushed back from the window and shook his head. "You guys run. I'll stay with Quentin."

"But—"

"Go!" He shoved Basil toward the stairs. "They've seen us, they know where we are, this is where they'll come. You have to get out of here, now!"

Wood splintered behind him, and he turned just in time to see the door finally give way, blown out into the corridor in a shower of shards and trailed by a few scraps of lettuce and a slice of bread. The fragments of door were like daggers, and several slammed against the glass windows and blew them outward into a rain of lethal hail.

"That's our cue," Eric muttered, and he ran for the stairs. "I can hear them coming. Either we go up, or we try another turret."

"They'll use the closest," Laurence breathed. "Try another turret. One at the back of the fortress. You should be able to move more freely there. Go—"

He broke off as a creature with spiraling horns and cloven feet rushed up the stairs and straight at Eric. Eric darted out of the way before the creature could make contact, and he backed up toward Laurence.

Laurence turned just in time to see another monster enter the corridor from the far end.

"Fuck," he muttered. "I guess we fight our way out."

Basil fumbled with his satchel straps and dug out his book, holding it close so he could read it as he flipped through pages. Jon reached into the bag and found a Sharpie and popped the cap off.

Eric continued to back up slowly, his hands held high in surrender, though Laurence doubted his dad really intended to give up so easily. Laurence would do the exact same thing —

pretend to be subdued until he saw a chance to strike — and he grinned. Apparently, his dad's instincts were alive and well, even if the rest of him wasn't.

Basil grabbed the Sharpie and began scribbling on the floor.

"That's my cue," Eric muttered. "Let me know when the coast is clear." He ducked into the room, head down, arms over it.

"Dad!" Laurence ran to the doorway automatically, but could have kicked himself. What was he worried about? Dad was already dead, and Laurence doubted getting hit by a flying chair would change that.

Except, in the howling of the winds, Quentin's screams had stopped.

Laurence raised an arm to shield his eyes. "Quen? Baby? We gotta run! Gwyn's coming!"

"Is he?" Quentin's voice was hoarse again. "Let him."

Laurence risked a peek below his arm and found Quentin walking toward him, a blot of darkness in the already dimly lit room.

"You need to count to ten," Laurence said. He took a step back, trying to stay out of the worst of the storm.

"I don't think I do." Quentin paused to kiss him, and Laurence felt sure there was something tender in there, if only for a second. "Where is he?"

"Outside," Jon said.

Laurence stared at Quentin's back. The armor had leaked through the gashes in his coat and begun to harden, forming plates and spikes of ink the color of Quentin's hair.

For something made of nightmares, that didn't seem to be good news.

More glass shattered and spewed out into the air.

"Gwyn ap Nudd!" Quentin bellowed.

"Oh my god, what is he doing?" Basil whimpered.

Laurence hurried out of the room. "Giving us a distraction," he said to Basil. "Keep going, we don't have much time."

Basil nodded and fought to hold the pages of his book steady enough so that he could refer to them as he scrawled.

"That *is* what you're doing, right, baby?" Laurence kept his voice low as he looked at Quentin.

Quentin only sneered in response. He turned that sneer on Laurence — and then Laurence felt the familiar hold of telekinesis settle around his body. From his head to his feet, every part of him was bound so tightly that he couldn't even breathe.

Panic seared through his thoughts. His heart raced, and set his pulse rushing in his ears.

"Quentin," Eric said, warning in his voice.

Dad, no! Laurence couldn't even move his jaw. His diaphragm fluttered to keep him supplied with the thinnest stream of air possible. But words weren't coming. All he made was a strangled moan.

Basil's spell ricocheted along the corridor, tendrils of blue snaking out and coiling around the creatures that were almost on top of them.

And Eric.

Laurence whimpered as his dad got caught up in the trap, inches from freedom.

"Shit!" Basil gasped. "Eric! I thought you were—"

Laughter boomed around them. It wasn't natural, wasn't human. Laurence tried to look at the courtyard, but he couldn't turn his head enough.

"I told you that you would be mine, Warrior."

Gwyn stepped out of the stairwell, pushing his way past monsters who were trapped in pale blue coils of magic. Litter bounced past his feet, and he ignored it, his eyes glittering like distant galaxies when he stopped in front of Quentin.

Quentin snarled. "You were wrong."

"I don't think so." Gwyn gestured toward Laurence. "Release him, and I will allow you to live."

Laurence's eyelids fluttered.

Was Gwyn really trying to protect him from Quentin?

"He is mine," Quentin growled.

"And you are mine," was Gwyn's retort. "Allow me to remind you."

Nothing happened for a moment, and then Quentin's eyes screwed shut, and he dropped Laurence just as he himself fell to the ground, howling in anger. His armor grew plates at an alarming rate, but it didn't seem to do anything to stop Gwyn.

Laurence rolled aside and gasped for air. "Stop!" he groaned. "Gwyn, stop! Leave him alone!"

"You don't seem to understand," Gwyn said, looking down at Laurence, his long hair blowing in the winds. "I cannot hurt you. I can only protect you." Then he flashed a dark smile. "But he can do whatever he wants to you." He spread his fingers toward Quentin.

Quentin roared as he surged to his feet. His eyes locked on Laurence.

"And I have to protect you," Gwyn added as he reached to his own waist.

Laurence could see it all play out in his mind's eye without needing to look into the future.

Gwyn had turned Quentin into a grenade, and the only way to stop him going off was to make it so he couldn't.

Gwyn's fingers closed around a hilt that wasn't there a moment ago, and he began to draw his sword.

"Quen! No!" Laurence launched himself at Quentin, desperate to use his body as a shield. If Gwyn couldn't hurt him, he couldn't cut through him to kill Quentin, either.

Quentin's eyes flashed a silent apology, and he grabbed Laurence out of midair, then twisted on the spot.

"You cannot have him!" Quentin snarled.

Laurence saw the window coming toward him, and he screamed, bringing his arms up to cover his head as Quentin tossed him through it.

He saw a gout of fire. Gwyn's sword.

He saw Quentin's face, a fragment of desperation in the rage.

He saw the shards of glass scatter through the air around him as he began to fall backwards toward the courtyard.

And the last thing he saw was the blazing sword as it drove into Quentin's side.

Laurence screamed and plummeted toward the ground.

40

LAURENCE

THE AFTERIMAGE OF THAT FLAMING SWORD SLIDING INTO Quentin's armor seemed burned into his retinas, but as Laurence's scream ran out of breath, there was something even more pressing that demanded his attention.

He was falling from one of the fortress' highest windows.

He had a split-second decision to make. Did he want to see his death race toward him, or not? But before he could even consider his options, he had begun to twist through the air, like a cat righting itself.

Below him, the bottomless waters of the moat.

Laurence gritted his teeth. Had Quentin intentionally thrown him out directly above the water, or was this coincidence?

No time.

He'd dived off a mega-yacht that was about as high as the window he'd been tossed out. He could do this. He didn't have a moment to spare, though.

Laurence kicked his legs out and drove his arms down, straightening out for a dive. He could only flatten one hand, so he twisted the other to ensure that the end of the iron would hit the water before his flesh. It might not seem like much, but it was essential to break the water's surface with as small a surface area as possible if he was to survive the fall.

A second before impact, he took a deep breath, then closed his eyes.

He hit the water like an Olympian at first. For a split second, everything was going well.

Then his fist met the moat's surface, and pain shot through his wrist. He felt something snap. Air rushed from his lungs as his fingers twitched apart.

Laurence let out a garbled yell and opened his eyes. He could see the iron bar, falling through the water almost as fast as he was. He cradled his right hand against his chest as he contorted himself to try and reach out for it with his left.

The moment his feet were below the water, he slowed down, and the bar began to overtake him.

His lungs strained for air and his eyes stung with tears. His right wrist was on fire, and he knew without a doubt that he'd fractured something.

But if he lost that bar, it was all over.

He kicked himself toward the iron and bumped fingers against it. It tumbled as if in slow motion, tipping so that it was vertical.

Once it was, it sank faster.

Laurence grunted and kicked again. He grabbed for the bar, and this time he caught it between two fingers, pinching it just enough to stop it vanishing into the blackening depths. He drew the iron back toward his body and used his right arm to help pin it against his chest. He adjusted his hold, righted himself, and kicked toward the surface.

It was a fight. With no air in his lungs, he wasn't at all buoyant anymore. If he wanted to reach air he had to strike out and pray that he was going the right way, but he saw a glimmer of light through the murk and hoped that it led to oxygen.

Waterlogged clothes dragged him down. He couldn't use either hand. And he was running out of strength. There was nothing left but for him to push every last ounce of effort into making it to air.

His head broke free from water and he sucked down a deep breath, intentionally filling his lungs so that he could float. There was no way he could stay here, though, so after a moment's respite, he submerged and swam toward the drawbridge.

Once he was beneath it, he'd be safe from prying eyes, and he could figure out what the fuck that look in Quentin's eyes had meant, because from where Laurence was right now, it looked a hell of a lot like he'd known he was committing suicide.

He scrambled up out of the water, flopping onto hard ground just beneath the drawbridge's hinges, and lay on his back gasping down air that tasted sweeter than candy right this very second.

Moving his right arm was next to impossible without jolts of stabbing pain shooting along it to his elbow. He'd had broken bones before, and he was in no doubt that something in his wrist had snapped when he hit the water like a sack of potatoes.

Laurence sat up slowly. He didn't have a whole lot of space. The drawbridge was barely three feet above the bank of the moat, and the bank was only a foot wide, so he dangled his feet back into the water for now and sat hunched over. He gripped the iron bar between his knees so that he could dig the stolen rope out of his pocket, and then he made a loop at one end of the rope with teeth and fingers. Once he was satisfied, he dropped the loop over one end of the bar and tightened it, then turned the bar the other way up and wrapped another loop around the far end of it, the rope tight between the two loops.

He needed a splint, and he needed to not risk losing this bar again, so he made sure he could kill two birds with one stone by shoving the bar up along the inside of his coat sleeve and then wrapping the rope around his forearm and hand, up and down several times until it was tight and he was out of rope. The end of the bar that butted against his palm was sharp and would no doubt slice into him over time, but there was nothing he could do, short of taking a sock off and using it as padding, and he wasn't going to waste time like that.

He tied the rope off in a knot under his thumb and studied his handiwork. It would do for now, though he'd never dream of sending ribbons like this out to a customer.

Laurence sagged, elbows against his knees. It had taken a startling amount of effort to splint his own broken wrist after nearly falling to his death after the man he loved had drained the life out of him, and he needed a few moments to catch his breath.

His eyes stung again, and he sucked in quick breaths, struggling not to make a sound even though he knew damn well he couldn't stop crying. Whatever Gwyn was doing to Quentin looked like it had pushed Quentin over the edge he'd been struggling to drag himself back from ever since Freddy had made him remember everything his dad had done to him; and yet, deep down, something of Quentin still remained. Laurence was sure of it. The way Quentin had looked at him once his back was turned to Gwyn…

Laurence couldn't shake that image. It haunted him. Quentin's desperation, Gwyn's sword, all of it.

No way would Quentin have tossed him like a rag doll if he didn't know the moat was there, right? He must've seen the only way for Laurence to survive, and taken it, even though it meant—

Even if it led to—

Laurence buried his face in his working hand and hiccuped.

Fuck, he couldn't afford to do this. Not right now. Gwyn's monsters were still out there, and if any of them heard him, he'd be toast.

But the only thing that stopped the hiccups was Dad's lousy jokes, and Dad was trapped in Basil's spell, a sitting duck for Gwyn now that he was done with Quentin.

Is bad? Windsor reached out with worry.

Laurence tried to hold his breath to make the hiccups stop. *Yeah. It's bad. I'm sorry, Windsor. I didn't know any of this was going to happen.*

Windsor made some sort of comforting rumble across their connection. *You not to blame. You are in Otherworld?*

Yes. He hiccuped again. *I don't know what to do, Win. I've lost everything. Quen, Dad, Basil, Jon. I can't do this.*

Windsor clucked at him. *You are Hunter.*

Laurence couldn't help but snort in derision. *Fat lot of good it's doing me right this minute. Gwyn ap Nudd is a Hunter too, Win. He's a Hunter, he's fair folk, he's a king, and he's got my dad.* He rubbed his eyes. *Is Mom there?*

Yes!

Laurence nodded to himself. *Tell her I love her. Tell her I saw Dad.*

Okay!

He'd seen Windsor try to communicate things he didn't yet have words for. It was like watching a really bad mime try to explain quantum physics.

On second thought, he said to his familiar, *tell her I'm okay.*

Windsor sounded unimpressed. *Is a lie!*

Laurence forced himself to smile. It, too, was a lie, but he was willing to fake it until he made it.

Yes, he replied. *It is. But I'm going to go do my best to make it true. Wish me luck.*

Luck! Windsor still sounded worried. *Love!*

Laurence nodded. *Love you too, Win.*

He looked toward the edge of the drawbridge and kicked his brain into gear.

Gwyn's monsters weren't Hunters. They were terrifying, but they weren't descended from gods.

They might not have what it took to notice Laurence, if he moved with the full force of the gift of stealth, handed down to him through the generations. His only obstacle would be Gwyn himself, and so far as Laurence knew, it would take a single touch from the wrought iron to kill him. All the conditions were correct. Gwyn was in Otherworld, as was the iron.

Passing through the fortress would be painstaking, but not impossible. His problem would be getting the iron into contact with Gwyn. A frontal assault probably wouldn't work, and it wasn't the Hunter's way anyway.

A sneak attack, then.

Laurence chewed on his thumb while he battled to keep his grief at bay. He would have time for that once he rescued his dad and killed Gwyn, but for now he had to keep going.

It didn't seem like much of a plan. Find Gwyn, stab him. But it was the kind of thing that had worked well for Laurence thus far, so why try to get fancy?

Satisfied, he lifted feet from the water and slowly crawled along the narrow embankment until he could get up into a crouch, and then he painstakingly, silently, pulled himself up onto the drawbridge and sneaked over the threshold.

So far, so good. Now he just needed to search an entire fortress without getting caught.

Piece of cake.

41

QUENTIN

Quentin knew what Laurence would do. He saw it in the Hunter's eyes. Gwyn began to pull a sword from nowhere; Laurence would use himself to shield Quentin from the blow, and Quentin wasn't willing to rely on Gwyn's willingness to adhere to his word.

But he also knew that for Laurence to be here, right in the center of everything, effectively hamstrung him. He was not a close-quarter combatant. His wits were his weapons.

Those, and the iron he held.

It was a brash decision, borne of desperation and fury. He would *not* allow Gwyn to control Laurence, even if it meant sacrificing his last shred of self-determination. He had full faith that if anyone could rescue him in the future, it would be Laurence.

And so he threw Laurence out of the window.

Quentin punched the glass out a split-second before Laurence would have struck it to prevent it tearing his body to shreds, and then he tossed Laurence far enough away from the castle wall that he would land in the moat. It had looked deep enough to hide an army, and Laurence was a powerful swimmer.

As Laurence fell from his line of sight, screaming with every bit as much anger and fear that Quentin felt, the sword finally hit him.

And yet it didn't hurt.

Quentin looked down. Flame licked from the blade, crackling in the air, but fire was no concern to him. The tip was buried in Quentin's armor, and the armor had turned to tendrils of black, lashing out to ensnare the sword.

Where it touched metal, it doused the flame.

Gwyn snarled and pulled, but the blade didn't break free. Quentin rooted himself to the floor, lest he be pulled off-balance by someone twice his size yanking on something he was attached to.

The armor drew the sword further into itself, yet still the tip never reached Quentin's skin.

Was it his imagination, or was his anger beginning to subside?

Gwyn snarled and released the hilt as the armor consumed the rest of the blade, and the fire extinguished with a soft *shhhht*.

Quentin grinned at Gwyn and turned to face him. "If I were you," he hissed, "I would run for my life."

"You cannot kill me!" Gwyn roared.

"I have long since learned that there are worse fates one may inflict upon one's enemies," Quentin seethed as he stepped closer. "Look at what you have done to the dead in your care. What you have done to me. What on Earth makes you think that I would be satisfied by *killing* you?"

Gwyn took one step back, but lifted his chin. "Unless you do, you cannot leave Annwn. You will be trapped here."

Quentin laughed. It bordered on hysterical, but he didn't care. "Your throne sits empty. I will hardly be bored." He reached out and flung Gwyn back toward the stairwell, slamming him into the stone wall so hard he was satisfied to hear something crack.

His armor spat out the hilt of Gwyn's sword, and it clattered to the ground. Now the armor looked like plate mail made from jet, and still it was rippling and building itself.

"Will you run?" Quentin tilted his head like a child burning the wings off a fly with a magnifying glass, his gaze laser focused on Gwyn's eyes. "Or do you wish to see what I am truly capable of?"

Gwyn snarled, but glanced at the dead still snared within Basil's spell. Without so much as a parting threat, he turned and darted down the stairs, disappearing in a flurry of steel and cloak.

The corridor was quiet but for the ragged breathing of three living people.

Quentin turned and swept his gaze over the monsters, who were doing their best to cringe away from him. Even Eric looked ill, trapped as he was, every bit as much a prisoner as the creatures he was ensnared with.

He turned his gaze on Basil and Jon. Basil, who was hanging on to his book as though it were a shield, and Jon who stood with insouciance.

"What did you do?" Basil finally squeaked.

Quentin ignored him and turned to the window to look down at the moat.

There was no sign of a body, neither floating in the water, nor on the ground either side of it.

It was a huge relief. Tossing Laurence out into the air from this height had been a calculated risk, but a risk nonetheless, and he might have lost what little remained of his heart if it had failed.

"Gwyn's goal is to kill Arawn," Jon said. "But Arawn is trapped in the real world."

Quentin nodded and made his way toward a monster. It gibbered in terror, but he placed his hand against its chest and closed his eyes. "But we have the facility to travel between the worlds," he said. "If Gwyn leaves here, we can hunt him down."

"If he is willing to expose himself to the existence of cold iron so soon," Jon said. "It may benefit him instead to wait out our lifespans and only then bother to hunt Arawn."

"So we're better off killing him while we can?" Basil sighed. "But Laurence had the iron."

"And you threw him out the window," Eric said quietly. "Tell me you had a plan, Quentin."

Quentin ground his teeth and counted down from ten.

Surprisingly, it seemed to help a little.

"Yes. I had a plan."

"Do you mind sharing it with the class?"

Quentin opened his eyes and regarded the monster beneath his hand. "Laurence is the only one who can kill Gwyn, but he is at his best when he has room to maneuver. Gwyn now expects the threat to be gone, and will do his best to rally his troops, many of whom are trapped here with us." He paused, staring at the creature.

Nothing seemed to be happening.

"I need some quiet," he added as he closed his eyes again.

Thankfully, everyone kept their mouths shut. He could hear Jon and Basil shuffling around in the corridor, feel the wind as it blasted back and forth, listen to the litter that was blown with it, but nobody spoke.

He needed to regain control.

In, two, three, four.

Out, two, three, four.

There was little use paying attention to time. Meditation took as long as it needed to. He focused only on his own breath, in and out, rhythmic and calming, until the winds died away.

He gasped as a pang of fear crept through him, and he jerked his eyes open and ran to the window to look down.

What had he done?

Oh, God, what had he done! He'd thrown the man he loved out of a bloody castle, on the off chance that Laurence would notice the moat and then safely dive into it? Was he bloody *insane?*

He gripped the edge of the windowsill as he stared down toward the awful-looking water. There *had* to be a body if

Laurence hadn't made it, surely? Quentin couldn't face the possibility that he had been the one to kill Laurence.

No.

No, Laurence *must* be alive, and Quentin had done everything in his power to ensure it. He just required a little faith.

"Bloody hell," he whispered. "All right. Thank you. Where was I?"

"Tossing Laurence off buildings," Jon muttered.

Quentin frowned faintly, but he was able now to see this from Jon's perspective. Though they were strangers to Quentin, Jon and Basil had done whatever they could to bring Laurence here, and now that they had finally met the man Laurence had travelled all this way to rescue, Quentin must seem like a psychopath.

He licked his lips and nodded a little; then a bottle of water caught his eye, so summoned it into his hand and twisted the lid off to gulp half of it down in five seconds flat.

Christ, that was better.

"You brought food and drink," he realized, once he had drained the whole bottle.

"It seemed logical," Jon said. "There is none here."

"Thank you." He placed the bottle upright on a windowsill, then turned and walked back to the creature he had initially touched.

Quentin drew a deep breath and released it slowly. He could do this. Or, rather, the armor could. It had drawn the nightmares out of Iolo ap Huw. It could do so again.

He met the eyes of the poor soul trapped in this monstrous form and placed his hand against its chest. "It's going to be all right," he murmured.

There was a moment of quiet, a moment in which Quentin thought he might have the wrong end of the stick after all, but then tendrils extended outward from his armor and coiled themselves among the creature's scales, and the poor thing began to scream.

"What are you doing!" Basil ran toward him, book still held against his chest, his eyes wide in horror. He stopped by Quentin's side and squinted like he couldn't quite see, then put his book in his bag and tried to pull on Quentin's arm.

His effort was hardly worthy of Quentin's attention, but Quentin shook his head faintly. "One moment, please, Basil. Trust me."

"How can I trust you? You're a maniac! Jon! Help me!"

"Wait," Eric said. "Oh, wow! Basil, back off!"

"What?" Basil's grip loosened.

Quentin bit his lip and remained focused on the person beneath his hand, whose eyes implored him to stop.

And then the armor retracted, and the monstrous body mutated and reformed into that of an elderly man. A man with ragged hair and pale white skin, and yet a now-human appearance.

"Thank you," the man sobbed. "Oh, Goddess, thank you!"

Quentin inclined his head.

He felt a little more of the blackness around his heart slough away.

"It's the armor," Eric breathed. "Holy shit, it's *feeding*!"

Quentin nodded faintly. As much as he despised being unable to sleep without plunging into a nightmare, his armor had darkened each time, and he had been able to function after with remarkable alacrity. It was as though the armor were doing its best to draw out the poison, except that Gwyn had overloaded it.

It took time to extract all the fury that Gwyn had unleashed in him, and it was still very much in progress. Quentin could feel that he was operating on a tight temper margin.

Unless he could feel compassion for these people, though, the armor would draw nothing from them, and it had taken a long while to chip away at Quentin's rage enough for his capacity to feel anything but wrath to return.

It was a ray of sunshine, proof positive that what Gwyn had

done was not yet permanent. A light at the end of the tunnel that would allow Quentin to do what needed to be done.

He stepped up to the next creature and made eye contact.

"This will hurt," he said softly. "I'm sorry."

He began to draw out the nightmares.

42

LAURENCE

Laurence crept silently through the castle, moving at a snail's pace, and it didn't take him long to realize that wasn't his only likeness to one. Everywhere he went, he dripped a trail of moat water. His thick winter coat had soaked up so much of it that it felt like an endless supply.

He could hide himself, but sooner or later that trail would give him away, so he ducked in through the first door he could find and closed it, then eyed the room he'd snuck into.

It was long and narrow, lined with dark wooden racks that had numerous holes carved into them. A few of the racks still held a weapon — a sword here, a pike there — and at the far end of the room was a second door. Otherwise, there was no décor in here, and no windows. Laurence had to make do with the thin sliver of light that crept in beneath either door.

The armory would do for now. He crouched down with his back to the wall so the puddle that spread out under him didn't leak its way under the door. He hissed as he cradled his arm across his lap. Moving his wrist around was hardly comfortable, but if he was going to ditch the coat, he had to remove his splint.

Waiting wouldn't make it more pleasant, so he dug in, using a combination of his nails and teeth to unfasten the knots he'd been so pleased with a few minutes ago. Once he had the end loose, he could work backwards and unravel the rope.

Goddess, it hurt. He bit down on his left hand a few times as his bones shifted around, and once the iron was free, he placed it carefully on the floor.

The hard part came next.

Laurence stood and slowly hung his arm down in a straight line, then unzipped his coat and struggled to wriggle out of it without being able to use his right hand and while trying not to jostle himself around too much.

Something scratched against stone outside, and he froze.

It had to be one of the monsters out there, patrolling the castle like a guard dog. He could hear it whimper with each step, and the scratching was a constant, as though claws scraped along the floor.

Laurence held his breath and prayed.

Goddess, please, if you can hear me, if you can reach Annwn, please. Don't let it see the water. Don't let it find me. If I never ask anything ever again, please, I need this one thing to go right.

He heard snuffling at the door.

The creature didn't stop, and soon the dragging and sniffing left him alone.

He let out his breath in a rush and gulped down air. "Thank you," he whispered.

It took a tremendous effort to drag the heavy, sodden coat down over his broken wrist without screaming, and even then, it was no easy feat to re-splint his arm over the sleeve of his shirt. He tucked the rod up inside the cotton and bound the rope tight, then squeezed his own fingertips to make sure he hadn't cut off the blood supply.

Satisfied that he'd done the best he could, he spread his coat out and searched through the pockets, cursing when he dug out his cellphone. There was no way it had survived the dive into the moat, and no amount of rice would save it, even if he could find some in this place.

Thank the Goddess that Quentin had more money now, because Laurence was burning through cellphones like they were going out of fashion. Still, it had his SIM card in it, and if there was any hope of the device being saved it'd be better than leaving it behind, so he stuffed it into his jeans. He grabbed his wallet and tucked it into another pocket after squeezing water out of it, then padded along the length of the armory to the far door, grabbing a sword as he went.

He paused just inside the door to listen, but heard nothing, so he tucked the sword under his arm and silently eased the door open. A quick peek outside and he was in the clear. He closed the door again just as silently, took the sword in his hand, and made for the stairs.

SINCE HE'D BEEN FLUNG out of a high window, he figured Gwyn might still be up there, horribly tormenting everyone left behind by Laurence's rapid departure, but the turret stairwells were narrow. It would be impossible for him to hide if someone or something came down them while he made his way up, so once he reached a stairwell, he hunkered down and closed his eyes.

He slowly lowered himself into the stream of time and directed his attention to the here and now, to the immediate future from where he hunkered to the stairs above. When he caught sight of himself, he dove into the vision, but it didn't take long to be sure that so long as he moved now, he would be clear, so he darted up the stairs as quietly as possible without sacrificing speed, and then he popped out at the second story and into another bedroom.

The hunt required patience and precision. He would check his path until it was clear, and then move on, but first he looked at the bed and had a better idea.

He still moved quietly. There was no way he was going to get caught by something dumb like making a sound, so he kept it nice and slow as he peeled a sheet off the bed and tucked a corner under his right armpit, biting his tongue when he had to move his arm to clamp down on the sheet.

Laurence stretched it out with his left foot, then used the sword to slice a line from one to the other. It took some repositioning as he went; once he had a strip of cloth, he cut it down to size, sawing through it as accurately as he could, which wasn't all that great with his off hand. Still, he managed to pull together something that was about the right size to use as a triangular bandage, and he knotted the ends together, then rested his arm in the fold and popped his head through the knotted ends.

It was a bit short, and held his hand up across his heart, but it would do. With his arm strapped up, it wouldn't bounce around so much when he moved, and he could focus on getting where he was heading without worrying about trying to cradle his broken wrist as he went.

Laurence snuck back to the door and dipped back into the stream of time until he was sure it was safe for him to go, and then he hurried up the stairs to the next floor.

That was when things started to get weird.

HE SLUNK along the corridor he'd emerged into and looked both ways. The hallways were near-identical. Glass windows stretched along the outer walls, tapestries along the inner, and not a soul in sight. Laurence peeked out of a window, but this was the back of the fortress, and all he saw below was moat and outbuildings. He slipped past the turret to check out the other window and found the fortress' outer wall, stretching out ahead and curving to the left.

This had to be the right-hand side of the fortress, then, and if he picked this corridor it would lead to the front, to where he'd left Quentin.

Well, more like where Quentin had tried to kill him.

He gritted his teeth and made his way toward the front of the building. Quentin wasn't himself, and Laurence couldn't blame him for the broken wrist.

No, it all came back to Gwyn, and Laurence was going to make him pay for everything he'd done.

He heard low voices as he approached the corner, so he paused to listen.

"We can't really ask them to fight for us, can we?" Basil whispered. "Haven't they been through enough?"

"They have free will," Jon murmured. "What harm does asking do?"

"Well, what if they feel obligated? This whole thing is like, pure medieval. What if they think their chivalric code or whatever forces them to do what he asks?"

Laurence blinked. That didn't sound like Gwyn was here, so he peeked around the corner.

That didn't clear up a whole lot about the situation. He could see Basil's spell, curling down the corridor like a mass of brambles, but half of the souls trapped within it looked human now.

Basil and Jon were only five feet down the corridor, their backs to Laurence as they muttered to each other. Beyond them lay the mass of spell, souls, and creatures. Eric looked on patiently within the confines of his own part of the spell, and Quentin's armor had turned into some weirdly intricate full plate made of glossy black metal.

That was a whole lot of naked people, and Quentin didn't seem to be flipping out. Laurence watched as he approached a monster and laid his hand somewhere in the assortment of limbs and ichor, and then he winced as filaments of armor leaped out and latched onto the trapped soul, which began wailing in pain as Quentin murmured softly to it.

And then the monstrous façade melted away, leaving a middle-aged woman weeping in its wake.

"Holy shit," he breathed as he stepped out into the corridor.

Everyone turned toward him. Basil even hopped a couple of inches off the ground, and Jon had to catch him before he lost his balance.

Laurence gestured to the vista before him with his sword as casually as he could. "So is this a private party, or, like, can anyone join in?"

"Cricket!" Eric tried to take a step, then gritted his teeth against the spell. "It's good to see you, buddy!"

Quentin blinked as he looked toward Laurence, and locked eyes with him, but he didn't smile. Instead, he closed his eyes. "Thank God," he breathed.

Laurence eased down the corridor, nodding to Basil and Jon. "What's going on?"

"We think the armor feeds off negative emotions, nightmares, anger, that kind of thing." Eric nodded toward it. "It's draining all the horrible crap out of these people. I figure once they aren't gonna attack us anymore, we can kill this spell."

"Right," agreed Basil. "I don't think they're going to let us just walk away from here if we leave some behind."

"I would not be comfortable leaving them when we have the means to help," Quentin said quietly.

Laurence nodded to himself as he continued to approach. Quentin was still off, still had his eyes closed. "Baby?"

Quentin slowly opened his eyes, and this time they were creased in pain. "I'm so sorry," he breathed. "I couldn't see any other way." His eyes fell to Laurence's makeshift sling. "You're hurt."

"Broke my wrist. Had to splint it up." Laurence didn't dare say what with. There were still people in this corridor on Gwyn's side, and Gwyn might be able to turn Quentin back into a rage-monster at any moment. "Where is he?"

"He ran," Jon said. "Quentin threatened him, so he ran."

Laurence frowned.

There was nothing a mortal could say to a fairy that would be truly frightening, surely? Quentin might be scary when he got going, but not to an ancient king of the fair folk.

No. It didn't sit right, so he stepped across to the window and glanced out.

There weren't any bodies in the courtyard anymore. Not lying prone, at least. They had returned to their feet – or limbs that bore the same purpose – and were all facing the fortress.

Laurence peered further down, closer to the wall.

There, on the drawbridge, was Gwyn.

He didn't look scared at all.

He looked like a general rallying his troops.

43

QUENTIN

God, this was horrible. Laurence was so close, and yet it felt as though he were light-years away.

Quentin couldn't touch him, couldn't kiss him. Hell, he could barely speak to him. The fury bubbled and crackled inside still, despite slowly ebbing away, and he'd already done more harm to Laurence than he ever wanted to.

Laurence moved to the window, breaking their eye contact, and Quentin's relief was immense. He stepped past and approached the next of Gwyn's tortured souls, and softly apologized to them for the pain he was about to cause.

"What's going on?" Basil crossed to the window and looked out. "Oh, shit. You think he's gearing up to come kill us?"

"I don't know," Laurence said. "Maybe?" He hesitated, then added, "What do you think, Quen?"

Quentin took his hand away as the creature became human and walked over to check the scene below.

Gwyn was gesturing with a new sword, addressing his amassed troops, though Quentin couldn't hear a word of whatever was being said. He glanced toward the direction the sword was pointing and frowned.

"No," he said quietly. "He is not coming for us. Without the iron, we are no threat. He is rallying his forces to take Arawn's castle while Arawn is gone."

"Then we can leave," Jon said.

Quentin ground his teeth and shut his eyes. He would *not* unleash the anger that had flared toward his lips at those words.

Ten. Nine. Eight. Seven.

"We can't leave," Laurence said quietly. "The dead over there aren't tainted. But the more of Gwyn's forces that gather in one place, the more power he has over corrupting others. Even if everyone over there is pure as fresh snow, he'll wear them down."

Quentin opened his eyes and moved on to the next corrupted soul to let his armor do its work. "I'm sorry," he breathed. Then he looked at Laurence. "If we wish to stop him, we may need to move soon. I doubt he will wait around."

"What makes you say that?" Eric asked.

He drew a breath and released it, then took another with which to answer the question. "If he waits, he gives us time to hamper him somehow. He gives Arawn opportunity to find another way back here. But if he moves now, he has surprise on his side. He leaves us with the belief that I have been at all effective in making him go, when in actuality I was no such thing." He hesitated, then shook his head. "Were I in his position, knowing my enemy was powerless, I too would press on with my primary goal."

"Yeah." Laurence lingered like he wanted to say something else, but then he shook his head. "Okay. If he leaves the outer walls, they'll be able to spread across the mountainside."

Quentin lifted his hand away from the person he was trying to help as the anemone-like tendrils of his armor withdrew, and nodded to her gently when she thanked him. "That's true. They will be more able to control the situation." He moved on to the next, made his apologies, then laid his hand on their head.

"Then we separate him from his army," Jon mused. "They cannot all pass through the portcullis at once."

Laurence sucked air between his teeth and backed away from the window at last. "Man, that's risky. It means one of us has to sneak off without being noticed."

"Splitting the party," Eric agreed. "I'll do it."

"Dad, no!"

"I can move quiet when I gotta, Cricket."

Quentin nodded a little. "Every bit as quietly as you, Laurence," he confirmed.

Bloody hell, it felt weird to not call him *darling*.

He had to stay focused. More than simply losing control of his gifts, if he failed to keep hold of his compassion, the armor would not remove the darkness from the souls here.

"What if he goes outside in front of his army?" Basil, too, stepped back from the window. "There's no enemy over there. Won't he want to lead from the front, so he looks badass?"

"Any attempt to reach him will be thwarted by our already having closed the portcullis," Quentin sighed. "And, regardless, without the iron, we are doomed to failure, and potentially also death."

"I might have another option," Laurence said, avoiding Quentin's gaze. "Okay. Can we distract him once the gate's down?"

"I dunno how long for." Eric clicked his tongue. "Also, it only takes a few minutes for his people to get airborne as a Wild Hunt. If you've got an ace up your sleeve, it'll have to be quick."

Laurence nodded. "Okay, then here's what we're gonna do. Dad, you get to the gatehouse, ready to hit that portcullis. Jon, you go with him, in case there are any guards there. I don't want to hear about it," he added when Eric opened his mouth. "If you pop out of nowhere and lower the portcullis the guards will attack you, and Jon can get rid of them."

"I can't move silently if I've got a Child of Arawn on my tail," Eric reasoned.

"How is it we can't hear him?" Basil peered out of the window again.

Quentin frowned and moved on to the next victim of Gwyn's evil. "Magic?"

"Glamour?" Basil suggested. "He's fair folk, right? That could be how he pulls swords out of nowhere, too." He clicked his tongue. "Nothing we can use, then."

"Whatever." Laurence set off toward the end of the corridor he'd originally come from. "Separate Gwyn from as many of his people as you can. Drop the portcullis. Then I'll take him out of the picture, and we can go home."

"They're on the move!" Basil breathed.

"We have to release Eric," Quentin said.

"But—"

"Leave them to me." Quentin gestured for Basil and Jon to head toward Eric as he himself walked to the sigils Basil had drawn on the floor. "If you don't hurry, Laurence will be outnumbered and overpowered, and I will be..." He paused to suck in a deep breath. "*Quite* upset," he finished, as levelly as he could manage.

Basil let out a little *eep*.

"Yeah," Eric said. "He's intense, right?"

Quentin used his armored foot to scrape at the ink until it flaked away enough to break the spell. He looked up in time to make eye contact with Laurence.

He wanted desperately to say *I love you*, but his heart wasn't yet able to squeeze those words out past his lips. And then the remaining handful of monstrous souls rushed him, and the moment passed.

Laurence slipped away down the stairs, and Quentin prepared himself for the onslaught.

He had to take them two at a time, one with each hand, as he held the other three telekinetically to stop them chasing after the others.

He was on his own.

All he had to do was hold fast and allow the armor to do its work. There were five souls, and the armor was already feeding on two.

Laurence doesn't love you.

He gritted his teeth and tried to tamp down on the panic.

One of the souls was free, so he dragged another in and set his armor loose on it.

Or maybe it's you who don't love him anymore.

You should feel something, shouldn't you? He's alive, he's come and gone without even a touch, and you said nothing.

The tendrils wavered and began to retreat.

One of the souls slipped his telekinesis and charged at him, and Quentin backtracked a couple of steps to improve his stance in readiness, but aikido was not meant for a practitioner in full plate armor.

The soul collided with him, and he reapplied his hold to himself, to stay on his feet, upright, as another slipped free and charged.

The woman he had freed already turned to tackle a third for him, and then he was surrounded by naked bodies throwing themselves into the fray, besieging the suddenly outnumbered tormented souls and peeling them away from him.

He had a *feeling*. It wasn't anger or irritation. It wasn't hatred or loathing.

It was hope.

He blinked quickly as his eyes smarted.

These people, these *strangers*, had come to his rescue. Because they were free. Because they were decent people beneath all

Gwyn's tortures. Because he had saved them, and now they were returning the favor. It didn't matter *why*.

What mattered was that surge of warmth in his chest, the feeling that was borne on the kindness of people whose names he didn't even know.

There were people who needed his help, and once he was done, he could move on and protect Laurence, just as they were protecting him.

He smiled faintly. It was a small thing, but a good one, and he stepped back toward the fray, reaching out for the next soul to be saved.

"Thank you," he said as the armor got to work.

"You are our liege," said a middle-aged woman with deep brown eyes. "It's the least we can do."

"What is your name, my lord?" asked a younger man, who had wrestled a monstrous soul to the floor.

Quentin waited until his armor drew the bitterness and hate out of the soul he was in contact with, and then he regarded them all.

"I am Quentin d'Arcy," he murmured. "Earl of Banbury. Heir apparent to the Dukedom of Oxford." He paused, then added, "Warrior."

The word felt comfortable. It might actually fit after all.

44

LAURENCE

There was that *look* in Quentin's eyes again. Desperation. Could be something else, too. Something more.

Laurence couldn't stay. That look threatened to sink barbs into his heart, and now wasn't the time to get held up. They could figure all this out later.

Assuming there *was* a later.

He pre-checked the stairs after the first couple of steps, then darted down them, pausing at the next landing to pre-check again.

It was a cautious process. Stop, scan the future, delay or move accordingly, repeat. Stealth and caution took time, and even though he only had to avoid three guards on his way to the main entrance, those were three more guards than he was prepared to get into any kind of fight with, even without a broken wrist.

Crossing the drawbridge without incident would be the greatest test of his skill yet. It was one thing to hide in a crowd or under cover of darkness, and another to cross an open bridge, alone, in the closest thing to broad daylight available in Annwn.

He slowed by the entrance, molding himself to the wall like he was a tapestry, and paused to peek into the stream and see whether this would get him caught.

The army was on the march. Halfway through the gate, Gwyn at their head, they marched in the closest they could muster to some kind of order. Some of the monsters tumbled as they moved, but it seemed to be part of the way they were structured. Others couldn't keep up, and as they began to lag behind, others had to move around them.

Laurence was free to run across the drawbridge if he wanted to, because there wasn't a damn thing looking back at him.

He opened his eyes. "Fuck!"

Footsteps echoed down the corridor and he looked toward them in time to see his dad emerge from the stairwell — silent — followed by Jon and Basil — anything *but* silent.

"Dad!" he hissed.

Eric looked his way, then smiled and stood up, sauntering over at a more relaxed pace. "Hey, Cricket," he whispered. "What's up?"

Laurence jabbed his finger toward the entrance. "They're already leaving. Gwyn's passed the gate. They're outside, Dad!"

"Oh, this is bad," Basil breathed. "I might be able to trap some of them? Start splitting *their* party for once?"

Laurence swapped a look with his dad, then nodded. "Not a bad idea, and it's all we've got. Let's go!"

He peeled away from the wall and used his left arm to stabilize his sling when he broke into a jog. Little stabs of pain still jolted up his right arm, but he figured it'd be way worse if he let go and let the sling swing as he moved, so he kept hold of it and bolted across the drawbridge.

Footsteps clattered behind him. Neither Basil nor Jon were at all used to moving quietly, it sounded like, but that wasn't their fault. Engineers and journalists probably didn't also need to be ninjas.

He darted across the half-deserted courtyard, drawing his

team toward the outer wall rather than running directly at half an army. Even someone like Jon could hide against a wall, surely?

"Okay," he gasped. "Basil, we're gonna try and get you into the gatehouse, okay? Cast inward, toward the fortress. Stop as many of them from leaving as you can. Jon, protect him. Dad, you're with me."

There were nods all round, so Laurence hurried from the wall until he could join the tail end of the army and blend in, and he glanced at his dad as Eric did the same thing.

Except Eric went one step further. His body began to transform, shedding skin and hair and clothing, becoming rotten and dark.

Laurence had to look away. It was a horrific sight that turned his stomach, and he never wanted to see it again.

He focused on moving forward through the army, taking advantage of the cumbersome march and unpredictable movements. All he had to do was slip forward here, quickstep there, and he was passing beyond the fortress gates in no time.

But he couldn't look around for Eric. Not without seeing... *that*... again.

He heard a chorus of bellowing break out behind him, and the entire army beyond the gates stumbled to a halt to look. Laurence glanced back, too, and grinned in satisfaction as he saw the flimsy blue tendrils that held at least a third of the army fast.

Movement high up caught his eye, and he tipped his head back to get a good look.

It was Quentin.

His armor was terrifying now. A helmet had developed, obscuring his face. His hands were buried in thick gauntlets. He was a black spot that climbed out of the shattered remains of the third story window and stood on the sill for a second, surveying the situation below.

And then he jumped.

Laurence's heart hammered as he stared.

Quentin was a blot on the sky as he sailed toward the courtyard, his arms wide, legs stretching toward the earth. He almost seemed to be traveling in slow motion.

Then Laurence realized that was *exactly* what he was doing.

He was making himself a target.

Some of the army had begun to turn, to surge back in through the gates.

"Stop!" Gwyn bellowed.

The army stumbled to a halt, confused.

A stream of naked souls flowed out of the keep's entrance, over the drawbridge, rushing toward the gates and Gwyn's army.

"With me!" Gwyn roared. He sounded genuinely furious.

Quentin landed, and the ground shook, as though from the force of it. Another trick, using his telekinesis to make a bigger impact, to draw more attention.

"Goddess, you're fucking amazing, baby," Laurence breathed.

He tore his gaze away as Quentin began reaching out to the nearest trapped souls to drain the poison from them, and he grinned at the chaos it had caused. It made slipping around unnoticed way easier.

Gwyn roared in fury and began to stride back toward the fortress. "Get out of my way! Ignore him!" He raised his sword toward Quentin, and bellowed, "Warrior! You will pay for this!"

Quentin, to his credit, completely ignored Gwyn.

Then the portcullis came down.

Laurence grinned again. He hunkered down and bided his time as his prey began to scream at his troops to back away from the fortress.

It looked like an army consisting entirely of souls ruled by the most negative emotions imaginable were really bad at following orders that didn't involve getting into a fight right away, and Gwyn's troops only half milled away from the portcullis, while the other half still tried to claw at the metalwork.

Laurence watched as Gwyn began dragging souls away and hurling them in the direction he wanted them to go. It was a task he couldn't rush, and the more he tore from the gates, the more managed to get it into their heads to turn around of their own accord.

They really did move like a school of fish, twisting and turning to stick to the majority. Laurence merged back into the flow, and hoped that his dad had done the same, because he'd now totally lost sight of Eric.

Gwyn smacked several souls away with his sword as he hurled more away from the gate, and then he seemed to decide that he had enough for his invasion, because he turned his back on Quentin and pushed through the army, pointing toward the far castle once more. "March!"

It had taken what felt like ages but was likely only a few minutes, but finally the scattered remains of the army was moving the right way, and Gwyn pushed toward the front, blackened features twisted in an ugly snarl.

Laurence sidled closer. There was no rush, but he didn't want to wait until they were all halfway down a mountain in case the souls turned on him once Gwyn was dealt with, so he closed in on his prey and readied himself to strike, searching for any gaps in Gwyn's armor.

There were none that he could see. Like Quentin's, it was full plate, but even beneath the straps that bound front and back together, there was the glint of metal. Laurence didn't know a whole lot about armor, but he figured from the look of it the stuff was chainmail, and he wasn't going to be able to jam a footlong rod of metal in there and reach skin.

The only part of Gwyn's body that was unarmored was his head, so that's where Laurence would have to go. He gripped the edge of his sling so that he could start easing his arm out of it.

Gwyn halted abruptly and turned, void-black eyes scanning the ranks of his army.

Laurence hunkered down and used a soul as cover, hiding behind the hideous body to the best of his ability.

"You!" Gwyn bellowed suddenly. He raised his sword to point with it. Laurence figured most people would just use a finger. "Stand up!"

The monster he was pointing at looked startled, and slowly straightened its back.

Laurence frowned. Was Gwyn the kind of guy who randomly executed his people to motivate the survivors?

Gwyn laughed and approached the soul, then clamped a hand around its neck and lifted it clean into the air. "I haven't seen you in forever, kid!" he bellowed. "How's it hanging? I see you died!"

Eric gritted his teeth and resumed his more familiar shape, dangling in Gwyn's grip like a broken doll. He didn't bother grabbing Gwyn's hand or trying to fight the hold.

"Hey, Gwyn," Eric said with a smile. "Long time, right? Shame you owe me a debt or something."

Gwyn smirked, then laughed. "I offered to *transfer* that debt to your son, and he accepted. That means it is no longer with you."

Laurence's heart hammered in his chest. The look on his dad's face said everything it needed to.

They'd made a mistake. Without even knowing it, they'd been screwed right from the start.

"Where are you, Laurence?" Gwyn called. He shook Eric about for emphasis, and Eric grabbed Gwyn's hand and clung on. "Come out here, or I'm going to turn your father inside-out and make him worse than your black-hearted lover!"

Eric kicked at Gwyn's chest. "Ignore him, Cricket!"

Gwyn's smirk was satisfied, and Laurence grit his teeth.

Eric had just gotten tricked into blowing his son's cover, and now there was no way Laurence could hide, so he stood and raised his good arm in surrender.

"Fine," he called out. "You want me? Here I am. Come and fucking get me."

He regretted his boldness the moment Gwyn turned to face him.

45

QUENTIN

THE MORE HE DRAINED, THE FASTER IT GOT. QUENTIN WADED through the souls imprisoned by Basil's magic, and taking the darkness out of them grew swifter with each and every one.

At his heel, the army of freed souls grew, gently reassuring each other that they would be safe soon, that the evil was gone, that Quentin was their savior.

He would rather have argued that last point. If it wasn't for the armor, he wouldn't be able to do this, and he couldn't be sure how much more it could take.

His world was down to a thin slit across the eyes, all that he could see now that the armor had grown a helmet to protect his head. He had to step with care, careful not to bump into anyone else, because it felt oddly as though the armor continued to gain bulk, and he was growing taller as it built more of itself anywhere that it could.

The army beyond the portcullis had become a total shambles, and Gwyn was yelling at them to try to make them regroup, but to Quentin's eye it was already over.

Gwyn had lost his balance.

Quentin smiled faintly and continued with his task. The more souls he could free now, the less power Gwyn's army held. More importantly, the sooner everyone's suffering came to an end.

Movement caught his eye, and he looked up in time to see Basil and Jon sprint from the gatehouse and run toward him, darting around flailing limbs that tried to grasp them whenever they got too close.

Quentin had *definitely* gotten taller. Both Basil and Jon were looking up toward his head as they skidded to a halt.

"Quentin?" Basil sounded as doubtful as he looked, and he squinted like a man whose eyesight wasn't a hundred percent.

"Yes," he confirmed.

"You, uh." Basil licked his lips. "You got taller."

Jon looked down and pointed somewhere Quentin couldn't see. "It's the armor," he said, as though it were no more interesting than a leaf on the ground. "The more it absorbs, the bigger it gets."

Basil blinked, then laughed. "It's turning into mecha?"

Jon snorted. "I hope not."

"Dare I ask?" Quentin reached for another soul.

"It's a cartoon thing, don't worry." Basil bit his lip and started to rifle through his spell book. "I don't know if I have anything else that can help. If there were ghosts here, it'd be a totally different situation." He sighed and shook his head. "Are you okay doing all this by yourself?"

"Absolutely." Quentin nodded a little, then realized they couldn't see it. "And I'm sorry if I, ah... behaved poorly when we first met."

"You weren't yourself, I guess?" Basil sighed. "But it'd be nice to get to know who you actually are at some point."

"Likewise." He moved further into the trapped army. "Would you be so kind as to keep watch for Laurence and Eric? I don't wish to disrupt their hunt, but I also don't wish to stand here all day if they need any of us."

Jon inclined his head. "This seems wise," he said, and turned away without another word.

Basil stuffed his book away, eyed Quentin some more, then trotted after Jon as he buckled his satchel.

Quentin continued, focusing on the work at hand, because the sooner it was done, the sooner the spell could be removed.

"Uh… Quentin?"

Quentin looked toward Basil. He was over halfway through the trapped forces now, and Basil looked so small.

Basil waved frantically, then pointed through the portcullis. "I don't know what's going on, but it sounds bad?"

"It is bad," Jon agreed. He kept his back to Quentin. "Gwyn has found Eric."

Quentin heard a distant shout that was unmistakably Laurence's voice, though too far away — or the helmet was too dense — for Quentin to make out the words. He could pick up the tone, though.

Laurence was angry.

Quentin moved with care toward Basil and Jon, easing between bodies until he could see through the portcullis for himself.

Gwyn had Eric by the throat.

Laurence was standing in the middle of a widening circle of Gwyn's army with one arm held high, palm toward Gwyn.

"I think Laurence just surrendered?" Basil blinked up at Quentin. "What do we do?"

Quentin licked his lips briefly. Was this part of Laurence's plan? He doubted it, as it placed Laurence in exactly the situation he had been in before all this happened.

Out in the open.

Exposed.

Visible to his enemy.

No, something had gone wrong.

"Step back," he said.

Jon finally turned, blinking up at him in confusion, but Basil grabbed Jon's arm and pulled him out of the way.

"Thank you." He reached out and gripped the portcullis and then, with a judicious application of telekinesis, hefted it out of the ground and rolled it back up into the wall, holding it over his head as he strode outside, and then he let go of it and allowed it to fall. Without any tension in the chains, it slammed straight back down at high speed, and rang out across the mountaintop like a bell when it hit the ground.

"Gwyn ap Nudd," he bellowed as he made his way directly toward the fairy king. "I've about had enough of you. Surrender now!"

Gwyn tore his attention from Laurence, thank goodness, and sneered at Quentin. "Come one step closer and I will destroy Eric!"

Eric turned his head toward Quentin and grinned, then gave a little wave. "Oh, hey, dude! Don't mind me. Fuck his shit up, it's cool."

Quentin tilted his head, then hunkered down and launched himself at Gwyn at full speed. The less time he allowed for Gwyn to do anything to Eric the better, and he leaped clean over the scattered army between himself and his target.

Eric's form essentially melted out of Gwyn's hand, sloshing to the floor and rushing back out of reach like a small stream before he began to take shape again, and by the time he'd grown arms, Quentin had landed and thrown a punch straight at Gwyn's face.

Gwyn snarled and used his sword to bat Quentin's arm away, then charged in like a rhinoceros, yelling wordless anger and reaching for Quentin's helmet.

Except this time, they were the same size as each other.

Quentin slipped a foot back and blocked Gwyn's arm, but instead of dodging, he took hold of wrist and bicep and twisted to throw Gwyn a good ten meters, where he landed in a heap among tormented souls.

"Thanks, baby," Laurence gasped.

"Of course." He tracked Gwyn and raised his hands in readiness. "Hadn't you both best disappear?"

Neither Riley said anything, and Quentin focused on Gwyn through the slender slit in his helmet

Despite a good first round, Quentin couldn't take down Gwyn alone, and he certainly wouldn't be able to fend off two thirds of an army he didn't wish to harm.

For now, though, Quentin was more than capable of throwing a few shattered trees at Gwyn's head as Gwyn ordered his army to swarm Quentin.

The army charged him, and while he could hold some off, others quickly figured out how to blip out of physical form just long enough for him to lose his grasp on them. It was like watching an avalanche approach, in that it seemed to be moving toward him so slowly, and yet within the blink of an eye it was on him, and all he could do was stand fast in the rush of bodies against his armor.

The armor ensnared who knew how many of them. The visor gave him very little range of vision, and it was as much as he could do to remain upright as more and more of them climbed over each other to bury him under a mass of bodies.

Irritation stirred deep within him. It had to be an issue of mass, but there was nothing he could do about it short of leaving the arena altogether, and he couldn't do that. Nor could he hold out against the corruption which was seeping its way through the armor and into his soul. His only hope was that the armor could drain the darkness more quickly than the overwhelming number of tainted souls could have their inevitable effect on his own heart.

He closed his eyes and began to meditate in the hope of prolonging his resistance as much as possible.

Whatever Laurence's plan, it had better bloody work, because Quentin was running out of time.

46

LAURENCE

To Laurence's eye, it was like a scene from some horror movie where someone got totally swarmed by zombies, and he had to ignore that it was Quentin under the pile that was twice Laurence's height, because Quentin had been his usual flashy self to buy Laurence time.

Which meant Laurence had none to waste.

He blended and flowed between what few trees Quentin had left standing, choosing his moments with care. He had to wait to be sure Gwyn's attention was either on Quentin, or on searching away from where Laurence was, and every time Gwyn's gaze swept back toward him he molded himself against a tree and waited, quickly taking snapshot glimpses into the future to determine the best moment to move.

"Where are you!" Gwyn bellowed.

"Right here!"

Laurence peeked past the trunk. The voice was familiar, but not because it was his dad's.

No, it was his own.

Dad was walking toward Gwyn, but this time the shape he'd

taken was Laurence's own. Younger, shorter, slimmer, blonder. He even had a fake bar of iron in his left hand, and his right was in a makeshift sling.

Laurence slipped to the next tree as Gwyn's attention was on Eric.

"You're trickier than your father," Gwyn muttered. "Throw the iron down and step away."

Eric shrugged. "What's in it for me?" He thumbed back toward Quentin. "Call your people off him, and we'll talk."

Gwyn bared his teeth, but his gaze was on the iron.

"You can't harm me," Eric added, like he was reminding Gwyn of the deal that bound him. "And if you don't pull them off Quentin, I've got no reason not to harm you."

Gwyn hissed, then swept an arm toward the pile. "Leave the Old One," he yelled.

Laurence used the sound to mask his approach, doubling back on Gwyn from behind and evaluating how exactly to get this right.

The army was as uncoordinated as before, and only a few of them managed to obey Gwyn's order.

Laurence didn't have much time. Soon Gwyn would wade in, like a teacher trying to split up a schoolyard fight, and his stride was far longer than Laurence's.

He turned himself over to instinct and broke into a run, closing the distance in seconds just as Gwyn took a step forward, and Laurence leaped off the ground, planting a foot against the back of Gwyn's calf and using it as a stepping stone to push himself higher.

He grabbed the shoulder of Gwyn's cloak just as Gwyn swung violently on his heel, and Laurence hung on as he was thrown sideways.

Gwyn roared and swung his sword up over his own shoulder, and the blade came toward Laurence's face.

He ducked so that Gwyn's own armored shoulder protected him, then kicked himself upward again, screaming as he dragged his right arm out of its sling at speed. The pain was bordering on unbearable, but he swung his right hand toward one of Gwyn's short antlers.

Gwyn threw himself to the ground and rolled, and Laurence was crushed beneath his weight, pinned.

Unable to breathe.

Gwyn snarled in irritation and lifted himself off Laurence, and Laurence gasped for air.

"It's over," Gwyn said. "You have lost. And for your trickery, I will allow your lover to succumb." He shrugged. "After that, you may take him if you wish. I will take Arawn's throne. When you die, I will be waiting for you, and I will make your afterlife miserable and eternal. You cannot escape your fate."

Laurence rolled slowly onto one side, and the tang of blood hit his senses. He looked down to his palm, pooled with blood. The sharp edge of the iron had dug into his palm in the crush and sliced it open.

Laurence ran his tongue along his teeth, then slowly hauled himself to his feet and affected a deep sigh as he hung his arms by his sides.

Despite the army crawling over Quentin, he could still hear the *pat pat pat* of his blood hitting the forest floor.

"You're right," he said, slumping his shoulders slowly. "You're right. I've lost. But *you* have broken your deal."

Gwyn's gaze followed Laurence's as Laurence raised his hand and looked at it, the back of his hand toward Gwyn.

"You hurt me," he said, quietly, "when you swore not to. You have broken your bond."

Gwyn shook his head. "That... that was an accident!"

"You know that is not how the promise of a Tylwyth Teg works," Laurence murmured. "You must allow me to cut you in return, or far worse will come to pass."

It was a gamble. Surely *something* bad had to happen if a fair folk broke their word, otherwise why would it be so binding to them?

Gwyn hissed through his teeth, but sank to one knee and bowed his head. "One cut," he growled. "And then I will kill you."

"Yeah," Laurence breathed. "But first, the cut."

He used his left hand to guide his right, and to help shield the iron from Gwyn's view should Gwyn suddenly raise his head, and then he rested his fingers against Gwyn's ear and dragged the end of the iron forward, along his cheek.

Gwyn screamed. He lashed out, but Laurence threw himself back and kicked himself further away before Gwyn's sword could reach him.

Gwyn fell forward, and his screaming became horrific, sinking several octaves until Laurence no longer heard it, and yet felt it in his bones. Gwyn's armor broke apart and turned to dead moss, which fell away and left Gwyn naked.

He threw himself at Laurence as cracks began to appear across his skin.

Laurence kicked himself away, slipping in the loose, dead earth until his head hit a tree, and before he could try to roll aside, Gwyn's weight was on him again, breath like soured milk, hot against Laurence's face.

Gwyn grasped a broken shard of tree from the forest floor and drove it toward Laurence's side as off-white started oozing from the cracks in his skin.

"You die with me, Hunter," Gwyn gurgled as white foam specked his lips.

Laurence couldn't move away, and his only weapon was strapped to his underarm, his hand across one end. If he wanted to end Gwyn before Gwyn killed him, he had to do something that would hurt like fuck.

He twisted his hand until the iron poked out between his

thumb and pointer finger, and the agony almost made him black out. For a second, he lost track of everything.

Then the wood speared into his side.

Laurence jabbed his arm up into Gwyn's body. It might wreck his wrist for good, but if he couldn't kill Gwyn right now, that wood was going to kill him.

Hell, it still might.

He was going to be sick. The pain from his wrist far outshone that from his side, and hot, wet warmth surrounded his hand as he continued to thrust the iron deep inside Gwyn's chest. Wherever the bar went, flesh seemed to puree and give way, and Laurence had no choice but to keep pushing.

The cracks became chasms. Gwyn's blackened face was streaked with milk-white blood that poured from every crevasse, until there was nothing left but the freakish blood and the shaft of wood hanging out of Laurence's body.

The white stank of soured milk, and it drained off Laurence in rivulets, sinking into the thirsty ground until there was nothing more than a powdery white stain.

Laurence panted heavily as he struggled to get his arm back in the sling. The pain made him feel sick to his stomach, but he couldn't let himself faint just yet. There were still two-thirds of an army to deal with.

Although the pile did seem to be slowly diminishing, as more and more untainted souls broke free of it and clustered together to help each other. Combined with Quentin's armor just getting crazy huge now, perspective was something he couldn't rely on any more, so he slumped down against the ground and sat with his back to a tree, trying to stay conscious.

Eric retook his own shape and hurried over, crouching by Laurence's side and gripping his left shoulder. "You okay, Cricket?"

"No?" Laurence chuckled weakly. "Oh Goddess, Dad, I didn't think we'd make it."

"Nah. You gotta have more faith," Eric snorted as he began to examine the wood sticking out of his son's body. "Still had the iron, huh?"

"Yeah. Been using it for a splint." He thought about turning his arm to show his dad, but the pain already thrumming through his wrist made him decide against it. By the time he got back to where he belonged, his wrist would be swollen like crazy. From here, he might be able to make it to Avalon to heal, but he didn't want to drop in like it was a day spa. That seemed disrespectful.

It wasn't ribs again, and for that he was grateful. He could cope with his arm in plaster for three weeks. He looked down to the wood, then up to his dad. "Is it ok?"

Eric laughed and shook his head, but his laugh was weak. "I don't think it's hit anything vital. You're still breathing okay. I don't hear any fluid or anything in your lungs. Best I can do is pull it out and hold my hand over the wound."

Laurence nodded. "Yeah. Please."

Eric hesitated, then slowly drew the wood out, placing his hand across Laurence's skin once he'd removed the makeshift dagger. Laurence eyed it and quickly looked away again. Six inches of it glistened with his blood, and he didn't want to start imagining all the unseen damage it had probably done.

"We should help Quen," he sighed.

"Don't think we need to," Eric murmured. "He's winning. It's just down to waiting for him to finish, then go clean up whatever's left inside the fortress. He's gonna be like thirty feet high once this is done."

"Great. He can carry us back to Arawn's castle on his back or some shit." Laurence laughed, but it shifted his arm, and he whimpered instead.

"You rest, Cricket," Dad said. "Your mom always knew you'd turn into a great man, and she was right. I'm proud of you."

Laurence smiled a little, but his head lolled back against the tree, and he closed his eyes. Just for a second. That was all he needed.

Just one.

47

QUENTIN

QUENTIN LOST TRACK OF TIME. FOR A MOMENT THERE, HE thought he might also lose track of himself, but he hung on, meditating in silence, until his sense of self began to return, and then he waited.

And waited.

He could see Laurence, so far down, passed out against a tree, and Eric by his side with his arm around his son's shoulders. He saw Jon and Basil scurry out from the fortress now that the portcullis was raised once more, and was satisfied with how they attended to Laurence right away.

And, eventually, his armor was still.

He was surrounded by an awful lot of naked people, all bowing before him, though some gestured toward the fortress, and Quentin knew why. There were still souls left behind that he had not cleansed, and that meant he had work to do.

There was no way he could walk beneath the portcullis, so instead he leaped over it to continue his task.

Naked souls rounded up guards and brought them to the armor. By the time Quentin was done, he had no idea how he was supposed to take the bloody stuff off, but the moment he thought about it, the arms raised and lifted the helmet away, and the gap it left behind was wide enough for Quentin to climb out of.

He leaped from it and landed lightly on his feet, then looked back up at it.

Hollow and empty, it was like a statue to some forgotten king, standing guard over a deserted fortress, and that seemed a fitting way to leave it, but he gave it a light pat regardless.

"Thank you," he said.

Maybe it understood, maybe it was inert; but it was best to be grateful rather than make any assumptions.

He turned his back on it and went out into the petrified forest to find Laurence.

"How is he?" He whispered the question as he came to a halt by Laurence's side.

Eric nodded. "Exhausted. Other than that, he'll be okay. He needs to get his hand seen to when you get back home. And this." Eric gestured to a wad of cloth that peeked out from a blood-stained gash in Laurence's coat. "Gwyn tried to skewer him with a stick. I've rolled up his t-shirt and tied it tight as a really shitty bandage, but he needs actual medical care at some point."

Quentin crouched and lowered his head to rest one ear to Laurence's chest, and he listened. There was no crackling in his lungs, and his heart was steady, so he rested back on his heels and laid fingertips against Laurence's shoulder. "What do we do now?"

"I guess we lead all these people to a safer place?" Basil squinted to the circle of souls that surrounded them. "Especially since they all seem to be bowing at your feet?"

Quentin glanced around.

They were indeed, to the last one, down on one knee with their heads bowed.

"Are you all right to travel?" he murmured.

Basil nodded. "Sure. You want us to hike up a mountain, right?"

"I do." Quentin inclined his head. "But first, we must hike down this one."

"Oh boy," Eric said cheerfully. "This was so much fun last time, too."

Quentin smiled a little and raised Laurence to his chest. For all that he had been throwing his gifts around with abandon in this place, it was down to ill temper and unrestrained anger, and he was not going to make a habit of it.

He kissed Laurence's forehead softly as he rose to his feet, then raised his chin.

"Onward," he said quietly.

As one, hundreds of souls raised to their feet and waited for Quentin to lead them, but the soul that mattered to him the most lay fast asleep in his arms.

"So, like, who are you?" Basil asked as he walked alongside Quentin.

Quentin spared him a glance, but he already knew how treacherous the footing was around here, so he soon had his gaze back on the ground ahead, searching for obstacles. "My name is Quentin," he murmured. "I am the Earl of Banbury, but please, don't allow that to color your perception."

"If you didn't want it to affect what I thought of you, why'd you mention it?" Basil grinned.

Quentin pursed his lips. "I don't know," he admitted. "I

suppose because it's all I have been for most of my life. I'm not entirely sure how to be anything else."

"There's always more to someone than can be explained in three words. People are complex." Basil squinted up at him. "Even you. Don't think I don't see that expression."

Quentin's nose remained scrunched up. "And who are you?" he asked, hoping that Basil's response might give him a few clues about the kind of answer Basil might prefer.

Basil shrugged. "Well, I'm a journalist. Arts sub-editor, actually, but I do ghost-hunting on the side. I'm from Vermont, but I moved to New York to find work…" He took a breath. "And get away from my dad. He was devastated when he found out I was gay, and…" Basil shrugged. "I wasn't welcome for a while. But I met Jon, and once I realized he had a really sharp sense of humor buried away in there, we hit it off. Now we hunt ghosts together." He beamed widely. "Your turn."

Sodding hell, Basil had completely seen through him.

Quentin pressed his lips together, then inclined his head. "I have no employment. I was born in Princes Risborough, a few miles from Oxford in England, and lived there until my mother died when I was nineteen. After that, I drifted around London for a while until I was disowned by every friend I had, and so I decided to travel further afield. After some time in Europe, I came to the United States, drank my way across it to San Diego, and met Laurence." He smiled softly to the sleeping man in his arms. "And there I stayed."

Basil stuffed his hands into his coat pockets as he listened, and then he was quiet a while before he spoke again. "There's more than that, though, isn't there?"

Quentin shrugged. "Of course. There's more to everyone, I think, than can be summed up so briefly. But depending on how long we have when we return to New York, perhaps we can discuss more over dinner."

Basil beamed. "Sure. Uh, I mean…" He trailed off. "Nowhere too fancy, right?"

"My treat," Quentin murmured, "but nowhere too fancy, if that is your wish."

"Great. Somewhere we're allowed to push our own elevator buttons would be a great start."

Quentin blinked, then smiled wryly.

"Deal," he said.

THEY HAD HIKED for hours before Laurence began to stir, and Quentin watched his eyelids slowly flutter open.

"Shh," he whispered. "You're quite safe. I have you."

Laurence groaned and lifted his head to look up, his gaze guarded. "What's going on?"

"We are leading a few hundred people to Arawn's castle," Quentin explained. "I'm not sure that I could fly them all at once, and it seemed quite rude to leave them behind, especially as they have been imprisoned for so long."

Laurence gazed up at him, then gave a slow, weak smile. "Welcome back, baby."

"Laurence, I am so sorry—"

"It wasn't you," Laurence whispered. "He did something to you. And sure, he might have drawn out something that was already in you, but that doesn't mean it *was* you. You've got every right to be angry." Laurence closed his eyes for a moment. "But you're a better man than to let your anger define you. I'm glad you're back."

Quentin gazed down at him and wondered, not for the first time, how on earth this man could be so generous with his heart, so firm in his belief that Quentin was who Laurence pictured him to be. What had he done to earn such unshakeable devotion?

How could he do more of it, to ensure that he never lost Laurence's faith in him?

"You've got your thinking face on," Laurence murmured as he leaned his head against Quentin's chest, tucking himself up beneath Quentin's chin.

"Would it be too difficult for Arawn to meet us here, rather than force us to go on a three-day hike?" Quentin muttered.

Laurence chuckled and said nothing. There was no need to. They were both fully aware that Quentin didn't want to talk about it right now, and would get around to it later.

But really, it would be nice if Arawn could save them an awful lot of time when Laurence's wrist was swelling up like a grapefruit.

IT TURNED out not to be three days at all. While it was difficult to measure time in a world with no sun, hunger had not even begun to set in when they approached the outer walls of Arawn's castle.

Quentin blinked, in case he had managed to switch himself off at some point, but Basil and Jon seemed equally surprised.

Perhaps Arawn had saved them some time after all.

"Quentin!" The skeletal guard at the gate waved him forward with cheer. "Ah, and the others. Eric!" they added, with another wave.

"Hey," Eric grinned.

"Is that—"

"Yeah-huh," Eric answered, before the guard could finish asking.

"Amazing! Please, come in! Everyone is welcome!" The guard bowed to Quentin, and then to Jon.

"Thank you. Arawn has returned?" Quentin asked.

"He waits for you," the guard replied. "Please, come with me."

"I can walk," Laurence croaked.

Quentin looked down at him, an eyebrow raised.

"Baby, I'm not gonna let you carry me into a god's throne room," Laurence added sheepishly. "I can walk it."

Quentin inclined his head and placed Laurence on his feet with care, only releasing his telekinesis once he was sure Laurence was steady.

Laurence winced as his arm shifted a little, and he cradled it with his left hand to steady it, but then he gave a faint nod to show he was ready.

They walked up the cobblestoned streets toward the castle side by side, and for the first time in weeks, Quentin felt as though there might be light at the end of the tunnel.

THE NEWLY-RESCUED army waited in the courtyard outside the castle, since the throne room was not large enough for them all, and the guard continued on inside with only the living and Eric following.

Arawn was, it was a great relief to find, no longer wearing Quentin's face. He had reverted to his enormous, antlered self, and rose from his throne when his guests were led through the seemingly-eternal semi-naked party to meet with him.

"Thank you," Arawn said to the guard. "You may go."

The guard bowed and cast Quentin a nod before they left the hall.

"You have done well, Warrior," Arawn announced as he regarded Quentin.

Quentin inclined his head faintly. "Had you informed me that Gwyn ap Nudd was not here, I would still have willingly aided you," he chided, only softly. "But thanks to Laurence's quick thinking, the situation is..." He hesitated. "Resolved," was the word he selected, because *we murdered a fairy king* sounded truly awful if he stopped to dwell on it too long.

"Yes," Arawn agreed. "Mortals have matured since I engaged with them last. Will you accept my apology?"

Quentin nodded. "Of course."

Arawn's lips twitched. "The torc suits you."

Quentin blinked. Bloody hell, he still had it on. He quickly raised his hands to begin removing it, but Arawn raised a hand, so he hesitated.

"I owe you a debt," Arawn murmured. "Name your reward."

He blinked. Was Arawn suggesting that Quentin keep a trinket in exchange for all that he had done? True, it might well be a priceless artifact, but it was a status symbol from a people he did not belong to, and to view it only as wealth did it a grave insult.

He used his gift to expand it enough to remove, then lifted it over his hands, closing it once more, and offered it to Arawn. "This is not mine," he murmured, "and I have no right to claim it. But there is one thing that I would ask of you."

Arawn's smile was enigmatic as he took the torc. "Name it."

Quentin glanced at Laurence, and then down to his feet. It was an audacious request, but he was an audacious man, and if he didn't ask, he certainly would not get.

He raised his head and looked Arawn in the eye. "I have no faith," he murmured. "I am an atheist. It is my understanding that this will not allow any opportunity for my soul to unburden itself after my passing."

"That is correct," Arawn said.

"My soul has a lot to unburden, and I cannot guarantee I will succeed within a single lifetime." He swallowed tightly and paused to blink. "It is my wish, should you be so gracious as to grant it, to be brought to Annwn after my passing, so that I may save any future lives this burden." He paused, then added, "And to be with Laurence."

He heard Laurence's intake of breath but dare not look toward him, lest Arawn take that as some sort of signal to deny Quentin's request. Now that he had given voice to his plea, it was suddenly all too real, and the prospect of Arawn refusing it was horribly unthinkable.

Arawn gazed down at him for a few seconds, then bowed his head. "You are wise already, Warrior, and you are only at the beginning of your journey. I will honor your wish. When it is time, I will collect you personally to ensure that you reach Annwn."

An incalculable weight lifted from his shoulders, and Quentin bowed. "Thank you, Arawn."

"Thank you, Warrior," Arawn said. Then he looked at Laurence, and added, "You were perceptive and true, as all great Hunters must be. You offered yourself freely to aid in this task, and you have suffered for it. Please, ask of me what you will."

Quentin turned to face Laurence, and watched as his lover licked his lips.

"Well," Laurence began.

48

LAURENCE

Laurence was reeling from so many things. Staying upright with the twin pains of wrist and side was enough of a challenge, but then Quentin had asked to spend his afterlife with Laurence, and that...

Well, it was pretty fucking overwhelming, and Arawn expected him to be able to speak when he was still grappling with the massive commitment Quentin had just made. Quentin didn't just want to spend the rest of his life with Laurence, he *expected* it.

Goddess, it was... it was a relief, but also so frightening. This was already the longest relationship he'd ever been in; he'd spent so long worrying about whether Quentin might leave him, and Quentin was always so confused about why Laurence might think that way.

Now Laurence could see why. Because Quentin had already committed to a whole life spent with Laurence, even if he hadn't ever phrased it that way.

But Arawn was still waiting, so Laurence struggled to gather his wits in time to take a once in a lifetime opportunity.

"Can I just, like, spend some time with my dad?" He licked his lips again, then swallowed. "I'd really like to talk to him before we have to leave, and that's…" Laurence shook his head. "That's what I'm asking for, if it's okay?"

Arawn dipped his head. "That is your wish, and it is a wise one also. You are well-matched." He reached forward and brushed a fingertip against Laurence's chest. "There is irony here," he added. "That a Hunter filled with life brings death, and a god of death holds domain over life itself. My Children are skilled healers, and yet those of Herne never are."

Laurence held his breath as pain slowly drained from his side, and the swelling in his wrist eased little by little. The swelling began to go down.

"That will be enough," Arawn murmured. "You must take care with your wrist until it is fully healed, but it will be painless enough for your conversation to be more relaxed." He stepped back and looked at Basil. "I have already given my Child a gift. Will you allow me to bestow one upon you also?"

Basil blinked rapidly, then nodded. "Sure! I mean, I'd be honored! If you want to, I mean…"

Arawn chuckled and placed his hand on Basil's forehead, and thankfully Basil didn't fall over dead. Instead he blinked a few times, then gasped. "Oh my God! Seriously? Thank you!"

Laurence glanced at Quentin, then down to his own arm. The swelling was gone, so he began to untie the rope and pulled the iron out the moment he could. "Should I leave this with you?" he offered. "In case, some day, another Tylwyth Teg comes to Annwn?"

Arawn reached for the iron and took it. "A fine plan. Thank you. Would the rest of you like to be returned home while the Hunter speaks with his father?"

Basil and Jon looked at each other, then Basil shook his head. "Can we wait here?"

Arawn looked at Quentin, who inclined his head. "Naturally, I choose to wait."

"Very well. Explore as you wish, return when you are ready. Blessed be."

"Blessed be," Laurence murmured. He turned to Quentin and leaned in to whisper, "May I?"

Quentin nodded. "Please do."

He closed his eyes for the kiss and allowed Quentin's presence and warmth to fill his world for a moment, and then he broke away. "I'll be back."

"Of course."

Laurence smiled a little, then headed for the door, taking off the rest of the rope and pulling his sling off overhead as he walked. Eric fell into place by his side, and together they went out of the hall.

ERIC LED him through the castle and to a small annex with a window that overlooked the courtyard. He sat on the wide windowsill, and Laurence perched beside him, setting down the rope and makeshift sling in a little pile between them.

Laurence rested his hands in his lap and looked out the window a moment, watching all the people they'd saved as they began to speak with people from the castle, as well as one another.

Yeah. They'd done good things here. Things to be proud of.

He looked toward Eric and smiled weakly. "I don't know if I'm ready to say goodbye again," he said, his voice barely above a whisper.

"Yeah," Eric mused. "We weren't ready the first time, huh?"

"No," Laurence agreed.

Eric's lips twitched into a gentle smile. "C'mon. Tell me how you've been doing. What've you been up to? How's Myriam? How'd you meet Quentin? Fill me in, Cricket."

"Oh, you know." He shrugged. "Selling flowers, helping Mom on the farm, Mom's great, she misses you..."

Eric chuckled and held up his hands. "You in a rush?"

Laurence blinked, then laughed and shook his head. "No. Goddess, Dad, I'm sorry. You're right. Can we go for a walk?"

"Sure! Let's go outside!"

HE WALKED with his dad through cobblestoned streets, finally relaxing into talking the way they never really had while Eric was alive. Sure, Dad had known his son was an addict, but Laurence could talk about it now in ways he never could back then.

He figured it was because they knew the root of it all now. Dad's addiction to chocolate and candy, Laurence's addiction to drugs, it all stemmed from their heritage — their need to hunt, and their distance from it — and that knowledge provided Laurence with some coping strategies that gave him hope for the future.

They talked about Myriam, about how she still loved Eric very much and looked forward to seeing him again, about how she was back to her role as a Priestess among the community, and how she still only looked like she'd just turned forty.

He spoke about how he'd met Quentin and some of the adventures they'd had since, though he didn't want to get into all the stuff about the duke. It'd only make them both angry, and Laurence didn't want to leave his dad with anger about a problem he couldn't reach, never mind try to solve.

He talked until his throat got sore, and he listened while his dad offered jokes or advice or even just a sympathetic murmur. They walked through streets populated by people in all kinds of states of decay and undress, until seeing a corpse or a skeleton seemed almost normal. And all the while, he silently thanked the Goddess for his good fortune.

"Tell me about your future," Eric said as they drifted back toward the castle.

Laurence hesitated, then said, "I don't really look."

"I can't say I blame you. Life is for living, not watching from afar." Eric grinned at him. "But have you thought about what you'd like to find there? A handfasting, maybe?"

Laurence gawped at him. "Dad! Goddess, what is it with everyone telling us we should get married?"

"Let me tell you something about love, Cricket." Eric stuck his thumbs into his belt loops as they dawdled along. "Everyone else can see it. When there's true love, when it's powerful and kind, everyone around you can see it in you. People are only responding to the way you two look at each other when they suggest this, you know. Think about it, 'cause he already has."

Laurence stopped dead in his tracks and stared. "Did he talk to you about it?"

Eric didn't stop. He just shrugged as he continued along the path, and Laurence had to jog to catch up.

"We might have exchanged a few words," Eric said.

"Dad! How could you!"

Eric gave a deep, hearty laugh. "My son's happiness on the line? How was I gonna pass that up?"

"Urgh." Laurence threw his hands up, then winced when pain flared through his wrist. Arawn *had* said to take it easy. "Fine. I'll... I'll think about it, okay?"

"You do that." Eric pulled a hand free so he could grab Laurence in a one-armed hug. "Next time you're in Annwn, I wanna see pictures."

"You mean, like, when I get caught up in weird shit and happen to be here, right? Not when... you know."

"Sure. Hey, you already came here once, and your buddy has the spell to bring you back any time." He released Laurence and turned to face him, looking serious for a moment. "I figure Arawn will view it as trespassing if you arrive without his permission, so just find a way to ask first. This isn't goodbye, Cricket. Understand?"

Laurence took a deep breath as the weight of his dad's words settled around him.

He'd viewed this whole conversation as the goodbye they'd never had. But Dad hadn't.

Laurence broke into a smile. "You asked me to take care of Mom," he said. "And I will."

"Good. Now make me another promise."

He nodded. "Okay."

"Take care of *you*, Cricket." Eric drew him into a tight bear hug. "If you're gonna get into fights with gods all the time, don't forget to take care of yourself, too. Sometimes you need to remember to breathe, so promise you will, okay?"

Laurence clung to him and held on just as tightly, and he smiled as he did so. "Yeah," he said. "I will. I promise, Dad. I'll take better care of myself."

"Good. How about we go send you home, and I can get back to partying naked in the streets?"

Laurence blinked, then laughed, and they started walking together for what might be the last time.

But it wasn't goodbye.

49

QUENTIN

QUENTIN watched as LAURENCE left the hall with his father, and briefly envied him. Not the fact that Eric was dead, of course, no; but to have such a loving relationship with *both* parents was forever beyond Quentin's reach.

He took a breath, then murmured, "If it is quite all right, I too would like to go for a walk."

"Certainly." Arawn nodded.

Quentin bowed faintly, then turned and wandered around the edge of the partying crowd, not wishing to disrupt their antics, and it was only once he was crossing the drawbridge that he realized he was being followed.

He slowed and glanced back, and saw that Basil and Jon were tailing him, a few feet behind, so he waited.

"Oh, we didn't mean to intrude or anything," Basil began as they caught up.

Jon just stared at Quentin. It was enough to unsettle even in small doses, but Quentin supposed that as a Child of Arawn, some of that heritage was bound to have some less desirable effects.

The descendants of gods all seemed to have inherited the good and the bad, from what he could tell. Laurence might be full of life, have gifts and magic at his disposal, but his innate need to hunt had pushed him into drugs and awful relationships, and his teenage years had held more than enough misery for a single lifetime.

Jon's bearing was that of a man weighed down by how much the world rejected his very existence, his connection to a god of death making him inherently off-putting to every living thing, and that had to be an awful experience, especially if Jon had spent any time not knowing where his gifts came from.

Quentin smiled softly and gestured for them to accompany him. "I wished to say farewell to those we rescued from Gwyn," he explained as he began to walk again. "They may wish to thank you both, too."

"I didn't do anything," Jon muttered.

"You are a Child of Arawn," Quentin countered. "I think perhaps this is a good opportunity for you to understand what that might mean."

"To you?" Jon didn't blink.

"To *you*," Quentin replied.

Jon didn't answer, so Basil stepped in.

"I think it's a good idea," he said.

Quentin nodded and continued off the drawbridge and into the mass of people, who immediately began to drop to their knees and bow their heads.

He stopped once it became apparent that they all wanted to stay there, waiting for some response from him, so he considered his words and then raised his voice.

"Everyone, thank you. Please, I would like you to stand."

Heads turned, surreptitiously at first, as people glanced at each other, and then to him. Slowly at first, they began to rise, though they kept their heads lowered.

"You owe me no allegiance," he called out. "You have been imprisoned, forced to obey a false king, but now you are free. I'm here if anyone wishes to talk, but otherwise I would like to remind you that you have all the time in the world to recover and to find your own peace. You need no leaders."

There was no resounding cheer. Not even a half-hearted clap. The crowd stood eerily still, until a few managed to raise their heads.

And then a few more.

And then someone stepped forward to hug him.

Quentin smiled and hugged her tightly, and whatever had gripped these people broke away. Those who couldn't hug Quentin hugged Basil or Jon instead, none pausing or hesitating to treat Jon exactly the same as they treated Basil or Quentin.

Quentin's world became a string of hugs and gratitude. He moved forward so that he could reach more people, and ensure that nobody at the back felt left out, and he asked questions. Names. Memories. Loves. He asked people to recall their lives and their deaths, to remember that their entrapment under Gwyn was not who they truly were.

To each and every person, he insisted, "You are not a monster."

"You will always be our liege," one said to him. The soul's name was Gavan, and he bore the crow's feet and graying hair of middle age.

Quentin laughed gently. "I am flattered," he replied. "But you are here so that you can find yourself, and then move on."

"And if following you helps me find myself?" Gavan countered.

He considered the question, then dipped his head. "Then it is an honor to be part of your journey."

"And I wish you well on yours," Gavan said.

Quentin bowed his head, and then continued on.

He was in no hurry.

———

By the time he and the crowd separated, more of Annwn's residents had come into the courtyard and begun to speak with the new arrivals, and Quentin was satisfied that these people would begin to find themselves in a place where they were welcomed and protected.

It was something they were long overdue.

A rotting corpse wandered up to him and smiled widely. "Warrior!"

Quentin gave an equally wide smile to the merchant who had gifted him with armor. "I never asked your name," he said as he offered his hand.

The merchant chuckled. "I gave up names a long time ago. They are as malleable as the rest of us, but once you let them go, you realize how much power they have over you." He reformed some skin so that he could shake Quentin's hand. "I hope it served its purpose?"

"And more," Quentin said. "I owe my life to your gift." He gestured toward the crowd. "They owe their freedom to it."

"Nobody owes anyone anything." The merchant chuckled. "But I'm glad that it kept you warm."

"It did quite a lot more than that," Quentin insisted.

The merchant shrugged and tapped a finger to Quentin's chest, directly over his heart. "Warriors always risk becoming tyrants. But you remain warm. For that, I am glad to have been of service." Then he backed away and grinned again. "Take care, Warrior. It was an honor to meet you. Now, if you will excuse me, I have some new friends to go and meet."

"Take care," Quentin said as he too stepped back.

He watched as the merchant drifted away into the crowd, and as Basil and Jon stumbled out of it. Jon even seemed to have an expression on his face, even though the closest word Quentin could pick to describe it would be bemusement.

"This is so amazing," Basil enthused the moment he got near. "These people are all so wonderful."

"It is…" Jon blinked. "Uncommon," he finished.

"Are you all right?" Quentin asked of Jon.

Jon frowned at him.

Quentin simply nodded. "It must be rather a shock to the system," he murmured. "If you wish to talk about it, I am more than willing to listen."

"I don't," Jon muttered.

"I understand." Quentin smiled, then looked at Basil. "And you?"

"It's hard," Basil admitted. "People think death is so scary, but it's not. It's just change. And it's really nice to see concrete proof that the things we do — me and Jon — are just mopping up shadows, and not harming anyone's soul. We find ghosts," he added, "and we put them to rest, but they aren't really the people themselves. They're like echoes, trapped in cycles or moments, and it's good to know we aren't, like, ending actual people."

Quentin nodded at that. "That must be a relief," he agreed. "Thank you," he added. "I'm sure I will hear how Laurence met you and you came to his aid, but I don't wish to wait until then to thank you for doing so. I would be dead without your assistance, and none of these people would ever be free. If ever there is anything that I can do for you, please do not hesitate to ask."

Basil rubbed his nose and huffed, then crossed his arms and glanced away. It took a few seconds for him to look back up at Quentin. "I'm sorry I thought you were a psycho."

Quentin lifted an eyebrow.

"I thought maybe Laurence was all head over heels with this guy who turned out to be absolutely the worst, but that wasn't you, and I'm really glad I got a chance to find that out." Basil bit his lip. "Though you're still pretty scary. You know that, right?"

"I know." Quentin slid his hands into the pockets of his coat and sighed softly. "Sometimes intentionally, usually not."

Jon glanced at him, then shrugged. "Some people are intimidated by the weirdest things. Intelligence. Confidence. Power.

Combine two, and some fear you. Hold all three, and enemies will always find you."

Basil gawped up at Jon, then grinned at him and hugged his arm.

Quentin simply chuckled. "Then I should be grateful I have none of those."

"Bullshit," Jon said flatly.

Quentin pursed his lips and turned his gaze on the crowd.

"All right." He raised his chin a little. "Then perhaps a few enemies are the price of doing the right thing."

If that was the cost, he paid it gladly.

50

LAURENCE

They reappeared in the hotel room, in the very spot Basil had transported them to Otherworld from, although the sheet was gone, and the chairs were back in their places. Housekeeping must have seen some weird shit in their time, but Laurence hoped they weren't too freaked out by what they'd found here.

Home! Windsor's voice blasted through with such excitement that it made Laurence take a step back.

Yes! Home! Safe and alive! I'm so proud of you for waiting! he answered.

I will see you soon?

Yes. He smiled faintly. *You will. Not long now.*

Okay! Windsor settled down, leaving Laurence with the sense that he was being fussed over by a room full of teenagers.

He wanted to get his damp, bloodstained, torn clothes off right away, but that felt insensitive, since Basil and Jon still had to get home, so instead he looked around for some kind of indication of what day it was.

The view outside was crisp and sunny, with settled snow and pathways cleared through it. Traffic was moving, and the snow-banks either side of the road already had dirt spattered up them.

Quentin pulled his phone from his pocket and switched it on, whereas Basil and Jon pulled theirs out and immediately began to gripe about dead batteries.

Laurence laughed. Quentin, of all people, had thought to turn his phone off in a world that had no signal. The man who a year ago didn't even own a cellphone, and sure didn't know how to use one, had adapted fast.

Goddess, he was so smart.

"Hm." Quentin finally looked up from the screen. "I make it two days?"

"Though time works differently in Otherworld, so who really knows?" Laurence shrugged. "Still, at least we're back before the hotel took our stuff away." He looked at Basil. "Do you mind if I ask—"

"My eyes," Basil laughed. "Would you believe it? He fixed my eyesight! Do you know how much money that's gonna save me?"

Laurence shook his head.

"A lot," Basil confirmed.

"I'm so sorry." Quentin set his phone down. "How far is it for you to get home?"

"Oh, like, half an hour on the 6 train. I'm in East Harlem." Basil shrugged. "It's okay."

"No. I'll have a car take you." Quentin gestured to the state of Jon's clothes as he reached for the room's phone and hit the button for concierge. "Then perhaps, before Laurence and I leave for San Diego, we can meet up under better circumstances, and I can thank you properly for all your assistance."

"Oh, that won't be necessary—" Basil began, but he cut himself off as Quentin started talking into the phone, and Basil shot Laurence a look that Laurence understood far too well.

"Yeah," Laurence chuckled. "He's always like this. Once his mind's made up, he just hits the gas until it gets done. Don't worry about it. He's right. It would be nice to see you again before we leave town." He looked around, then grabbed a notepad and pen off the desk and offered it to Basil. "Can you write your number down in case my phone's destroyed it? I, uh. I landed in a moat."

Basil's cheeks pinked, and he nodded quickly. "That was pretty scary," he said as he scribbled on the paper. "I think I'm gonna be hyped for weeks after all this." Jon rolled his eyes, like getting sent to Annwn happened every day, and Basil laughed and slapped his shoulder, then offered the notepad back to Laurence. "Phone, email, address. Any time you get a ghost problem, you call us."

"Deal." Laurence tore the top sheet off, then wrote his own details down and offered them back to Basil. "And if you get a problem with the weather, call me."

Basil grinned and stuffed the sheet into his satchel.

"Right," Quentin said as he hung up. "The car will be ready in ten minutes. We shall get some sleep, and then be in touch. Is that all right?"

Basil nodded eagerly and offered Quentin his hand. "That'll be great. See you soon."

Quentin shook Basil's hand, then raised an eyebrow at the state of Basil's nail polish.

"Don't worry," Basil laughed. "I'll get it fixed by then."

Quentin just laughed, then shook Jon's hand. Laurence stepped forward to do the same with both while Quentin went to open the door for them.

Laurence saw them to the elevators, and grinned as the attendant did his best not to notice all the dried blood and torn clothes between them, then strolled back to the hotel room and waited for Quentin to close and lock the door.

Finally he could take his coat off, only to find that the weird, tight sensation around his ribs was his own t-shirt, tied like some eighties crop top. "What?"

"That was Eric's notion of first aid," Quentin protested, "not mine."

"Oh, man! My dad did this?" He shook his head, then blinked at Quentin.

"Myriam," they both said as one.

"Can I?" He gestured to Quentin's phone.

"Of course." Quentin summoned it to his hand, then proffered it to Laurence.

Laurence didn't have much scrolling to do to find his mom's number. Quentin had fewer than ten people's numbers in his phone book, and it was so weird seeing "Myriam Riley" next to "Neil Storm" in a list.

He shook his head and dialed, then put the phone on speaker.

"Quentin?" Myriam sounded concerned.

"Mom!" Laurence said. "Hey, it's both of us, you're on speaker. We're alive, we're in New York, everything's okay!"

She chuckled nervously. "Oh my goodness, Bambi, you frightened the life out of me. Windsor was screaming his head off!"

"Are you at the house?"

"I am, dear. Soraya wanted to look for you, but she couldn't find you."

"Yeah. Mom..." He licked his lips and glanced at Quentin. "Mom, we went to Annwn."

His mom was so quiet that Quentin finally added, "Myriam?"

"I'm sorry, dear," she said. "I'm still here. Annwn?"

The question was as obvious as it was unspoken, and Laurence said, "He's there, Mom. He's waiting for you."

"He says that he loves you," Quentin added.

"Oh... oh, Goddess..."

Laurence could hear her gasp, the hitches in her breath that suggested she might be holding back tears, and he bit his lip. "I just wanted to tell you that right away. We literally just got back, and I didn't think it should wait."

"I appreciate that," she breathed. "I imagine you have things to do."

"The usual," Quentin murmured. "Buy Laurence a new phone, for a start."

Myriam laughed quietly. "Oh, you two are so much trouble. Go on, fix yourselves up. I'll wait to hear back from you about what actually happened."

"Okay. Love you, Mom."

"I love you too, Bambi. And you, Quentin."

Quentin opened his mouth, then blinked. "You also," he managed to confess.

Laurence grinned. "I gotta shower. Speak later, Mom."

He hung up and picked apart the knot in his t-shirt, then pulled it off over his head, and eyed Quentin. "Did Dad tell you to pass that on to Mom?"

"He did, yes. Asked me to promise to do so, and I gave him my word that I would." Quentin began to unfasten his own coat, then he hesitated. "Shall I join you, or would you rather..."

Laurence eyed him and wondered what could be making him pause, but then his gaze fell to the gashes all over Quentin's coat, and he figured Quentin might still want to hide the gift from Laurence, so they could carry on with life like normal tomorrow, so Laurence smiled.

"Why don't I go fill the tub, and you can join me if you want to?" he offered.

Quentin smiled gratefully and nodded. "Thank you."

HE WAITED for Quentin to settle into the water behind him, and then leaned back against his chest and closed his eyes. His hands drifted down through the water to rest on Quentin's legs, remaining still once there to avoid tickling his scars, and Quentin began to tenderly smooth soap across Laurence's skin.

"Are you ready to say it, baby?" he murmured.

He half expected Quentin to ask for clarification, to dance

around the subject until he finally decided to talk, but this time he didn't. "I was wondering," he said softly, "how I could possibly have earned the love of a man as wonderful as you, because if I could work that out, I would know what to do more of, so as to make sure that you never lost your faith in me."

Laurence's eyes fluttered open, and he shifted aside so that he could tip his head back and look up at Quentin.

Quentin smiled shyly and glanced at Laurence's shoulder, watching it intently as he scooped water to wash away lather. "That is all," he added.

Laurence settled back against Quentin's chest and let his eyes close again. "Baby, even when you weren't yourself, you couldn't hurt a hair on my head."

"I threw you out of a window, darling!" Quentin protested.

"And you're gonna buy me a new phone, too." Laurence sighed.

The temptation to lie was great.

But lies got them nowhere in the end.

"It scared me," he admitted quietly. "Seeing you like that. And I want to say 'it wasn't you' until I'm blue in the face, until you believe me, but I don't know how healthy that would be. Maybe it's healthier to say that we know neither of us ever wants that to *become* you." He hesitated. "Gwyn didn't create something from nothing. I think the best way to protect you from what neither of us want you to be is for us to get some help once we're home. And I know, it means we have to find a therapist who'll keep quiet if you ever move their furniture around during a session, but..." He sat up carefully so that he could turn and look Quentin in the eye. "I'm willing to spend the time, checking out futures, finding one who won't ever betray us. If you're willing to see one."

Quentin searched his gaze for a moment, and then he dipped his head. "I agree. Oh, thank God, Laurence. I don't... I don't ever—"

"Yeah, I know. And you won't ever be him, baby, I swear to

you." He took Quentin's hand and squeezed. "And I wanna see one, too. A therapist," he added. "I've got some things to work through. You know, Mikey stuff." He hesitated, then added, "and Freddy put me through the wringer, too. Nothing physical," he added at the sudden flash in Quentin's eyes. "But I think I want to work it all through in my head and come to terms with everything we've been through, and I have literally no experience in dealing with my problems in any healthy way." Laurence laughed weakly. "I wanna stay off the heroin, baby. For good. And if it means I have to work for it, well... that's a price I'm happy to pay."

Quentin lifted his head again, then let out a breath slowly. "Christ, how did we get this way?"

"By leading amazingly shitty lives with people who abused us?" Laurence offered a gentle smile. "It's okay. I'd be more worried if we weren't damaged by all the bullshit we've been through, you know? I never want that to become *normal*."

Quentin bit his lip faintly, then leaned forward and met Laurence's gaze. "I'm going to do better," he insisted. "You wanted me to woo you, and I have been... frankly, hopeless at doing so. But I would like to try again, and as you said you wished for it to be ongoing, I hope you do not mind?"

Laurence laughed gently and leaned closer. "I don't mind at all. I'm still obviously worth it."

Quentin leaned in, then kissed him softly, and Laurence sank back against his chest as Quentin's arms wrapped around him.

They'd have their Christmas, meet up with Basil and Jon, then go home and start working on themselves until they became better. And maybe it'd never be perfect, but they would move forward together.

It was more than Laurence could have hoped for a year ago.

51

QUENTIN

There were no nightmares.

Quentin woke as he should, as he missed doing, and he felt rested for the first time in months. As he listened, he heard New York traffic and Laurence's breathing, the quiet hum of the room's refrigerator, and distant sounds of an elevator's ding.

It was glorious.

He laid an arm across Laurence's chest and nestled up against his body, and Laurence made a faint, mumbling sound as he slipped his arm around Quentin's shoulders without waking up.

If his life had required every single step he had taken to reach a moment such as this, then it had all been worthwhile.

"Hey, baby," Laurence whispered.

Quentin blinked, then laughed a little. "Good morning, darling. Merry Christmas."

Laurence stretched and yawned, then rolled onto his side and opened his eyes. "Merry Christmas. Do I get a Christmas kiss?"

Quentin drew nearer so that he could press his lips to Laurence's, and they remained with their lips touching for several seconds, until Quentin withdrew.

"Mmm." Laurence grinned. "Okay. What do you wanna do first? Breakfast, or gifts?"

Quentin's smile faltered.

Gifts.

Bloody hell. He had only had time to buy one thing before he was kidnapped, and even that was damaged now.

"Hey." Laurence lifted his eyebrows. "You want to give me something that's literally been to another world and back? All I got *you* was stuff from stores."

"But—"

"Otherworld," Laurence insisted. "Nobody else on the planet has one. It's unique, whatever it is."

Quentin jutted his lip out like a toddler, then huffed. "Very well. But first, breakfast."

Laurence grinned at that. "I'll let you order, since you're wooing me."

He eyed Laurence, then laughed and eased out of bed to fetch the menu.

THEY SAT around eating breakfast in their pajamas while overlooking Central Park, where much of the snow had already begun to turn to slush. It remained beautiful, full of far more life than had existed in Annwn, even though the trees looked bare and wildlife was hardly anywhere to be seen.

Beneath the surface of the trees and ground, new life waited for spring. Between snowbanks, people walked their dogs or took part in their morning jog, or simply strolled along enjoying the scenery. There were, Quentin reflected, a myriad of ways to view the world, and each of them revealed different facets.

"Man, even the breakfast in fancy hotels is amazing." Laurence spread some preserves on his toast and stuffed it into his mouth. "Where does jelly like this even come from?"

"Fruit, sugar. I imagine there is more to it than that." Quentin sipped his tea as he watched Laurence. It had to be love when even watching the man chew toast was an absolute treat, he supposed.

Laurence grabbed his juice and used it to wash the toast down, then leaned back and patted his stomach. "Man, I'm stuffed. I didn't realize how hungry I was until I started." He eyed Quentin's plate, then added, "I guess you were too, huh?"

"Apparently one cannot exist on energy alone," Quentin agreed.

"Nutrients," Laurence said, without further explanation. He stood and wandered to the closet, then pulled out a couple of bags and carried them back to the table, sitting down and resting them in his lap. "Okay. I got you this. I'm sorry it's not wrapped." He peeked into a bag and sheepishly plucked out a receipt, then offered Quentin the bag.

"Oh, allow me to—"

"Nuh uh. Me first," Laurence insisted.

Quentin smiled a little, then took the bag. "Thank you."

It was light, yet the contents were stiff and slender, like sheets of card. Or of card backing to paper. He raised an eyebrow, dipped his fingers inside, and found a familiar sensation.

Shrink-wrap over card and paper.

Sheet music.

"Laurence!" He drew the music out of the bag with growing excitement, and set the bag aside so that he could see what was inside it.

Piano solos, from a composer he had never heard of.

Quentin tore the shrink-wrap free from both and placed it on the table, then began to skim-read the first of the compositions, hearing it form in his head as his eyes danced across the printed notes.

"It's beautiful!" he realized. "Is this modern?"

"Uh huh!" Laurence was grinning ear to ear. "Do you like it?"

Quentin nodded. "I love it, darling! Thank you!" He had to fight the urge to keep reading long enough to set the music aside. Instead, he reached for the drawers beside the television and tugged open the lowest of them. He drew out the bag, sliced by bone as it was, and pulled the gift-wrapped book from it, careful not to destroy the wrapping any further. He offered it to Laurence with his brows creased in apology. "If it is too damaged, I can always—"

"I'll keep it anyway, baby," Laurence said as he took it. His face was without any trace of a smile. He was deadly serious. "This meant enough to you that it helped you cling to who you were, and nothing can replace that."

Quentin felt the temperature in his cheeks rise and folded his hands together in his lap, over the remains of the bag.

"Let me see." Laurence used the gash in the paper to tear the rest of it off, then his eyes widened, and he took in a light gasp. "Oh Goddess! Is this..." He turned it over and ran his hands across the leather.

The cut was, Quentin noticed, along the back of the book, and was not deep enough to cut all the way through to the paper. He released a quiet sigh of relief.

Laurence opened it and stared at the pristine pages, then raised his head and gazed at Quentin.

Quentin blushed again. Laurence had that hungry look in his eye.

Who ever knew that a book could have such an effect?

"It's perfect," Laurence whispered. "Goddess, Quen, I love everything about it. Thank you!"

"You're very welcome." He finally set the bag aside, then blinked as Laurence lifted the other bag he'd brought over with him into his lap. "What's this?"

"Well, uh." Laurence cleared his throat. "I went back to that store and bought a few things."

It took Quentin a moment to work out which store precisely

Laurence meant, and then he had to shift in his seat to get a little more comfortable. "Oh? As a gift?"

"Kinda? For both of us?" Laurence coughed into his hand, then laughed a little. "Want me to show you?"

Quentin bit his lip, then chuckled. "I would like that very much."

"Okay. Wait right here!" Laurence put the book down and bounced out of his seat to dash into the bathroom with his bag, and he shut the door after himself.

Quentin tidied. He returned all the breakfast items to their tray, then took the tray to the door and set it down outside. Once the door was closed, he locked it, and put all the rubbish in the bin beneath the desk. Once he was satisfied that everything was as it should be, he waited.

What could Laurence possibly have bought? Nothing too extreme, he hoped. But hopefully something just extreme enough. The hunger in his deep, dark eyes was enough to stir Quentin's own interest, and as the bathroom door opened, he looked at it with interest, curious to see what on earth Laurence had in mind.

Laurence stepped out and raised an arm to lounge seductively against the wall, and he grinned. "What do you think?"

Quentin wasn't thinking. Not that he could tell. There was so much to take in all at once. The mesh gave the appearance of decency, and yet Quentin could readily make out Laurence's muscles, his curves, his half-hard cock pushing against the see-through material.

He couldn't work out how this was sexier than Laurence naked, and yet it was.

"Bloody hell," he said. It came out of him like a growl.

"I thought so too," Laurence murmured. He began to prowl toward Quentin, his hips swaying lightly as he ran his hands down his sides and tugged on the hem of the shirt to make it even sheerer against his flesh. "You want me, baby?"

There were things Quentin wanted. God, so many things.

Whether they had names, he couldn't say, but he knew how to describe them.

The question was one of courage.

He stood slowly and tugged on the belt of his bathrobe to unfasten it, and as it fell loose he stepped toward Laurence and slowly brushed his fingertips over the mesh of the shirt, marveling at how soft it felt, and how it molded to Laurence's body so well now that Laurence held the hem.

"I want," he breathed softly, "you to stop asking me for permission to kiss me."

Laurence blinked at him.

"That's what I *want*," Quentin added, as their chests finally came into contact. "I would like to try it, to be sure that it does not lead to… ill effects," he said with care, "but ultimately, what I want is for us to be able to engage with one another as the mood takes us." He hesitated, then added, "In part, I suppose, because I already know that you will not press should I *not* be in the mood, but I would like to remove that barrier, because I trust you."

Laurence's lips had parted, and the playfulness was gone from his eyes. They were turned to serious now, and he nodded briefly. "Okay. Okay, we can try that out, if you're sure."

"I'm certain." He dipped his head forward and rested his lips against Laurence's jaw, so that he could murmur nearer his ear. "I want to touch you. Lose myself in your presence. I want to hold you and never let go." He slipped his fingers around the hem of the shirt and up beneath it until he found soft, warm skin.

Laurence shivered under his touch, and the hardness against Quentin's groin grew firmer still.

Quentin closed his eyes briefly. The final hurdle felt tantalizingly close, and all he had to do was leap over it. He counted down from ten.

"I want you," he whispered, "inside me."

Laurence's whimper was exquisite. His hips moved and

pressed their lengths together, making Quentin's own breath sharpen.

"Goddess." Laurence's breath hitched as he whispered the word. "I want to fuck you so much, baby. I want to show you what it can be like, what it *should* be like. If you really want to do this, I think we should..." He hesitated, then groaned a little. "After we get home. I think it's something we ought to talk about first."

Quentin sagged and let out a small sigh, finally opening his eyes. He didn't know how he felt now. Had he really thought they might simply fall down onto the sheets and begin... whatever it was? *Fucking?* After it had taken such planning and preparation to share a bed or a bath together?

Or was he grateful that, yet again, Laurence had been the one to insert a small dose of reality into the mess in Quentin's head? Was Laurence ever going to grow tired of always being the one to figure out the logistics in these situations?

Quentin would try harder. He already was. These things wouldn't be rushed, and Laurence held knowledge and experience that Quentin did not. He had to stop being so horrible to himself.

"Baby?" Laurence said.

He smiled faintly and kissed Laurence's jaw, then pecked tiny kisses down the side of his neck and began to run his hands up Laurence's sides beneath the shirt.

"Until then," he murmured, "I would very much like to hear you scream my name."

That would definitely do for now.

52

LAURENCE

LAURENCE FELL BACK AGAINST THE BED AS QUENTIN PUSHED HIM toward it, and he quickly squirreled his way up the sheets until his feet were off the floor.

Quentin shed his robe while he gazed down at Laurence, haughty and aloof as he began to unfasten his pajamas.

Fucking hell, the man was so goddamn hot, and he wanted Laurence to fuck him, and for a moment there, Laurence had hoped for *right now*. Maybe Quentin had meant that, too, but it was far too huge a risk.

He hated being the one to put the brakes on, but there was no way he dared screw that up.

Quentin parted his shirt and allowed it to slide down his arms and then flutter away to the floor, and Laurence's thoughts couldn't wander any more. He dropped his gaze to Quentin's groin as Quentin pushed his pants down, and nothing else mattered.

There was fire in Quentin's eyes. His features were hard with lust. As he placed one knee against the mattress and began to fall forward to his hands, he never broke eye contact.

He was in charge, and he wanted Laurence to know it.

Laurence arched his back and laid his arms together above his head, entwining his fingers and tensing his muscles to show himself off. The brush of mesh over his skin as he moved was like a hint of what would come soon enough. Enough of a hint to make him gasp.

Quentin lowered over him until their cocks and mouths crushed together. Like a tsunami smashing against rocks, Quentin's presence was all-consuming, drowning Laurence beneath it, that breathtaking force of nature constrained within a single human body.

Quentin's hands pushed his shirt up to his collarbones, thumbs stroking across his nipples until they were as hard as his cock. He sucked on Quentin's tongue and slid his fingers through Quentin's hair, releasing wordless pleas as his cock strained against the mesh of his pants.

Those hands on him were masterful and firm. They knew where to touch, where to squeeze, where to stroke so lightly that they made his skin shiver. Laurence had no choice but to give himself over to the pleasure that burned through him and chased away every doubt and fear he clung to.

"Quen," he gasped when those lips lifted away.

Quentin's body undulated against his, fingers merciless as they played Laurence's weakest spots. "Louder," he breathed.

Laurence looked up into Quentin's eyes. Gray, laden with promise, narrowed in intense focus. Focus Quentin was applying to Laurence, to giving pleasure, to making Laurence lose himself.

He gasped and rolled his hips against Quentin's, hanging onto his hair as his cock's urgency increased. "Fuck," he gasped. "Fuck yes! Oh, shit, Quen, fuck me!" His voice grew louder, and he wasn't going to try and stop it. "Quen! Fuck, that's so good!"

Quentin's lips twisted into a smirk and he dipped his head to Laurence's neck, teeth scraping against skin while his fingers and thumbs began to slowly pinch Laurence's nipples.

Laurence cried out. His orgasm leaped a whole lot closer, and the mesh was a frustrating barrier, like he could feel the heat from Quentin's cock, but the touch was a fraction of an inch away, and the torment was horrendous.

He loved it.

Goddess help him, he loved it. And if Quentin didn't get them off him soon, he was gonna make a mess in these pants, and he'd only just put them on.

The mental image was too much. He parted his knees a touch further, as though he could beg for climax without words.

But words came anyway.

"Fuck! I'm gonna come! Quen! Quen! Oh, fuck, I'm-oh!"

Quentin's teeth sank against his skin. His fingers had slowly built to a pinch that was almost too much. Laurence teetered on the precipice, and every part of him thrummed with need.

"Quen!" He screamed it. His head fell back, and he screamed it again. "Fuck! Quen! *Quentin! Que—*"

His orgasm was an inferno, and it robbed him of breath with its fury. It consumed all that he was, all that he could be, and he came hard, each jerk of his cock sending shockwaves through his body.

He became a wreck. A creature without bones, stranded on the rocks as the tide began to recede. His world had blacked out for an eternity of bliss, and now that it came back, he lacked the power to do anything about it. His arms fell to the sheets, and he gasped for air.

Quentin's hands were still on him, but there was no pinch. His teeth still rested against Laurence's skin, but there was no bite. And his cock was still pressed against Laurence's own, but it was gently softening.

They lay together, breathing, because breathing was as much as they could manage.

THEY TOOK A SHOWER TOGETHER, and once they were dry, Quentin suggested they head out to enjoy the remaining snow."

The idea of enjoying cold weather was near-anathema to Laurence, but he agreed, and Quentin kept them warm while they strolled arm-in-arm through Central Park and down to the Rockefeller Center.

Quentin taught him to ice skate, though Laurence was sure that Quentin was way more graceful than he could ever be, and afterward, they stopped off at a cafe for some hot chocolate.

They sat overlooking the rink, cradling their mugs for warmth, and Quentin idly curled one leg around Laurence's as their elbows rested comfortably together.

They would fly home soon. Quentin seemed more at peace than he had in weeks, and Laurence wanted to get back to a normal life – one without gods or unexpected journeys to the lands of the dead. Just him and Quentin. And Windsor, and the dogs, and a house full of teenagers. And Mom, and the shop, and the regular, everyday kinds of things that used to drive him nuts, but now were like a balm to him.

Right now, he was the happiest man alive. He had love, great sex, and hot chocolate, and even though it was the heart of winter, he felt like things were looking up. When he got home, he would find his dad's Book of Shadows and discover the source of all his father's terrible jokes.

He groaned to himself.

Quentin pursed his lips and glanced at Laurence. "Hmm?"

"I bet that's what it is," Laurence chuckled. "Dad told me where to find his old Book of Shadows. I bet it's just full of really terrible jokes."

Quentin laughed lightly and shook his head. "I wouldn't put it past him," he said. "Although, perhaps his jokes are not *all* bad."

He eyed Quentin, then looked out the windows as light flurries of snow began to fall. "No," he agreed. "Maybe not the worst."

He sipped his chocolate and savored the moment, watching

the snowflakes drift toward the ground in no particular hurry, and then he looked at Quentin.

"Merry Christmas, baby."

Quentin laughed and set his cup down, then eased a hand across Laurence's thigh.

"Merry Christmas."

EPILOGUE

ELSEWHERE

HE REGARDED THE DOSSIER FULL OF PICTURES. PHOTOGRAPHS taken around the world, some by professionals with long lenses and some by tourists with cellphones.

As a couple, they were sickening.

He supposed that New York had a black dog or two due to the graves full of English dead. The mass graves on Hart Island, those from the yellow fever outbreak, and the dead from British rule in the seventeenth century were all ripe for the formation of such a creature. While most of the English might have been Protestants, all it took would be for a handful of families to have older faiths.

Legends sprouted up around people, not the other way around.

Riley was impossible to target directly, but that was all right. Summoning a dog and showing it some pictures worked just as well, and now he had a better idea of Riley's resources and capabilities.

Days after the black dog took one, the other had disappeared, and yet here they were.

Ice skating.

Getting in a cab.

Entering JFK airport.

It had done nothing to draw Grant out of his solitude, and he had to wonder whether Rufus was even aware that his student had been involved in anything.

If throwing Riley into a pit wasn't enough to entice Grant out into the open, then more persuasive means must be employed.

"Marcella," he called.

She was at his side in moments. "Yes, master?"

He closed the folder and handed it to her. "Put Angela in play."

"Yes, master." She bowed as she took the folder. "Will that be all, master?"

"Yes."

For now.

*~ **Inheritance** continues in **Sigils of Spring** ~*

ACKNOWLEDGMENTS

I must thank my freshest ever cheesebags for helping me through the roughest couple of years of my life. There were some unpleasant moments, and it's fair to say that I wouldn't be here now without their help.

Thanks as always to Jen, without whom Inheritance literally would not exist. Jen is like the little angel / devil combo on my shoulders, except there's just one entity, and they like to shout "That's great, NOW WHERE'S THE REST OF IT?" whenever I try to slack off. But more importantly there are ideas and characters in this series who wouldn't exist without Jen, so what I want you to do is tell all your friends to buy all these books so I can shower Jen in dolla dolla bills, ok?

Rites of Winter was mostly fueled by IAMX, Assemblage 23, and Mesh, in what I think is possibly the shortest playlist I've ever assembled for writing to. Food-wise, I have to say it was mostly built on layers of cake and frosting, with the occasional bag of crisps. I blame Eric.

Thanks again to Mum, who keeps harassing me to write "good books", because "all the other ones I read are rubbish."

Until next time!

ABOUT THE AUTHOR

AK Faulkner is the author of the *Inheritance* series of contemporary fantasy books, which begins with *Jack of Thorns*. The latest volume, *Sigils of Spring*, will be released in November 2019.

AK lives just outside of London, England, with a charismatic Corgi. Together they fight crime and try not to light too many fires on the way.

Find out more at akfaulkner.com

Sign up for the *Inheritance* newsletter at discoverinheritance.com/signup

INHERITANCE

Season One:

Jack of Thorns

Knight of Flames

Lord of Ravens

Reeve of Veils

Page of Tricks

Season Two:

Rites of Winter

Sigils of Spring

Visit discoverinheritance.com to learn more about the characters and world of Inheritance, and sign up to the newsletter.